DRAGONS IN OUR MIDST

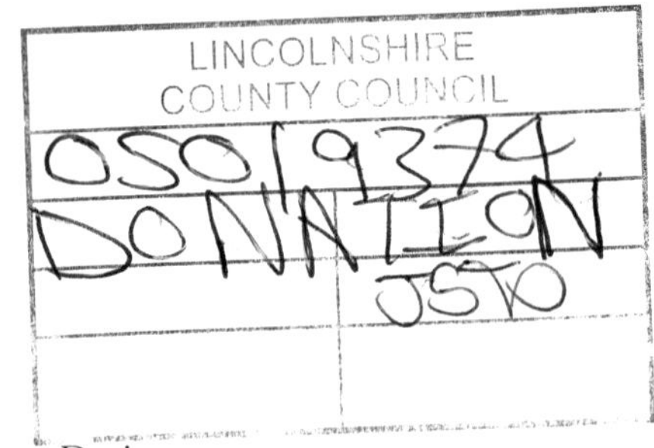

Circles of Seven

This edition published in the UK in 2009 by Candle Books
(a publishing imprint of Lion Hudson plc),
Wilkinson House, Jordan Hill Road, Oxford OX2 8DR
Tel: +44 (0)1865 302750 Fax: +44 (0)1865 302757
Email: candle@lionhudson.com
www.lionhudson.com

Published in the USA by Living Ink Books,
an imprint of AMG Publishers
6815 Shallowford Road
Chattanooga, Tennessee 37421

Distributed in the UK by Marston Book Services Ltd,
PO Box 269, Abingdon, Oxon OX14 4YN

Circles of Seven is the third of four books in the youth fantasy fiction series, *Dragons in Our Midst.*

ISBN 978-1-85985-793-9

This book has been printed on paper independently certified as having been produced from sustainable forests.

Printed in Malta by Gutenberg Press
First printing 2009
10 9 8 7 6 5 4 3 2 1 0

Recap of ***Raising Dragons*** and ***The Candlestone***

If you haven't read the first two books in the series, you'll need a briefing before you read this one. My name is Professor Charles Hamilton, former Oxford professor and now a private tutor for the children in this story. Since I am intimately acquainted with their amazing adventures, I have been asked to relate them to you.

During the sixth century, most dragons were evil, giving dragon slayers reason to kill them. Merlin, of King Arthur fame, used a miracle to transform the good dragons into humans, thereby protecting them. These anthrozils, as they were called, retained dragon genetics, and a few married into the human race and produced children. Among these were Billy Bannister (whom I always call "William"), who is able to breathe fire, and Bonnie Silver, who has dragon wings.

One slayer, Devin, survived through the centuries, using the healing photoreceptors in dragon blood in combination with a gem called a candlestone. This stone is able to absorb energy from a dragon, thus weakening it and providing power for the slayer. Devin killed all the anthrozils except for one, William's father, Jared, who was known as Clefspeare when he was a dragon. After Devin slew Bonnie's mother, Irene (Hartanna as a dragon), Bonnie fled Montana and located William in West Virginia. Devin, taking the guise of William's school principal, discovered William's dragon past and tried to kill both him and Bonnie.

Through many harrowing adventures and narrow escapes in the wilderness, including a miraculous use of Excalibur, William and Bonnie survived (with substantial help from myself and William's friend, Walter Foley). During the escape ordeal, William's father transformed back into a dragon, and we found a strange book, Merlin's ancient diary.

Later, Bonnie's father, Dr Conner, located her and claimed that her mother had only been severely wounded and was still alive, so Bonnie went home with him to Montana. When I uncovered his deceit, we – William, William's mother, Walter, and I – flew to Montana to find them. Strangely enough, Merlin's diary helped us. Cryptic words appeared in poetic verse, a guiding light of sorts. We also found Excalibur, which Bonnie had used to dispose of Devin in the climax of her battle in the wilderness but later dropped while flying to safety. The sword is able, in the right hands, to create a beam that transforms people into light energy, a process called translumination. If that energy is not immediately confined in a structure such as the candlestone, it disperses, killing the unfortunate victim.

Dr Conner told Bonnie that he transluminated her mother and stored her in the candlestone until he could find a way to heal her. It was up to Bonnie to dive into the stone and retrieve her. This retrieval process was the brainchild of a young genius, Ashley Stalworth, whom Bonnie befriended, along with several orphan girls who lived in Dr Conner's underground laboratory. When Bonnie dove into the candlestone in the form of light energy, she discovered that Devin was actually trapped there instead of her mother, and she became trapped herself.

When we arrived in Montana, Palin, Devin's henchman, kidnapped William and took him to the laboratory. Once there, William escaped, and, with Ashley's help, ventured into the candlestone to rescue Bonnie. After finding several others in the stone, knights from ages past, including a splendid chap named Sir Barlow, William helped everyone escape in the midst of a ferocious tumult – earthquakes, sword battles, and the collapse of a mountain overhead.

My part in this effort, after being transluminated myself, was to escort the escapees into a restoration chamber. I pulled William out, but he was unconscious, his brain addled by the process. When I placed Excalibur in his hands, however, he suddenly revived, receiving an amazing infusion of light energy from above, having finally learned the secret behind Excalibur's power.

Devin also escaped the candlestone, becoming an enormous, lightning-spewing monster. William battled him in a titanic struggle, finally defeating him with Excalibur's unbridled energy. When all had settled, I revealed to William that he was Arthur's heir and that he must come with me to England to fulfil his destiny, to battle the ultimate evil in the Circles of Seven.

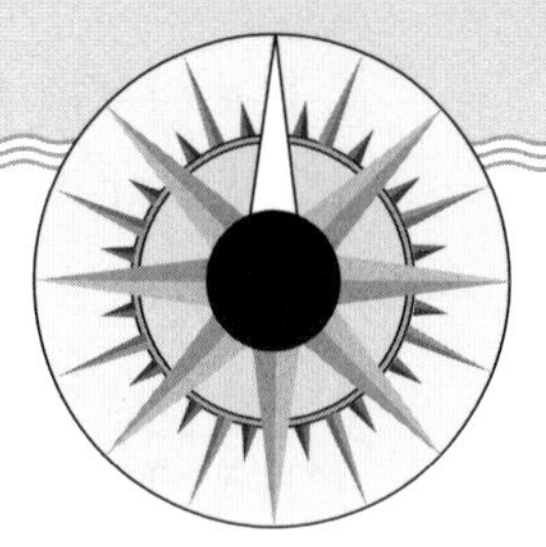

Contents

CONTENTS

All hail the true "Once and Future King",
the ever-present light we follow, whose blood is our ally
in the great battle. As we rescue the enemy's prisoners in
our circles, show us the light that will lead us safely home.

The Glastonbury Tor

Photo by Kevin Redpath, Glastonbury, England

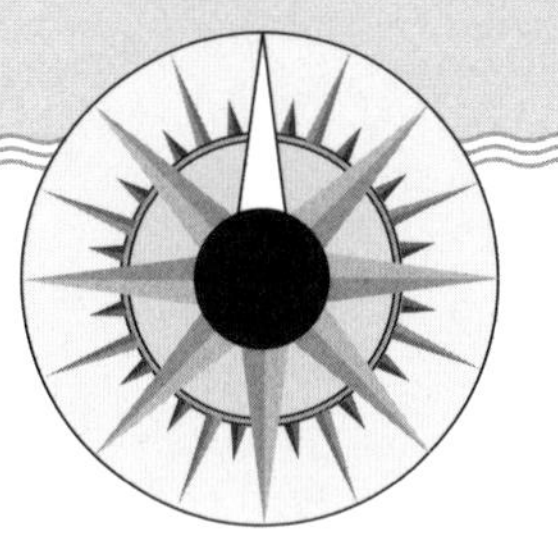

Acknowledgments

To my faithful wife and best friend, Susie – without you, I would not know the meaning of "Welcome Home".

To my AMG family – Dan Penwell, Warren Baker, Rick Steele, Dale Anderson, Trevor Overcash, Joe Suter, and all the staff – thank you for daring to be different. Your desire for excellence is unmatched.

To my editor, Becky Miller, thank you for hanging in there with me. Thank you for listening to the voice of the King.

Thank you to Lynne Stephenson, the talented young creator of the "Apollo" sketch, and Kevin Redpath, who provided the stunning photo of the Glastonbury Tor.

A special thank you to Dr Spiros Zodhiates for teaching me the meaning of *autarkeia*. (see 1 Tim. 6:6)

"Apollo"

A prototype sketch by Ashley Stalworth

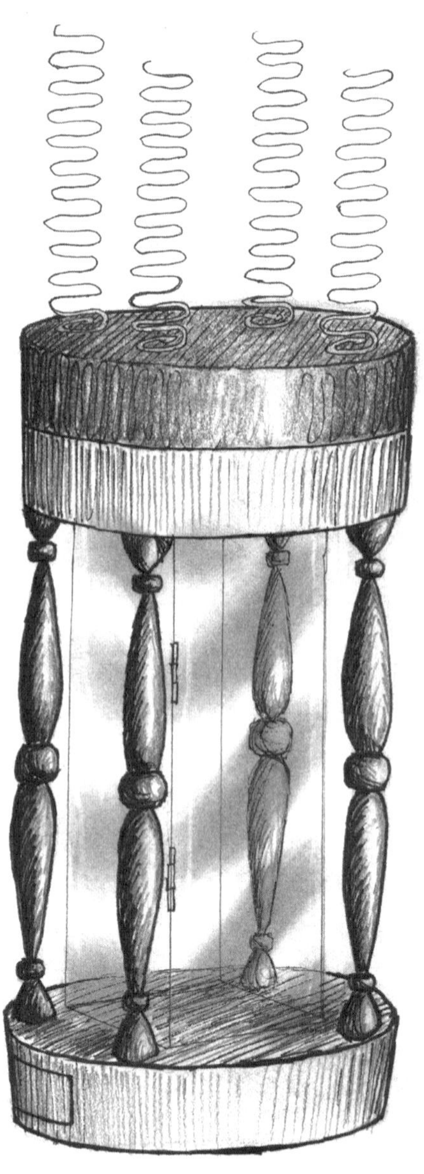

Merlin's Song

With sword and stone, the holy knight,
Darkness as his bane,
Will gather warriors in the light
Cast in heaven's flame.

He comes to save a remnant band,
Searching with his maid,
But in a sea of sadness finds
His warriors lying splayed.

A valley deep, a valley long
Lay angels dry and dead;
Now who can wake their cold, stone hearts
Their bones on table spread?

Like wine that flows in skins made new
The spirit pours out fresh;
Can hymns of love bring forth the dead
And give them hearts of flesh?

O will you learn from words of faith
That sing in psalms from heaven
To valley floors where terrors lurk
In circles numbering seven?

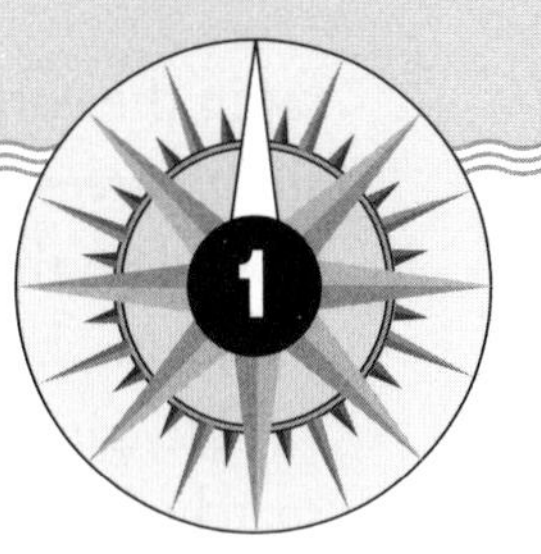

CHAPTER 1

The Monogram

Danger!

Billy's internal alarm blared. Something evil approached, creeping up slowly through one of the hallways of the huge English mansion. Sitting back in an easy chair, he closed his book and flicked off the floor lamp at his side. He waited, allowing his eyes to adjust to the dimness of the unfamiliar bedroom. Only a ray of moonlight seeped in from the window on the opposite wall, its yellowish white glow casting odd shadows across the oak floor.

He slowly rose to his feet, cringing at the sound of the creaking boards under his heels. He tiptoed to the door and pushed it silently closed, carefully releasing the knob and begging the latch not to click.

Icy dread crawled along his skin. The sense of danger grew in intensity with each creak from the bowels of the centuries-old house. Not able to sleep, he had decided to read a book of King Arthur lore borrowed from his teacher, Professor Hamilton. As he sat in the corner, he had thought the post-midnight noises were simply trees brushing the windows or maybe his host puttering around on the first floor. Now, as the clock on the wall ticked past 3:00 a.m., he knew better.

He glided across the room with long, quiet strides and snatched Excalibur's scabbard from a belt hanging around the bedpost. Grasping the hilt, he slowly drew out the blade. The sound of metal sliding on metal drilled courage into his heart, and the sword's illuminating glow chased the shadows from the room.

Holding the sword with his arms extended, he planted his feet and kept his body perfectly still . . . waiting . . . listening. The clock marked the seconds – tick . . . tick . . . tick. Cold sweat seeped through his pores, dampening his oversized T-shirt and raising goose bumps on his arms. The air in the bedroom felt heavy . . . suffocating, creating a sense of desperation, like being stuck in an underground cavern with a dying flashlight.

A stuttering creak sounded from the hallway. Was it a floorboard bending under a skulking footstep? The door hinges grating, ready to fly open at any second?

Billy's eyes riveted on the door. The creaking stopped, but a spine-tingling alarm kept blaring in his mind. What could be lurking out there? Professor Hamilton was supposed to be sleeping in the next room. Had the approaching menace already paid him a deadly visit? With a dozen bedrooms lining the hall on this second-storey wing, maybe it – whatever it was – had passed the professor by.

Billy licked his lips. *Should I call Prof? Should I go check on him?*

The door creaked again. He regripped Excalibur's hilt and tensed his arms. In the dimness, he could see no movement, only shifting light as the sword vibrated in his trembling hands. He didn't feel scared – not much, anyway – mostly just cold in the spacious, drafty bedroom. His sweatpants and damp T-shirt weren't enough to ward off the chill.

As he watched for a hint of movement, an unusual scent drifted past his nose, a sweet blossom of some kind, not pungent like perfume, more like the soft fragrance of gardenias or jasmine. It was pleasant, soothing, even peaceful.

Billy yawned. His eyelids drooped. His brain felt light . . . tired . . . sleepy. He backed up a few steps and bumped into his bed frame. It was the middle of the night, so why not just go to bed? That noise wasn't really anything. This spooky old mansion probably creaked all the time.

A vague sense of danger still lurked in the back of his mind, but he shooed it away, yawning again. It was nothing; there was no danger. He sat down on the bed and breathed in the wonderful aroma, sweet flowers . . . so peaceful . . . so relaxing. He imagined lying in a bed of soft rose petals on a sunny day, a cool breeze caressing him to sleep. Was he really lying down now?

Yes, I must be. It's so soft, so comfortable.

Consciousness began slipping away.

There's that creaking noise again. But it's nothing . . . just the wind blowing through this old house.

His sense of danger faded, vanishing in a whirlpool of images – his friends, Bonnie and Walter; the dragon Clefspeare; his mother – all mixing into a confused dream.

More creaking? Footsteps? Mum, is that you?

He felt a cool hand softly touch his neck. He smiled. *Okay, Mum. I'll get up. I just have to—*

A wild shout pierced his senses. "William!"

Billy shot upward, but a strong grip shoved him back to the bed, iron fingers squeezing his throat. He couldn't breathe. A hooded form, a shadow in the dimness, pressed close to his face, almost eye to eye, as he straddled Billy's body, choking his life away.

The dark figure suddenly lurched back, releasing its strangling grip. Wearing a long, black robe, his attacker looked like a spectre flying away from his bed. Loud bumps erupted from the floor, and the professor's voice shouted, "William! . . . I require . . . your assistance . . . immediately!"

Billy sat up, caressing his throat and blinking away the mind fog. The professor and the dark intruder rolled on the floor, their arms and legs intertwined, the professor's white hair tossing wildly. Billy's senses came roaring back, and he threw himself into the mix, punching the assailant with both fists, then gouging his hooded face with his fingers. It was no use. He seemed impenetrable.

The man pulled the professor into a bear hug, and his muscular arms squeezed the elderly teacher's chest. The professor grunted. "The sword. . . . Use . . . the sword!"

Billy jumped up and searched for Excalibur. Where had he put it? He threw back the covers on the bed. *Ah! There it is!*

He grabbed the hilt and summoned Excalibur's transluminating beam, a laser-like shaft of radiance shooting out of the tip. Although he had practiced using it countless times, he wasn't sure he could strike the intruder with the disintegrating ray without hurting the professor. One touch would send this dark burglar into oblivion, making him nothing but a holiday sparkler, but he didn't want the professor to become part of the fireworks.

With a savage thrust of his bare foot, Billy kicked the hooded man in the ribs.

"Arrgh!" The man arched his back.

The professor pulled free and rolled away like a log on a steep hill. Rising to his knees the teacher called out, "Now, William! Now!"

Billy swung the sword's beam, slamming it against the intruder's torso. The shaft of light sizzled across his body, and sparks popped like water droplets on a hot frying pan. The man's black robe absorbed the fiery light, framing his shadowy form with a flashing halo.

The intruder sprang to his feet and kicked the professor in the head with a heavy boot, sending him sprawling to the ground. The black hood slowly turned. Two eye slots rotated to the front with a hate-filled glare blazing through.

Billy stepped back, stunned. Blood oozed from the side of the professor's head as he lay crumpled on the floor. Was he breathing? A hard lump grew in Billy's throat. He couldn't swallow it away.

The hooded man snorted. "Not so brave when your ultimate weapon fails, are you, Dragon Boy?" He blew on his hand with a mocking puff and laughed. "How about your fire breathing? Doesn't it work? Why don't you give it a try?"

Billy felt a good blast of fire growing in his belly. But should he use it? Excalibur's beam didn't work on this creep, and his challenge probably meant that fire wouldn't faze him either. But what could it hurt?

He took a deep breath and hurled a stream of fire from his mouth. The orange tongue of flame splattered against the intruder, but he just spread his arms as though he were basking in sunshine, allowing the blaze to caress his black suit, making it glow like a heated stove-top coil. As the colour faded to a dull orange, he crossed his arms and laughed. "I guess the mongrel's bark is worse than his bite."

Billy raised Excalibur to an attack position and bared his teeth. "I have not yet begun to bite."

"Oh, that's a good one," the intruder scoffed. He pulled a sword from under his cloak. "Let's see if your blade is as sharp as your wit."

Billy pulled his sword back and charged. With a hard, two-handed sweep he lunged at the intruder's neck. The man parried, blocking the swipe with his own silver blade. With a turn on his heel, Billy threw his body into a three-sixty spin, ducked low, and hacked at his opponent's ankles. The man hopped deftly over the blade and chopped downward at Billy's neck.

Billy lurched to the side and rolled away. The attacking blade sliced into the wood floor, wedging tightly.

As the intruder tugged on his hilt, Billy jumped to his feet and swung Excalibur like a baseball bat, aiming for the man's waist. Still hanging onto his sword, the man slid his feet forward, facing upward and ducking under the deadly swing. After Excalibur swiped harmlessly above his face, the intruder sprang back to his feet with the help of his recoiling sword. He finally yanked the blade out of the floor and straightened his body, his feet set and arms flexed.

With sweat dripping from his hair, Billy stepped back and stared at his opponent's fierce eyes, his chest heaving and his arms trembling. He gripped Excalibur tightly with both hands. Even if the beam wouldn't disintegrate the intruder, he knew Excalibur had to give him an advantage. It was more than just a sword; it was a holy sabre, generating its magnificent light energy only for certain people. It must have been guided by a greater power, an intelligence above and beyond his own.

The hooded man charged, his sword swinging. Billy blocked it with Excalibur, and when the two blades met, Excalibur's glow burst into a glorious blaze, so bright he had to squint.

The intruder held out his hand to block the brilliant light. Fear and agony flooded his eyes. With a wild, one-handed swipe, he waved his sword high. Billy ducked just in time, feeling the blade swish above his head. The intruder dropped to his knees and swung again, this time aiming low. Billy jumped, and the razor edge passed under his bare feet like a chilling wind. The intruder slumped, his cloaked head drooping. He seemed drained, exhausted.

Billy leaped at the chance. He slammed Excalibur's flat side against the man's skull. A burst of electrostatic energy covered the intruder's hood and ran across his black suit like a swarm of lightning bugs, buzzing and flashing in chaotic twinkles. His arms stiffened, and he toppled to the side, his head smacking the floor with a sickening thud. The black mass of body, cloak, and hood lay motionless at Billy's feet.

The twinkling died away. Billy, his eyes wide, lowered Excalibur, letting its point rest on the floor. The sword's light diminished, yet still retained enough radiance to illuminate much of the room.

He dashed to the professor's side and dropped to his knees. He placed a cool hand on the old man's wrinkled face and across his lips. The teacher's shallow breaths warmed his fingers. *He's alive!*

Billy set Excalibur on the floor and gently patted the professor's cheek. "Professor!" he called in a loud whisper. "Wake up!"

"Nonsense!" the professor replied, his eyes still closed. "There are no gardenias in these gardens. Roses and daffodils, yes, but no gardenias."

Billy shook his teacher's shoulder. "Professor. It's me, Billy. You're dreaming. Wake up."

The professor's eyelids fluttered open. "William!" His eyes darted around the room. "The assailant. Where is he?"

Billy gestured with his head. "On the floor over by the door. I think I knocked him out cold."

The professor struggled to his feet and retied the sash on his grey terry-cloth bathrobe. When he lifted his head, he seemed to be in a daze, and his body swayed.

Billy grabbed the professor's forearm and steadied him. "That guy really gave you a hard lick with his boot." He stepped into the bathroom, snatched a hand towel off the rod, and gave it to his teacher. "But it looks like the bleeding's slowed down."

The professor dabbed the wound gingerly and examined the splotch of red on the otherwise white towel. “Yes, William. I don’t believe I will require stitches.”

A bump sounded from somewhere in the house, then padded footsteps and whispered commands. The professor waved his arm at a dresser next to the door. “Block the entry! Hurry!”

Billy dashed to the door and pushed it closed. Then, with a quiet grunt, he shoved the waist-high dresser under the knob and pressed his ear against the door panel. “I hear noises, like people running on tiptoes.”

The professor knelt next to the intruder’s sprawled body and slid his hood off, revealing a young man with a wispy brown moustache and goatee. He pressed two fingers against the man’s neck, then looked up, his brow wrinkling. “He appears to be dead, William.”

“Dead? But I only hit him with the flat side! I didn’t even draw blood!”

The professor felt the intruder’s wrist and pressed his ear against his draped chest. He raised his head again. “Flat side or no, he is certainly dead.”

Billy picked up Excalibur and rushed to the professor’s side. “Have you ever seen him before?”

“No.” The professor lifted one of the intruder’s black-sleeved arms. “We must hurry. Help me get this cloak off.”

The professor rolled the burglar to one side while Billy tugged at a cloak sleeve, pulling it off the assailant’s arm. Repeating the motions, they slipped off the other sleeve and carefully slid the cloak out from under the man’s body.

When the professor rolled the intruder to his back, he paused and stared at the newly exposed forearm. He reached for Billy and pulled his arm, sword and all, toward the corpse. The sword’s light cast an iridescent glow across the man’s skin, changing its colour to pale blue. The professor put his finger on a strange monogram, dark blue lines in the shape of the letter *M*.

"William! He bears the mark!"

"The mark? It just looks like an *M* to me."

"Exactly!" The professor guided Billy's wrist, manoeuvring the sword's glow. As the light passed over the monogram, the outline of the *M* brightened to a phosphorescent purple. The professor kept his voice low. "It's the mark of a New Table knight, your opposition. It can only be seen within a narrow range of light frequencies, and I suspected that Excalibur might emit such a frequency."

The professor rose abruptly and began pulling off his robe. "Get dressed! Hurry!"

Billy leaped toward the dresser and popped open a suitcase that sat on top. "How are we going to get out of here?"

The professor, now dressed only in long, thermal underwear, pushed an arm into the sleeve of the intruder's cloak. "By stealth, William."

Billy dug into his suitcase and tossed out a pair of calf-length socks, his off-white cargo trousers, and a brown long-sleeved shirt. While he threw on his clothes, the professor peered into the suitcase. "May I borrow a pair of socks?"

Billy balanced on one foot, reaching down to tie a shoe. "Sure, Prof."

The professor fished out a wadded pair of socks, then picked something else out of the suitcase and slipped it into his pocket.

Billy grabbed his jacket and gloves. "What did you take from my—?"

"Aaaiieee!" A scream rifled through the room, freezing Billy in place.

The professor's eyes blazed. "The master of the house!" He threw the black hood over his head and pushed the dresser out of the way. "We must go! Now!"

Billy thrust Excalibur into its scabbard and fastened the belt to his waist. "That cloak may get you out of here, Prof, but I'll stick out like a mouse at a cat party."

The professor snatched up the intruder's fallen sword, then raised a finger to his lips. "Wait here while I fetch my keys." He slipped out the door and disappeared into the hallway shadows.

Billy waited in darkness, the ticking clock providing the only sound in the room. A dead body lay near his feet. Was he an advance scout of some kind? How many more of them were searching through the house?

A door slammed. Footsteps pounded in the hallway, louder and louder.

Billy shivered. They were getting closer. Would they catch the professor? He slid Excalibur from its scabbard. The sword trembled in his hand. Should he try to make a run for it? Should he obey the professor and wait? He took a deep breath and pulled the door open a crack.

A new voice sounded from the hallway, barely audible. "Did you find the boy?"

"Yes," another voice replied, whispering. "All is in hand."

Billy tried to peer through the crack. *That sounds like Prof!*

"Is Foraker dead?" the first voice asked. "Do they have his cloak?"

"Yes and yes."

"Good. Exactly as planned." The first man's voice lowered to an even quieter whisper. "Let them out of the room, then chase them to the front door. We'll kill the old man and dump the kid at Patrick's doorstep. Remember, just scare them out. Morgan wants the Bannister boy deposited unharmed with the cloak."

The conversation ended. Billy moved away from the door and waited. Seconds later, the door swung open. A black-cloaked figure stepped inside and jerked his hood off, revealing the professor's familiar face. His skin had turned ashen, and his wild white hair stood almost on end.

The professor closed the door and pressed his back against it, holding his hand on his chest and breathing heavily. "I fooled him . . . for now . . . but we must escape . . . by a way other than the front door."

"Yeah. I heard." Billy returned the sword to its sheath. "How long till we're supposed to meet Bonnie and the dragons?"

The professor took a deep breath and exhaled slowly. "About two hours. Five-thirty to be precise. We have plenty of time."

"Maybe, but if my dad's still like he was before he turned back into a dragon, he'll be early." Billy pointed at the window on the opposite side of the room. "Feel up to walking on the roof?"

The professor lifted his foot, displaying a mid-top hiking boot. "I managed to get my trousers and shoes on, and I collected my gloves, so I suppose I'm properly equipped." He squatted and began tying the laces. "But I have a splitting headache, which may indicate a concussion. I'm not sure what will happen if I exert myself."

Billy opened the window and leaned out into the misty darkness, turning his head from side to side. He left the window up and hustled back to the professor, a cool breeze following in his wake. "Looks like it's all clear in the backyard."

The professor stood up, holding his hand on his head. "Then perhaps we'll make it if I can move slowly enough."

Billy zipped up his jacket and stuffed his gloves into one of the pockets. "It's a cinch. I've done it at my house a hundred times." He bounded to the window and vaulted onto the sill. "Come on," he said, waving his arm. "The roof's flat enough." He crawled onto the shingles and helped the professor squeeze through the window.

"Now to find a downspout or a trellis." Billy bent over and skulked to the edge of the roof, careful to keep Excalibur from dragging. He dropped to his knees, planted his palms on the gritty surface, then leaned over the side. The professor scooted on his knees, nearing the edge while Billy scanned the ground level. Directly underneath, two black-hooded figures stood next to a car, one with his hand on the hood.

Billy whispered. "Two more goons right below us."

"Two that we can see," the professor whispered back. "There may be more."

"Is that your rental car?"

"Yes. Don't you remember it?"

"No." Billy lowered his voice even further. "I was tired when I got in, and I slept all the way from the airport."

The professor's tone matched Billy's. "It's a Vauxhall Vectra Elite, a fine British motor car."

"Well, it might as well be a unicycle without pedals. It's down there, and we're up here." Billy reached back and grabbed Excalibur's hilt. "Getting to it would be easy if I could just trans-luminate them. I wonder what went wrong."

The professor rubbed his fingers across his black cloak. "Very strange. It feels like a network of wires on the surface, as fine as silk thread, a metallic mesh of some fashion. And it's warm to the touch."

Billy passed his hand across one of the long sleeves. "Maybe the wires protected that guy. Excalibur's beam didn't faze him, and when I blasted him with fire it just made the wires light up like some kind of heating grid."

The professor stroked the mesh again. "Remarkable. It seems to carry a faint residue." He rubbed his finger and thumb together and brought them close to his eyes. After sniffing the fine powder, he brushed it away with his other hand. "I believe it could be rust."

"Rust? You mean like from iron?"

"Yes. Hydrated ferrous oxide of some sort."

Billy straightened his back, keeping his knees firmly on the shingles. "So if I can't zap these guys, what're we going to do? If we try to climb down, they'll see us for sure."

The professor sat up on his haunches with his hand on his chin. "Then we will conquer them with a tried and true, surreptitious approach."

"Sir Who?"

The professor rose to his full height and helped Billy to his feet. "I'll take the one on the left," he said. "Are you ready?"

"Ready? Ready for what?"

"Jump!" The professor leaped off the roof, pulling Billy with him, and they plummeted toward the two men in black.

CHAPTER

DRAGONS

The ocean surface glittered in Bonnie's eyes, reflecting the gibbous moon's shining disk. She was accustomed to flying through dark skies, a necessary skill for a girl with dragon wings. Darkness had helped her avoid obvious dangers in the past. During flights around her neighbourhood, her swooping profile had alerted dogs that barked and howled until she flew into the safety of the moonless shadows.

Although she yearned to fly boldly in the light, darkness had become her friend. It was a cloak of protection that hid her prominent features. But would tonight's gloom provide enough of a shield? With two huge dragons accompanying her over the Atlantic Ocean, a Navy radar operator might spot them and scramble a jet to check out the strangest UFO he had ever seen. Their danger was real, so the three flew swiftly through the silent night sky, gliding so close to the sea's undulating surface, the dragons' wings would sometimes graze the crests of the waves.

Although Bonnie's wings had been injured earlier in the year, it wasn't long before she was flying again. The photoreceptors in her blood, a genetic trait passed down from her mother, carried healing energy throughout her body. She had worked out strenuously over the past few months to get her wings, and herself, back in shape. Her longest flight to date topped three hundred miles, but this new journey stretched over an entire ocean and spanned several days. During daylight hours, one dragon submerged up to its neck while the other floated with only a mattress-sized portion of its back exposed, providing Bonnie a place to sleep while curled up in her wings. At night, they travelled as quickly as possible, still allowing breaks along the way and occasional back rides for Bonnie when she tired. As powerful as the dragons were, she didn't want to burden them too much.

At times the cool, moist air brought a chill in spite of her layers of clothing, a sweatshirt over a long-sleeved pullover shirt and a pair of blue jeans over thermal underwear. The wing holes she had sewn into her shirts had shifted in flight, allowing the breeze to find its way to her skin. Still, the leather gloves kept her hands warm, and the ski cap over her braided hair and ears helped a lot. Professor Hamilton had instructed her to wear cotton or wool clothing for a possible translumination, but she had decided the synthetics in the cap wouldn't pose a problem.

She looked down at their shadows on the bumpy ocean. Barely visible in the meagre light, the beating wings waved at her, each ghostly pulse reminding her again of her beastly appearance. For years she had tried to hide the deformity that had shrouded her in secrecy from school to school and foster home to foster home. A mere backpack had veiled a feature that would have made mothers scream, babies cry, and other kids run in fear or call her horrible names.

Bonnie shook her head hard. Her wings were a gift, not a curse! They had saved both her and Billy more than once, and they made her . . . well . . . unique. And every gift from God had a purpose, even strange, scaly gifts.

Clefspeare, the male dragon on her left, called out, "Do you need another rest?"

Bonnie clutched the front of her sweatshirt and let out a tired gasp. "How much longer to shore?"

"Probably a couple of hours."

"I guess I'd better take a break. Whose turn is it?"

Hartanna, the female dragon, glided closer. "My turn. Hop on. We'll take a rest, too."

Bonnie rose a few feet and hovered over Hartanna's back. With a graceful flutter of her wings, she settled gently on the base of the dragon's neck, behind one protruding spine and in front of another.

Hartanna descended to the ocean surface, skimming across the waves like a seaplane. When her huge body splashed down, she paddled to keep her back well above water. Clefspeare copied Hartanna's move and settled in next to her.

"Let's take a long break, Bonnie," Hartanna said. "We're way ahead of schedule."

Clefspeare took a deep breath as his armoured body rose and fell on the ocean's restless surface. "Not too long. We don't want to make the professor and Billy wait." He used his teeth to lift a blue denim backpack off one of his spines and stretched his neck to give the bundle to Bonnie. She slid the pack over her shoulder, and he nodded toward it. "You should eat now. It's been too many hours since your last meal, and you need your strength."

Bonnie pulled a wrapped sandwich from her backpack, fumbling over the plastic Ziploc with her gloved hands. "It's a good thing we're almost there. I'm down to my last sandwich. What about you and Ma—I mean, Hartanna? I haven't seen either of you eat since yesterday."

Hartanna reached a wing over her back and caressed Bonnie's arm. "It's okay to call me Mama. I really don't mind."

Clefspeare's eyes darted back and forth across the waves. "Yesterday's catch was large enough to last for two days, but with so much uncertainty lying ahead, we should take another meal." The dragon dipped his head in the water and pulled out a wriggling fish. He offered it to Hartanna, who shook her head. Clefspeare crunched the fish's body with his powerful jaws, and it disappeared into his gullet. With a satisfied smack of his lips he turned back to Bonnie. "Ahhh! Raw fish is such a healthy snack, especially with fins and scales still attached." He stretched his neck forward, and his maw widened in a toothy grin. "I could get one for you. I think I see a fat, juicy pollack up ahead."

Bonnie grimaced, then laughed. "Uh, no thanks." She finished half of her sandwich and rewrapped the other half. She pulled a water bottle from her pack and took a long drink. "I've had enough," she said, fastening the cap on the bottle.

"Would you like to ride on my back the rest of the way?" Hartanna asked. "You've already flown farther than anyone could expect."

"I guess so." Bonnie stretched her arms and yawned. "I'm getting pretty tired."

The two dragons unfurled their massive wings and lifted into the air as one. Bonnie used her own wings to help herself balance on Hartanna's scaly back. As their flying forms again painted shadows on the ocean surface, Bonnie wondered what would greet her on the other side of this massive sea. Even the dragons had not seen the British coast in many years. Would they know how to avoid detection and how to find shelter? Their caves had likely been searched out dozens of times since they last flew these skies. Would they have homes at all?

Bonnie hugged Hartanna's protruding spine, keeping her head low to duck under the jet stream of cold, wet air. With her gloved fingers gripping the plate-like skin, she wondered what it must be like to be a full-fledged dragon. Surely her mother must have longed to return to her dragon's domain. It wouldn't be the same, though. The days of Arthur were long gone. The night Merlin changed her into the lovely Irene would stand as the last night she would know as a dragon princess. Her future as the chosen queen of all dragons had been shaken by the slayers of old as they hunted dragons to near extinction. But in a single moment, a miraculous transformation from dragon to human had ended her plans, and those of the dragon race, forever.

Bonnie had only recently learned that Hartanna was once betrothed to Clefspeare. They had begun a period of separation from each other to prepare for their eventual union. The transformation ended their dreams. They gave up a kingdom – one they realized would be short-lived – to become human. When they began sailing once again over familiar lands, would sad memories or regret come to mind? As they lay alone in separate caves, would they lament, wondering what might have been? Or would lying on a bejewelled bed in the splendour of a regeneracy dome heal their spiritual wounds as the bouncing light massaged away their regrets?

After daydreaming for a while, Bonnie lifted her head into a stiff breeze. Now, instead of endless ocean, lights appeared in the distance. "Is that England?" she asked.

"Yes," Clefspeare replied. "If the stars have not changed significantly, that is the south-west peninsula. We will be at the rendezvous point soon."

The dim coastline slowly took shape, moving closer with each flap of Hartanna's wings. The dragons were flying faster than before. Bonnie knew they had slowed their pace for her when she was flying solo, and now they seemed to rocket through the air like scaly eagles, rising in altitude as they approached the misty shore.

A bank of clouds greeted them a few miles inland, and the dragons skimmed just above the puffy grey tops. Every once in a while Clefspeare dove below the bank to get a look at what lay below, searching for landmarks that would guide their way.

"I can barely see the great tor on the horizon," he finally announced, "so the hill underneath us is likely to be Camelot's resting place. But there is a problem. I sense danger when I fly at the lower levels."

"I felt something, too," Hartanna said. "Just a faint impression." The scales on the she-dragon's long neck caught the moon's glowing disk, reflecting a dozen, fiery replicas. "Clefspeare," she said, "Bonnie must fly with you to the meeting place. I will stay out of sight. If danger presents itself, I will be able to attack with stealth."

Clefspeare straightened his wings in a horizontal spread and slowly descended. "Very well. Keep watch and judge what you must do according to the Maker's guidance."

Hartanna nodded. "May His light guide you."

Clefspeare's body dipped below the cloud surface, his head still poking up. "Come child," he said, before disappearing into the mist.

Bonnie lifted her wings into the passing flow, filling out her leather-like canopies as she elevated inch by inch over Hartanna's back. Now flying freely, Bonnie forced a confident smile, and with a quick goodbye wave dove head first into the cloud bank. As soon as she dropped below the mist, she stretched her wings again and caught the air, slowing her descent. Between her and the ground, two scarlet orbs glided through the air in a lazy circle,

Clefspeare's eyes looking up at her. The veiled moon barely revealed his enormous silhouette trailing his ruby headlights.

Bonnie dropped quickly to join him, mimicking his circular pattern, and they approached a grass-domed hilltop. She landed near the edge of the field just a second or two after Clefspeare, running as her feet settled on the ground. Ankle-high grass covered the expansive summit, bordered by steep drop-offs and a dense forest.

The dragon turned his head in all directions, twisting his neck and sniffing the cool, damp air. His voice stayed low, a growling whisper. "Danger is near." He lumbered to the trees, and Bonnie followed. "Stay in the forest while I keep watch. Although we are considerably ahead of schedule, Billy may arrive soon. He is quite aware of my habit of being early."

Clefspeare continued sniffing the air. Bonnie tried to detect any unusual odours, but she noticed only a tinge of smoke from a distant wood fire. Maybe the dragon's sense of smell was more acute than hers. She whispered her question. "Do you smell something?"

"Flowers," he replied in a low rumble. "Yet I saw no gardens or wildflowers nearby. It is a familiar odour, but the memory is a distant one from centuries long past."

Bonnie sniffed again. This time a slight aroma drifted by, the buttery sweetness of some kind of blossom, maybe gardenia.

A voice called from the opposite side of the clearing. "Hail, Clefspeare!"

Clefspeare's neck straightened, and his ears twitched. "Who calls for Clefspeare? Friend or foe? Show yourself."

A figure appeared in the clearing, striding quickly forward and offering a formal bow. "I am Markus, servant and apprentice to Sir Patrick, steward of the Circle of Knights. I have come as his herald to welcome you and conduct you and the initiate's colleague to his side."

Clefspeare snorted a plume of sparks. "The initiate was to greet us personally, along with his mentor."

Bonnie kept her eye on the young man, but she couldn't stifle the need to yawn. The aroma of gardenias filled the air – sweet, intoxicating. A shadow of sleepiness filtered into her mind, and her vision blurred as she tried to refocus on Markus. He bowed again. "We have detected a hole in our security, so I have come to warn you and escort the girl to safety."

"But that was not the plan," Clefspeare argued. "There is danger afoot, and Billy and his teacher must not face it without me."

Markus turned his head from side to side. "There is no time to fret about plans gone awry, Great Dragon. If you sense danger, then I suggest we be off at once. Morgan would have the girl in her clutches, and we must keep the two of them apart at all costs."

Clefspeare took in a deep breath. His voice slowed, growing laboured. "Yes. . . . Danger is . . . very close. A s-s-sinister . . . presence." The dragon's head swayed, and his body tipped to one side. As he began to topple, he turned to Bonnie, his voice reviving in one desperate call. "Fly, lass! Find Hartanna!" With a tremendous thud, Clefspeare fell to the ground.

Bonnie unfurled her wings, but they drooped to the grass, heavy and limp. She could barely raise them above the level of her dizzied head. She tried to jump, but her legs collapsed. A curtain of black closed across her eyes, and she dropped to the grass. A strong hand gripped her wrist and pulled. She fluttered her eyes open and caught a glimpse of Markus's face and two hooded figures running toward them with swords in hand. As she struggled to get up, a stream of fire blazed behind Markus, but her arms and legs fell numb, and her mind faded into darkness.

Billy dropped from the mansion roof like a sack of rocks, his arms and legs flailing. He steadied himself just in time to smash his heels into the hooded goon's shoulder blades, crumpling the man's body into a heap. Bending his knees to cushion the impact, Billy pushed off to the side, his momentum propelling him into a barrel roll. The professor lay on his back next to his rental car, while the second goon sprawled over the edge of the gravel driveway, his face half-buried in the mud. Billy's victim writhed on his belly, clutching handfuls of pebbles and trying to push to his knees.

Billy jumped to his feet, planted his foot on the man's back, and slammed him down. Grabbing his sword from its scabbard, he lifted his victim's hood and pricked his neck. "Play dead, and I'll let you live."

The man cursed, then growled, "I don't take orders from dragon mongrels."

Billy lifted his foot high and thrust his heel into the man's head, driving his face into the gravel. When his victim's arms and legs fell limp, he stepped aside. "Then have a nice nap." He sprang toward the passenger's side of the car, threw open the door, then sprinted back to the professor. Letting out a low grunt, he lugged his teacher to the vehicle, half-lifting, half-carrying his body.

The professor's head wobbled. "Do you smell gardenias?" he asked groggily.

"It's all right, Prof. I'll get you out of here." Billy tucked the professor's legs inside, fished for the keys from his cloak pocket, and quietly closed the door. He dashed around to the driver's side, unhitched the scabbard from his belt, and tossed both the sword and scabbard into the back seat. He slid behind the steering wheel, hurriedly surveying the controls. Fumbling with the keys, he finally thrust one into the ignition and started the engine. Leaving the headlights off, he shifted into gear. As the car crept down the driveway, he glanced from side to side, watchful for moving shadows.

A cloaked figure jumped down from the mansion's elevated front deck and sprinted ahead to intercept them.

Billy slammed the gas pedal down. The car lurched forward, fishtailing as it surged past the man, its wheels spinning in the gravel and slinging a hailstorm of pebbles into his face. The tyres finally gripped the surface and catapulted toward the estate's entrance, a closed, metal-framed gate.

Billy ducked his head. The front bumper smashed through the barrier, launching the gate's frame over the windshield and sending it tumbling behind them. He spun the steering wheel to the right and careened onto a deserted road, tyres squealing as he jerked into the lane.

Billy turned on the headlights, then nudged the professor. "Prof! You okay?"

The professor pushed himself upright, slowly shaking his head. "Is it time for tea?"

Billy let up on the accelerator, settling the car into a comfortable cruising speed. "No, not exactly teatime." He adjusted the rear-view mirror, relieved that no headlights glared at him from behind. "How do we get to the meeting place?"

The professor blinked his eyes. "William? You're driving?"

"Yeah. I got my permit when I turned fifteen. Mum's been teaching me." He tapped the steering wheel with his hand. "It feels weird driving on the right side of the car though."

The professor laid his head back against his seat and exhaled slowly. "I believe an emergency flight from savage murderers will trump the law in this case. As long as you're comfortable driving, it's for the best." He dabbed his scalp wound with the tips of his fingers. "My head is killing me."

"Well, I hope I don't meet too many cars on the road." Billy nodded toward the windshield. "But I see some headlights up ahead."

The professor's eyes shot open. "William! You're not on the right side of the road!"

"What do you mean? Of course I'm on the right side of the road!"

"No!" the professor shouted. "Left is right! Right is wrong!"

Billy shook his head. "Professor that kick must've really—"

The professor lunged for the steering wheel and pulled it to the left, sending the car squealing into the opposite lane just as an oncoming truck roared past, its horn blaring. He pushed the wheel back, steadying the car in the left-hand lane. "Keep it . . . here," the professor gasped. He leaned back again, holding his hand on his chest, still breathing heavily. "In England . . . the left lane is the right . . . ahem . . . the correct lane . . . for driving."

Billy nodded. "Left is right. . . . I knew that. . . . Just forgot in all the excitement."

"Now," the professor continued, "I believe there will be a roundabout coming up. When you get to it, you'll want to take the road on the right, but first you must go to the left, and circle around until you get to the street that was originally on your right, though it will be on your left when you get to it. Do you understand?"

Billy wobbled his head between a shake and a nod. "I think so."

"Good." The professor took a deep breath and ran his hand along his sleeve. "Because of the unexpected attack on your person, we'll use our travel time to discuss a number of issues – this cloak, for example." His fingers paused at the cuff. "Strange. Why are there so many lumps in the lining?"

"Lumps?"

"Yes. Rectangular lumps." With a quick jerk, the professor ripped a hole at the cuff's lining seam and bent the material back. "I do believe they're microchips!"

Billy slowed down as he approached a circular intersection. "A computerized cloak? Sounds like a bad secret agent show on television."

"Perhaps, William." He pried one of the chips out and held it close to his eyes. "But bad television or not, this discovery could be vital."

Coming to a full stop at the intersection, Billy reached over and felt the cuff. At least six chips made a circle around the professor's wrist. "I'll bet Ashley could figure out how the cloak works."

"Yes, of course! Miss Stalworth's talents are perfectly suited for such a task." The professor lifted the bottom hem of the cloak and reached underneath for his cell phone. "I'll call and see if she is able to join us. It's late evening in West Virginia, so she may still be awake. Early morning departures to England are few, but one might be available."

Billy drove clockwise three-quarters of the way around the traffic circle and onto a new road. "That'll be great. When Mum gets done helping Sir Barlow, maybe she can drive down from Glasgow, and we'll all tour London when this mission thing is over."

"I don't see why she cannot join us," the professor replied, punching a number into his phone. "Sir Barlow will be able to handle the museum soon enough, and I'm sure we can find accommodation for your mother." He held the phone to his ear. "Busy. Apparently Miss Stalworth is awake." He set the phone down again and brushed some of the rust from his sleeve. "I am not sure, however, how long it will take to complete your mission. Sir Patrick is in charge of that, but he has kept the details to himself. For example, I, myself, was shocked when he delayed our journey here by six months. To this day he hasn't explained the reason. He also insisted that you have one helper, and only one helper, on your mission." He set a hand on Billy's shoulder. "He is a very mysterious fellow, but I trust him without reservation, and you should as well. His deeds have proven him an honourable gentleman." The professor pointed toward a roundabout up ahead. "Turn left at the next intersection."

Billy made the turn and proceeded slowly. Tall hedges bordered the narrow road on both sides, leaving no shoulder or even the thinnest strip of grass between the edge of the road and the foliage. With the lack of traffic at this early morning hour, he steered the car to the middle of the road. "Do you think the microchip will tell us something about the guy who attacked me?"

"Perhaps, but there is much I have already deduced. His youthfulness indicates that he is only in the second or third level of the New Table order, too young to be a master. He was probably hoping this mission would qualify him for consideration in joining the upper circle of seven."

"The upper circle?"

The professor pushed his hand into the cloak's deep pocket. "Yes. I assume with Devin's departure, there is now a vacancy. You see, there are multiple circles, and the highest level makes up the New Table, a group of seven who—" His jaw clenched. "What's this?" He drew out a small cylinder that looked like a slender candle, about eight inches long with one melted end. He ran it by his nostrils, then jerked it away again, his nose wrinkling.

Billy sniffed the air. "It's that smell, that gardenia smell that knocked me out."

"Yes, William." He placed the candle in his open palm. "This is a scentser, spelled with 'scent' as in the scent that a bloodhound would follow."

Billy pursed his lips. "Soooo . . . what's a scentser?"

"It's a weapon of a New Table warrior," the professor replied, holding the scentser close to his face again. "I heard of such a device years ago, but I learned much more about it from the books in Devin's library. This particular scent is obviously designed to put an opponent to sleep, a useful tool for a burglar or some other deceiver who wishes to disable his victim. Other scents are used for other purposes."

"Well, it worked on me. How did you fight it off?"

The professor returned the scentser to his pocket. "When you recognize an enemy's weapons, they are easier to resist. If you are caught unaware, however, they are much more effective. I suspect that dragons are more sensitive to the aroma. At least the legends tell us so. You, being a dragon of sorts, are probably more susceptible than I." He tapped Billy on the arm and pointed toward a gap in the hedge on the left. "Turn in here and park, please."

Billy guided the car through the gap and into a deserted parking lot, stopping at the closest space. He shut off the engine and gave the keys to his teacher. "Is this the place we're meeting my dad—I mean, Clefspeare?"

The professor hooked his finger through the key ring. "Yes, at the top of a hill on the other side of the road. It's called Cadbury Castle, though there is no castle there now. It is believed to be the location of Camelot, and remnants of a fortifying wall still exist on the border of the summit."

After Billy refastened Excalibur to his belt, he and the professor walked across the road and found a trail leading up the hill. Flanked by tall trees that blocked the moon, they scaled the path slowly, barely able to see their own feet. Billy stumbled on a rock but caught himself before he fell. He unsheathed Excalibur and cast its glow on the path.

The professor fished his cell phone from the cloak's pocket. "Since we know our secrecy has already been compromised, it may be important to maintain silence at the top, so I will try Miss Stalworth again before we get any closer."

Billy shifted Excalibur, illuminating the professor as he dialed. "With all those goons running around," Billy said, "I wish Sir Barlow could travel with her."

The professor's face wrinkled with a wide grin.

"What's so funny, Prof?"

"The thought of Sir Barlow flying in an airplane amused me. After spending over a thousand years inside the candlestone, he's not likely to keep his thoughts to himself should he peer out the window from thirty thousand feet."

"You got that right. When Mum flew with him to Glasgow, he fell back in his seat, kicked his food tray in the air, and grabbed a flight attendant, shouting at the top of his lungs, 'By all that is holy! This iron bird is sure to plummet at any moment!' "

The professor laughed as he punched the buttons on his phone. "Perhaps Walter would be a better companion for Miss Stalworth. He is a trustworthy young man, and they could watch out for each other."

"Yeah. Walter would never tip over a food tray, at least not one that still has food on it."

While the professor chatted with Ashley, Billy guided Excalibur's energy field toward the bordering forest. He thought he had heard twigs popping earlier and assumed any number of small animals could have been scurrying around in the undergrowth, but now his sense of danger pricked his mind. The sword's glow painted shifting shadows as each tree cast a dark stripe against another, criss-crossing into a patchwork of black phantoms.

Billy pulled on the professor's sleeve. "Prof, we'd better get moving."

The professor held up one finger. "Very well, Miss Stalworth. We'll see you when you arrive. Goodbye." He slapped the phone closed. "Danger, William?"

"Yeah," Billy whispered. "And it's growing."

The professor waved his hand at Excalibur. "Douse the sword. We'll have to take our chances without its light."

Billy slid Excalibur into the scabbard, plunging everything back into darkness.

The professor hiked up the trail, his outline barely visible as he swung his arm forward, whispering hoarsely, "Onward and upward, William!"

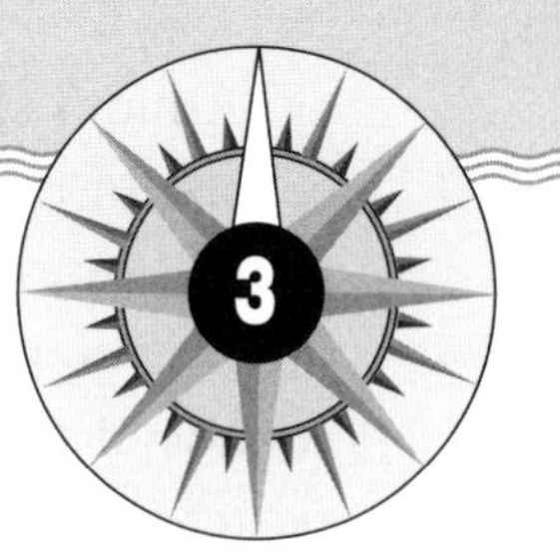

CHAPTER 3

England's Call

Ashley hung up the phone and propped her chin in her hand, rubbing her index ring against her jaw. With a deep sigh she lowered her hand and caressed the ring's gem with her thumb, polishing the rubellite's smooth surface. *I guess a girl's gotta do what a girl's gotta do.* She gazed into the gem and caught a glimpse of her warped reflection and whispered, "Or what a dragon's gotta do."

She rose from a plush sofa in the family room and walked slowly through a hallway toward her computer laboratory. A gallery of photos lined the freshly painted walls – Jared and Marilyn Bannister, their son, Billy, and Marilyn's five new foster children: Ashley and her four sisters, Karen, Rebecca, Stacey, and Monique.

The air in the newly rebuilt house was still tinged with the aroma of fresh paint and varnish. The stench of burnt flesh and scorched insulation had been bulldozed months ago, along with the remains of the old house the dragon slayers had burned down.

Ashley's shoes squeaked across the tile floor, and the noise echoed in the quiet corridor. Once she entered the computer room, however, everything changed. As soon as she swung the door open, a low-pitched hum bathed her ears in the exciting sounds of technology. Computer displays, digital meters, and poster-sized flowcharts covered the walls. A ten-foot-long work table abutted one wall, its top boasting at least five disassembled computers, their innards strewn across every square inch of space.

The drone of power supply cooling fans filled the room, and the refreshing breeze from an air conditioner wafted across Ashley's face. Karen sat in a glass-enclosed chamber, her bright orange hair bobbing as she pecked at a keyboard while watching a huge video display. The chamber's transparent walls enveloped the rear half of the computer room and housed Ashley's greatest creation, a revolutionary supercomputer, a ceiling-high box of metal and plastic covered with notched dials, flashing diodes, and plasma monitors.

"I thought I told you to go to bed," Ashley called.

Karen replied from behind the glass, her voice muffled. "Can't. If I don't finish this software installation, I'll have to start from scratch tomorrow." She rose from her chair, her eyes still glued to the screen. "Who was on the phone?"

"Professor Hamilton." Ashley gestured to her sister. "Come on out."

Karen's freckled face beamed as she slid the chamber's glass door open. "The professor? What's up?"

Ashley ran her fingers through her thick brown hair and walked slowly toward the chamber wall, staring blankly at one of her flowcharts. "He wants me to meet him in England. Something about analysing microchips."

"So what's got you looking like that?"

Ashley swivelled toward Karen. "Looking like what?" She rubbed her cheek with her fingertips. "Did I get toner on my face again?"

"No. You look like you missed a question on a calculus test or something."

Ashley smiled and shook her head slowly. "Oh, it's just an impression. The professor said he's 'lost the veil of secrecy' or something like that. You know how literary he is. Anyway, he told me to be careful, that I should ask Walter to come with me."

Karen's green eyes brightened. "You're going to England with Walter? Lucky dog."

Ashley put her palm on top of Karen's red head. "You're only fourteen. Keep your mind on your studies." She slid the glass door closed and leaned against it. "I'll need your brain in gear to operate the board, and this'll be a great chance to test how far the photo-porter system will transmit." She walked to a desk and pecked the keys on a laptop computer. The screen responded with a series of Internet pages, and Ashley browsed through an airline travel site. "Let's see. There's a morning flight out of D.C. We'd have to leave real early to get there on time." She rubbed the mouse pad and clicked its button. "Look at that! Two seats left!"

"Better snap 'em up."

Ashley switched to a personal phone directory on the computer. "Not yet. I'd better call the Foleys first and see if Walter can go."

Karen picked up a stray circuit board from the table and pressed on its memory chips with her thumb. "He'll go. With the professor in England, there's no school for a while. I saw him this morning, and he's so bored without Billy and Bonnie around, he's bouncing off the walls."

"This morning? I thought you said you were collecting cans."

"I was," Karen replied, raising her eyebrows. "I was just passing by on my bike, and he came out into the yard."

"Yeah, right. He probably wanted to tell you one of his lame jokes."

"No. Walter's cool as cash." Karen waved the circuit board at Ashley. "You think he's a clown, but he's not. Just yesterday I helped him and his dad fix their car, and he didn't crack a single joke. . . . Well, maybe one, but his jokes are always clean." She set one hand on her hip and blew her bangs out of her eyes. "Just because he's not Mr Sober Sides like you doesn't mean you should write him off."

Ashley grabbed a cell phone from her belt clip. "I'm not writing him off. I'm asking him to go to England with me, aren't I?" She flipped the phone open and glared at it. "I just wish he'd act his age."

Karen poked a finger into Ashley's ribs, grinning. "Well, maybe you should act *your* age instead of being an ornery old curmudgeon all the time."

Ashley's frown melted into a smile. "Curmudgeon? Where did you pick up that word?"

"From Larry. He called me that today when I complained about his installation protocol." Karen edged over to the glass wall and peered inside. "He doesn't like me, you know."

"Yeah, yeah. I know. Larry's out to get you, a computer with a prejudice against redheads." She punched in a number and put the phone to her ear. "Walter! Glad you're still up. Sorry to call so late, but it's important. . . . Yeah. Listen. You want to go to England with me? . . . When? Tomorrow. . . . Yeah, as in, you know, tomorrow. Don't get all worked up. . . . Do you have a passport? . . . Super! . . . What did your dad just say? . . . A chaperone? . . . Sure. Tell him the professor's meeting us at London Heathrow. We'll be in good hands. . . . He said 'yes'? . . . Great!

. . . Yeah. Good idea. I need Karen to man the computer here, but the other girls can stay there. Thanks for asking. . . . Cool! I'll get the tickets and call you back. We have to leave real early, so start packing. . . . I don't know how long, so I'm just getting one-way tickets. . . . How should I know how many? Underwear is light. Bring all you have. . . . Later."

Ashley slapped the phone shut and clipped it on her belt. "I'll take the laptop, the circuit board equipment, and Apollo." She glanced around the room, her eyes finally resting on an electronics workbench in one corner. "The professor asked if I have a way of detecting electromagnetic frequencies. Is my old spectral photometer repaired yet?"

"Yeah. It took quite a hit, but it's as good as new."

"Good." Ashley pointed toward a metal briefcase on a tabletop. "Put it in my case, and I'll get packed."

"So you'll be gone tomorrow for Halloween. Do we have anything for the trick-or-treaters?"

Ashley shook her head. "I was going to get something in the morning. Just turn off the porch light and hunker down in the computer room with Larry. Sleep on the sofa if you want."

"Sure thing." Karen put her finger on her jaw. "Is the transmitter still embedded okay?"

Ashley bent forward. "Better check it for me." She opened her mouth wide.

Karen peered in, her eyes darting around. "Looks like it hasn't moved at all." She pushed Ashley's mouth closed. "Better test the alarm."

Ashley tapped the outside of her jaw with her finger. A low-pitched buzzer sounded, and a light on the main computer panel flashed three times. After a few seconds, the buzzing faded away.

Karen crossed her arms over her chest and grinned. "Works like a charm!"

Ashley rolled her eyes. "Okay, I'll give you credit. It was a good idea. But I still think we could've come up with a better location than one of my molars."

"Why? Does it still hurt when you chew?"

Ashley worked her jaw back and forth. "No. I just chew on the other side. The transmitter's designed to take a beating, but you never know what might get stuck in there."

"Yeah. When you're in England I don't want to hear crumpets and tea swishing around when I put the headphones on."

A man dressed in black stepped heel-and-toe along a rocky ledge, brushing against the mountainside. Although the ledge was wide enough for two men to walk side by side, he never strayed from a narrow strip of talus that crunched under his boots. Below lay a valley of littered bones, a dry riverbed between two sheer rock faces.

As the ledge narrowed, he ran his palm along the vertical slope and marched on, keeping his gaze riveted on a gaping hole in another mountain face that lay ahead. The ledge curved to the right, leading the man to a mammoth cave.

As he passed under the shadowy arch, the bright sunlight at his back withered and fell into weak streams, crawling past his stocky legs like a hundred wiggling electric eels. After taking three more steps, he halted, allowing his eyes to adjust to the eerie radiance in the vast inner chamber.

A dark shape drifted across the open area like a statuesque ghost. Streaming light bathed the image, highlighting a tall female, graceful and elegant. She stopped at the edge of a circular opening in the floor, a hole about six feet wide. The streams of light poured over the edge as the orifice sucked them into its depths.

A colourful aura floated above the surface of the pit, creating a vertical, egg-shaped corona. It resembled an oval mirror standing on end, with symmetric, rainbow images waltzing through the depths of its ghostly glow. More like a living hologram than a dull, flat screen, it cast shimmering rays of light, illuminating the woman's face with stripes of red, green, and gold and passing through her semi-transparent body.

She spread out her arms toward the aura and bowed her head. "Samyaza, we have captured the dragon. Clefspeare will soon become a powerful ally. He has entered our realm unprotected."

A low voice replied from the chasm, echoing as if far away. Every syllable vibrated the hovering oval's light as though the speaker strummed its rays like a harp. "Can you trust a mere human to take control? Can he really act as one of the Nephilim, as a true child of Samyaza and Morgan?"

"Yes, my beloved. Devin is as devoted as any of our children would have been. He will not let us down."

The voice weakened. "So be it." And its echoes drifted away. The colours in the halo faded into pastels, still swirling within the oval.

Morgan turned slowly, her eyes gleaming as she gazed at the man who had just entered the cave. When she nodded, he spoke, his shaky legs belying his steady voice. "Elaine reports that Markus and Hartanna have taken Bonnie Silver to safety. They now have access to the two cloaks, as you requested."

Morgan's silky voice replied in a soft melody. "Very good, Palin. Patrick will know what the cloaks are for. All is proceeding exactly as planned."

Palin took a few steps toward the hole but dared not peer into its depths. Sliding his feet to the side, he edged close to the lady. "Is our master well?"

A dark shadow passed across Morgan's face, and her lips thinned out. "Samyaza is my husband, not my master. You would do well to remember that."

Palin bowed his head. "Yes, my lady. Forgive me."

"Forgive you?" She grabbed a fistful of his hair and yanked him down to his knees. "Grovel at my feet, you little worm. If not for me, you would have trembled naked at the judgment seat." She released his hair, and her hand dissolved into a translucent vapour.

Palin's cheeks burned. "I . . . I had hoped my service would gain your kindness, my lady."

She straightened her back and squared her shoulders, her eyes ablaze. "If it is kindness you desire, you chose the wrong blood to be your ally."

Palin bowed his head. "I have more news. The cloaks have been reprogrammed with a simplified encryption, as you requested. Number seventeen fell to Hartanna, so they now have cloaks from him and number thirty-two, but . . ." Palin cringed. "But the old man, the kid's professor, got away."

A plume of black smoke erupted from the top of Morgan's head. "What!" she screamed. "Hamilton escaped?!"

Palin instinctively ducked, but the blow to the head he expected never came. He looked up, thinking Morgan might have ignited into a raging fire and disintegrated, but she stood calmly rubbing her chin.

She placed a hand under Palin's arm and lifted him gently to his feet. A smile softened her face. "Does Patrick know what happened to Clefspeare yet?"

"He will soon. Markus is not one to keep news from his master for very long."

"Good." Morgan nodded slowly and began pacing. "My plan rests on the fragile arms of deception, and it flies into action on the wings of haste. Wise counsel is our enemy, so we must separate Charles Hamilton from Patrick and the boy king." She pressed two fingers against her cheek. "The mind of Merlin abided too long with Hamilton's, and since only Merlin knows how to spoil my plans, I cannot take the chance that his silly songs still chant in the old professor's eccentric head."

"And how do you propose to separate them?"

"With deception, of course. The sons of light are so naive, they'll believe anything they're told." She shooed him away with the back of her hand. "Go back to the sixth circle. I'll send you word when I decide how to remove the old man."

"Yes, my lady." Palin turned to leave, but he paused. "Who should be our agent? Devin would have been perfect for this job. No one is more qualified."

"Put Devin out of your mind. He is unable to serve in that capacity any longer." She turned again toward the colours in the halo as though reading a message from its swirling bands. After a few seconds she finally spoke again, her voice low but firm. "We must hold back the seven until the king steps into my realm. We'll call on number eight. It's time to flex our muscles."

The professor pulled the cloak off and laid it next to a tree at the edge of the hilltop. He and Billy crouched, allowing the tree's arching branches to shroud them in darkness. "How long till sunrise, Prof?" Billy asked.

The professor pulled a chain from his trouser pocket and caught the watch in his palm, extending his arm beyond the shadows. The setting moon, nearly full and ghostly white, illuminated the thick blanket of clouds on the western half of the sky and cast a faint glow on the antique, analogue face. "About half an hour, William." He slid the watch back into his pocket. "The dragons' delay concerns me. With the sun rising soon, I fear their discovery." From another pocket he drew out a light brown beret. After running his fingers through his scattered white hair, he pressed the cap over his head. "It's getting cooler," he said, turning toward Billy.

"Yeah. I noticed." Billy felt drawn to the professor's insistent gaze and shifted his eyes toward his teacher. The early morning mist flecked the elderly sage's wrinkles with tiny dots of moisture.

"Do you still sense danger?" the professor asked.

Billy shook his head. "No. The feeling left a few minutes after we got here." Although the prickly sensation on his skin and the boiling in his stomach had subsided, he still felt an ache, a different kind of pain deep inside.

The professor laid his hand on Billy's shoulder. "I have something for you," he said, holding his other hand open. At the centre of his palm lay a wide gold band with a dime-sized red stone mounted in the centre. "William, I saw your rubellite ring in your suitcase. May I ask why you are no longer wearing it?"

Billy pulled a lace on his hiking shoe and retied it into a secure, double knot. "I guess it makes me think too much," he finally replied.

The professor held the ring in his fingertips. His wise, old eyes gleamed under his bushy brow. "This rubellite is more than a mere bauble, William. It is a symbol of who you are; it is a connection to your heritage."

Billy retied his other shoe, finishing with an emphatic yank on the lace. "Well, maybe that's the whole problem right there." He stood up and shoved his hands into his pockets.

The professor rose with him and gently grasped his forearm. "William, you probably think that I cannot possibly understand your pain. You have lost your father, yet he continues to haunt your life as a phantom in dragon form. How can the grief in your soul ever be mended when his every appearance scalds your heart as surely as if he pierced you with a blast of fire?"

The professor opened Billy's hand and slid the ring onto his index finger. "Never lose hope," he said, closing Billy's hand into a fist. "This ring appeared at the threshold of despair, at the very moment darkness met the dawn." The professor's hands trembled, and his voice dropped to a whisper. "Don't give in to darkness." His long fingers tightened over Billy's fist. "For the dawn will eventually break."

Billy's face grew hot. His eyes moistened. He couldn't refute a single word his teacher had spoken. Somewhere in that scaly dragon named Clefspeare the spirit of his father lived on, though the voice that growled past the sparks and flames denied that he was any longer Billy's true father.

The professor patted Billy on the back. "William, as your heart aches, remember this: 'Weeping may endure for a night, but joy cometh in the morning.' "

Billy lowered his head. He balled his hand into a fist and rubbed his ring's gemstone with his thumb. The rubellite was cold. It was lifeless. But it was all he had remaining of his father's touch.

The professor walked slowly out of the stand of trees and stood atop a low berm that encircled a huge, grassy field.

Billy followed and mounted the embankment at the professor's side. With his hands in the pockets of his pleated trousers, the professor gazed up at the sky and let out a long stream of white vapour. "Many people are offended when I speak freely about my faith, but I trust, now, that you are not."

Billy shrugged his shoulders. "No, I'm not offended." He followed his teacher's line of sight; the clouds had drifted to the west, exposing the northern sky. "What's on your mind?"

The professor pointed into the darkness. "Do you see that star?"

"The one that looks kind of yellow?"

"No. I believe you are referring to Kochab. Look more to the left."

"Okay. I think I've got it."

"That's Polaris, the North Star." He glanced down at Billy. "I assume you've heard of it."

"Sure. It's always due north. Sailors used it for guidance back before satellites came around."

"And many explorers still use it." The professor moved his finger in an anticlockwise circle. "If you could see a time-lapse film of the night sky, all the stars would stretch out into a stream and draw concentric circles with Polaris at the centre, yet, for all practical purposes, Polaris would remain a single point – unmoved, always guiding, a light that never changes."

A fresh breeze blew across the field, biting through Billy's flannel shirt. He zipped up his jacket and bounced on his toes. "I think I've seen a picture like that before, but I don't remember where."

The professor shifted his finger up to the right. "And you probably recognize that constellation."

Billy ducked under the professor's elbow and followed the angle of his arm. "I see the big dipper. Is that what you mean?"

"Yes. Ursa Major. We call part of it 'The Plough' here in England, and in ancient times, it was called 'King Arthur's Chariot.' Do you see how the two stars in the dipper make a line that points toward Polaris?"

Billy pulled a pair of gloves from his jacket pocket and began slipping them on. "Sure, Prof. I've seen that before. I used to go out and look at the stars with Dad and . . ." Billy clenched his gloved fingers together. "So what's all this got to do with your faith?"

The professor drew out his own gloves from his back pocket and put them on, keeping his eyes on his fingers as he slowly pushed them into the holes. "Much of what you have learned about faith, you have learned from me, but where you are soon going, I cannot come." He pulled out his watch again, fumbled the latch open through his thick gloves, then, after reading the time, snapped the casing shut. He kept it in his closed fist as he shifted his gaze to the northern sky. "God always provides a guiding light, William. No matter how dark it seems or how terrible the situation, you can always count on finding a glimmer, a spark of light in the deepest blackness that will tell you which way to go."

Billy watched the twinkling north star, imagining a lonely explorer looking up at the same star a thousand years ago, counting on its never-changing position to keep him on his charted course. When he turned to the professor, his teacher's sad, deeply set eyes were trained directly on him.

"Do you understand?" the professor asked.

Billy nodded. "Yes." He then looked back at the sky and wrapped his arms around his chest to battle a new gust of wind. "I think I know exactly what you mean."

The first hint of dawn appeared on the eastern horizon, and the professor stepped down from the berm onto the grassy field. "Now we can finally search the area." His long legs stretched into a quick pace. "Bring Excalibur, William."

Billy hustled the few steps back to the tree where he had left Excalibur. He strapped the scabbard to his waist and vaulted over the embankment again, following his spry teacher into the circular field. He searched the grassy dome, scanning both the ground and the brightening sky. The clouds had moved in from the west again, but they couldn't keep the sun's rays from spilling across the hilltop as the horizon dawned clear and sparkling blue.

Within seconds a huge shadow covered the hilltop. Billy jerked his head up toward the eastern sky. "It's a dragon! Is it . . . Dad? . . . No. It's Hartanna!"

Gusts of wind bent the grass and whipped Billy's hair while two madly flapping wings settled Hartanna's enormous body onto the hilltop. "Billy! Professor!" she growled. "Climb onto my back! We must fly!"

Billy scrambled up Hartanna's flank and straddled her back between her shoulders. The professor extended his long arms and grasped one of Hartanna's spines to pull himself up. With a final push, he boosted himself aboard, just behind Billy.

Two seconds later, her wings beat the air again. "Hold on!" Hartanna shouted. With a sudden vertical lift, the great she-dragon took off, heading straight for the clouds to the west. Billy wrapped the fingers of both hands around a two-foot-long spine and held his breath. The g-forces were so great, he felt his brain pushing into his sinus cavity.

After they passed upward through the cloud bank and slowed their ascent, Billy looked back at the professor, mounted like a seasoned warrior with a steely gaze. Billy understood the professor's serious countenance. If he had a mirror, he'd probably see the same expression on his own face. One dragon alone meant trouble.

Hartanna shouted through the wind. "Clefspeare, Bonnie, and Sir Patrick's squire were ambushed by two of the New Table's so-called knights. I rushed down and killed one of the fiends, but the other held a knife at Bonnie's throat. He demanded Clefspeare's promise to go with him quietly, and he would treat him as a prisoner of honour."

"A prisoner of honour?" Billy yelled. "What's that?"

"We used that term back in the sixth century. It means he won't kill his prisoner without giving him a fair fight, and the prisoner must agree to go peacefully. When Clefspeare gave his word, the coward let Bonnie go and led Clefspeare away. I guided Bonnie and the squire to a safe place."

The professor leaned over and shouted, "Sir Patrick's squire? That must have been Markus. Is he still with Miss Silver?"

"No. When I dropped them off, Markus insisted on reporting to his master, but Bonnie refused to go with him, saying that she wouldn't trust anyone but her teacher and me. I agreed and sent Markus away, but since tracking Clefspeare was an urgent matter and great speed was necessary, I decided to leave Bonnie behind. I sensed no danger, even while Markus was present, and Bonnie assured me that she would fly away if she heard or smelled anything strange. Unfortunately, I have been unable to find Clefspeare and his kidnapper. I can't imagine how they disappeared so quickly."

Although the wind buffeted the dragon's words, Billy understood the gist. "But what was Patrick's squire doing there? He wasn't even supposed to know about the meeting."

"My question exactly," Hartanna replied, "but I was in too much of a hurry to interrogate him as thoroughly as I would have liked."

A sudden gust of wind knocked the dragon to the side. Billy tightened his grip on Hartanna's spine and hung on until she righted herself. The professor shouted again. "It seems that we're in for a rough ride in more ways than one, and we won't get any answers until I have another talk with Sir Patrick."

Ashley sprinted through the airport corridor, waving an arm as she ran. "Come on! That was our boarding call!"

Walter lugged a heavy, carry-on suitcase and shuffled into a laboured jog. "What'd you put in this thing? Dumb-bells?"

Ashley stopped and waited for him to catch up. "I'm not going to comment on 'dumb-bells' ." She took the briefcase and ran ahead, apparently oblivious to the weight. "I told you I'd carry it," she shouted back. "You're the one who wanted to be Mr Chivalry."

Walter slung his backpack over his shoulder and tried to catch up, but he kept falling farther behind. He straightened the baseball cap on his head and grumbled under his breath. "She's a dragon, Walter. Get used to it. She's stronger and smarter."

Letting out a grunt, he urged his legs into a dead run. "I'll bet she can't fish with a fly rod or spar with a sword or jump across Saddler's Creek without getting wet."

Walter finally caught up to Ashley at the gate. As soon as he arrived, she tugged at his backpack. "I hold my high school's record for long jump," she said, fishing in one of the pockets. "I know I put the tickets and passports in here somewhere."

He turned to make it easier for her to search. "Long jump? How did you know what I was thinking?"

She pulled out two envelopes and handed them to the attendant. "What do you mean, what you were thinking? I was just explaining why I can run so fast. I did the long jump in high school, and you have to get up a huge head of steam before you can plant and jump."

"I was just thinking . . . Oh, never mind. But you sure creep me out sometimes."

"Yeah, I know." She wagged her head as they hustled down the jetway. "I've heard it before. Ashley reads minds. She's a space alien."

After finding their row in the crowded plane, Ashley slid her case under the seat in front of her own and helped Walter get his backpack off. "My brain reacts so quickly to all sensory input," she continued, "everything from facial expressions to posture to personality, it can anticipate what people are thinking. It makes people think I can read their minds."

Ashley took a window seat on the right side of the plane, and Walter slid into the middle. He hoped the seat to his left would remain empty or at least be taken by someone under four hundred pounds. He tilted the video screen embedded in the seat back in front of him, eyeing the line of passengers stowing their luggage in the overhead racks.

It was easy to tell the Americans from the Brits. Those heading home to England looked drained from their 'holiday' ordeal, ready to fall asleep, while those embarking on a vacation adventure in Europe greeted Walter with bright, cheery faces. A thin, pale man plopped down next to him, buckled his safety belt, and leaned back without a word, immediately closing his eyes and easing into a gentle snore.

Walter mumbled under his breath. "Seven hours of snoring ahead!" He pulled the flap of the seat pocket in front of him and rifled through the magazines. *Aha! A comic book!* Walter leaned back and flipped open the pages. After reading it for a few seconds, he burst out laughing.

"Walter!" Ashley scolded. "Settle down!"

"Just a minute! Listen to this joke. There was this fish who loved to play golf—"

Ashley snatched the comic book from his hands. "Shhh!" She pointed toward Walter's neighbour. "He's trying to sleep."

Walter frowned and crossed his arms. Ashley pulled the airline magazine out of the seat pocket and flipped through the movie schedule. Walter found the plastic bag that held the video headset, tore it open, and slid the earpieces around his cap. He adjusted the speaker pads on his ears and grinned at Ashley. "So what am I thinking? My brain can't leak through my ears now."

Ashley lifted her index and middle fingers. "Two things I would guess. Your most pressing thought is 'I wonder when breakfast is served on this flight.' " She then gestured toward her carry-on luggage under the seat. "The second is, 'She still hasn't told me what's in that heavy briefcase.' "

Walter yanked off the headset and moaned. "You're three for three!" He leaned back and closed his eyes. "I can tell this is going to be a long trip!"

Ashley pulled the bill of Walter's cap down to his chin. "Then sleep all the way to London, and I'll experiment with Apollo by myself."

Walter jerked up and straightened his cap. "Apollo? What's Apollo?"

The airplane began backing up, and Ashley checked her seatbelt buckle. "I'll show you when we're at cruising altitude."

Walter fastened his seatbelt, then used his shoe to nudge the briefcase that was neatly stashed just in front of Ashley's toes. "You're always the one for mysteries, aren't you?"

Ashley yawned and leaned back in her seat, closing her eyes. "Get used to it. It's like I always say, 'Too much information can make your brain choke.' "

"Maybe. But not enough information makes for a lot of dead cats."

Ashley opened her eyes and squinted. "Dead cats? What in the world are you talking about?"

"You know, 'Curiosity killed the cat.' And I have enough curiosity to start a feline genocide."

"Feline genocide?"

"Yeah. If you don't explain Apollo, the cat kingdom will crumble. Cats all over the world will suddenly plop down in unmoving masses of fur, their food will dry up in smelly chunks of liver and fish, and when people call, 'Here kitty, kitty, kitty,' no cats will come running; they'll just—" Walter suddenly stopped. A blank expression covered his face.

Ashley poked his ribs with her finger. "What's wrong? Cat got your tongue?"

Walter stared straight ahead. "I just realized . . . if all those things happened, no one would even notice the difference."

Hartanna broke through the clouds and zoomed downward in full daylight, hurrying to conceal her presence in the woods below. Billy and the professor held on, bracing themselves for a sudden landing. Having found an open space in the canopy of beech and ash trees, she settled to the ground with a surprisingly soft touch amid an enormous flurry of wings.

Billy and the professor climbed down, dropping to the mat of dead leaves with a muffled crunch. Hartanna stretched her long neck toward a western slope. “My old cave is nearby, but it’s too close to populated areas now for me to use.”

A twig popped somewhere in the forest, followed by rustling and the sound of running footsteps. A pair of hands parted the thin branches of two short trees in the distance, revealing Bonnie stepping high over a muddy patch. With her wings now hidden in her backpack, she glided through the remaining brush with ease. When she looked up, her eyes brightened. “Billy!” she called. “I heard Mama coming back, but I didn’t expect to see you!” She greeted him with a warm hug. “I’m so glad she found you!” She then hugged the professor and stepped back. “Did you enjoy your ride?”

The professor pulled down his sleeves and squared his shoulders. “Indeed we did. Quite exhilarating!” He ran his hand through his tousled hair. “But I seem to have lost my favourite beret.”

Bonnie’s head drooped as her smile faded away. “Did you hear about Clefspeare?”

Billy snapped a stick under his hiking boot. “Yeah, and wait’ll I tell you what happened during the night where we were staying.”

“Save your story for a moment,” the professor said. “First we must find our way to civilization and back to our rental car at Cadbury.”

“A town is close by,” Hartanna said, “but I cannot safely fly you there. It is not more than a half hour’s walk, and I saw a major road running through its centre, so finding transportation back to Camelot should not be a problem. Since I am able to sense Clefspeare’s presence, I will continue my search for him before the trail gets too cold. When you get to your car, make haste back to Glastonbury and alert Sir Patrick."

The professor raised his hand to his chin and gazed blankly at a heavily knotted old tree. "Yes . . . We must go to Glastonbury." He grabbed his cell phone from a belt clip and punched in a number. "William, I'm calling your mother to see if she is able to meet Ashley and Walter at Heathrow. It's a six- or seven-hour drive from Glasgow to London, so she could get there in plenty of time. You must prepare for your mission while Sir Patrick mobilizes our men to help Hartanna search for Clefspeare. Our veil of secrecy has obviously been torn to shreds, and any delays may further endanger our efforts." He paused, lifting the phone to his ear. "And our lives."

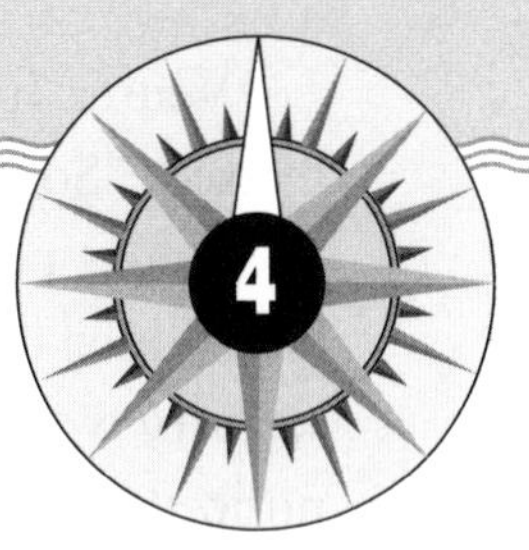

CHAPTER 4

The Compass

Ashley unlocked the hefty briefcase and opened the lid. With careful hands she pulled out what looked like an old-fashioned hourglass, except that the glass enclosure separating the top and bottom circular platforms was rectangular and had no constriction in the middle. Four, foot-long wooden dowels surrounded the glass, one at each corner of the rectangle, and one of the rectangle's glass faces had tiny hinges on one edge as though it could act as a door to the inside.

Next, she drew out a black cylinder, which she attached to the top of her hourglass gadget with a quick twist. The cylinder, about double the thickness of a hockey puck, carried four protruding springs on top, each about six inches long with a marble-sized plastic bead swaying back and forth at the upper end.

Walter narrowed his eyes at the strange device. "That's Apollo? The top looks more like—"

"A hockey puck with springs for hair?" Ashley interrupted.

Walter fumed at her correct guess, but he kept his face relaxed. “Something like that.”

Ashley popped the beads off the springs, gathering each into her cupped hand. “I put the beads on to make it look like a toy so security wouldn’t ask a bunch of questions, but they never even noticed it. The wire coils are antennae that serve to transmit and receive data.” Ashley pulled two headsets from the briefcase and handed one to Walter. “Put this on. It’s wireless, so you don’t have to plug it in anywhere.”

Walter stretched the headset’s saddle apart and slipped it over his head. “What am I supposed to be listening to?”

Ashley put on her own headset and placed the hourglass device on the seat tray in front of her. “You’ll see.” She flipped a switch on the side of the communications “puck” and a barely perceptible whirring emanated. She then tapped her jaw with her finger. “Are you there?”

Walter adjusted his headset. “Of course I’m here.”

Ashley put a finger to her lips. “Shhh! Not you. Karen.”

A voice crackled in Walter’s ears. “Sorry. I was in the kitchen making breakfast.”

Walter closed one eye and reached for Apollo. “You’re talking to Karen through a high-tech hockey puck?”

Ashley batted his hand away. “Karen, how am I coming through?”

The scratchy voice returned. “There’s a lot of static, but you’re hitting six on the meter. Not bad.”

“I expected the static,” Ashley replied. “Walter’s doing mental somersaults, so he’s probably jamming the circuits.” She smiled and gave Walter a friendly shove on the arm. “I think we’re at about 37,000 feet, but I can’t guess what our electromagnetic reflection angle is. I’m sure Apollo will work better at ground level. We’d better not try a material generation until we’ve landed.”

Karen's voice buzzed again. "How about something small? What could it hurt? It only absorbs light, not power. The plane engines won't feel a thing."

"Okay . . . I guess you're right." Ashley pressed her index finger on her bottom lip. "Use the same program I wrote when we transmitted from the transfer box to the kitchen. Maybe if you keep Gandalf away from the power grid, it'll work this time."

"Don't worry. He hasn't set a paw in the computer room since the infamous tail-fire incident."

Ashley rotated Apollo until a rectangular metal flap on its base faced her. "Good. Let's try sending the button again."

Walter sat up straight and pushed the headset tight against his ears. "This is cool! Beam the button up, Scotty!"

Ashley slid the metal flap to the side and spun a tiny dial. "She can't hear you, Walter. Just watch the bottom of the glass enclosure."

"I've got you locked in," Karen buzzed. "Are you ready?"

A light flashed down from the top platform, illuminating the inside of the glass rectangle, a strange, sparkling light, thick and green, like an electrified, emerald mist. The lights from the airplane's overhead panel dimmed, and a shroud of grey shadows enveloped their seats. Seconds later the sparkles congealed, falling to the bottom of the glass rectangle, a shimmering green snow shower in a crystal cage. The particles spun around at the bottom like water swirling down a drain, throwing off their jade pigment and finally settling into a small, round disk.

The light switched off. At the bottom of the enclosure sat a small white button, like those on the cuffs of a man's long-sleeved dress shirt.

Ashley tilted Apollo back and peered into the enclosure. "Karen, didn't you use the blue button?"

"Yeah. The blue one. Just like last time."

Ashley squeezed her lips together and shook her head. "The spectrum encoder must be on the fritz."

"Could be. I'll ask Larry."

Walter mouthed, "Larry?" but Ashley ignored him.

"No," Karen continued. "Larry says it's on your side. It's the decoder, not the encoder."

Ashley shook her head again. "No way. I checked it this morning. Put Larry on." She turned Apollo, bringing the door of the rectangle to the front, and placed a finger on her left ear pad. "Larry. It's Ashley. What's the deal with the spectrum translator?"

An electronic voice sputtered, "You're the genius, Ashley. If you think it's the encoder, then why don't you fix it yourself?"

"Don't get smart with me, Larry. I'll have Karen bust you down to a Windows machine faster than you can say Microsoft."

"You programmed me. If you don't believe what I'm telling you, you're calling yourself a liar."

Ashley slapped her palm against her forehead. "Oh, why did I have to go and put a logic booster in his AI unit?"

Walter grinned. He thought Larry was a hoot. "AI? Artificial Intelligence?"

Ashley opened the door to the glass rectangle. "Yeah. Larry's almost like a real person. Sometimes he gets on my nerves."

"A talking computer with an attitude problem? Haven't I seen that in a dozen B-grade, sci-fi flicks?"

"Of course. Where do you think I got the idea?" She picked up the button, but it crumbled and fell in a tiny pile of glittering dust. "Oh, no! The bonding factor must be way off!"

A new voice broke in. "Excuse me." A female flight attendant peered at them from the aisle surrounded by several wide-eyed adults and children.

Ashley brushed the button dust away and smiled at the attendant. "Yes?"

The tall brunette smiled. "Some of our passengers saw you playing with that toy. It's a long flight, so they were wondering if you could explain how it works and maybe let them try it out."

Walter flashed a wide grin and leaned back with his hands behind his head. "I'm sure Ashley would love to explain her little toy!"

Ashley cleared her throat and held the device up with both hands. "This is an antimatter, tachion reversal engine made by Stalworth Enterprises. Lots of fun, but you have to be qualified to use it. I'll have to lecture you in quantum physics and antimatter theory for at least two hours and then give you a thorough written exam." She glanced around at the onlookers. "Who's up for that?"

The crowd began to disperse, several people shaking their heads and laughing, but one little old man who smelled strongly of cheap cigars and used gym socks stayed put. With his wispy grey hair blowing in the draft of the plane's circulating air, he nodded slowly. "It's been a while since I wrote my doctoral dissertation on antimatter theory, but I'm willing to spend a few hours polishing up what I remember."

Walter got up and squeezed past his sleeping neighbour. He motioned for the little old man to sit, then strolled down the aisle, grinning back at Ashley. Her face had wrinkled into a tight, red fire alarm. "Have fun," he called. "I'm going to find another comic book."

"Walter!"

After hiring a van and driver in Yeovil, Billy, Bonnie, and Professor Hamilton endured the short drive back to Cadbury Castle. They rode in physical comfort, though not in peace.

The chauffeur, a leather-skinned man in his seventies, battled verbally with the professor over every subject that could possibly concern a British citizen, from the value of the British pound versus the Euro, to the congestion charge in London, to the importance of the royal family in government. They disagreed on everything, the driver rattling on in a cockney accent and the professor responding in the quiet dignity of an Oxford sophisticate.

The chauffeur flicked his tweed driver's cap higher on his brow. "I mean it's so bleed'n obvious, innit? The queen's useful as a nine-bob note, all dolled up wit' nowhere to go."

"But you must understand, my good fellow, that Her Majesty is more than merely a cultural icon; she represents the hopes of the whole country. She is the symbol of our past and our future. And, trust me, the future of the monarchy is getting brighter every day."

As the two talked in the front, Billy told Bonnie about the burglars, the sword battle, and the strange microchip-embedded cloaks, although he had to keep his voice down to protect their secrets and lean close to her ear to compete with the incessant chatter.

When they arrived at Cadbury Castle, they searched for the body of the man Hartanna had killed, following directions she had provided. They found him on a steep slope in a dense thicket about a hundred yards from the grassy field. Like Billy's night-time attacker, this one wore a black hood and robe coated with wire mesh.

Kneeling on the surrounding undergrowth, the professor stripped off the hood to reveal a tawny-faced man with high cheekbones and a short, trimmed beard. He looked a few years older than the previous attacker, but he still seemed young, too young to die in the service of this "New Table" conspiracy.

The professor sighed. "Another sacrificial lamb, I'm afraid."

Bonnie stepped away from the body and folded her hands behind her back. "Sacrificial lamb? What do you mean?"

The professor draped the hood over the man's face. "Whoever is sending these men into battle must know they are too inexperienced to deal with fire-breathing dragons and a paladin who wields Excalibur."

Billy shoved his gloved hands into his coat pockets, a hot flush surging into his cheeks.

The professor rubbed his fingers along the man's black cloak. "The microchips in this garment," he continued, "may explain the mystery."

The professor and Billy removed the cloak and draped it over the dead body. The professor then stood and flipped open his cell phone. "Please excuse me while I make a call." He walked up the slope and stood behind a pair of oak trees.

Crouching next to the body, Billy picked up a stick and twisted it into the ground. He couldn't tear his gaze away from the morbid scene, a dead, young man covered in the funeral trappings of shimmering black. Although he didn't know how Hartanna had killed the man, his crumpled body gave evidence that she may have crushed his bones. Perhaps his strange robe protected him from her streams of fire, and she resorted to bashing him with her powerful tail.

The professor returned, clipping the cell phone on his belt. "If we take the cloaks with us, our pursuers might be able to track us enroute, so I called one of my compatriots to arrange for their transport to Sir Patrick's residence. He will also take care of the corpse. If the chips don't identify him, perhaps his fingerprints will." He motioned toward the path leading to his rental car. "We must hurry to Sir Patrick's. Clefspeare's life hangs in the balance."

Without the cockney cabby around, the trip to Glastonbury was much more peaceful. Bonnie related her flight across the Atlantic and gave more details about the ambush in the forest. She was a masterful storyteller, providing Billy with vivid images painted in bright colours across the canvas of his mind. He drank in every word, leaning his head back and closing his eyes, sometimes peeking at Bonnie to catch her facial expressions while she untied her braids and brushed out her hair. Her excited eyes were always fun to watch as they widened and narrowed with the highs and lows of her tale.

After the story, Billy had a hard time concentrating on anything. Thoughts of Clefspeare kept bursting into his mind. He tried to shoo them away, arguing in favour of indifference. This dragon wasn't really his father anymore; he was a . . . a dragon. Dragons could take care of themselves, couldn't they? Clefspeare didn't really need anyone to watch out for him . . . or to rescue him. Not really. His arguments barely made a dent in his anxiety. The shivers running up and down his spine proved that he wasn't very good at lying to himself.

When they arrived in the outskirts of Glastonbury, they drove along a narrow road that meandered into a beautiful rural setting: perfectly manicured lawns the size of a dozen football fields bordered by meticulously trimmed hedges intermingled with tall, robust oaks. Far in the distance a green hill stood alone amidst the lush, flat fields. On its apex, a tall monument towered over the valley, like a stone shepherd standing erect and vigilant. The protruding hill seemed out of place, high and steep in a land of low-lying farms.

"That's the Glastonbury Tor," the professor explained. "A very strange landmark, filled with mysteries and legends. My favourite story involves two natural springs that flow from a chasm under the hill. One deposits a reddish sediment, an iron compound of some kind, while the other leaves a white residue, calcium carbonate, I believe. After your mission, I should like to visit Chalice Well Gardens where the red spring emerges, and there I will explain the legend."

After driving to the end of the narrow road, they followed a long, winding driveway leading into one of the magnificent fields of green. Autumn flowers – myriad pansies and chrysanthemums of purple and yellow – lined the pristine, brick path, as though a colourful carpet of greeting had rolled out in anticipation of their arrival.

The professor pulled the car to a stop in front of a wrought-iron gate bordered by two massive stone columns that looked like totem poles, each one chiselled with eight gruesome faces, vertically stacked. The face on the top level looked more feminine than the seven below, and they all scowled with equal malevolence, as though they had been placed there to discourage visitors.

The gate opened by itself, apparently monitored from within, though there wasn't a trace of a hidden camera or any telltale cables. Billy wondered if the eyes of one of those ugly totem faces doubled as the eyes for a security guard inside the house. He also wondered at the professor's strange countenance, troubled and distant, as though he were doing battle in his mind.

The professor drove forward, following the driveway up a hill toward a palatial mansion at the top, a modern-day castle, complete with at least three turrets and a short drawbridge that lay open over a narrow moat.

"Sir Patrick's residence." The professor nodded toward the massive house.

At the foot of the drawbridge, he stopped the car. "We walk from here."

Billy and Bonnie climbed out and joined the professor at the edge of the moat. With a huge castle standing against a sparkling blue sky and a pristine lawn of emerald green spreading out toward a distant forest, the atmosphere crackled with the feel of old England. Billy could almost see armoured knights riding muscular steeds on endless fields of grass and stones. Dragons flew into the misty woods in the distance, carrying glittering gems to their caves, always wary of trailing treasure hunters who might be seeking their lairs.

The chime from the professor's cell phone brought Billy back to the twenty-first century.

"Charles Hamilton speaking. . . . Yes, Marilyn, we've just arrived. We have quite a story to tell you. You see— . . . Yes, I am able to meet them. . . . No, I think I should introduce William and Bonnie to Sir Patrick first. I have plenty of time to do that and still make it to Heathrow. . . . What? . . . Yes, I understand, but I must tell you about Clefspeare. He— . . . Very well. . . . Goodbye."

The professor pressed a button on his phone and eyed the screen. "How strange!"

Billy leaned over to take a look. "What's up, Prof?"

"No caller ID. Your mother must have called from a blocked line. I wanted to tell her about your father's capture, but she cut our conversation short. She didn't even ask to greet you."

Billy reached for the phone. "Here. Let me call her cell." He punched in the numbers and waited through eight rings before shaking his head and handing the phone back to his teacher. "Nothing. The battery might be dead. But I thought I'd at least get her voice mail."

"I don't think it was an imposter. Her voice was quite clear." The professor clipped the phone back on his belt. "In any case, her vehicle has broken down, so she is unable to meet Miss Stalworth and Mr Foley at the airport. She is trying to procure a replacement, but the rental company says it will be several hours before they can accommodate her."

"So we have to go to London?"

"Not 'we'. I will go. We will meet Sir Patrick, and he and I will explain your mission. Because of the loss of secrecy, it's important that we prepare you as soon as possible." He turned and gazed at the driveway behind them, and Billy followed his line of sight. The twin totem poles at the bottom of the hill kept watch over the quiet country road in the distance, and their eerie vigilance gave Billy a shiver. The professor continued. "I have a feeling that even more trouble lurks, but I cannot say why. We must be on our guard and trust no one but those who have proven their love and loyalty."

Palin slid each of his feet backwards a step, biting the inside of his cheek and keeping his eyes glued to the cave's theatric display. The colourful aura over the floor chasm floated like a levitated tapestry. The swirling colours painted a photo of a lonely figure standing on a remote hilltop, a solitary woman in a desolate field. "I see our agent," Palin said, "but is this the past? The future?"

Morgan swept one arm across the front of the luminescent screen, and the scene began moving as though a movie director had called, "Action!" She trained her dark eyes on the display, her lips barely moving as she spoke. "The recent past, Palin, only a few minutes ago. Our number eight has completed part of her assignment. Listen."

A middle-aged woman with an angular jaw held a cellular telephone like it was a beloved musical instrument. Her throat grew taut as she pursed her lips to create a precise sound, like a flautist searching for the perfect note. Her voice played in time with the vibrating aura, distorting the view. "Wait. I'm glad you made it, but please hold your story until later. Listen, my car broke down, and the rental company said it might be several hours before they can get another one to me. Can you meet Ashley and Walter at the airport? There's no way I can make it in time."

After the phone exchange ended, the display's colours melted into their previous pattern of twisting ribbons. Morgan waved her long, slender arm toward the halo again, and the glow faded to bright white. "Now that we have arranged for Merlin to separate from Arthur, our real work can begin. Our knights must be in position when the boy king steps into our realm. He has no idea what he'll be facing, and Merlin won't be around to whisper any last-minute poems in his ear."

Morgan's dark form slowly shrank, her bare feet hovering inches off the ground. Although her body maintained human proportions, she stiffened, and her shrivelling skin seemed to morph into shiny, black porcelain. After shrinking to about a foot tall, her body suddenly began shaking. Her arms and head thickened, and her nose stretched to a hardened point. When the shaking ceased, a raven stood in her place, its feathers puffed out to double its size. With another quick shake, the black feathers smoothed out, making the bird indiscernible from other ravens.

With a low-pitched "Caw!" the raven flew up to Palin and landed on his shoulder. It croaked into his ear. "Soon I will send you back again to the sixth circle, where you will await your turn to meet the young king. I know how you yearn to get your revenge, but you will follow my instructions to the letter. Understand?"

Palin just nodded, sweat pouring down his cheeks.

"Good. And now I must pay a visit to my friend, Sir Patrick."

The raven flapped its coal-black wings and zipped through the cave entrance, vanishing in mid-flight.

Billy and Bonnie followed the professor up a short flight of stairs to a marble-tiled porch that skirted the entire wing of the huge mansion. With the professor marching at a brisk pace, the younger pair had to quicken their stride to keep up, their shoes squeaking on the walkway's tactile floor.

As they passed one of the many tall white columns, Billy rubbed a finger across its smooth, mirrored surface. He glanced from side to side. Something about this place bugged him. It felt like they were being watched, like those weird totem poles out front had unseen cousins probing them with camera eyes.

Bonnie tugged his sleeve. "What's wrong? You're as nervous as a politician hooked to a lie detector."

Billy kept his voice low. "Yeah. I feel like something's not right, like we're being watched."

"We probably are. A place like this must have lots of security."

"Yeah," Billy said, letting his voice grow a bit louder, "this guy must be rolling in cash. If he's one of the good guys, why is he wasting money on a marble-coated castle?"

The professor stopped at the massive front entryway, a solid oak door with carved panels and a stained glass window near the top. "Your judgment is premature, William. I suggest that you withdraw your comment and wait for further evidence of Sir Patrick's character." He grasped the huge door knocker just below the glass panel and gave three loud bangs.

After a few seconds the door swung open revealing a grey-haired man dressed in faded blue jeans and an Oxford University sweatshirt. In one arm he carried a young, dark-skinned child, a smiling, walnut-eyed boy who looked to be about a year old. The man's youthful complexion belied his grey hair. His smile exuded the vigour of a teenager, yet the gravity of his brown eyes made him appear as old as England itself.

"Merlin!" he shouted in a strong, dignified British accent. "You made it!" With a sweep of his free arm, he motioned for them to enter.

"Yes, Patrick," the professor replied, "but just barely, I'm afraid."

Patrick put a strong hand on the professor's shoulder, and his brow created a shadow over his deeply set eyes. "The Circle's network buzzed with rumours of an attack, and Markus reported his escape with Bonnie and the capture of the great dragon. I have already dispatched Sir Bradford and his company to help Hartanna seek Clefspeare's whereabouts. I'm so glad you weren't also a victim." He knelt, let the boy down on the floor, and with a love pat on the child's back, shooed him away. The boy pattered across the tile, and an elderly woman scooped him up into her arms, then disappeared into a hallway. "We retrieved your luggage from our safe house," Patrick continued. "I apologize for its lack of safety."

The professor cupped his hand under Patrick's elbow and gestured toward Billy and Bonnie. "Sir Patrick of Glastonbury, I would like to introduce you to William Bannister and Bonnie Silver."

When Sir Patrick cast his gaze on Bonnie, his jaw fell. He swallowed hard, took a step toward her, and knelt, gently gripping the fingers of her hand as though he would give her knuckles a formal kiss. With a bow, he closed his eyes for a brief moment, then stared at her, his lips trembling to match his voice. "Young lady," he said, tears filling his eyes, "it is a pleasure to be in your presence. Stories of your courage precede you, decorating you with honour and bringing glory to the great God whom you serve."

When he rose, Bonnie blushed and smiled. "I'm delighted to meet you, Sir Patrick."

He then turned to Billy. With his hands spread out, he dropped to one knee and bowed his head again. "Has Arthur finally made his presence known? If you are the Once and Future King, I submit myself to your service, Your Majesty."

Billy had no idea what to say. A string of words came to his mind, and he tried to formulate a coherent sentence before opening his mouth. "Sir Patrick, the offer of your service is . . . um . . .

a treasure beyond words. I trust that as I . . . embark on this mission . . . I won't really foul things up." He cringed. He hoped he didn't sound too ridiculous.

Sir Patrick rose again. The nervousness in his smile was easy to read. "Merlin, our compatriots have discerned great danger. That's why I sent Markus to find Bonnie. I have a well-placed spy in our enemies' ranks who learned that our secrecy was compromised. Since your rendezvous point was already known to them, I dispatched my own squire to head them off." He took a deep breath and gazed at Billy and Bonnie. "The mission has taken a dangerous turn. Our enemies may have infiltrated my staff, so I can trust only Markus from now on."

"Agreed." The professor reached into his shirt pocket and withdrew two microchips, displaying them in his open palm. "I extracted these from dark cloaks worn by our attackers."

Sir Patrick pinched one and drew it close to his eyes. "Yes. My people brought the cloaks to me just a few minutes ago. The New Table has had cloaks and ID chips for years, but this is a new technology."

The professor extended his palm, and Sir Patrick returned the chip. "I have an expert coming from the States," the professor explained, "who will help us analyse them thoroughly. In fact, after we reveal the details of the mission to William and Miss Silver, I must be off to collect my expert and her travelling companion at Heathrow. They arrive during the evening hours, so I'm afraid I will have to leave before William's appointed time."

Sir Patrick raised his eyebrows. "Is that so?" His concerned expression then vanished as quickly as it came. "I can handle the monitoring on my own until you return."

"Yes, I'm sure you are able, if our assumptions are correct. I wanted to be on hand, but these circumstances prevent me from attending at least the first circle. I shall return as soon as possible."

Sir Patrick added a dose of cheer to his voice. "Then let's all make the journey to the compass room, shall we? You still have several hours before you have to leave."

As they moved deeper into the recesses of the huge mansion, the sound of laughter drifted through the hallway, children playing somewhere in the distance. Bonnie reached down and scooped up a cloth-bound book from the tile floor. She thumbed through its barnyard scenes as she walked. "How many children do you have, Sir Patrick?"

Patrick smiled and looked back. "Last count, I'd say about seventy-five."

"Seventy-five!" Bonnie repeated, reaching the book toward him. "Your poor wife!"

He stopped and took the book from Bonnie. He hesitated as if he was going to say something, but he just folded the book and pushed it into his pocket before continuing his march down the hall.

"Sir Patrick inherited this estate," the professor explained as he kept pace, "and converted it into an orphanage of sorts. He rescues the neediest element of society – abandoned, abused, or otherwise forsaken children – and uses his wealth to house them here, complete with the best teachers and counsellors in England." He nudged a plastic bat out of the way with his foot. "Patrick, how many children have passed through this home?"

"Over the years? About three thousand, I would guess."

More signs of children cropped up – three wooden letter blocks, a jump rope, and an assortment of scattered puzzle pieces. Billy shook his head in wonder. "You've helped three thousand orphans? That's awesome!"

"Well, orphans and displaced children." Patrick stopped at an intersection to another hallway. "My motivations aren't altogether altruistic, William. My wife and I were bereft of children, so we filled that void in our own way. Just before she died, she made me promise to continue our ministry. I told her that heaven and earth would have to collapse before I'd abandon the little ones."

Patrick turned to his right and walked quickly through a narrow corridor that signalled a sudden change in the house's architecture. With a lower ceiling and rough plastered walls, it seemed older and less polished. He picked up a flashlight and an oil lamp from a shelf along the way and stopped at an old oaken door, the end of the hallway. He handed the lights to the professor, then pulled an old-fashioned brass key from his pocket and inserted it into a hole under an octagon-shaped knob.

After turning the key, Patrick raised his hand. "Before I open this door, I want to warn you not to touch anything. This part of the castle is essentially the original building, dating from the fifth century. It has been restored only once in all those years, so even the walls are fragile. Please walk softly and take care."

Patrick turned the ornate knob and pulled. The massive door creaked open, revealing another corridor with an even lower ceiling. The professor flicked on the flashlight and pointed the beam into the dim hallway. Patrick set a match to the lamp's wick, then ducked his head and entered the passage. The others followed, also ducking as they trailed the flickering lamp.

The grey stone ceiling was about six feet high, with thick wooden beams that bent toward the floor here and there, as if ready to splinter under their load. As Billy walked, he detected a strange odour in the air, like the smell of the forest on an autumn day when the fallen leaves are just beginning to deteriorate.

The fragrance of nature blended with something else, maybe rusting metal or some other chemical corrosion that years of solitude had birthed. Billy hoped to see suits of armour lining the walls and standing to attention, but no ghosts of knights haunted these ruins, at least not in their silvery, cast-off shells.

The long corridor ended at a doorway that opened into a much larger room, dimly lit by sunshine filtering through an air vent in the vaulted ceiling high above. The skylight seemed roughly cut into the stone roof, a rectangle perhaps ten feet long and eight feet wide. Traces of soot stained its edges, evidence that it had once served as an exhaust port for fires that had heated the chamber an untold number of years ago.

Leaves had fallen through the opening and littered the floor, some crumbling to dust as the visitors stepped on them. The debris sprinkled a symmetric design, etched with a multi-pointed star in the centre. Sand and crushed leaves filled each engraving, making the lines blend with the surrounding floor, muting the image.

Sir Patrick swept the area with his shoe. Within seconds the design became clearer, an eight-pointed compass with narrow spires stretching north-east, east, south-east, south, and so on. At the end of each spire, a basketball-sized circle enclosed an illustration.

Patrick knelt and blew the debris away from the lines in the north-east circle. He set the oil lamp at the edge and nodded at the image. "The creation of man."

The simple etching displayed a man and a woman standing with a fruit-filled tree between them, and in the midst of the tree a miniature dragon perched on a branch, his eyes focused directly on the woman. At the edge of the circle, a string of strange words lined the inside of the arc. Billy squinted at the words. They seemed indecipherable, though some resembled English.

The professor stood at his side. "It's Latin, William. It says, 'In principio erat verbum et verbum erat apud deum et deus erat verbum,' which means, 'In the beginning was the word, and the word was with God, and the word was God.' "

Bonnie knelt and rubbed her fingers across the impression, pausing briefly on the woman's bare back. She looked up at Patrick. "Adam and Eve before the Fall?"

Sir Patrick nodded. "True innocence – undefiled, without even the memory of sin. You might even call it a holy naivety." He walked over to the eastern spire. "You could learn a great deal by analysing these in depth, but we can't afford to take the time. I'll just show you each one as we make our way around the compass." He stooped and blew the dust away from the circle, revealing two swords crossed in battle and under the swords, a bag of spilled coins. Two of the coins carried tiny portraits, one with a crown on his head and the other with long, flowing hair.

Billy and company followed Patrick from circle to circle. The south-east point held a drawing of two men, one taller than the other. The shorter man carried an axe with the sharp edge positioned at the taller man's heels. The taller man held a mirror, and he gazed at himself, apparently unaware of the shorter man's actions. Within the mirror, the reflection showed the face of a dragon.

Patrick walked by the southern circle, waving at it as he passed. "This one is best left covered. I have not cleared debris from it since I first viewed its image, and I shall not describe it to you. But I will tell you that it represents one of the deadliest enemies of men, and I mean 'men' in the gender sense, not as in 'mankind'."

Billy paused at the edge of the circle's muddy covering. Years of dirt and rotted leaves had mixed with rain from the open ceiling. He swiped a bit of the mud away with his shoe, but all he could see was a bare foot in the dim light. He leaped past it and hurried on.

On the south-west circle, Patrick pointed out a feast scene, a rack of meat over a fire next to a table covered with piles of indistinguishable fruits and vegetables, yet only a single man sat at the table's bounty while a child knelt begging at his feet.

The circle on the west side needed only a quick sweep to reveal a clear etching. A dragon spewed a stream of flames at a male figure so small that he seemed to be a child. The boy carried a short, thin sword, useless and pathetic against the monstrous dragon. A girl sat close by, watching the battle.

Billy shivered. He knew the image carried a profound message, yet he couldn't figure out what it was. He just wanted to move on.

When they reached the north-west point, Patrick pulled a handkerchief from his pocket and scraped away a thick layer of damp silt. The smudged drawing showed a bridge spanning two mountains with a valley underneath. There was little detail, only the bare cliff walls and a valley floor teeming with a mass of haunting, forlorn faces intermixed with tiny, winged creatures.

Finally, at the north end of the compass, Patrick placed the lantern at the circle's edge. Most of the debris had already been cleared, and when the professor highlighted the circle with his flashlight beam, the deep etchings sharpened. A man sat on a regal throne, a river gushing out from a hole under the base. A dozen crowns lay scattered around the man's feet, hundreds of tiny worshipers bowed in reverence, and a child sat in his lap.

"Heaven?" Billy asked.

The professor aimed his flashlight at Billy's chest. "We believe so, William. It resembles a paradise scene from the book of Revelation. It is the eighth circle, not part of the seven to which you will journey." He lowered the beam and cast it on the other circles in turn. "Have you figured out what the other circles represent, if not heaven?"

Billy's tongue suddenly dried out. The question seemed too easy, yet the answer caught in his throat. "Hell?"

CHAPTER

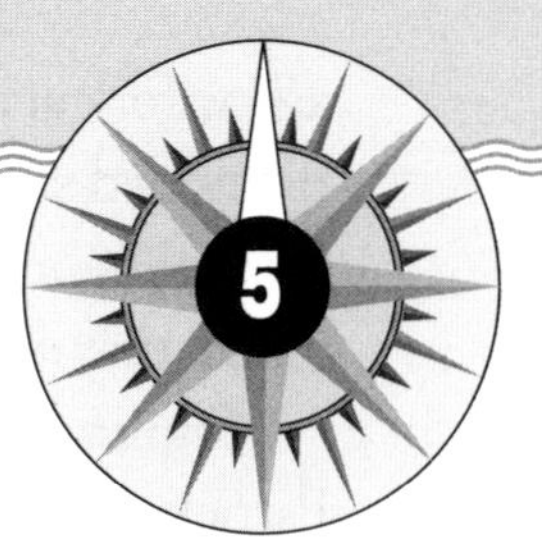

MERLIN'S WARNING

Perhaps not exactly hell," the professor explained. "The circles are not the final lake of fire, you see—"

"Ahem! We shouldn't recount terrifying stories yet, Merlin." Sir Patrick waved his arm toward a circular table at the back of the room. "Since you were only a little late this morning, our noon meal can commence as planned. I would guess that a girl who just flew across the Atlantic Ocean must be starving."

Bonnie placed her hand over her stomach. "I wasn't going to ask, but I could eat a horse."

"And since I already know about your wings, may I also suggest that you remove your backpack and make yourself more comfortable?"

Bonnie began slipping the straps off her shoulders. "Sure. That would be great."

Patrick pulled a handheld radio to his lips and pressed a button on the side. "Markus, please tell the kitchen that we're ready. Thank you." He walked back to the wooden table and straightened an askew fork at one of the four perfectly placed settings of stoneware plates and stainless steel utensils.

Pulling out one chair, he gestured for everyone to sit. "Miss Silver, may I?"

Smiling at Billy, Bonnie slid into the chair and allowed Sir Patrick to seat her. She folded her hands in her lap, her silky hair falling in front of her shoulders. Billy sat across from her, while the professor pulled up his chair at Bonnie's left and faced the chamber's back wall of logs and stone. A cot sat against the wall next to a kneeling bench and a three-foot-tall wooden cross.

"Who sleeps here?" Billy asked.

Sir Patrick sat in his chair and pulled it up to the table. "That's my bed."

Bonnie leaned forward in her chair, making more room for her wings. "Why do you sleep here? It can't be comfortable without heat in the winter."

"With all the children coming and going, the bedrooms have new occupants on a monthly basis. At times I would give up my own bedroom and move my personal items from place to place. I decided it was easier just to camp out here. It's a bit cold at times, but I am content. I have all I really need."

A tall, thin man wearing a white uniform entered pushing a wheeled table that rattled with teacups, drinking glasses, and an assortment of carafes and bottles. On top he balanced four pizza boxes.

Sir Patrick moved the stacked pizzas to the table and placed his palm on top. Closing his eyes he prayed, "We thank you, Maker of all things, for the gift of nourishment. We know, as you stated yourself, that we live not by bread alone, but by every word that you speak. We humbly ask you to bless this delicious bounty. Amen."

"Amen," the others chorused.

Patrick slid the box off the top. "I did my research." He set a pizza in front of each of his guests in turn. "Extra cheese for Bonnie, sausage for Billy, and mushrooms for Merlin."

Billy flipped up his box lid and took in a long sniff. "All right!"

Bonnie opened her box and pulled out a slice. Long strings of melted cheese stretched from her hand to a greasy spot at the bottom of the box. "Thank you, Sir Patrick. What kind is yours?"

He lifted his lid a crack and peeked inside. "A dangerous combination – goats' eyes, camel's tongue, and . . ." He glanced at each guest, a hint of mischief in his gaze, "earthworms!"

Bonnie's eyes bulged just as she bit into her slice. Billy burst out laughing.

Sir Patrick threw the lid open. "Will you look at that? It's pepperoni! They got my order wrong again!"

Billy picked one of the sausages from his pizza. "Looks like they put it on mine instead!" He tilted his head and lifted the morsel over his mouth. "One camel's tongue down the hatch!"

Bonnie tried to chew and laugh at the same time, her face turning crimson as a string of cheese dangled over her chin.

Professor Hamilton winked at his two students. "It seems that when the postman delivered a box of maturity to Sir Patrick's house, he was out hiding in the barn."

Patrick raised a slice of pizza as though he were proposing a toast. "And may the crippling corpse of the sedentary curmudgeon never find me! My kids need me to stay young at heart."

The four ate pizza and talked for a couple of hours, sipping soft drinks and tea while going over Billy's and Bonnie's life histories. The professor told of his academic career at Oxford, but Sir Patrick kept deflecting questions about his own past. He would just wave his hand and say, "Oh, I'll tell you some other time."

The patter of a late afternoon shower interrupted their conversation. Raindrops found their way through the roof opening and dripped on the floor's compass design, filtering through the sand and disappearing into an unseen drain. The diners, seated far from the exposed area, relaxed and listened to the cooling rain in comfort and silence.

Billy stretched his arms and let out a yawn. Bonnie stood and extended her wings fully, joining in with a yawn of her own. Sir Patrick pulled a radio from his belt. "Markus, is Miss Silver's bed prepared?"

A scratchy voice replied, "Yes, Sir Patrick."

"Please show her to her room. Take the back hallway to bypass the children." He raised a finger. "Oh, and bring the New Table cloaks."

He picked up Bonnie's pizza box and neatly folded it in half. "Miss Silver, you've had a long journey, and you must get some rest before your next one."

Bonnie smiled, her tired eyes blinking. "Thank you. I'd like that."

A few seconds later, Markus came in and laid the folded cloaks next to the wall by the entry door. After handing him the empty boxes, Patrick whispered in his ear. Markus nodded and led Bonnie toward the exit, her backpack hanging limply over her shoulder. Just before passing through the doorway, she waved at Billy with one of her wings.

The professor patted Billy on the back. "William had a difficult night as well. I suggest that he also gather his strength."

"As should you, Merlin, but I don't have another available room."

"I can nod off in my chair, but I would sleep better if William had a bed."

Sir Patrick extended his arm toward his cot against the wall. "Will my bed be sufficient?"

Billy slid out of his chair and shuffled to the spindly bed. He yawned again and sat on the edge. "I think I could sleep on a bed of nails if I had to." He stretched out on his back and intertwined his fingers behind his head. Within seconds of closing his eyes, he was dreaming, floating over dark clouds in a star-sprinkled sky. He had experienced this dream a hundred times before, flying with dragon wings over high-topped thunderheads in the middle of the night. It seemed so real, yet he knew he was dreaming, predicting the events before they occurred. Next came his usual dive into the clouds and then farther down into the stormy air currents below.

Three dragons flew past. One of them, Clefspeare, his father in dragon form, circled back. It orbited him three times, then zoomed away and joined the other two.

Billy finally landed on a forest path, rain pelting his head and forming puddles across the muddy trail. Next, if the dream went according to plan, a penguin with an umbrella over his head would walk by and offer it to him. Yes, there he was, waddling down the path, propping the umbrella up with his narrow black wing. It raised the umbrella toward Billy's hand and opened its mouth to speak, but the words that came out were new. On most nights he said, "Here, my umbrella never leaks." This time, he croaked a low-pitched warning. "Great danger awaits. Beware of the Watchers." He then shuffled past Billy and disappeared in a flash of lightning and a thick curtain of driving rain.

As had become common in recent months, a familiar character appeared, Billy's old nemesis, Palin. The dark knight stood in his path, wielding a sword. "Come on! Fight me face-to-face! Or are you still a coward who can only attack from behind?" As Billy drew nearer, Palin vanished, but his voice echoed in the darkness, "You're just like me, boy. You're just like me."

Billy ventured on in the gloom of his dream, trudging through muddy water in a cemetery littered with bones. As usual, a white glow appeared on a distant hill. He hurried toward it, but a fence of shining light dropped down to block his way. He had seen this fence in other dreams, and he knew that touching it would jolt his skeleton right out of his skin. No matter how evil his pursuers, no matter how bright and wonderful his destination, this fence always prevented him from escaping death and darkness. He was never able to figure out how to open it.

A new sound rang out in the dream, the clanging of metal on metal. He spun around. Two men fought with swords, but they looked strange. Their bodies were normal, but they had the heads of lions, complete with sharp teeth and thick manes. One of them roared, yet the roar transformed into words as his bright blade smashed against his opponent's. "Patrick, he cannot enter the circles. It's too dangerous!"

The other lion-man countered with a swing of an equally bright sword, and when the two blades met, each one flashed like the sun. "He must go, Merlin! Without him, the prisoners will be trapped forever!"

Another clash sent a current of light through Merlin's sword, making it too bright to watch. As the blades rubbed together, Merlin gritted his teeth. "Would you exchange their freedom for William's life? And what if the Watchers are set free? Would you risk the safety of the entire planet?"

Suddenly, the dream took another new turn. The earth collapsed beneath Billy's feet, sending him plunging downward in a swirl of bright lights. His body throbbed, and a horrible squeal pierced his ears and sent numbing shock waves through his brain. He landed on his feet and stood alone in darkness. Above, he could still see the hole he had fallen through, so far away it seemed like a solitary star in an ink-black sky.

A loud crack jolted Billy out of his dream world, and his eyes snapped open. The sun had already set, leaving only early evening twilight peering in through the hole in the ceiling. A single lantern sat on the floor between him and the centre of the room, shedding dim light throughout the chamber. The professor and Sir Patrick stared at him, each man sitting in one of the dining chairs, their elbows resting on the arms. Their faces seemed tense, locked jaws around tight lips.

Sir Patrick's complexion had turned grey, making him look much older. He rocked his head upward. "Merlin, I think we should inform William of the danger and let him choose. I will abide by his decision."

Patrick's words mixed with the sound of heavy rain ripping across the floor at the centre of the room. A peal of thunder answered, and a gust of wind swept a blanket of mist across the faces of the two gentlemen, relaxing their tense cheeks.

Professor Hamilton wrung his hands together, then tightened his intertwined fingers. "William, Sir Patrick has revealed to me that your mission is more dangerous than I knew. He believes it is vital and that you should go anyway, but since we cannot wait for your mother's counsel, the decision is up to you and Miss Silver."

Billy searched the professor's sad grey eyes. Prof was definitely worried, more worried than he had ever seen him. After a few seconds, his teacher's countenance suddenly brightened. Billy swung his head around. Aha! Bonnie was standing just inside the doorway. The lantern's flickering wick cast dancing shadows across her smiling face, covering her blonde tresses with orange ribbons of light.

Patrick rose from his chair, and the professor and Billy followed suit, each giving her a gentlemanly nod. Patrick beckoned her in. "Please come and join us. I assume you are more rested now?"

Bonnie glided toward the chairs, clutching her empty backpack in one hand. "Fit as a fiddle." She sat in the dining chair Patrick had vacated. "I was snoozing like a log until that thunderclap rattled my window."

Patrick placed his hand gently on her shoulder. "A startling yet effective alarm clock indeed. But it's good that you've come. It's time to tell both of you about your mission." He stepped over to the cot and sat next to Billy, folding his hands in his lap. "We have long believed that a king in Arthur's mould would come at our time of greatest need, and your professor believes that you, Billy, have proven yourself to be the one, both by virtue of your lineage and your deeds."

Billy pinched the edge of the cot's blanket. "But I can't possibly rule a country. I can barely keep my own room clean."

Patrick grinned and patted Billy's back. "Don't worry, son. You are not called to rule; you are called to rescue. You are to journey into a strange land that we call the Circles of Seven and rescue some prisoners there. As your professor has noted, we suspect that this land has some connection with the afterlife." Sir Patrick glanced at Professor Hamilton for a moment before turning his gaze back to Billy. "Your mission should have been simple in concept, but complications have arisen. The knights of the New Table plan to coerce you into using your power and authority for their purposes. They aim to trick you into releasing their allies who are also trapped there. The details are sketchy, but they need you to use Excalibur to destroy their prison."

Billy stood and shoved his hands into his pockets. "So there are prisoners I need to rescue and prisoners I don't want to rescue. How do I tell the difference?"

Patrick reached for a night table next to the cot and retrieved a tape recorder. "Your professor recorded Merlin's song, which I believe he sang to you several months ago. We have a few clues in the lyrics and a few more in a poem that I will show you in a moment." He pressed a button on the player. "Listen while our modern bard sings the old prophet's song."

The recorder's tiny speaker replayed the sound of a chair being dragged and the professor clearing his throat, then crooning the song in his melodic tenor.

With sword and stone, the holy knight,
Darkness as his bane,
Will gather warriors in the light
Cast in heaven's flame.

He comes to save a remnant band,
Searching with his maid,
But in a sea of sadness finds
His warriors lying splayed.

A valley deep, a valley long
Lay angels dry and dead;
Now who can wake their cold, stone hearts
Their bones on table spread?

Like wine that flows in skins made new
The spirit pours out fresh;
Can hymns of love bring forth the dead
And give them hearts of flesh?

O will you learn from words of faith
That sing in psalms from heaven
To valley floors where terrors lurk
In circles numbering seven?

The haunting words sent a cold shiver all across Billy's skin. He remembered the song. It had the same effect on him the last time he heard it.

Patrick waited through a soul-searching pause, then rose to his feet. "Apparently the prisoners you'll be looking for are helpless and in great need. I get the impression that they will be in a weakened state and desperate, while the allies of the New Table will be in some sort of impenetrable confines that only Excalibur can destroy. Otherwise, the knights would have released them long ago since they hold sway over that domain. They need the Once and Future King and Excalibur to set their evil company free."

Patrick gazed at the kneeling bench and cross next to the cot. "Even the greatest king of all time turned down an earthly crown to rescue a host of captives." He leaned over and grasped Billy's shoulder, his deeply set eyes drilling a laser stare. "Everything else pales when compared to securing freedom through courage and personal sacrifice. From what I have heard, you risked your life to set prisoners free from a candlestone."

Billy dropped his gaze. "Well . . . yeah . . . I guess so."

Patrick straightened his body and stepped back. "So this mission is similar, except that it is on a larger scale and more dangerous." He curled his finger, beckoning for Billy to follow. "And now I want to show you something that will astound you." He walked toward the north side of the room where a thick green drape veiled the entire wall. Reaching behind the veil, he pulled down on a rope, drawing the curtains apart. A rectangular window appeared, framed by beams of varnished hardwood. The window seemed wide open, no glass, no screens, just a bare hole that led to a dark forest, a tropical jungle of massive trees and dense, fern-like undergrowth.

Billy couldn't remember seeing any landscape so lush when he arrived at the castle, only bright green fields of perfectly manicured grass stretching out over countless acres. A few majestic oaks had dotted the expansive estate, but nothing like this virtual jungle now before his eyes. Had the long corridor led to a part of the mansion they couldn't see when they drove up? Was it just a movie projection? It seemed so real, as though they could walk right into the screen and just keep on going, stepping through a maze of age-old trees and green long-leafed ferns.

"We believe this is the first circle of your journey," Patrick explained, "the first of the seven circles. We know very little about what you will face, only the instructions that Merlin left with us, apparently written over a thousand years ago."

Billy placed his hand on Excalibur's scabbard, fingering the engravings in the metal. Somehow the touch brought him comfort as he gazed at the mysterious forest. Nothing seemed to move inside, yet he could tell the place was alive, as though the air was filled with voices that beckoned him to enter and discover its mysteries. "So do we just crawl through that window?" he asked.

"If only it were so simple." Patrick placed his palm flat against the forest scene. "It's a solid barrier, as far as we can tell."

Billy touched the wall with his fingers. It felt cold, and a mild vibration, an electrostatic buzz of some kind, massaged his hand. "So what do Merlin's instructions say?"

The professor angled the flashlight beam to the right of the forest scene. "Apparently, Merlin etched this message in stone, employing his usual poetic scheme of simple rhyme and metre, but I'm afraid the meaning is far from simple. Merlin decided to be more cryptic than he ever was in his diary. But what is truly astounding is that he must have foreseen the lettering and word usage that would make sense in this present age. The verbiage is hardly ancient, but Patrick's scientists have verified that it has been there for at least a thousand years." He stepped back and allowed the light to expand over the entire message. "Read it for yourself."

Billy leaned forward and narrowed his eyes. The letters were small but perfectly shaped, as though chiselled by a laser stylus. He read out loud.

Young Arthur holds the window's key
To ancient realms that bear his quest.
The circles know where lie the beasts
Who crave the light, who crave their breath.

The beasts conceal the ancient truths
That dwell behind divided tongues,
But dragons' hearts reveal their flame
From shining light and psalms well sung.

The prison world awaits a king
To rescue souls who have no hope,
Yet evil spirits also wait
To ride the sword's redeeming stroke.

In circle one there lies a belt,
The camera's eye to watch your tale,
A tale as old as man's first tears
When Adam donned the devil's veil.

The stone recalls the tale of threats
That lie in circles deeper still.
In letters giving aid and hope
They guide the souls with steadfast will.

You cannot bear this test alone
For faith is edified in pairs,
And bearing witness two agree
Survival rests on faithful prayers.

Beware of mirrors found within
To quell your rival's fiery darts,
For mirrors sketch our shallow shells;
They cannot fathom human hearts.

Yet mirrors can reflect the truth
And overcome the darkest night;
The perfect law resides in those
Who live by faith and not by sight.

When thinning shadows fade to black
Polaris greets the standing bear,
Then raise the sword to pierce the veil
And strike the pose of saints in prayer.

Billy rubbed his eyes and followed the flashlight beam back to the professor. "Is that why you mentioned Polaris to me this morning? Because it's in the poem?"

The professor aimed the beam at the line about Polaris. "I knew about the poem, William, to be sure, but I used Polaris to illustrate light and guidance, which I'm sure many teachers, like Merlin, have done in the past. Here he seems to indicate your departure time. I looked up the astronomical charts for tonight, and it seems that Ursa Major will be standing completely upright at about seven o'clock. It will be quite dark by then, so all shadows will have faded to black."

Bonnie lowered her backpack to the floor, hanging on to one strap. "I guess Merlin's talking about me when he says, 'faith is edified in pairs'."

"I think that's a fair deduction," the professor replied, "considering that the song also refers to searching with a maid. It's a dangerous journey, but I assume you won't be changing your mind about accompanying William."

Bonnie smiled and shook her head. "After what we've been through together? Not a chance." She lifted the backpack a few inches. "What do you think? Should I leave this here or take it with me?"

The professor pressed a finger on his lower lip. "Because of the danger, I think you should probably be ready to fly on a second's notice." He turned to Sir Patrick, raising his brow. "Agreed?"

Sir Patrick stood with his arms crossed, tapping his foot on the stone floor. "All souls are laid bare in that domain. Even perceptions of the mind become visible to the eyes."

Flashing a half-smile, Bonnie dropped the backpack. "I guess that means 'leave it here'."

The professor gave Sir Patrick a quizzical stare but kept silent. He then placed both hands on Billy's shoulders. "William, as far as we know, these prisoners have been waiting for many years, and no one else is able to rescue them. That's why I approved of your participation. Lives are at stake. But now we know about the increased danger, and I am concerned, very concerned, yet I also have confidence in Merlin. It is apparent that he has intimate knowledge of what lies ahead, and his counsel is trustworthy. In the end, of course, it's up to you to decide."

Billy shrugged. "I think it's a no-brainer. A thousand-year-old prophecy painted a bullseye right on my forehead, so I'd better get the job done."

The professor withdrew his hands and held his head erect. "Very well." He pulled out his pocket watch and glanced at it. "It seems that I will not be able to stay here and await the alignment of the bear. Walter and Miss Stalworth will arrive at seven-thirty, and I must be there to greet them."

Sir Patrick laid his palm on the wall's forest view. "It's a shame, Merlin, that you won't be able to witness what you have waited so long to see, the piercing of the veil."

The professor dropped the watch back into his pocket, his chin tightening. "I accept my fate. It seems that I am called to another task. Perhaps when I return tonight, I will be in time to see wonders so great that neither one of us could have imagined them." His face turned red, and his eyes glinted with tears. With a quick spin he headed toward the exit. "I'll see myself out." A second later, he disappeared into the narrow corridor.

Billy shifted his weight from one foot to the other. "Uh . . . bye, Prof."

Bonnie's wings shuddered. "Something's really bothering him."

Sir Patrick's gaze fixed on the dark exit hall as the sound of the professor's footsteps faded. With his arms crossed and his toe tapping the floor again, he seemed to be waiting for something.

Billy lowered his voice to a whisper and leaned closer to Bonnie. "I have a bad feeling about this."

Bonnie joined the whisper. "Danger?"

"Yeah. And it's growing fast. It's a good thing Prof trusts this guy so much. Otherwise, I wouldn't be so sure."

Sir Patrick swivelled his head toward them and reached for his back pocket. "I almost forgot to give you something." He withdrew his wallet and pulled out a plastic card. "If you'll remember, the poem mentioned a stone that will aid you as you navigate the circles. We've assumed that you'll learn exactly what that means once you're inside, and I've copied the entire poem onto this card so you can reference it during your journey and possibly receive help from it right away."

"Got it." Billy read the poem again, slowly this time, trying to memorize as much as he could, then slid it into his back pocket. "How long till the constellation is ready?"

"It's difficult to determine the exact moment. Polaris is likely already visible, and Ursa Major is already rotating toward an upright position. But I have no idea how upright it has to be to be considered 'standing.' It's possible that everything is ready for your departure already."

Loud clopping sounded from the entry corridor. Markus appeared at the doorway, then leaned over with his hands on his knees, breathing heavily.

Patrick ran to meet him. "Markus! What's wrong?"

Markus held his palm against his chest. "Couldn't . . . call on your radio. . . . Normal frequencies jammed. . . . The dark sorceress . . . has been seen."

Patrick grabbed Markus's arm and helped him stand. A purple vein ridged across Patrick's temple. "Who saw her?!" he shouted. "Where?!"

Markus blinked rapidly. "Our outposts saw her with two of her knights near the tor, and now she's coming this way."

"Did Merlin get out safely?"

"Yes. I think he left undetected."

Patrick pulled Markus close, but his rasping whisper carried across the room. "Don't inform the staff. Use the stealth drill procedure, and lead the children into the tunnels yourself. When they are settled in the bunker, pull the alarm."

Markus bowed his head. "The children are safe in my hands."

"Go now! I will barricade this door."

Markus nodded, turned, and ran through the dark hall.

"William!" Patrick called, waving from the doorway. "Come!"

Billy sprinted to the passage. He and Patrick heaved the massive door closed. Bonnie flew to them and helped lift a thick wooden beam into the locking brackets. It dropped into place with a secure clump.

Patrick rested his arm on the beam, trying to catch his breath. "I don't know . . . if this will be enough to keep her out."

Bonnie pushed on the slab of solid oak. It didn't budge. "But how will the professor get back in?"

Patrick's eyes darted around the room. "Markus can monitor the building's perimeter, even from the bunker." He patted a radio on his belt. "Now that we know of the danger, we'll switch to coded communications and alert your professor by cell phone when all is clear." He turned an iron key below the knob. "*If* all is clear."

Billy jerked his head up. His danger meter suddenly shot into the red zone. "Do you hear something?"

Bonnie pointed toward the hole in the ceiling. "It sounded like a crow."

Patrick's eyes flared. "You must go now!" He ran toward the image on the wall. "Follow me!"

With two beats of her wings, Bonnie zoomed toward the wall. Billy raced behind her, grabbing Excalibur's hilt. "What do I do?"

Patrick puffed, holding his chest. "What the original Merlin . . . commanded, 'Raise the sword to pierce the veil and strike the pose of saints in prayer.' " His head spun toward the door. "I heard a screech!"

Billy nodded. "Yeah. It's just the crow again."

Patrick's cheeks turned fiery red. "It's your enemy! Draw your sword and kneel! Now!"

Billy slid Excalibur from the scabbard. The blade flashed from hilt to point with a brilliant white light.

Patrick laid a hand on each of their heads, whispering, "Godspeed my children," then backed away.

Billy grabbed Bonnie's hand and heaved Excalibur upward, its glow brightening by the second.

Three banging knocks sounded at the entry. “Patrick, son of Nathan!” a female voice shouted, “Open this door!”

Excalibur’s light expanded into a halo, surrounding Billy and Bonnie with a spherical envelope of luminescence.

The banging continued, each thud sounding like a sonic boom. “Patrick! If you don’t open this door, its splinters will pierce your skull!”

Glittering specks within the sword’s halo attacked their bodies, like sparkling locusts eating away their flesh and transforming them into light energy. The huge room bent out of shape, warping like a circus sideshow mirror.

Bonnie’s grip tightened on Billy’s fingers, and the sword grew as light as a plastic baseball bat. Billy felt himself being absorbed into the window, his body stretching out, morphing every sight and sound into a chaotic swirl.

Seconds later, the bending world straightened out, snapping back into shape like a tightened blanket. Billy knelt in the middle of a forest, the very same stand of trees he had seen through the window of the compass room. He glanced at his right hand. Excalibur was still there, a residual glow casting faint light all around. He jerked his head to his other side. Bonnie was gone!

CHAPTER

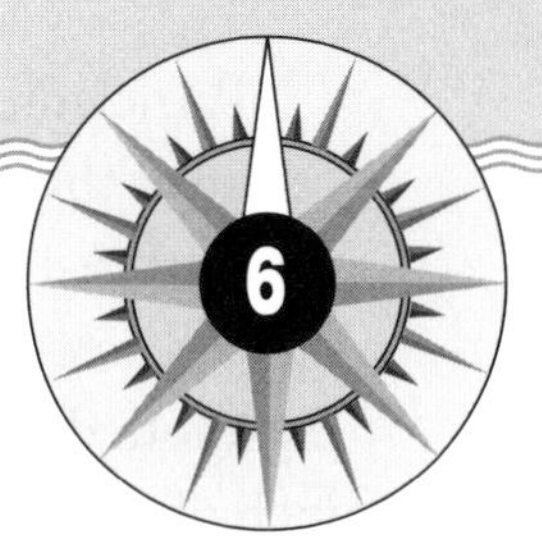

Morgan's Threat

Patrick raised both arms, shielding his eyes. Billy and Bonnie dissolved in an eruption of sparkling light, each of their bodies crystallizing and melding with Excalibur's pulsing halo. The radiance swallowed the sword itself as glittering shards swirled around, forming a horizontal tornado that rushed into the window like a whirlpool of luminescence.

The banging on the door grew louder. Each boom shook the floor and sent a shower of crumbling debris from the ceiling.

As soon as every sparkle vanished, Patrick turned toward the door, crossed his arms over his chest, and shouted, "Morgan, I suggest you take your foul vapours to the dung heap where they belong. You are not welcome here."

Silence descended on the chamber, followed by a low, feminine voice streaming past the door. "Patrick, I am not welcome in many places, yet I walk in them unhindered. Will you let me in, or must I display a bit of unsavoury force?"

Patrick drew the curtain across the window and hustled to the centre of the room. "Do your worst, Witch!"

A thin, black vapour oozed under the door and spread upward across its inner face. It hugged the door as if painting over the knotted wood with smoky dust. When it finally covered every inch of ancient oak, the door shimmered, and vibrations rattled the latch, the jambs, and even the locking bar and brackets until splinters popped out all across the surface.

With a sudden burst, the door exploded into the inner chamber. Needle-sharp spears of wood catapulted in every direction. Patrick dove to the floor, covering his head with his arms. Dozens of wood fragments pelted his body, but nothing pierced his clothes or skin.

When the tapping of falling debris ceased, Patrick looked up. The black smoke collected into a column under the doorway's arch, fashioning into the curves of a slender woman. A smile bent back her pale cheeks. "Security is a fleeting fantasy, don't you think?" She leaned over and picked up one of the door's broken locking brackets, then tossed it back to the floor. When the metallic clatter faded, she continued. "I appreciate your prostrate position, Patrick, but it's a bit premature, isn't it?"

Patrick jumped to his feet, brushing the dust from the front of his shirt. "It's your thinking that's premature, Morgan. Mastering vapour resonance will not defeat the dragons."

She turned her head, acting surprised at seeing the spears of wood protruding from the demolished jamb. "Oh, that?" She pulled out a wood fragment and flipped it to the ground with an air of nonchalance. "That was just for show, an impressive little talent, but too slow for battle."

"Well, the show is over. I'm duly impressed." He extended a rigid arm, aiming his finger toward the doorway. "Now get out."

Morgan walked to the wall and picked up one of the black cloaks. She held it up, her nostrils flaring. "How could you send them in without the cloaks? I'm sure you figured out how to track them, didn't you?"

"No one who is covered by Excalibur's light needs a cloak. They were sufficiently protected. And I know your malice well enough not to trust what wearing them might do to their minds."

She threw the cloak back to the floor. "But I notice that you still wear yours when you venture into the circles. Have you lost your fear of its influence on you?"

"Those who recognize your arts are equipped to fight them, so you have no power over me. You might as well change to that black chicken costume and fly the coop."

Morgan glided toward Patrick with long, graceful strides. She passed her fingers along his outstretched arm and teasingly caressed his face. "My dear Patrick, you know that I hold the ultimate dagger over your head. Don't you think you should offer me just a wee bit more graciousness?"

He grabbed her wrist and pulled her arm down. "Cut the pretense, Morgan. What do you want?"

Morgan's wrist dissolved into vapour and slipped from his grasp. The dark mist floated to her side, rematerializing into a thin, pale arm. Her smile faded, stretching into a tight line across her face. "I want to negotiate a trade."

Patrick crossed his arms and scowled. "What kind of trade?"

Morgan walked around Patrick in a slow, graceful circle. Patrick swivelled his head, keeping an eye on her as she spoke in a firm, matter-of-fact tone. "You know what the members of the New Table really want, don't you?"

"Of course. Dead dragons and worldwide domination. It's such a small request." Patrick raised his eyebrows and smirked.

"I think the world's leaders should just agree to your demands and give up all authority, don't you?"

Morgan stopped and brushed a wood chip from his shoulder. "Sarcasm doesn't flatter you, Patrick." She continued her slow orbit, now in a tighter circle. "But you're right. Those are the goals of my little underlings. But you also know what I want for myself, isn't that true?"

Patrick swallowed hard and tried to keep his voice from trembling. "Yes. Yes, I'm afraid I do."

"As we speak, my knights are entering the circles. You know their power. You know their craft. Young Arthur and his princess cannot possibly defeat them unless I lend a hand of protection."

Patrick broke from Morgan's stalking circle and strode toward his kneeling bench. He stood firm and grasped the top of the cross. "How did you find so many entries to the circles? I know of only one, and it leads to the rocky vestibule, not to the land of the dead."

Morgan followed, gliding on silent steps, but she stopped several feet short of the bench. "You only know what Merlin taught you. And what is Merlin?" She waved the back of her hand at the cross. "A weak prophet for a weak god. Merlin floats about like shining pixie dust and leaves pathetic doggerel on ancient walls."

Patrick bent over and extended his arms toward the altar as if inviting her to kneel. "If God is so weak, then why do you keep your distance?" He straightened his frame and squared his shoulders. "Does the presence of the cross remind you of your greatest defeat?"

She let out a spiteful snort. "Hardly! Since your dead messiah took his dirty little lambs away, the other world has been mine. Young Arthur's mission to rescue prisoners is a fool's errand.

It's nothing but Merlin's misguided dream and the folly of dragons who shouldn't have trusted him fifteen hundred years ago. Their dry bones testify against the singing prophet to this day, and some dragons still have never learned."

Patrick ground his teeth. "State your business plainly. Then get out."

Morgan took a step back. "Very well, Patrick. But beware of what you ask for. My plain speech may sizzle your ears." She raised her arms, allowing her loose sleeves to fall to her elbows. Her bare limbs looked more like whitewashed bones than human flesh. With sweeping motions, she gathered darkness from the air and moulded it into a black sphere. She cradled the gloomy mass as though it were a nursing infant. "Look, Patrick, if you dare. See the fate that awaits young Arthur and his betrothed."

Patrick turned his back to her and crossed his arms over his chest. "Your arts tell lies. I'd rather look at a bloated skunk."

Morgan laughed. "Who is the liar? The one who spins dark oracles, or the one who tells tales? You know what is required for her to escape, yet you led Arthur to believe he could rescue your lost little waif."

Patrick clenched his fists. "No! I never mentioned her. The mission is about the other captives." He lowered his gaze, and his voice weakened. "I can't expect William to forfeit his life."

Morgan repeated his words in a mocking tone. "I can't expect William to forfeit his life." She laughed again, louder and longer. "Let me guess. You sent him wandering into Hades in search of unnamed prisoners with only Merlin's songs to guide him, because if you gave him too much information he would retreat before the battle ever began. And if he just happened to come across a certain girl, maybe, just maybe he would give his life to save her, a noble sacrifice that would be immortalized in song by inane bards for all eternity. Is that pretty close to the mark?"

Patrick scowled as her acidic words burned into his brain. "Your accusations spew from the pits of hell, you venomous vulture. You're fishing for secrets, and I will reveal none."

"Oh, please forgive me!" she continued. "Certainly such a selfish scheme never entered your mind. You plan to rescue the girl yourself when William returns, because you've found your own way into the circle that holds her captive."

Patrick whirled around and faced her again. "As if you didn't know! I've tried to enter the upper circles ever since you stole her from me. I've followed every rabbit trail in that forsaken pit, I've quoted every ancient prayer, I've tried every recipe in a thousand old wives' tales. There's no way to cross the bridge over the valley of bones! None!"

Morgan flashed an evil smile, still caressing her black, swirling bundle. "Yes, I know it appears that way, and your torture has been delicious. Yet, I know how to enter the sixth circle, Patrick, and I offer passage to you if you will simply deliver what I want."

Patrick kept his gaze averted from the dark sphere in Morgan's arms. "What do you want from me?" he asked, crossing his arms again. "I hold no seats of power."

Morgan's smile vanished. "Perhaps not, but your circle was able to hide a valuable secret for centuries. Fortunately, one of your members finally succumbed to one of my favourite instruments of torture. He revealed that the young dragon you call Bonnie Silver is a legal heir to the king. All I ask is that you deliver her to me. Dead or alive, it matters not."

Patrick tightened his fingers into a fist. "Have you been drinking your witch's brew again? You can't use her body. Without Billy's permission, she is impenetrable to your black arts."

Morgan frowned and spat out her reply. "Your naivety concerning my arts is laughable." She continued to stroke her "baby" and slowly regained a smile. "Until young Arthur completes his mission, your authority surpasses his, so you can do what I ask. My knights will make sure that Bonnie Silver is in no shape to give you any trouble. Simply deliver her body to me, and I will show you where and how to enter the circles."

"You're mad!" Patrick shouted. "I would never hand her over to you!"

Morgan lowered her eyelids, covering half of her blazing orbs. "Shall we discuss why you've never told anyone in your circle of seven about your past and what happened to your wife and daughter? Do you think I am incapable of bringing the same fate to your precious orphans?"

Patrick glared at her. Her cunning smile froze his heart, and when his gaze wandered to the bundle in her arms, pain knifed through him. Within the black sphere a girl lay motionless in the middle of a valley filled with bones. A boy knelt at her side, weeping.

He jerked his head to the side. "Leave me now, Morgan."

Morgan spread out her arms, and the black swirl evaporated. "Very well. You have some time to consider my offer. But when Arthur and his bride meet their doom, it will be too late to reconsider. I need her body intact, either alive or freshly dead."

The professor hustled into the terminal building, his long legs striding across the flat carpet of the seemingly endless hall. A tune played in his head, and he marched to its lively beat. After a minute or two, syllables began mixing into the melody, combining with notes until they strung themselves together into rhythmic sentences to match the tune's iambic metre.

Once the song completed its self-composition, it replayed until it seemed to come from the airport speakers and float around his ears. But he didn't mind. The words created a mysterious poem, something for his brain to chew on while he watched for Ashley and Walter.

A sign in the distance announced his journey's end – British Airways baggage claim. He pulled out his pocket watch, took a reading, and searched the arriving flights display. *Ah! Flight fifty-six. On time.* He glanced at his watch again. *I'm two minutes late.*

As he approached the baggage conveyor, he surveyed the sea of rushing passengers. Sidestepping a man barrelling down the hall with a suitcase in each hand, the professor bumped into a lady standing next to the luggage queue. He pivoted and bowed his head. "I beg your pardon. Please forgive—"

"Professor Hamilton?" the lady interrupted.

The professor lifted his head. "Marilyn?" He brushed back his unruly hair. "I didn't expect to see you. Were you able to hire another vehicle after all?"

"Another vehicle? What are you talking about?"

The professor put a hand on his cell phone, his arm shaking. "You called me. Your rental car broke down and—"

"I called you?" Marilyn furrowed her brow. "Professor, are you all right?"

The professor took a heavy step, dizziness overtaking his balance. Suddenly, a strong hand gripped his arm and supported his body. "Steady there, my good fellow. Your legs are as limp as wet noodles."

The professor pulled himself up on his helper's sweater sleeve and grasped his beefy biceps. "Sir Barlow!" With a gentle touch, he laid his palm over the bump on his scalp. "I took quite a blow to the head this morning, and it seems that the shock of seeing you has triggered a fainting spell."

Marilyn stood on tiptoes and peeled the professor's hand away from his wound. "Oooh! That *is* nasty!"

The professor flinched at her touch. "No worse than the injury to my dignity, Marilyn. It is clear that I have been hoodwinked by one of the scoundrels of the New Table. Someone imitated your voice – quite well, obviously – and sent me to collect Walter and Miss Stalworth."

"But why?" Marilyn asked. "Are Billy and Bonnie okay?"

The professor smoothed his hair back again with a gentle stroke. "They are. Sir Patrick is with them. I think they're safe."

"You *think* they're safe?"

"I'm not as sure as I used to be. Patrick keeps many secrets, more than I ever realized before." The professor leaned over and whispered. "And now that Clefspeare is a prisoner of the New Table, my confidence in Patrick is waning."

Marilyn's eyes lit up with alarm. "A prisoner! How?"

The professor glanced down the corridor and pulled Sir Barlow into their huddle. "It's a long story, and I prefer to give the details in private after Walter and Miss Stalworth arrive." He swung his head back and forth. "A song keeps going through my mind, perhaps something Merlin left with me. I'll reveal its words soon, but the bottom line is simple. Clefspeare is in the hands of the enemy, and William and Miss Silver may also be walking into her lair."

Walter draped a jacket over his arm and slid his thumb behind the strap of his backpack. With his free hand gripping a waning MoonPie, he marched down an endless hall while chewing a sticky mouthful, trying to keep up with Ashley. She tilted to one side to compensate for a heavy briefcase, her hair bouncing in sync with her lively pace.

Walter took another bite and spoke through the marshmallow goo. "How was I supposed to know? That old guy seemed nice enough."

Ashley halted and spun around, her face aflame. "You try to survive five hours of cigar breath while listening to cockamamie theories about the 'spiritual conduits' of quantum mechanics."

"I was in his seat up front," Walter said, shrugging his shoulders. "You should've said something."

"I was trapped, Walter. You were reading Captain Marvel and eating lunch up in First Class while I was pinned to the window seat in row forty-one!" She pulled an apple out of her jacket pocket and held it in front of Walter's face. "It's a good thing I brought this. Dr Weirdo even ate my lunch!" She bit into the apple like an angry pit bull.

"So why are you mad at me? I didn't steal your sandwich."

Ashley swallowed her bite of apple. "Right! You had steak!" She closed one eye and held the apple up again. "Supposedly you came along to protect me. Don't you know what chivalry means?"

Walter lowered his head. "Sure. I know what it means." He slowly lifted his eyes and extended his half-eaten MoonPie. "Want a bite of this?"

Ashley let out a growling huff and spun back around. She hiked up her briefcase and stormed down the hallway.

Walter stood and watched her for a moment, shaking his head.

"Brilliant and filled with fire, isn't she, Walter?"

Walter jerked his head around. The smelly old man from the airplane stood at his side, chewing on an unlit cigar. Walter pulled his backpack higher and let out a nervous laugh. "I guess so. But she has a good heart."

"Oh, no doubt, no doubt." The man pulled the cigar from his mouth and spat out a fleck of tobacco. "Just keep in mind what she said about chivalry, son, and you'll do fine."

"Uh, okay. . . . I guess." Walter squinted at the old man's widely set brown eyes and his two-day white beard. "What did she say about chivalry?"

"That you're supposed to protect her, son! She's a strong, young woman, but she'll never respect you until you prove yourself to be a strong, young man. The key is to be gentle with her and a warrior against anything that might do her harm."

Walter stood still, blinking at the stranger.

He grabbed Walter's shoulder, turned him around, and gave him a firm shove. "So get going!"

Walter ran forward to keep from falling. After catching himself, he looked back at the bizarre old man and gave him a quick wave, then stuffed the rest of the MoonPie into his mouth and sprinted down the corridor.

When he reached Ashley's side, he grabbed her briefcase handle. "I'll get this," he said, his mouth still full.

Ashley stopped in her tracks, resisting for a second before letting it go. "Look, Walter, I'm . . . I'm sorry for giving you such a hard time."

Walter swallowed hard to dispose of his sticky snack. "No problem. I deserved it." He nodded toward a moving walkway. "Let's forget about it and go find Prof." He led the way into the baggage claim area and spotted the professor and his two companions. He angled his head back toward Ashley. "Did you expect Mrs B and Sir Barlow?"

Ashley narrowed her eyes. "That's weird. I thought they were in Scotland."

They picked up their pace, swerving in and out of lines of trench coats and travel bags. When they reached the three adults, Walter set the briefcase down between his feet and extended his hand toward the professor. "What's wrong, Prof? You look like the queen just died or something."

"No," the professor replied, shaking Walter's hand. "Her Majesty is alive and well – at least I assume so if she hasn't met a certain van driver from Yeovil." He bowed toward Ashley, his hand fishing something from his pocket. "Miss Stalworth, your services are needed more than ever."

Ashley pushed her fingers through her hair. "I'll do what I can, Professor Hamilton."

The professor held out his open palm, revealing two microchips. "If you can decipher the encoding, perhaps we will not be fooled in the future." He closed his fist and set the chips gently back into his pocket. "There is much to explain, but since time is of the essence, I shall tell the story in the car. We must get to Sir Patrick's house as soon as possible."

Ashley strode toward the luggage conveyor belt. "Then let's get going. The microchip equipment is in my checked baggage."

After a few minutes, a square box fastened by metal buckles and a wide leather strap appeared on the conveyor. Walter dashed to the front and lugged it down to the floor. "I got it," he grunted. He nodded toward the line of baggage. "Barlow, will you get my duffle? It's the blue one with the orange trim."

Barlow grabbed Walter's bag and helped him carry the equipment case to the airport's rental car area. Marilyn returned her rental, and the five proceeded to the professor's car in the main parking lot. Marilyn climbed into the front passenger seat, and Walter, Ashley, and Sir Barlow settled into the back.

Walter looked around at all the sombre faces. "Hey, I read a great joke on the plane. There was this fish who loved to play golf, see, and—"

"Hush, Walter," Ashley said sharply. "No one wants to hear your fish joke. It's probably not funny anyway."

"But it is. This fish—"

"Mr Foley," the professor interrupted, "please tell us the joke later. I believe my tale is more crucial right now." After leaving the airport's access loop, the professor told the whole story, from the time of the dragons' arrival with Bonnie to their planned entrance into the view window. He explained Sir Patrick's theory that the New Table would try to persuade Billy to set their own prisoners free. "I believe," he said, gripping the steering wheel tightly, "that Clefspeare is now being held somewhere within the circles. If the New Table dragon-nappers threaten to kill the dragon, perhaps William will feel duty bound to do as they wish in order to save his father.

"But a song has entered my mind that has opened a new line of thinking. Listen."

The professor gave a low "ahem" and pursed his lips. He hummed a quiet bar, then started again, adding words to the melody.

A dragon chained in darkest pits
Will not behold pure freedom's light,
For dragons claim a lofty perch,
Yet cannot reach the highest height.

For even now in pits of gloom
The dragon's pride will never bow,
Until redemption's sword sets free
The dragon's heart to kneel and vow.

The professor paused while negotiating the car through a busy roundabout. "I think," he said, accelerating onto a main road, "that William's mission is supposed to include rescuing Clefspeare from some sort of pit. It is essential, therefore, that I find a way to deliver the message to him. I'm not sure how the details of the song figure in, but if William doesn't even know to search in a pit, he might miss the assignment altogether and leave his father stranded. I have already tried calling Patrick's home and cell phone, but there is no answer." He cocked his head back. "Miss Stalworth, have you made any progress on the chips?"

Ashley looked up with a start. "Oh! Sorry. I was kind of distracted by your song." She inserted the two microchips into a small, flat grid, fitting each prong into a tiny hole. "Here," she said, placing the grid in Walter's hand. "Hold this." She ran a short cable from the grid's panel to the computer on her lap. After she tapped a few keys, thousands of numbers flew across the screen. Her eyes followed the river of data, darting left to right and back again dozens of times. "Now this is interesting." She pulled a headset out of her laptop case and slipped the pads over her ears. "I'm sending the data to my supercomputer." She then pressed her finger against her jaw. "Karen? You there?"

"Karen?" the professor repeated. "Your sister?"

"Yes." Ashley clicked the mouse button on her laptop and pulled off her headset. "I'll send the response through these speakers so everyone can hear." She touched her jaw again. "Karen, pick up right now! I know you can't be far. I told you to stay close to Larry."

"Ah!" the professor exclaimed, raising a finger in the air. "Larry is your supercomputer! But how are you speaking to Karen?"

Walter set the grid in his lap and pulled a foil bag of peanuts from his backpack. "She has some supersonic connection through a transmitter in her tooth."

"In her tooth?" The professor scratched his head. "Well, that's a new—"

A loud voice blasted through the computer speakers. "I'm here! What's all the fuss?"

Ashley slid a dial on her laptop. "I need to talk to Larry. Can you patch me through?"

"Sure. No problem." Karen's quieter voice was followed by three muffled clicks. "Okay. You're on."

Ashley looked up toward the car ceiling. "Larry, it's Ashley. I need the latest research in traversing metaphysical dimension portals."

"Metaphysical? Did you hear that, Karen? Ashley's going New Age on us."

"It's not New Age, Larry. Get a life."

"No can do, Ashley. I'm just a machine with a vivid imagination. No life for me."

"Just cut the jokes and send the research to my laptop. I need the photoanalytical data for purported transdimensional windows, anything that would help me understand a possible migration environment. I'm going to set up some equipment that will analyse the various invisible spectrums in an interdimensional portal, and I need to know what to look for."

"Coming right up."

Walter popped a peanut into his mouth. "Translated," he said, grinning, "Ashley wants to know what the light was like in places where people claim to jump from one dimension to another. She's going to let her machines stare at that weird window Prof talked about to see if there's a match."

Ashley glared at him. "Thank you, Walter."

Larry's voice returned. "Do you want the results of the microchip analysis you sent?"

"Did you break the code?" Ashley asked.

"Ashley, it's me. Of course I broke the code."

"So you're a cryptological genius. Big deal. You still have a lot to learn about grammar and humility."

"So sue me. You wrote my grammar engine. As far as humility goes, I'm merely pointing out the obvious."

"Okay, okay. Just send me the decoded stream."

"Coming right up again, most excellent martinet."

Ashley balled her hand into a fist. "Karen, do you know how to check Larry's vocabulary level? It needs to be turned down a notch."

"Yep. No problem. I don't know how to adjust his sarcasm meter, though."

CHAPTER

A World within a World

Bonnie sat upright in a lush garden paradise. Daylight filtered through a tropical canopy, casting its brightest beam toward a nearby pond. She was alone in the eerie quiet. Not a puff of wind moved the sweet-smelling air, a humid blanket of jungle warmth that coaxed beads of sweat from her forehead and neck. She rose to her feet and mopped her brow with her sleeve. *This sweatshirt has to go!*

After unfastening the Velcro closures at the back, she pulled the sweatshirt over her head and tied it around her waist. She then smoothed out the picture of a roaring lion imprinted on the front of her long-sleeved shirt and set her hands on her hips. *Okay, now where am I?*

She remembered the ride to Sir Patrick's castle but nothing after that. Was she in one of the estate's gardens? Had she fallen asleep on the way, and the others left her here to rest? Maybe if she had a look around she would remember what was going on.

Bonnie walked slowly toward the circular pond, a crystal clear pool no bigger than a Little League baseball diamond. A bushy tree with a broad, twisted trunk grew near the opposite edge, reaching as high as a telephone pole. Wide, velvety leaves covered its branches, almost completely veiling the tree's woody limbs in greenery. A single fruit dangled near the end of one branch, a red, pear-shaped fruit about the size of a large apple.

When Bonnie reached the water's edge, she heard voices, more like singing than speaking. The varied pitches blended in sweet harmony, the melody seeming to radiate from the tree branches, as if each leaf had a part in a youthful choir. She walked around the pond on a bed of soft grass and approached the tree. The music sounded oddly familiar, like the haunting chant from a dream that begs to be believed. But this was too real. It couldn't be a dream.

When she came within ten feet of the trunk, she stopped, and, as if silenced by her hesitation, the song faded away. The leaves rustled from one side of the tree to the other as though a stiff breeze had passed, but she felt no hint of moving air in the steamy glade.

A new sound arose, the pleasant voice of a young male. Although he spoke with the inflections of normal speech, his words seemed to carry the cadence of song. "Bonnie Silver," he said with a cheery tone.

Bonnie swivelled her head from side to side. "Yes. Who . . . where are you?"

"I'm a friend, and I'm close by. I'm glad you've finally arrived."

Bonnie scanned the scenery, from forest to pond to strange old tree, watching for any movement. "Finally? Have you been expecting me?"

"Oh, yes. For a very long time. Merlin told me of your coming."

Bonnie tried to peer into the tree without seeming too obvious, but she couldn't find the speaker. "Merlin told you? How could he know I'd come here?" She glanced around and spread out her hands. "Wherever 'here' is."

The speaker's voice grew more serious, but still friendly. "Merlin's prophecies about you are well known. Even back in his day he would sing songs about your coming."

"In his day?" Bonnie tilted her head, still trying to peek through the leaves. "How old are you?"

"Prepare yourself. I am coming forth." The tree rustled again. A section of branches parted to reveal the head of a dragon.

Bonnie gasped and stepped backwards.

"Don't be frightened. As you can see, I am of your kind. I am a dragon, the first dragon, your principal ancestor." The dragon emerged from the tree and seemed to float to the ground, his huge clawed feet pressing holes in the soft grass. "Most humans flee at the sight of me, but since you're a dragon, you have no need to fear."

Bonnie felt plenty of fear. Her legs trembled, and she could hardly breathe, but she knew she had to stand her ground. She tried to keep her voice from shaking. "But . . . but I'm not a dragon . . . not really."

The dragon seemed to stifle a laugh, and his voice remained friendly. "Not a dragon?" His long neck stretched toward Bonnie's back. Bonnie followed his head with her gaze but kept her body as stiff as a number three pencil.

The dragon gave a gentle snort, and tiny sparks fell to the grass. "I've never seen a human with such beautiful wings before. Are you sure you're not a dragon?"

Bonnie glanced back at her wings. "I . . . uh . . . I'm sort of a dragon, fully human and fully dragon."

The dragon nodded. "An anthrozil."

"You know about that word?"

"Anthrozil? Oh, yes. I am aware of your father's work and his alliance with that crafty Devin fellow. Anthrozil is a perfectly fine word, but they were mistaken about you. You are much more dragon than you are human. I heard that you wore a backpack to hide your wings, but with all those scales, I'm surprised you ever fooled anyone."

"Scales? What are you talking about?"

The dragon cocked his head. "Why, your facial scales, of course. We dragons have scales instead of skin. The reddish ones around your eyes are especially lovely. It's too bad the rest of your body isn't the same."

Bonnie threw her hands up to her cheeks. Her skin was tough and slick like a snake's hide, separated into imperfect squares by a network of fissures. "How did I get scales? This is terrible!"

The dragon's facial lines turned downward. "Terrible? Why is it terrible? Do you find dragons ugly?"

Bonnie caught her breath. She pulled her hands down and tightened her fists into nervous balls. "No . . . No, not ugly. It's just . . ."

The dragon nodded sympathetically. "You're ashamed. You're accustomed to human skin, and you fear what others will think of your dramatic change."

Bonnie pulled on her bottom lip with her teeth. She didn't know how to answer. Maybe she was ashamed. Was it wrong to be embarrassed about having dragon scales? Was it wrong to be concerned about her appearance at all?

The dragon motioned toward the pond with his head. "My pool is not the best of mirrors, but it is adequate. Look for yourself. You are more beautiful than ever."

With a hand on her cheek, Bonnie took a step toward the pond, but when she caught a glimpse of the surface, she planted her feet. *A mirror. I remember something about a mirror.* As she rubbed her skin again, her ring dipped into a crevice between two scales. She pulled her hand down and glanced at the rubellite, then did a double take and stared at the stone. *It's pulsing!* The stone changed colours in a rhythmic beat, its hue alternating between two shades of red.

A flood of memories roared into Bonnie's mind – her mission with Billy, Merlin's poem, a warning about mirrors. But she couldn't remember the exact words. Her voice quaked, and she averted her eyes from the pond and from the dragon. "I . . . I don't want to look."

"Do you fear what you might see?"

The simple question seemed almost like a playground dare, yet more subtle, more enticing. A new idea crept into Bonnie's mind. She added up her surroundings – a dragon, a tree, a tropical paradise . . . a tempter. She raised her head and stared defiantly at the dragon. "Who are you, anyway? Why are you trying to get me to look at a mirror?"

The dragon raised his brow and pulled his head back. "I care nothing for my own benefit. I thought you'd want to see how beautiful you've become. Look, or don't look. I care not."

Bonnie gazed at the twisted old tree. Could it really be that old? How could she find out who this dragon really was without giving away her suspicions? She folded her hands behind her back. "So, Mr Dragon, if you're my ancestor, I should call you by your name, don't you think?"

The dragon held his head high. "Mr Dragon is quite appropriate, for I am the first dragon, and I will likely be the last. But, if you wish, since I am the first and the last, you may call me either Alpha or Omega."

Bonnie stifled a gasp. She had heard those Greek letters before. Alpha and Omega were the names of the entrance doors to her father's cave laboratory. Was it a coincidence? What could it all mean? She tried to dig deeper. "So, uh, Alpha, what's with that tree? Is it as old as you are?"

"Yes. It has been my home for thousands of years."

Bonnie eyed the solitary "apple" hanging on the end of a branch. "Does it ever bear much fruit?"

"It does, more than you can ever imagine."

She lifted her finger toward the tree. "Why is there only one on it now?"

The dragon raised his foreleg and opened its claws. A fruit identical to the one on the tree materialized in his scaly palm. "As soon as one appears, someone plucks it." The fruit suddenly vanished. "At one time the tree was filled, but only two people ever walked this garden in those days. Now, with billions of people around, the tree is constantly harvested."

"Billions of people? I don't see anyone."

"They are here. They walk in the world of the living. They cannot even see the tree, yet they pluck its fruit just the same."

Bonnie folded her hands behind her back again. "Why am I able to see it? And why hasn't anyone taken that one?"

The dragon stepped forward and pressed one of his clawed feet into the soft turf. He then pulled it back, allowing the grass in the imprint to slowly rise, but the blades were unable to regain their former height. The outline of the dragon's claw remained. "You have stepped out of your realm and into my world. In this place you see things as they really are, exposed, without superficial coverings. The tree is veiled in your world, though people take its fruit readily. They are even at this moment passing all around you, but they cannot pluck this particular piece. It exists only here, in the world of revelation. Only you may take it."

Bonnie waved her hand at the tree and began to turn away. "Well, I don't want it."

"Very well. It will still be here when you do want it."

She pivoted back again. "But I know what it is. I'll never want it."

The dragon winked. "So you say. I've heard it all before. Everyone eventually reaps my harvest. I know for a fact that you've taken fruit from my tree in the past. It's just a matter of time until you take it again."

Bonnie crossed her arms over her chest and squinted at the dragon. "I've got you figured out, *Mister* Dragon. You're no alpha or omega, but I do believe you are the first dragon, the original fallen angel."

"Dragon? Yes, I am a dragon, as are you. And fallen? Yes, again, as are you." The dragon moved his head to within inches of Bonnie's, and his eyes blazed into hers. "As you conform to my image, you will learn that my ways are not what you think. I'm sure you've heard people say 'there are dragons in our midst.' Well, they think there are dragons living among them – ruthless gangs in urban jungles, crooked politicians in seats of power, child abusers in darkened alleys. The truth is that there is actually a dragon within every human on earth, and you have the unique opportunity to see it unveiled on your very skin." The dragon pulled his head back and winked again, nodding his head slowly. "You were born taking my fruit, you have taken it every day of your life, and you will take it again today. It's only a matter of time."

Hot blood rushed through Bonnie's face. Tears formed in her eyes. She had to fight this lying beast. He was subtle – vague and pointed at the same time, spinning falsehoods and mixing them with pulpit sermons.

She felt the urge to run to the pond and see the scales, yet she knew doing so would bring the dragon an easy victory. She decided to use her best weapon, and she spoke boldly, with her eyes fully open in defiance. "The Bible says, 'Resist the devil and he will flee from you.'" She pointed toward the pool. "If you want to see a foul, ugly dragon, go take a look at yourself. Just leave *me* alone."

"Very good, Bonnie," the dragon replied, chuckling. "Keep making those hilarious quips, and keep quoting the Bible. You'll eventually get to the passage that names me as the master of this realm. I am the king of all dragons, and since you're one of my subjects, you'll never escape my influence. You'll keep plucking my fruit for as long as you live, so you might as well admit it. You love the taste, the satisfaction it gives, the autonomy of a mind set free."

"No!" Bonnie shouted, backing away. "You're a liar! I don't want any part of you or anything you say!" She took three full steps back before stopping. For some reason she felt compelled to listen to the dragon's reply.

"But, Bonnie, dear child, I'm just stating what you must have heard many times before. Haven't preachers told you that you were born eating my fruit and that you cannot escape it? Ever since Eve listened to my voice in the Garden of Eden, her sons and daughters have heeded my call. Even your own parents have proven their allegiance to me. Your father conspired to murder your mother, and your mother has returned to her dragon state. Can't you see that your nature was embedded in you before you took your first breath?

"And now you are alone. You are trapped between earth and hell. In this place where all masks erode, your nature seeps through your pores and reveals who you really are. It makes no sense to reject the obvious. If you will just view your true nature and accept it, you can stop your fruitless struggles. The truth will set you free."

Before Bonnie could answer, the dragon floated back toward the tree. Seconds later, he disappeared into the greenery, and the leaves rustled once again, their song seeming more inviting than ever before. Every note made the fruit appear brighter and more enticing.

Bonnie placed her hands on her cheeks again. The scales were more pronounced than ever. Deep cracks ran in criss-cross patterns all over her face. Just thirty feet away a glassy pond would tell her the truth. Its crystal clear surface mirrored the twisted tree as well as a few puffy clouds above, but from her angle, she couldn't see herself.

A breeze passed by Bonnie's ear, and a familiar voice rode on its whispering current. Her father spoke in hushed tones, a distant memory echoing from years long past that first came to a little girl sitting cross-legged with two rag dolls on her knee. "Wings?" the masculine voice said. "We can't have a daughter with wings! We won't be able to show our faces in public, not with a mutant for a daughter!"

Bonnie choked back a sob. A mutant? Her throat squeezed shut. Her skin rippled with stinging pain. A thousand invisible needles pricked her skin, goading her toward the pond. A million eyes stared at her, voices laughing and mocking. "Lizard face! Dragon girl!" The laughter turned into shrieks, children running away in fright. She was a hideous monster, a winged freak. She felt her cheeks again. Could it really be that bad?

The pool's crystal surface beckoned. Although Bonnie's entire body shook, and hot tears streamed down her cheeks, she refused to budge. "I won't take the fruit!" she shouted. "I won't!" She finally sank to her knees and, looking up toward the sky, cried out, "You promised me escape! I need it now!"

Billy jumped to his feet, gripping Excalibur with both hands. "Bonnie!" he shouted. "Where are you?" He glanced all around, shuffling his feet on the carpet of thick, long-bladed grass. The evening sky boasted a milky array of bright, familiar stars, adding to Excalibur's faint glow, and a wafer-thin moon hung low on the horizon. The faint smell of mould rose through the wet air, and Billy's forehead gathered drops of sweat and dew.

He stood still and listened. Silence. Heavy silence. Not a chirping bird or a rustling leaf interrupted the thick layer of musty air. He looked for the entry window but saw only trees and thick undergrowth with a single, narrow path leading into the midst of the dark foliage.

While holding the sword in front like a long, heavy flashlight, Billy followed the path, dodging or pushing aside branches that protruded from the dense forest. Within minutes he came to a clearing, a grassy area that led to a small pond. In the twilight he saw a pair of silhouettes standing between the pond and a strange old tree. One of the shapes was much larger than the other, but he couldn't figure out what they were. He tiptoed slowly into the clearing. His danger signals seemed jumbled, warning him one second, then calming him the next, as though someone was jamming his radar.

As he approached, the two shadows took no notice of him. He skirted the pond, keeping his eyes fastened on the sharpening images. A huge set of wings protruded from each of the shapes, but the smaller one was clearly a female human.

He dashed ahead. "Bonnie! What's going—" He halted. The other figure was a dragon! A big one! Billy could tell right away that it wasn't Clefspeare, but was it friendly? He surveyed his danger signals again, but they still sent contradictory messages. He ran up to Bonnie, stopping at her side. She had her hands on her cheeks and her lips were moving, but no words came out. "Bonnie. What's going on?"

Bonnie didn't turn to answer. She spoke to the dragon, and the dragon responded, but there was still no sound. They were like ghosts stopping by the pond to have a quiet chat.

Billy reached to place a hand on Bonnie's shoulder, but his fingers passed right through. He jumped back and stared at his hand. His face grew hot, and the dampness of new sweat moistened his clothes. He took a longer look at the dragon. It seemed to glance at him from time to time, taking millisecond looks while talking to Bonnie. Yet, he seemed to be a phantom as well. Excalibur's light passed through his semi-transparent body and illuminated the grass behind him.

Billy rested the sword's point on the ground and bit his lip. Was this the first test of the circles? It didn't seem to relate to Merlin's poem at all. He grabbed the card from his pocket and held it close to Excalibur's glow.

> Young Arthur holds the window's key
> To ancient realms that bear his quest.
> The circles know where lie the beasts,
> Who crave the light, who crave their breath.
>
> The beasts conceal the ancient truths
> That dwell behind divided tongues,
> But dragons' hearts reveal their flame
> From shining light and psalms well sung.

He slid the card back into his pocket and looked again at the huge phantom. *Dragons' hearts . . . I wonder . . .*

He stared long and hard at Bonnie and the dragon, trying to read their body language. Bonnie was obviously upset, and the dragon looked smug, deceitful, even dangerous. Billy raised Excalibur to get a better look at the dragon's face. His eyes shone with a reddish glow, and they glanced at Billy more frequently. . . . He was definitely watching.

Billy moved the sword lower. A shadow appeared in the middle of the dragon's body, a round mass that blocked the light. The dragon moved abruptly. He seemed to float backwards toward a tree that stood alone behind the pond. Billy followed, hoping to figure out what the dragon's inner shadow meant. Maybe this was his heart, the key to learning the truth, just like the poem said.

As he walked alongside the beast, Billy gently pushed the sword toward the dragon's body. Excalibur passed through his scales easily, but the blade stopped when it reached the "heart". The point of the blade pricked the heart's outer layer. Black scum slowly oozed out and dripped to the ground. The slime gathered on the grass into a twisting, vibrating mass, dividing into squirming, worm-like shapes that crawled away from the dragon.

Suddenly a burst of anguish splashed through Billy's mind, his familiar sense of danger roaring through his soul like never before. This was more than danger; it felt like imminent death, cloaked in the toothy smile of this haughty-eyed lizard. The heart of the dragon vanished, and the dragon floated into the tree, disappearing among the leafy branches.

Billy spun on his heels. Bonnie had covered her cheeks with her hands, staring wide-eyed toward the pond. He ran to her side, shouting, "Bonnie! Can you hear me?"

Bonnie dropped to her knees and seemed to wail, her head lifted upward and her mouth wide open in a soundless scream. Hundreds of tiny snakes, each with real, flesh-and-blood bodies, crawled all over Bonnie's phantom form. The dragon's gooey blood had transformed into vipers, and they bit Bonnie viciously, each one striking with a pair of long, needle-sharp fangs.

Billy pricked one with Excalibur and slung it away, then another. He lunged for a larger viper, but his foot slipped, and the blade swept through Bonnie's head and passed harmlessly to the other side. Billy then hacked at the snakes without care, ferociously swiping with both arms and stomping the wriggling bodies of those he merely wounded. Within seconds, every snake lay dead.

Billy thrust the sword back to its sheath. The sky brightened. A few puffy clouds appeared overhead, creating dark reflections of themselves on the spongy ground. Billy blinked in the sudden daylight and looked down at Bonnie, who had bowed her head and closed her eyes. She heaved a great sigh, and a relieved smile graced her lips as she rose to her feet. When she opened her eyes, she looked straight at Billy. Her smile burst into laughter and she jumped forward, wrapping her arms around his neck. "Billy! You're here! Thank God!"

Billy felt a new rush, the pure fountain of love. The feeling of danger washed away, replaced with relief, joy, and a wave of exhaustion. He returned the embrace for a moment, then pushed Bonnie away gently. "Did you feel those snakes crawling all over you?"

She scanned the ground. "What snakes?"

Billy rubbed his shoes across the grass. He expected to find dozens of mangled snake bodies, but the lush carpet was unspoiled. "Whew! This is a weird place."

"I did feel something," she explained, crossing her arms and rubbing her shoulders, "sort of like needles. But there weren't any snakes on me."

"I don't know how to explain it, but I saw them and whacked their heads off. I could tell you couldn't see me. It was like we were in the same place but in different worlds." He glanced at the tree. "What did that dragon say to you?"

"He said . . ." Bonnie held a hand up to her cheek. "Billy, what's wrong with my face? What does it look like?"

Billy squinted and cocked his head. "What do you mean? Your face looks normal."

She ran her index finger down her face from her eye to her chin. "I feel . . . ridges . . . something like scales."

Billy brushed her other cheek with his own finger. "I don't feel anything."

Bonnie tilted her head and gazed at the tree. "Hmmm. I wonder . . ."

Billy pulled out the prophecy card again. "I don't know what's going on, but I do know we have to find a belt of some kind lying around. At least that's what the poem says." He read it out loud while Bonnie looked on.

In circle one there lies a belt,
The camera's eye to watch your tale,
A tale as old as man's first tears
When Adam donned the dragon's veil.

"It mentions Adam," Bonnie said. "I'll bet this place is like the Garden of Eden."

"So this *is* the first circle. Now if we—"

"Billy!" Bonnie grabbed his elbow. "There are *two* of those strange fruits on the tree now. A few minutes ago there was only one."

Billy slid the card into his pocket. "That's weird. How could it grow so fast?"

"What do you think it means?"

Billy shrugged his shoulders. "Who knows? Let's just forget the tree and look for the belt. I don't see it around here, so we might as well look back in the woods."

Billy marched toward the forest with Bonnie at his side. She kept glancing back at the tree, but he riveted his own gaze on the ground. The green undergrowth was like a carpet of ferns with long fronds that covered all but a narrow path, forcing Bonnie to drop back and walk in single file.

Billy pulled out his sword and hacked away the thicker brush as he walked, making sure nothing snapped back to whip Bonnie's legs. He took his time, poking through every bush. The belt could be almost anywhere, and he didn't want to pass it by.

As they walked deeper into the woods, the path grew darker. Billy looked up at the thick tree canopy and held out his palm. "It's starting to rain."

Bonnie tilted her head upward and blinked several times to ward off the droplets. "We'd better find shelter."

"But where? Do you think there are any buildings around here, or maybe a cave?"

Bonnie shook her head. "I haven't seen either one."

A new voice sounded from behind them. "Would an umbrella do?"

CHAPTER 8

THE INVISIBLE VEIL

The professor threw back the curtain that hid the window portal, flooding the room with light. "Since the note Sir Patrick left didn't say when he would return, it makes no sense to wait for him. If the fiends of the New Table have found a way into the circles, as he wrote, they will not wait for us to act." He placed his hand on Sir Barlow's shoulder. "Thank you for bringing in the table and chair, my good fellow. Would you please station yourself in the corridor and stand guard?"

Barlow gave a polite bow. "Your wish is my command." The burly knight hurried into the hall, dodging the protruding spears of the shattered door jamb.

Ashley set her laptop on the table in front of the window and slid into the chair. "Is there an electrical outlet in this room?"

Marilyn pulled aside one of the curtains. "I don't see one."

"This is an ancient chamber," the professor replied, shaking his head. "Perhaps we can run an extension cord from the newer section."

"Want me to fetch one?" Walter asked. "I think I saw one by a hedge trimmer on the porch."

Ashley adjusted the screen angle as the laptop flashed to life. "It can wait. The battery will last for a while." After a few keyboard clicks, a series of eight horizontal bar graphs appeared on the display, each with a different colour. Next to the laptop, Ashley placed her new invention. "This device – I call it 'Apollo' – gathers and reads electromagnetic waves, much like my old photometer, but it does a lot more." After flipping a switch on Apollo's base, the computer's graphical bars became animated, their lengths changing constantly. "My computer is analysing Apollo's readings. I want to see how the data changes when it gets close to the window."

The professor pulled a pair of spectacles from his shirt pocket and slipped them on as he leaned over to read the screen. "I don't mean to question your strategy, Miss Stalworth, but how will that help us in our quest?"

Walter joined him, two heads, one young and one old, straining to read a series of cryptic numbers.

Ashley adjusted the screen's brightness with the press of a key. "Larry found a bunch of research on alternate dimensions, but since most of it was rubbish, he had to filter out all but a couple of instances of similar phenomena. Strangely enough, the remaining data is directly associated with this part of the world, stories about Glastonbury being the gateway to the world of the dead."

The professor pulled off his glasses and folded the earpieces. "Well, many theories abound." He slid the glasses into his pocket and grasped his chin. "The 'world of the dead', as you call it, has also been referred to as Hades or Sheol, and I, too, have heard tales about the town's reputation as a portal to that world."

"So we're probably on the right track." Ashley pointed to three rows of numbers near the top of the screen. "I've downloaded the characteristics of the spectral trails that were found in those purported cross-dimensional windows. You see, if there really is another dimension, it has to exist somewhere, in a real time–space continuum. Otherwise, Billy and Bonnie wouldn't be able to go there." She looked up at the professor. "Are you with me so far?"

"Yes, I believe so," the professor said. "Go on."

"I'm clueless," Walter added. "But go on."

Ashley pecked a couple of keys, and a diagram popped up on the screen that looked like a topographic map. "The microchips you gave me, Professor, have embedded transmitters that send location coordinates based on what I call magnetic reckoning. In other words, they keep track of where they lie in the earth's magnetic field and transmit the data using light-encoded signals." She traced a line with her finger through several flashing dots on the map. "I've programmed these blips to represent the New Table knights, but they're inoperative right now. Once I figure out how to correct the signals for the cross-dimensional rift, I might be able to read them and plot their locations on this map."

"Cool!" Walter exclaimed. "A computer eye on the bad guys!"

"Yes," the professor agreed. "It is . . . cool . . . but what benefit will that be?"

Ashley gave a shrug. "I'm not sure; I haven't gotten that far yet. But since information is power, I'm hoping we'll be able to use it. At the very least, we should get an idea of what's going on."

The professor gazed at the jungle scene. "Yes, if this window is a live viewport, we may have some idea eventually, but, for now, it's just a static image, no more useful than a framed photograph."

Marilyn stood next to the window with her hands on her hips. "It does seem like it's changing a little bit, maybe darker than it was just a couple of minutes ago, and it looks kind of misty."

"But no Billy and Bonnie," Walter noted.

The professor picked up a long, sharp splinter from the floor. "No, not a sign of them. Patrick's note indicated that they entered successfully, but the condition of the door does not bode well." He tossed the splinter to the side. "I hope my absence during their entry doesn't endanger their mission."

"Why would it?" Marilyn asked.

"The new song. It seems that the lyrics are crucial, and I have no way of communicating them to William. I'm confident that the timing of the song's arrival in my mind coincided with William's departure. If I had been here, I could have informed him and set him on the correct path to finding his father." He bowed his head and whispered, "What a fool I am!"

Marilyn hooked her arm in the professor's. "You're no fool. You did everything you could. You can't be everywhere at once."

Ashley snatched up Apollo and walked closer to the window. She motioned for Walter to join her. "Hold Apollo at this spot while I look at the readings."

Walter saluted and piped, "Aye, aye, Captain," then wrapped his fingers around one of Apollo's external dowels.

Ashley began to turn away from the window but stopped. She slowly pivoted back, squinting at the portal scene. "What are these white things on the ground?" She pointed at the lower portion of the window. "Right here by these ferns. Any idea?"

Walter dropped to one knee and leaned his head toward the tangle of ferns. "You got me. Bones, maybe?"

"That's what I was thinking," Ashley said quietly. "Bones."

Marilyn gently brushed one of the white, bone-like images with her fingers. "I don't know how to explain it," she said, "but it just doesn't feel completely solid. There's an odd sensation, like a vibration."

Ashley chose another "bone" on the window and copied Marilyn's movements. "I see what you mean, like a force field of some kind." She pressed her index finger against the wall. "Put Apollo right in front of where my hand is." Walter complied, and Ashley marched back to her laptop, pressing her hand on her jaw. "Karen, you with me?"

Karen's voice sputtered through the laptop speakers. "Like grease on an axle, Ash."

"Hook Larry up to my computer again, please."

"Two seconds." Karen's voice shrank, sounding farther away. "Okay, Larry, behave yourself, or I'll put your source code on a hackers' website."

Ashley suppressed a laugh. "Okay, Larry. Time to do your thing. Are you getting this spectrum data?"

"One moment, please, Ashley. I was just reading your email. Obviously your spam filter needs adjusting. Three thousand four hundred fifty-two messages. How did you get on an email list for herbal foot fungus remedies?"

"Never mind," Ashley snapped. "Just read the spectrum data."

"Cool your jets. I'm on it."

The professor and Marilyn looked over Ashley's shoulder at the computer-generated graph while Ashley directed Walter's position. "Okay, move Apollo slowly to the right."

She drummed her fingers for a moment. "This is too weird. The wavelengths shift like crazy with every inch of spatial change, almost like a steep slope on a contour map." She waved her hand at Walter. "Lower now, at the bottom and against the wall." She pointed again. "There! It bottoms out at that point and then starts the upslope again. It's like an electromagnetic depression. That wall is absorbing a narrow band of wavelengths, but it's not a one-way street. It's allowing the entire visible light spectrum to exit along with quite a bit of ultraviolet radiation."

"Absorbing?" Walter asked, still holding Apollo in place. "Like the candlestone?"

"Not quite. The candlestone traps all excited light energy, but this portal seems to absorb a much narrower range. The window is also producing a strange electromagnetic field that we can sense when we touch it."

"Are you able to find the New Table transmissions?" the professor asked.

"That's a job for Larry." She clicked a few keys, then held two fingers on her cheek. "Larry, I'm opening this data gateway directly to you. Can you tell me what the microchip transmissions from the cloaks would look like after passing through this vortex?"

"Certainly. One complex codex of vortex com-specs coming to your cortex vertex."

"What?"

"Translation – I'm sending the data to you now."

"Karen!" Ashley barked. "What's with the rhyming nonsense?"

"I tried to insert a new vocabulary range like you told me," Karen replied, "but the database must have included a rhyming dictionary."

"What's the matter, Ashley? Can't duplex your index?"

Walter laughed so hard, tears began rolling down his cheeks. "I think I need a Kleenex."

"Not you, too, Walter!"

Walter clapped his hand over his mouth. "Sorry," he said, talking through his fingers.

Ashley squinted at the screen, and her voice lowered. "Something strange is going on. Professor, is there some other source of light energy in this room?"

"Not that I know of, unless, of course, you count the hole in the ceiling."

Ashley looked up at the gap in the roof. "That couldn't be it. It's dark outside, and the data doesn't indicate a white light frequency." She swivelled her head and nodded toward the centre of the room. "According to Apollo, it's coming from that direction." She rose from her seat and walked to the compass design on the floor, gazing at the etchings in the circles. "What are these?"

"Representations of the circles in the other world," the professor said. "We assume that Merlin put them here centuries ago."

Ashley stooped at the edge of one of the circles. "How weird!"

"This is the Eden circle," the professor explained, "and the two people in the drawing are likely Adam and Eve." He dropped to one knee. "This is very strange indeed!"

Marilyn joined them and leaned over the circle. "What do you make of it, Professor?"

"Hey!" Walter called from the view port. "Let a guy in on the news, will you?"

Ashley waved him over. "You can put Apollo down now. Come and see for yourself."

Walter set Apollo on the floor and hurried to the centre of the room. He crouched next to Ashley and gaped at the sight. Although the etching of Adam and Eve was simple, he could tell they were facing outward as if they were looking straight at him. Their tiny eyes, each about the size of a pinhead, glowed, pulsing like scarlet beacons. Walter reached forward and touched Adam's left eye, feeling the slight rise in the drawing. It seemed as though a glass bead had been wedged into the floor, and a light from underneath poured a ghostly beam through the bead, making it look like a tiny ruby. He glanced around at the trio of worried faces, and his gaze landed on his teacher. "What do you think it means, Prof?"

The professor shook his head. "Very mysterious. I have no answer."

Marilyn knelt and placed her own fingers on Adam's eyes, rubbing them gently. "Call it a mother's intuition, but I think they represent Billy and Bonnie in the first circle."

Billy spun around. An elderly man stood on the path, his body erect and tall. With one arm he held out a candy-striped umbrella toward Bonnie, and under his other arm, pressed against his body, he held two other multicoloured umbrellas. Dressed in a black tuxedo, complete with tails, a frilly white shirt, and a broad cummerbund, he looked like an old-fashioned butler answering the door to a mansion or a maitre d' handing out menus at a fancy restaurant. Bonnie took the umbrella and popped it open, while the stranger extended a purple and gold one to Billy.

Billy stared at him for a few seconds, wondering how he appeared so suddenly and why he was there. The stranger opened the second umbrella and placed it over Billy's head. "What were you expecting, a penguin? Please, take it before you catch your death." The man opened a silver and black umbrella over his own head, gave a friendly smile, and bowed. "My name is Joseph, and I am at your service."

Bonnie bowed her head. "Pleased to meet you, Joseph. Thank you for the umbrellas."

"Yeah, thanks." Billy looked through a circular shield of dripping rain. "It's really starting to pour now." He replayed Joseph's "penguin" comment in his mind, tightening his grip on the umbrella's silver rod. How could this guy have known about the recurring dream?

"Oh, you're most welcome," Joseph replied. "I heard you were coming, so I put on my best tuxedo."

"You have more than one tuxedo?" Bonnie asked.

Joseph cocked his head, a pained expression on his face. "Well . . . actually . . . no." He passed his hand across the frilly shirt. "But this *is* my best one."

Billy slid his hiking boot across the expanding puddle on the footpath. "Do you always carry umbrellas around?"

"In this circle? Of course. Terrible downpours here. Just terrible. And you never know when a visitor might come through."

Bonnie turned her head back and forth, smiling. "Really? Do you have other visitors now?"

"Oh, no," Joseph replied, waving his hand. "Haven't had another visitor in almost forty years. But your presence proves you never know when one might drop by." He lowered his head and sighed. "Of course, thousands of souls come to this circle every day, and they pass directly to the valleys before I ever see them. They're not allowed here in the high places."

"The high places?" Bonnie asked.

Joseph twisted his shoe on the grass. "Yes. Up here on the solid ground. This part of the circle was once called Abraham's bosom, and many dwelt here, but they have been taken to their final home, and only the lost souls remain."

"Then why are you here?" Billy asked. "Are you a lost soul?"

"Me? A lost soul? Hardly!" Joseph spread his feet apart and straightened his body. "I am the guardian of the Holy Grail."

Billy caught a hint of mirth in Joseph's eyes. Was he playing a game, or was he dead serious? "The Holy Grail?" Billy repeated. "Like in the King Arthur legend?"

The corners of Joseph's lips turned up. "If you are asking if I guard the grail King Arthur long sought for, yes. But your modern tales have reduced the true grail to a common cup." He held out his hand as if he were holding a drinking glass. "A common cup! Can you believe it? There is a real cup, of course, but it is merely a symbol of the greater grail." His voice grew strong, and he slapped his hand over his heart. "The grail in which life is generated, the new wine creating flesh and sinews on dry bones." His eyes suddenly grew dark. "I can say no more. My sacred duty is to keep the grail's location secret until King Arthur's heir returns to find it."

Billy wrapped his fingers lightly around Excalibur's hilt. "Well, supposedly, that's who I am."

"Yes, yes. So I've heard. Time will tell. I will follow your progress, but your journey will be far more dangerous than you can possibly imagine. If you survive through the seventh circle, you will indeed prove your mettle."

Billy pulled the prophecy card from his pocket and scanned the verse. "Well, can you at least get me started? I have this old poem that's supposed to help me along. It says, 'In circle one there lies a belt, the camera's eye to watch your tale, a tale as old as man's first tears when Adam donned the devil's veil.' "

"Ah, yes. I recognize the poetry of my old friend, Merlin. He comes through here from time to time and sings a few of his verses."

Billy returned the card to his pocket. "So do you know anything about this belt?"

"Indeed I do." Joseph walked past Billy and Bonnie, gesturing for them to follow. "Come this way, and mind the puddles."

They high-stepped along the narrow path, veering around the growing puddles and vaulting over the streaming rivulets that crossed their way. Huge raindrops fell from the saturated tree canopy and slapped loudly on their umbrellas. Rather than shouting over the steady pounding, they followed the strange man in silence.

After about a half-mile hike, they entered a darker part of the forest filled with tall trees sporting wide trunks and deeply wrinkled bark. A mist hung in the air, floating in thin white layers, and the rain fell through without stirring the vapour.

Joseph held up his hand to halt the company. "Take care," he said. "This part of the wood is where pretenders are exposed and find their doom."

Bonnie stopped next to a long-stemmed fern and took a dripping frond between her finger and thumb. "Pretenders?"

Joseph faced them. "You have nothing to fear, William." He then added with a thin smile, "If you really are the coming king." He pointed into the underbrush. "There is one of the imposters."

Billy leaned over, trying to see through the mist and rain. He took a couple of steps into the ferns and halted. A lone skeleton wrapped in tattered clothing rested in the foliage. A torn shirt lay across his chest with gaping holes exposing his ivory ribcage. Loose breeches covered his bones from his hips downward, and an ornate belt buckle kept his oversized trousers in place. His greying skull displayed a gaping mouth, as though his last breath ended in a horrified scream.

Billy retreated a step and looked back through the curtain of water cascading from his umbrella. Bonnie held one hand over her mouth, her brow furrowed, but Joseph just tapped his foot in a puddle, a hand resting on his hip.

"Is that the belt?" Billy asked, pointing at the skeleton.

Joseph nodded. "It is."

"Am I supposed to get it now?"

"You are."

Billy drew in a deep breath and, lifting his feet high, took several long strides into the thick undergrowth until he straddled the skeleton. Looking around, he noticed dozens of bones, some still attached to other skeletons and some scattered about as though dogs had feasted on them and cast the remains aside.

With one hand still holding the umbrella, Billy grasped the buckle and pulled upward. The bones gave way, breaking and crumbling, and the belt and harness, which wrapped over the skeleton's shoulder, came away freely. Billy jumped back through the ferns, holding the belt in front of him. The strap seemed normal enough, a rough sort of leather that had somehow defied years of rain and rot. The metal buckle, on the other hand, held a strange jewel, a shiny red orb with a dark circle in its centre making it resemble a crystalline eye.

With the rain letting up, Joseph collapsed his umbrella and set it down. He took the belt, unfastened the buckle, and wrapped it around Billy's waist, throwing the harness over his shoulder. With expert hands, he moved Excalibur's scabbard from Billy's old belt to the strap on his back. "The crystal you see on the buckle is the other world's eye into this one," Joseph explained. "Whoever looks through Sir Patrick's window will be able to see what lies in front of you."

Billy slipped off his old belt. "How do you know so much? I mean, about Sir Patrick and me?"

Joseph took the old belt and slung it over his shoulder. "Merlin is a great teacher. His songs carry many stories about the world of the living. Much of it I find hard to believe, but I know he would never lie."

Bonnie adjusted the scabbard on Billy's back. "Billy, remember how Merlin told stories to Barlow and his men in the candlestone? It sounds like he can go wherever he wants."

"Yeah. I remember." Billy nodded toward the scattered bones. "Joseph, what happened to those 'pretenders'? How many were there?"

Joseph patted Billy on the back. "You are the seventh candidate, my boy, and the first in a very long time. And the others?" He picked up his umbrella and leaned on its curved handle. "Ah, yes. The others. They were drawn by the promise of power and wealth. They possessed impure passion, and all but one were forced back to this circle to be consumed by the dogs and vultures that frequent these woods." His shoulders slumped, his steely glare fading. "They followed their desires rather than the light of wisdom. One of them, however, was captured by the New Table, and, as far as I know, he still wanders aimlessly in a deeper circle."

Billy felt a pinch in the strap just below his shoulder blades. "How did they get in without Excalibur?" he asked, trying to reach the pinch.

Joseph straightened Billy's strap and patted it flat. "There are other portals, but those doors are known only to a small number of dark souls in your world."

Bonnie collapsed her umbrella and shook off the water. "How many portals are there?"

Joseph placed his hand on his chin and tilted his head upward. "There is one at the great tor that many know about, but few know how to enter it." He reached down, grasped a long stick, and began scratching the mud with it. "Other portals have been created by men, though I will never understand their desire to come to this forsaken land. Ridiculous, I think. The other six candidates failed, because their entry portal differed from the one the true king would pass through."

Billy folded his umbrella and let the rainwater drip to the path before handing it back to Joseph. "What's our next step?"

"To find the next circle," Joseph replied. "You have met the dragon, and you have already extinguished his first flaming arrow, but the trials of this circle are not complete. Your journey to the next level is still fraught with danger, and deeper still lie perils far worse than a few snakes. If you heed the path, you will avoid disaster."

"Heed the path?" Billy dragged a toe through the mud. "Do you mean this path?"

Joseph drew a circle with his stick. "The narrow path you are on travels through this forest in a wide circle. When you come all the way around, you will reach a passage to the next circle." He drew a smaller circle inside the first one. "Every succeeding circle will have a path, though they are not all circular and some will not be visible to your physical eyes. Somewhere along the path you will be tested, and every test will differ from the previous one." He smacked the stick on Billy's shoe. "But never forget that your mission is not merely to survive the tests; it is to rescue any physical captives you find in this realm. You see, there are myriad spiritual captives who only appear to possess flesh and bone, but they are out of your reach. Though you may pity them with a thousand tears, you will not be able to rescue them."

Joseph gazed into their eyes. "That is all I will say for now. If I reveal too much, your journey will no longer test your wisdom. Just remember, the dragon you faced is the father of lies, and your enemies are his children. Be wise. Their faces will shine with sincerity, but their words will drip with poison."

"Okay. Good advice." Billy placed his hand on his new belt and took in an encouraging breath. "So, what are we waiting for? We have prisoners to rescue."

Joseph collected Bonnie's umbrella and smiled. "I will not see you again in this circle. As long as you stay on the path, you will not lose your way. Just remember, God always provides a guiding light."

Billy and Bonnie turned and walked briskly down the path. Joseph called out, his words travelling across the space between them and seeping into their ears like a whispered song. "Remember the warnings in Merlin's poem. Temptations will creep in like the mists of the night. They will devour you like a gnawing cancer. So beware! Even the suffering of another soul will consume your life's energy and call on your spirit to bleed. Yes, even to death."

CHAPTER 9

Lost Souls

Walter rose from his knees at the edge of the compass design. "I don't know what's weirder," he said, stuffing his hands into his pockets and sauntering toward the view port, "watching those creepy drawings or this crazy window. I feel like a razor without a blade . . . useless."

The professor joined Walter and stared at the window. "Then I shall unite with you in futility. We shall be a two-sided razor, but I have hope that the blade will soon arrive."

Walter took a step closer to the view port. "I see someone!"

"Yes!" the professor cried. "It's William! He's approaching from the other side of the window!"

Ashley, still on her knees near the compass diagram, leaped up and ran back to her computer while Marilyn rushed to the window. Walter stretched his body and put his finger near the top frame. "And there's Bonnie with some old guy I've never seen before. They're all holding umbrellas."

Billy's hand drew closer, finally enveloping the entire view and covering the window in a dark brown shadow. After a few seconds, the other world reappeared, but the view jumped wildly. Treetops spun around a cloudy sky, then rocketed upward, giving way to a close-up of the green undergrowth being tromped by Billy's shoes.

A pair of hands partially covered the window again, moving rapidly for a moment, then falling to the side of a man's lower torso. As the man stepped back, more of his body became visible.

"The belt!" the professor exclaimed.

Walter's eyes darted all across the wall. "What belt?"

The professor grasped his own belt. "Merlin's poem told William to find a belt, that it would be the 'camera's eye'. It seems that he has put it on and we are looking at his world from the belt's vantage point. We are seeing what William sees."

Walter took a long stride backwards, away from the wall. "Yep. There's Bonnie again and that dude in a tux. Who do you think he is?"

"He doesn't appear to be a prisoner," the professor said. "The legends speak of a guide who might be in the circles, but I wouldn't expect a member of the Jewish Council to be dressed in a tuxedo."

"The Jewish Council?" Walter repeated.

"Yes. We covered it during the class on the Arthurian legends. Since it will be on our unit exam when we return home, you would do well to look it up."

"Could he be a New Table knight?" Marilyn asked.

Ashley's rapid taps on her computer sounded like a woodpecker on a bug-filled tree. "Since he's not wearing a cloak, I doubt he's a knight, but we'll know more in just a second." She punched in a final sequence on her keypad. "There! Now to start it up." Walter dashed back to the computer and stooped next to Ashley. The screen began drawing a detailed map, dozens of squiggling lines running through colour-coded land and water masses – forests, fields, ponds, and streams.

"It's a contour map," Ashley explained. "Sir Patrick's house is in the centre, and you can see about two miles of the surrounding topography."

Seconds later, faint, pulsing dots appeared on various parts of the map. Walter moved his finger across the screen, counting. "One, two, three . . . looks like eight."

"Yes, there are eight," Ashley said, "and I'll have their numbers in a second."

The professor approached the computer table and leaned on the corner. "Their numbers?"

Ashley pushed her hair out of her eyes. "Yes, each chip has an identification number. The encoding suggested a hierarchy, so maybe it represents the ranking of the bearer. With only two samples, Larry couldn't come up with a definitive solution, but with eight more, we should be able to crack the code." She angled her head toward the ceiling. "Okay, Larry. Is this enough data? Let's make sure we get it right."

The computer's voice buzzed through the laptop's speakers. "Ashley, to quote Alexander Pope, 'To err is human, to forgive, divine.' In other words, I do not make mistakes; I am but a machine. Yet in the spirit of forgiveness, I will provide my analysis."

Ashley turned the speaker volume down. "Karen, what have you been feeding Larry?"

"Not much. I let him browse your digital library for a snack. It looks like he ate *Bartlett's Familiar Quotations* and the works of Mark Twain."

Ashley smacked her palm against the table. "Oh, no! He'll be insufferable! Can you delete them?"

"I'm on it. He's been quoting Shakespeare with a southern accent for an hour."

Ashley studied the screen while drumming her fingers. "Okay, the numbers are coming in." Her finger hovered over a flashing dot. "According to Larry, this brightest one is number seven in the hierarchy." She slid her thumb on the mousepad, then clicked its button. "Now here's something interesting."

"What?" Walter asked, lowering his head close to the screen.

Ashley pushed the computer back a few inches and put her finger near one of the dots. "The weaker the signal, the lower the number. See? The dimmest one is encoded as number one."

Walter pointed at a dot on the opposite corner. "Here's one that looks even dimmer."

Ashley leaned closer and frowned. "You're right, but it's not transmitting a ranking." She guided the mouse cursor over the dot, and a series of numbers popped up on the screen. "Unless you call zero a ranking. The lack of intensity in the signal indicates weakness of transmission or lack of data. In other words, it's either farther away or something's distorting the stream."

"Ashley, my programming instructs me to inform you of an anomaly."

Ashley's head tilted upward. "An anomaly? What is it?"

"Anomaly—noun; deviation or departure from the normal or common order, form, or rule—"

"I know what the word means! Just tell me what the anomaly is."

"The encryption was much simpler than you anticipated. You could have broken it in your head." A series of numbers flashed across the bottom of the screen. "See for yourself."

Ashley followed the stream of data with her eyes. "It *is* simple . . . too simple."

"Why would they want us to break the code?" the professor asked.

"It's pretty suspicious if you ask me," Walter said. "Never trust an open door in your enemy's hideout."

The professor pointed at Walter. "Well put. Sir Patrick's computers have not been able to crack the code in the past, so whoever simplified it must realize that we would notice."

Marilyn placed her hand on the viewing window. The trees and fern-like undergrowth moved up and down in a rhythmic sway, the foliage passing by at the speed of a marching gait. Bonnie was nowhere in sight. "Please put it in simple terms, Ashley. What do you think we're seeing here?"

Ashley leaned back in her chair. With three creases furrowing her brow, she took a deep breath and crossed her arms. "I think we're looking at our own world and our own time. The window in front of us is a gateway into another dimension, and the belt is a kind of cross-dimensional camera port within that realm. As Billy moves with the belt, our view of the other dimension moves with him. Since we can't see Bonnie, she's obviously out of the camera's view, probably walking next to him." She moved one hand to her chin and slowly stroked it. "I think Billy and Bonnie are actually still in our world, just in a different dimensional sphere. Without this view port we wouldn't be able to see them or anything in their dimension, and they can't see us or anything in ours."

Marilyn's head bobbed in time with the window's image. "Does that make sense in your experience, Professor?"

The professor chuckled. "I have never personally experienced cross-dimensional phenomena, but I have read a reliable account of one." He leaned toward the laptop screen. "Do you have an electronic Bible on your computer?"

"Larry has one," Ashley replied, tapping the keys once again. "I'll have him send it across. What version?"

"I am most familiar with the King James. Please look up Second Kings chapter six."

"You got it."

After a few seconds Ashley turned the laptop toward the professor. He slipped his spectacles over his eyes and began reading.

"And when the servant of the man of God was risen early, and gone forth, behold, an host compassed the city both with horses and chariots. And his servant said unto him, 'Alas, my master! how shall we do?' And he answered, 'Fear not: for they that be with us are more than they that be with them.' And Elisha prayed, and said, 'Lord, I pray thee, open his eyes, that he may see.' And the Lord opened the eyes of the young man; and he saw: and, behold, the mountain was full of horses and chariots of fire round about Elisha."

The professor folded his spectacles and turned the screen back toward Ashley. "Another invisible dimension, Miss Stalworth? Was Elisha's servant granted a view port similar to this window?"

Ashley shrugged her shoulders. "Could be. Who knows? What I can deduce is that those microchips are in the other dimension, so their carriers somehow found another portal. And their brightness on my map indicates that our view port is getting closer to bad guy number seven."

She grasped both sides of the screen and tilted it farther back. "Although the map shows geographic features in our area, it also computes the location of the energy sources from the other dimension based on Apollo's readings. I digitally anchored the map in place based on light streams that appear to be static. In other words, there are sources of electromagnetic energy in the other dimension that aren't moving, so as Billy's belt moves within the anchored map, we can watch where he goes. Right now, he and Bonnie are about a mile and a half to our north-west, and they've almost completed a circular path."

The professor strolled to the view port, his hands behind his back. He stood next to Marilyn, watching the continued up and down undulations on the wall. "I believe it's imperative that we find Sir Patrick at once. It seems that a crisis arose while I was at the airport, and much is amiss. If I understand Patrick's interpretation of the legends correctly, he needs a dragon in order to deal with our enemies, so he likely has gone in search of Clefspeare." He withdrew a piece of paper from his pocket, scanned the words written on it, then slid it back in. "Patrick's note gives me an idea of where to look for them, Marilyn. Will you come with me?"

Marilyn swivelled her head toward Ashley and Walter. "What about the kids?"

"Sir Barlow is here, and from what I have seen, these two are quite capable of taking care of themselves. I, however, will most certainly need your assistance. We must find Hartanna, and our journey may be more than I can handle alone."

Marilyn nodded. "I'll go. You know as well as I do how much I want to find my husband." She lowered her eyes. "I mean, Clefspeare."

"Of course you do. And you may be the only one who can find him." He gestured toward the doorway. "Shall we go?"

After giving Ashley his cell phone number, the professor led Marilyn to the doorway, and they disappeared into the corridor.

Ashley returned her gaze to the computer map, shaking her head slowly. "Walter, I don't like this."

Walter crouched at Ashley's side. "Losing battery power?"

"No, that's fine." She pointed at the screen. "See here? Billy's half-angstrom signal is about to meet this four-angstrom electromagnetic echo."

"What?" Walter said, frowning. "Could you translate that into 'human'?"

Ashley pressed her lips together. "Sorry. I'm in data mode." She took in a deep breath, then spoke slowly. "If Billy and Bonnie keep travelling at their current rate, they'll meet a member of the New Table in about five minutes."

Billy slowed his gait, then halted. Bonnie walked up close behind, whispering in his ear. "Do you sense danger?"

"I'm not sure." He scanned the trees lining the path. The oaks were taller here with broad limbs spreading out as if inviting them into a welcoming embrace. Sunlight barely filtered through the leafy branches above, poking through with pencil-thin shafts of light. The sun began heating the atmosphere, raising prickles on his neck. He took a deep breath of the humid air and let it out slowly while stuffing his hands into his pockets. "Everything's so different here, I can't tell what I'm feeling. I don't sense danger, but something's not right. I just can't put my finger on it."

"Do you think it would be safe for me to fly up and look around? Maybe I could see where we're going – you know, check if there's anything to watch out for."

Billy searched the canopy above. "There's a hole in the branches. Think you could fit through that?"

"I'll know soon enough." Bonnie stretched out her wings and jumped. Seconds later she darted through the hole, the tips of her wings barely touching the woody fingers of the tallest trees. Billy tried to follow her flight, catching glimpses of her winged shadow as she soared over the forest. After a minute or two, she reappeared through the canopy rift. With a flurry of her wings, she settled a few feet in front of Billy. She held a hand over her chest, catching her breath, and her wind-blown hair fell over her eyes. "It's so beautiful up there!" she said, pushing her hair back. "I saw a huge river on each side of us, and they flow into an enormous, crystal blue lake. I wish we could explore it all."

"Yeah," Billy said, scooting one of his rain-dampened hiking boots through the moist dirt, "but I doubt that we're supposed to." He nudged a pebble. The grass was still far removed from the narrow trail of mud, but there were no prints, not even animal tracks. He kicked the pebble down the path and lifted his gaze. "Could you tell what's ahead?"

Bonnie waved her hand across the scene in front of them. "The trees thin out, and it looks like the path disappears into a hill, maybe a cave."

Billy craned his neck to see around the bend, but the path disappeared into the dark forest. Keeping watch over both sides of the path, he trudged ahead with Bonnie close behind. Overhead, the storm clouds raced away, and the tropical sun beat down. Beads of sweat gathered on his forehead, and damp circles appeared on the front of his long-sleeved shirt. He wiped his brow with his sleeve. This mission was like a jungle safari, not the hike across the British countryside that he had hoped for.

He glanced over at Bonnie. Rings of sweat dampened her shirt, and her occasional quiet grunts and red face revealed her own discomfort . . . or worry.

As they marched, the landscape began to change. The dense forest gave way to fields of grass and scattered stones. The terrain undulated with gentle hills guarding each side of their path, and the wind strummed the long blades of grass like a million invisible fingers on a whisper-quiet harp.

The hills rose more steeply the farther Billy and Bonnie travelled until it seemed they were walking in a shallow trench, unable to see over the bordering slopes on each side. The gap in between narrowed, finally ending at an imposing wall of rock.

The path led straight into the cliff through a low, dark archway flanked by piles of sand and pebbles.

"It's a cave, all right," Bonnie said, "but the hole's pretty small."

Billy set his foot at the base of a grassy knoll on their left. "Yeah. Let's climb this hill and go around. It's not very smart to go into a strange cave without a light."

"But we're supposed to stay on the path, and, besides, we do have a light."

"If you mean my fire breathing, I can't keep that up for very long. We don't know how far we have to go in the dark."

"But we have Excalibur. You're real good at keeping it glowing now."

"That's true, but it won't hurt just to take a look around up there." Billy vaulted up the mildly sloped knoll, taking several leaping steps to the top. The incline levelled off to a grassy plateau, giving him plenty of room to walk around. He shaded his eyes and scanned his surroundings, finally gazing back down at Bonnie. "This ridge follows alongside the mountain, but it gets narrow and goes out of sight around a bend."

Bonnie set one foot on the slope. "What's on the other side? There should be a river about a mile or so away, but I didn't notice anything closer."

Billy waved his arm. "C'mon up. It's cooler up here."

Bonnie ran up the hill, fluttering her wings to give her body an extra boost. She seemed to float to the summit, her churning feet settling softly on the grass as she slowed to a stop.

Billy signalled for Bonnie to follow. "Let's take a look." He jogged toward the opposite edge of the plateau, a span about the width of a football field. Bonnie joined him as he leaned over the side.

This slope descended at a steeper rate and plunged far deeper. Instead of a plush green carpet, the embankment was knotted with tufts of wire grass and littered with fist-sized stones and reddish clumps of clay.

Bonnie pointed toward the valley floor. "Something's moving down there!"

A stirring mass seemed to be climbing the ridge, lunging bodies and reaching arms taking shape as they drew closer. Billy pulled out Excalibur. "They're coming this way!"

Bonnie put her hand on Billy's arm. "Maybe they're prisoners. Maybe we're supposed to rescue them."

The climbing horde drew closer, their speed increasing as dozens of desperate hands dug long, skinny fingers into the clay.

Billy pulled away from Bonnie's hand, summoning Excalibur's beam as he drew back the blade. "I . . . I can't tell what they are. I don't feel danger. I feel—"

"Save me!" a haunting voice called out from below.

"Don't leave me here," another voice cried.

Excalibur's light spread across the forms, illuminating the bodies in an eerie glow, like fluorescent ink under black light. Contorted faces echoed a purplish luminescence, outlining every feature in startling detail and painting dark emotions on a writhing canvas – sadness, anguish, terror.

Billy swung the beam over their heads. "Stop!" he shouted.

The mass suddenly halted, every form shivering in a sloping field of glowing humanity. Unlike their faces, their bodies were indistinct, possessing head and limbs but no details, more like ghosts than people. Several had climbed within a few feet of the summit, and they reached with stretching fingers, not quite touching the top.

Billy inched his foot back from the edge. Were there hundreds? Thousands? They seemed to meld together, one body attached to the other like a carpet of intertwined anatomy.

He softened his tone, but only a little. "Who are you?"

Dozens of voices cried out at once, calling a variety of names. "Samuel Johnston!" "Beatrice Cooler!" "Teresa García-Ramírez!" "Roland Mattis!"

Billy shook his head. "No! One at a time!"

Names pummelled his ears again, this time louder and more intense.

He waved the beam again. "Quiet!"

Every voice fell silent, and the mass trembled like a litter of chilled puppies.

He let out a sigh. "Okay. I heard the name Samuel Johnston. Would Samuel Johnston please tell me who you are?"

A weak voice replied, "As I said, sir. I . . . I'm Samuel Johnston. I'm a civil engineer from Milwaukee."

Billy searched the sea of bodies for the source of the voice. "Are you a prisoner here?"

Hundreds of voices shouted in a cacophony. "Yes!" . . . "Save me!" . . . "Get me outta here!"

Billy screamed, "Samuel Johnston only! If your name's not Samuel Johnston, keep your mouth shut!" He let out a long breath. "Okay, Samuel. What's the deal?"

The voice grew a bit stronger. "I can't seem to get out of this valley, if that's what you mean. I try to climb the hill, and something keeps me from getting to the top, like I'm dragging a ton of weights."

Billy finally spotted Samuel, a quivering phantom in the first row of bodies. He was scratching at the slope with his head tucked near his chest. "What about everyone else?" Billy asked. "Who are they?"

Samuel looked up, a forlorn expression glowing from his bone-white face. "Everyone else? I haven't seen anyone else."

Billy waved his arm across the sea of bodies. "But they're all around you. They're attached to you on all sides."

"I don't know what you're talking about." The bony fingers scratched again at the ground and reached for the rim of the hill. "I just . . . can't . . . seem to get . . . to the top."

Bonnie lowered her arm toward the man, but Billy pulled her back. "Wait!" he said. "Let me!"

Billy returned Excalibur to its scabbard and reached his hand down. Samuel grasped for it, but his hand passed right through. He lunged, groping with outstretched fingers, but they spirited past Billy's like lines of white smoke. Samuel's face twisted in anguish. "No!" he shouted, his body shivering. He let out a mournful cry, "Nooooo!" and sank back into the blanket of souls.

Billy grabbed Bonnie's upper arm. "Let's get out of here before they start shouting again." He pulled her into a quick stride.

Bonnie hustled next to him, her wings beating to keep pace. "Isn't there any way we can save them?"

Billy just shook his head and hurried across the plateau. When they reached the opposite side, he bounced down the slope while Bonnie glided to the path. He stepped up to the cave entrance and pulled Excalibur out again. "There's no hope for them," he explained, summoning the sword's beam. "It's like they're all one big mass. They just keep dragging each other down."

Bonnie's chin hung low. "Joseph warned us about lost souls. It's so sad!"

"You're not kidding." Billy wanted to say something to lift Bonnie's spirits, but the image of all those mournful faces in the valley churned up only depressing thoughts. The names echoed in his mind, real names, real people, each with hopes and dreams now lost forever. What did an engineer from Milwaukee do to deserve this fate? What was lacking in the life of Teresa García-Ramírez that would leave her stranded in a valley of lost souls?

Billy shook his head hard, trying to cast off the phantoms. "Looks like you were right. Getting off the path was a bad idea."

He gripped Excalibur with both hands and held it in front of his body. "I guess we'll just have to see what this cave has in store." He took a deep breath and marched forward, Excalibur's light leading the way.

Ashley pecked frantically at her keyboard while Walter leaned on her chair, his glance skipping from the computer to the portal window and back. "Yep. They decided to go into the cave."

"Can't blame them for that," Ashley replied. "It beats messing with those zombies."

"What's to be scared of? They looked like gingerbread men that got too close together on a cookie sheet. Billy and Bonnie could've handled them."

"Well, their little excursion helped me calibrate my digital map." Ashley thumped the tabletop with her finger. "I'm sure one of the knights is in that cave." After several dramatic keystrokes she slid her chair back and threw on her jacket. "Walter, call Sir Barlow. We'll need him."

Walter rushed into the hallway and returned seconds later with the knight. His thick moustache twitched under his wrinkling nose. "I am at your service!"

Ashley held up a grey box about the size of a loaf of bread and began a series of drill-sergeant commands. "Walter, bring Apollo and put this photometer in its place. Barlow, you come here, too. You're going to learn how to communicate with my computer while you're watching the window. Walter and I are going on a little expedition."

Walter set Apollo on the table next to the computer. "An expedition? Aren't we going to keep watching what Billy's doing?"

Ashley lifted her briefcase from the floor to the table. "The mission is too dangerous. We have to help Billy."

"He knows it's dangerous, and he's got Excalibur."

She flipped open the latches and propped up the lid. “True, but he probably doesn’t know the New Table knights are in the circles, and do you think he’d be going in that cave with Bonnie if he knew one of them was lurking in there?”

Walter nodded. “That’s a good point, but I’m not sure we should be sticking our noses where they don’t belong.”

Ashley thrust her hand into her briefcase and rummaged through it. “It’s not like we’re going to mess up their mission. All we’re going to do is find a portal into the other dimension and warn them. It’s not right that the bad guys can interfere and we can’t.” She pulled out a handheld computer and attached a cable from it to her laptop. “I’m downloading a program to my handheld that will receive Apollo’s data. The other photometer will transmit to my laptop and then to my handheld, so we won’t lose track of them.”

Walter flicked his thumb toward the window. “Isn’t there any way we can use this portal?”

Ashley shook her head. “Patrick’s note said that Billy and Bonnie were transluminated by Excalibur and absorbed into the other dimension, and I don’t have any way to duplicate Excalibur’s beam. The black knights must have found another entry. Apollo and Larry will help us find the portal, and when we do, I’ll analyse it to figure out how the knights used it.”

Walter raised a finger. “I’ll bet those—”

“Black cloaks have something to do with it?” Ashley finished.

“There you go again! How do you do that?”

“It’s just deduction, Walter. Don’t have a cow.” She cocked her head toward the wall near the smashed door. “I saw the cloaks over there. We’ll pick them up on the way out.” She turned her laptop toward the knight. “Sir Barlow, get ready. I have a lot to teach you and not much time to do it.”

Barlow straightened his body and firmed his chin. “My mind is a steel trap, Miss.”

"Good . . . I think." She put her finger on the computer screen. "These flashing dots are the bad guys. The point in the centre is Billy, and, as you can see, he's getting close to this bad guy. It's your job to watch the portal window and tell me what's going on. Just talk to the computer. I'll hear you. And my voice will come through the computer speakers here." She put a hand on the knight's elbow. "Got it?"

Barlow bowed his head. "You can count on me, Miss."

Ashley snatched her handheld computer and scooped up Bonnie's backpack from the floor, slipping a strap over one arm and unzipping the pouch. "Walter, grab the cloaks and stuff them in the backpack. I'll carry that while you carry Apollo."

Walter gathered the cloaks into a wad. "Won't we need a flashlight or something?" he asked, pushing the bundle into the pack.

She dug into her jacket pocket. "I have a penlight on my keychain. It'll be enough."

The two hurried through the old corridor and found their way outside. Ashley jumped off the portico and ran ahead into a massive green expanse that stretched out over several acres, alternately watching her step and gazing at her handheld computer. Walter followed, keeping a keen eye on the woods that bordered the manicured lawn. Fog had settled in, shrouding the trees in a mantle of ivory mist, but the full moon gave enough light to keep them from colliding with the plant beds and decorative boulders that lay about the grounds.

He pulled his jacket closed and shivered. With all the talk of enemy knights, he wondered if some of them were watching the mansion and if they knew he was on Billy's side. Out in the middle of this glorified pasture he felt like he was wearing a neon "shoot me" sign on his back.

Ashley stopped and looked all around before turning toward the nearest border of the lawn. "That way." She sprinted toward the trees, her tennis shoes scattering droplets as she dashed across the fog-dampened grass.

Walter ran as fast as he could, still carrying Apollo. He finally caught up when Ashley slowed down just inside the forest edge. She gazed at the tiny screen on her computer. "Billy and Bonnie are still quite a ways to our south-east, but in our dimension we don't have a clear path like they do in theirs. We have to trudge through these woods."

"How about an update from Barlow before we go in?"

Ashley spoke into her computer. "Barlow. Anything new?"

A buzzing voice replied. "Young William seems to be deep inside the cave now. It's quite dark, but I can see the stony walls in the glow of Excalibur. He is moving slowly, and I assume the young lady is following behind."

"Maybe we can still catch them," Walter said. "Let's follow your gizmo and get moving!"

"Let me get a reading from Apollo first." Ashley studied the screen and then gazed at Apollo, shaking her head and muttering, "Strange." Her brow wrinkled into tight ridges. "The spectrum is all out of whack." She waved her free hand through the saturated air. "This whole place is like a swirling vortex of weird electromagnetic patterns, like someone has thrown in all the wrong ingredients in a pot and stirred it up."

"And we're part of the stew," Walter added.

Ashley tilted her head upward. "Karen? Are you listening in?"

Karen's voice came through the computer's speaker, sounding weak and far away. "You bet. You guys are the best show in town."

"How about Larry? You got him patched in to us?"

"Yeah. He's been reading Apollo's data ever since you turned it on."

Ashley gazed down at her computer again. "Larry, what do you make of it? Can you analyse this mess, or is Apollo ready to croak?"

"Apollo is not malfunctioning. It is simply showing that your illustration of a mixing pot was strikingly accurate. The data stream is consistent, but there is also an influx of extraneous light data. I will separate what is natural from what has been artificially added."

"Well, thank you, Larry. A compliment without a smart aleck remark. I'm impressed."

Walter kicked at a rock on the ground. "Just tell him to hurry up. We have a cross-dimensional party to crash before it's too late."

"I heard that, Walter. Here's your smart aleck remark." A rude "raspberry" sound blasted through the speaker.

"Larry!" Ashley scolded. "Behave yourself. Just give us the data."

"Your wish is my command, Ashley dear. I'll turn off your raw input and stream filtered data to you."

Ashley studied the tiny screen again. "That worked, Larry. Good job." She pulled the computer closer to her face. "There's a radiation signal here. It's not real strong, but it's significant."

Walter grabbed a leg-length stick from the ground and tried his weight on it. "Let's get going. I'll bet it's stronger where the New Table creep's waiting." He held Apollo in front of his body and marched into the woods, using his new walking stick and kicking through the dense undergrowth. "Just let me know if I'm going in the right direction. I have a feeling that we don't have a second to lose."

CHAPTER

The Second Circle

Billy stopped and sniffed the air. "You smell that?"

Bonnie raised her head and took in a long breath, closing her eyes, then exhaling slowly. "Onions?"

"That's what I thought, but how could onions grow in a cave?"

Bonnie's shadowy form looked like an eerie phantom in Excalibur's glow. She tapped Billy on the shoulder. "I hope you don't get tired of me asking, but do you feel any danger?"

"No," he replied, lowering his voice to a whisper, "but I don't know if I'd recognize danger here even if it stepped on my toes."

"That smell's getting strong," Bonnie said. "It might be some kind of natural gas. Maybe if we just keep going, we'll get past it."

Billy took two steps forward and halted abruptly. A sudden surge of fear buzzed up and down his spine like an electric shock. "I . . . I can hardly budge."

"Same here," Bonnie replied, her voice weak and trembling. "It's like my legs are made of clay."

Billy moved his sword from side to side, casting its glow all around. Wet gravel littered the flat stone floor at the sides, but the two-foot-wide path down the centre seemed clear and dry, as though regularly swept for passing travellers. He tried to hold his breath, both to avoid the odour and to listen for sounds deeper in the cave.

What was that? Crunching gravel? Footsteps? He forced his weakened legs to take a long stride backwards so he could stand in front of Bonnie, his sword ready to strike. A boiling rage churned within, worse than his usual danger sensation, but it didn't come from the fire in his belly. The fury seemed to radiate from every pore in his skin. "Who's there?" he yelled. "Identify yourself, or I'll cut your head off and gut you like a dead fish!"

"Billy!" Bonnie whispered hoarsely. "Why are you talking like that? It might be Joseph."

Billy detected a spike of anger in Bonnie's voice, maybe a rebuke, but he couldn't help what he felt. The rage burned so hot, his legs shook like toothpicks holding up an elephant.

A new voice oozed out of the darkness. "He's talking like that, Bonnie, because he's in over his head." A woman stepped into the light, but she kept her distance. Excalibur's glow washed over a tall, broad-shouldered body that tapered to a narrow waist. A shadow obscured her facial features, but the outline seemed thin and concave, her hair, blonde and shoulder-length. "He's trying to prove himself king," she continued, "but he's just a child."

Billy strangled Excalibur's hilt and gritted his teeth. Over his head? Just a child? The fire in his belly grew hotter by the second. "Who are you?" he shouted.

The woman smiled, her teeth eerily white in the darkness. "Calm down, child. I mean you no harm. I'm just here to tell you the truth. As you can see, you are too volatile to be a leader of the people. Your heart is filled with rage."

As she stepped closer, Billy raised his sword, his teeth grinding. "Get . . . back!"

The woman shook her head and kept walking. "Will the rage that murdered Palin in cold blood strike down an unarmed woman?" She stood toe-to-toe with Billy and let out a low laugh. "You think your faith purged your anger, but you were wrong. Anger is still your life's blood."

"Don't listen to her," Bonnie called. "I feel the anger, too. It's some kind of trick. We have to fight it!"

"Oh, yes," the woman said, chucking Bonnie under her chin, "the faithful princess never doubts her prince." She patted Billy on the head. "Why don't you both just turn around and go home? Joseph will show you the way out. Marry this lovely girl, Billy. Have a dozen children, and live happily ever after. Why risk what lies ahead? Why endanger this loyal young lady? Is your prideful pursuit of royalty worth risking her life? Is a tin crown really worth the price of her blood?"

Billy felt a catch in his chest. He tried to gulp air, but the taste of onions coated his tongue with every breath. His thoughts swirled. *Could she be right? Am I risking Bonnie's life just to get a crown?* He shook his head, trying to scatter the boiling cloud of anger and confusion.

"Billy," Bonnie said, "I made the choice myself. No one forced me to come with you." She pulled on his sleeve and whispered in his ear. "This is a place of darkness. Remember what you learned in the light!"

While the stranger stood with her arms folded over her chest, a smirk of satisfaction spreading across her face, Billy let Bonnie's words seep into his brain. *Remember what you learned in the light.*

His heart beat wildly as he fought against the unearthly, burning rage that threw every thought into turmoil.

An image of his earlier battle with the young knight of the New Table flashed across his mind, and then the professor pulling the melted candle from his pocket . . . the scentser that had lulled him to sleep with its gentle fragrance. He remembered the professor's words. *When you recognize an enemy's weapons, they are easier to battle.*

The rage slowly subsided. His mind cleared. He relaxed his biceps and lowered his sword. "We're going on." He reached back for Bonnie's hand and pulled her forward, allowing Excalibur to light their way. He wondered what the stranger might be doing, but he resisted the temptation to look back. The odour of onions died away, and all he could hear was the clopping of their shoes on the stone floor. He felt Bonnie's hand squeeze his three times. A silent congratulations? Maybe. Whatever it was, it surged through his body, chased out any remnant of anger, and flooded his mind with peace.

An echo reverberated throughout the cave, the voice of the stranger. "You think you've won, Dragon Boy, but the second circle makes the first seem like a picnic . . . if you can find it." A beam of light flashed from behind them. Billy spun around. For a brief second he could see the outline of the stranger, now completely shrouded in a black cloak and hood. In a brilliant explosion of sparks, she disappeared.

As if awakened by a blaring trumpet, thousands of bats erupted from the cave walls with furious wings and enraged, piercing screams. Billy and Bonnie swatted at them, Billy with his sword and Bonnie with her flailing arms and wings. Billy grabbed Bonnie's hand again. They plunged deeper into the cave, away from the madhouse of wings and razor teeth, then skidded to a stop. A wall of solid stone blocked their path.

Billy slapped his hand against the cold, dark barrier. "There's no way out!"

Bonnie backed up to the wall as far as she could. "The bats are coming closer!"

The shifting shadow of fluttering, shrieking bats began to envelop Excalibur's light. In seconds the black predators would be on them again.

Ashley held the computer at arm's length, trying to walk while studying the data. "We must be getting close. We're reading some of the same frequencies we had in Patrick's house."

"Good. Finally." Walter slowed his march through the forest thicket and turned around. "Did you hear something?"

Ashley aimed her penlight at Walter's face while looking down at her handheld computer. "Yeah. It sounded like Barlow." She pulled the computer up to her ear. "What did you say, Sir Barlow?"

The scratchy voice squeaked from the speaker. "William has met a tall woman, an unsavoury wench if you want my opinion."

Walter leaned close to the computer. "Barlow, is she armed?"

"Not that I can tell. They seem to have conversed, and now William has left her behind and moved on."

"Can you see—" Ashley began.

"Wait!" Barlow interrupted. "A flash of light!"

"What? What is it?"

"I don't know," Barlow replied. "It happened so fast. The cave is dark again. I can see only the sword . . . and now I see Bonnie. She looks quite well."

A blinding flash of light filled the woods. Walter pulled Ashley behind a wide tree trunk, and they peeked around opposite sides. A tall, feminine figure seemed to step out of nothingness next to a gorse bush. The stranger jerked off her hood, and blonde hair streamed down to her shoulders. She skulked away, disappearing into the dark forest.

Ashley whispered hoarsely. "Larry, did you pick up that flash of light?"

"Yes. A very strange anomaly."

"It's not an anomaly. I think it opens the cross-dimensional window. Can Apollo duplicate it?"

"Of course it's an anomaly, Ashley. Have you already forgotten the definition? Anomaly—noun; deviation or departure from the normal."

"Miss Stalworth!" Barlow yelled through the computer. "Bats! There are bats in the cave! They are attacking William and Bonnie!"

Ashley's eyes flamed. "Stuff the dictionary, Larry, and analyse the flash! Can you duplicate it?"

"Perhaps. It seems that you were physically displaced from the flash locus, and I can't determine the distance in order to establish the strength. You will have to provide an estimate of the relative coordinates between you and the centre of the light source."

Ashley punched a few keys on her computer. "How's that? Can you deliver a flash now?"

"One millisecond, please. Okay, Apollo is now programmed to release a similar flash in thirty seconds. Have a nice trip. Send me an electromagnetic postcard from the other world."

"Walter, let's get the cloaks on! Hurry!" She turned her back to Walter, and he yanked the cloaks from her backpack. She then spun around and helped Walter pull the black robe over his head. "Larry, we'll need another flash to come back to our world, so you'd better program Apollo for another flash two minutes after the first. Got it?"

"Two minutes. Got it. You now have twenty seconds before the first one."

Ashley dropped the backpack and grabbed her own cloak. "Walter, my turn." She threw the robe over her head and stuffed her arms through the sleeves while Walter pulled the hem down to her ankles.

"Ten seconds."

Ashley scrambled to the gorse bush while pushing her head into the black hood. Walter followed with Apollo in one hand, trying to put on his hood with the other.

"Five seconds."

Ashley set the computer on a log and yanked Walter's hood down over his face. As they stood side by side, a brilliant flash of light exploded from Apollo's centre. The light collected in a radiant stream and rushed to a point a couple of feet in front of Walter. It spread out in mid-air like an oil slick on water as though it had splashed against a transparent shield. The light barrier grew into a ragged-edged, vertical rectangle, hovering at least six inches off the ground and extending to a height of eight feet or more.

Ashley grabbed Walter's hand and lunged head first toward the pulsing light. "Jump!"

Keeping a tight grip on Apollo, Walter leaped with her through the portal. Tumbling to the ground, he banged his shoulder against a bowling-ball-sized rock and sprawled to his side.

"Ouch!"

He sat up. The light faded and shrank to a dim, buzzing square about the size of a cereal box. Ashley sat in front of him, massaging the top of her hooded head. "Remind me not to dive head first through any more interdimensional portals."

Walter yanked off his hood and rotated his throbbing shoulder. "I'll make a note of it." He spread his fingers in front of his face. "My hands feel like they're on fire!"

Ashley blew on her hands. "Mine too. They weren't protected by the cloaks."

In the fading light of the portal, a strange, undulating darkness flittered all around. "It's the bats," Walter whispered.

Ashley pulled off her hood and shook out her hair. "I see them, but I don't feel them."

"Yeah. It's weird. Too weird." He pointed at a glow in the distance and took a step toward it. "I'll bet that's Excalibur." Still holding Apollo, he stuffed the hood into his cloak pocket and reached for Ashley's hand. "Come on!"

The two stepped as quickly across the dim floor as they dared, glancing all around at the furious bats, neither feeling their wings nor hearing their squeals. Within seconds they found Billy and Bonnie backed up against the stone wall. Billy waved his sword, whacking at the bats as they approached, while breathing blasts of fire and making fluttering torches out of a few of the bigger ones.

Walter ran up to him, dodging the sword. "Billy!" He tried to grab his friend's shoulder, but his fingers clutched nothing but air. "Billy! Can you hear me?"

There was no response. Billy just swung Excalibur and smacked a grey bat with the side of the blade, sending it hurtling against the wall.

Ashley looked all around. "Why can we feel the floor and rocks but not Billy or Bonnie?"

"Or the bats," Walter added.

Ashley rubbed her thumb on the band of her ring. "I must have guessed our distance from the original flash incorrectly. The dimensional portal brought us only part way into this one. But we still have to figure out how to get them out of here."

"What about Billy's mission? If we take him out, won't it be a failure?"

Ashley swatted at a bat, but her hand passed through its snapping jaws. "Would you rather leave them here as bat bait? With the New Table knights running around messing things up, the mission's as good as over already."

Walter shook his head. "I guess you're right, but how can we get them through the portal? Aren't we pretty far from it now?"

"Yeah. Probably at least fifty feet, straight through the bats."

Walter lifted Apollo to his chest level. "We only have one shot at getting back ourselves. Can Larry adjust the flash somehow to stretch it this way?"

Ashley pressed her jaw. "Larry? Can you hear me?" She waited a few seconds. "Nothing. I guess I can't communicate by voice across the dimensional barrier."

"We're almost out of time. I'd better put Apollo back at the portal. Maybe when the window opens, Billy and Bonnie will see it and make a run for it."

Ashley shone the penlight beam into the flurry of bats. "Are you sure you can find the place we came in?"

Walter took the pen and leaned over, trying to direct the beam under the mass of beating wings. "Yeah. I'll remember that rock I landed on."

Billy swung his sword again, and Walter instinctively ducked, but not quite far enough. The blade sliced harmlessly through his neck. Billy then blasted a breath of fire into Walter's chest, and the stream surged through his back, engulfing a bat in flames.

Walter wiped his sleeve across his forehead. "Way too weird!" He then plunged into the sea of beating black wings, found the rock, and set Apollo on the ground. "How much time?" he yelled.

Ashley pulled her watch up close to her eyes. "About fifteen seconds!"

Walter jerked his hood out and pressed his head into it. "Put your hood on and get over here! And don't forget to wrap your sleeves over your hands."

Ashley pulled down her hood. "I want to know if the opening is visible from here. Maybe they'll be able to see it in their dimension and make a run for it."

"Won't they need cloaks?" Walter shouted.

The bats began closing in. Walter could barely see Ashley as the bustling vermin enveloped Excalibur's glow. "Good question!" Ashley shouted back. "I don't know!"

Suddenly the entire cave exploded with light. A stream of energy poured from Apollo, painting a new portal door within a foot of Walter. He cupped his hands around his mouth. "Can you see it from there?"

"Yeah! I'm on my way!"

"Hurry up! It's already getting smaller!"

Walter jerked his sleeves down over his hands, forming mittens over his fingers. He waved his arm frantically as Ashley dashed toward him. The portal's ragged edges contracted, the glowing rectangle dwindling to the size of a fireplace. When she reached his side, she pulled her sleeves over her hands and clutched them tightly. Walter snatched up Apollo, and they both dove through the hole.

Two seconds later the light evaporated, and Walter blinked away the spots in his field of vision. They were back in the woods where they had begun. Ashley sat on the forest floor, her arm around one knee, shaking her head. She slowly pulled off her hood and stared at Walter. "You were supposed to remind me not to dive through portals."

Walter propped himself up on his elbow and rubbed a crick in his neck. "Must have slipped my mind."

He jerked his head around. "Billy and Bonnie aren't here!"

Ashley rose shakily to her feet and lumbered toward the log where she had left her handheld computer. "Sir Barlow! What do you see? Are the bats still attacking them?"

Barlow's scratchy voice replied. "No bats, Miss. But it is an amazing sight, indeed!"

Billy swung Excalibur and sliced a bat's wing cleanly off, knocking down two more with his follow-through. The transluminating beam didn't affect them at all. He had to resort to old-fashioned slice and dice with the blade. "They're closing in!" he shouted.

Bonnie beat the air with both arms, slapping away a bat with every swipe. "If you have a plan, I'm listening."

Billy pointed with Excalibur. "What's that little red light?"

"I see it!" Bonnie shouted. "It's moving away through the bats!"

Billy lit up Excalibur's glow to full force. "Follow it! Hurry!"

They ducked their heads and charged through the screaming mass of flapping wings, Billy waving the sword frantically. "There's a door!" he yelled.

With bats snapping at their faces, they suddenly burst into a field of blazing light. The shrieks died away. The razor teeth vanished. Billy fell onto a patch of soft grass and rolled to a stop. He jumped up and rubbed his eyes, trying to adjust to the new light. A lush meadow stretched out for thousands of yards with thick green grass and purple and red wildflowers swaying in a gentle breeze. Bonnie sat only a few feet away, squeezing her eyelids closed.

Letting out a deep sigh, Billy returned Excalibur to its sheath and adjusted his belt. "You okay?"

Bonnie opened her eyes, stretched out her wings, and nodded. "I think so, but jumping through these portals is kind of painful. Did you feel an electrical shock?"

"A little bit." He reached down and helped her to her feet. "But Excalibur seemed to form an energy shield of some kind that sort of punched through that door. I was closer to the shield than you were."

She brushed off the seat of her trousers, and when she lifted her gaze, she thrust out her arm. "Look behind you!"

Billy reached for his sword and spun around, then pulled back, laughing. "Food!" he yelled happily.

A picnic table sat in the midst of the grassy field. A white cloth covered the top, and dozens of traditional picnic foods spread across it like a hungry teenager's dream come true – hamburgers, hot dogs, fried chicken, baked beans, apples and bananas, leafy green salads, corn chips, and a variety of bottled drinks. On one end of the table, two paper plates sat neatly trimmed with napkins and plastic utensils.

"Think it's for us?" Bonnie asked.

Billy spread out his arms. "Who else? There's nobody here."

Bonnie placed a hand on her stomach and smiled. "Well, I don't know about you, but I'm pretty hungry. Sir Patrick's pizza was good, but my trans-Atlantic flight burned a ton of calories."

"Yeah. And fighting those bats worked up an appetite."

They sat down side by side and began heaping their plates with a sampling of everything. Billy twisted open two bottles of root beer and handed one to Bonnie. Just before he could pull a leg of fried chicken up to his mouth, Bonnie nudged his forearm. "We have to give thanks first."

Billy nodded and bowed his head. "We're thankful for this food. Please bless it and strengthen us for the rest of our journey. And thank you to whoever left it all here for us. Amen."

"You're welcome!"

Billy looked up, startled by the new voice. Joseph sat on the other side of the table, now dressed in long khaki trousers and a striped polo shirt. He untwisted the cap on a bottle of water and took a long drink.

"Did you put this food here?" Bonnie asked.

Joseph set the bottle down and patted his stomach. "Yes. I hope these foods are to your liking. It's traditional American fare."

"Yeah, it's great." Billy scooped a pile of baked beans onto his plate and stared at Joseph. "You look different. Not just the clothes. . . . It's like you're younger or something."

"You look younger to me, too," Bonnie chimed in.

Joseph's bushy eyebrows twitched, and a hint of a smile wrinkled his lips. "Younger? Ah, yes. Not surprising. Perceptions change, always change." He swirled the water inside his bottle and nodded slowly. "Video games; once a pastime, now a waste of time. Grandma's stories; once a burden, now a treasure." He propped his foot on the bench. "Yes, flowers fade to ashes. Coal becomes diamonds. Such is life."

"So what's that got to do with you looking younger?" Billy asked.

Joseph waved his hand at Billy. "Now, now, let's not dwell on perceptions. You'll learn that perceptions are volatile in this place. Visible properties change without warning. What you see will often be generated by your thoughts and fears or by how you project those thoughts and fears onto others. What really matters is the quality of the heart, not the shell in which it resides."

Joseph slid a steaming casserole dish toward Billy. "Right now you must eat your fill. You will need your strength, and there will be no food fit to eat in the remaining circles." He waved his arm across the meadow behind him. "Your journey continues in that direction. The grass is still green, for this path is now rarely used, so you will have to watch carefully to stay within its boundaries. This will be the last circle that will have a physical path to follow. The remaining ones will be spiritual paths."

"How will we know how to get to the next circle?" Billy asked. "We just kind of stumbled into this one."

Joseph drew his head back. “Stumbled? I should say not!”

“Well,” Billy said, using his hands to explain. “I just followed this little red light through the cave. That’s all.”

“That’s all?!” Joseph repeated. “That’s everything!”

“Everything? What are you talking about?”

Joseph took a hot dog from a plate and squirted a line of mustard along the top. “Have you forgotten your lessons so soon? I thought the son of Merlin was a better teacher than that.”

“You mean Professor Hamilton? He’s the best!”

“Aha!” Joseph took a bite of his hot dog and spoke with his mouth full. “Then you did remember. You followed the light, just as he taught you.”

“Uh . . . yeah. I guess so.”

“Good.” Joseph swallowed, and his voice cleared. He raised a finger, and his brow seemed to arch farther out, shading his eyes. “Your journey will become darker, much darker. The light will always be there, sometimes dim, sometimes appearing only as words of truth, but it will be there.”

“What about the prisoners I’m supposed to find?” Billy asked. “Are there any in this circle?”

“No, no. Not here. Deeper realms, darker circles. You will see. But for now, you must eat, and I will take my leave. You will not see me again until your mission nears its goal.” Joseph stood and walked away, heading in the direction he had told Billy and Bonnie to go. His body shrank in the distance, more quickly than his pace should have allowed. In less than a minute, he was out of sight.

Ashley shoved the black hood into her backpack and held the computer close to her mouth. “Amazing, Sir Barlow? What’s amazing?”

"The cave is gone," Barlow replied, "and William appears to be sitting at a primitive banquet table in the middle of a battlefield. I saw a great deal of food, but since he sat down, it is now above my view. He turned for a moment, and I saw Bonnie sitting next to him."

Ashley helped Walter to his feet, still keeping the computer close. "So they're safe?"

"They appear to be quite safe, Miss."

"I guess our portal got them out of the bat cave." Ashley pulled a pair of twigs entangled in spider silk from her cloak and tried to fling them to the ground, but they stuck to her fingers. "So, how do you know it's a battlefield?"

"When William was standing, I noticed the way the grass was growing. The lawn is uneven in distinctive patterns, scalloped and thick in portions with nearly vertical divots that mark the gallop or rearing of a horse. Wildflowers have grown where the dirt was exposed, so I would guess that it's been three months or so since a battle took place there."

Ashley brushed the twigs onto a rock, then retrieved her backpack from the ground. "Barlow, that *is* amazing!"

"I am not expert in much, Miss, but I do know the battlefield. And there is a saying that red flowers mark the trail of blood. I'm afraid much blood was spilt in that field."

Ashley pointed, as though she were in the room with Barlow. "Go look at the compass circles and see if there are any lights in the drawings."

"One moment, Miss."

Ashley bit her lip, then brushed a leaf from her sleeve. "I guess they can go through the portal without cloaks. I wonder why."

Walter pulled a mass of web-entwined leaves from his own black cloak. "I'd rather not try to guess. I'm already more confused than a two-headed chicken."

After a few seconds, Barlow's voice returned. "Yes, Miss. The eastern circle has two coins, and the faces in the coins are glowing red."

"Cool!" Walter said. "It's about time we had some *change* for the better!"

"Stuff it, Walter," Ashley snapped. "This is no time for puns."

Walter held up his hands. "Okay, okay. Just trying to lighten the mood."

Ashley put a finger on her lips. "Now that I know they're both in the second circle, I can calibrate my readings to follow them." She hurriedly punched a series of keys.

Walter tried to peer at the handheld computer's screen. "So are there any bad guys around?"

Ashley gazed at the screen while pulling a cell phone from her belt. "Yeah. A bunch. I don't like this at all." She pressed a single button and lifted the phone to her ear. "Professor! Any news? . . . Good. You found Markus. . . . You're going where? . . . Isn't Avalon a myth? . . . I see. . . . I guess Markus knows where Patrick might look for a dragon. . . . Yes. Billy and Bonnie are fine. Just a run-in with a few bats. . . . It's nothing. Don't worry; we're keeping an eye on them. . . . Listen, any news on enemy movements? . . . Really? . . . No, actually that makes a lot of sense. . . . Sure thing. I'll talk to you later." Ashley re-clipped the phone to her belt.

"What makes a lot of sense?" Walter asked.

"Markus's spies say there's no sign of the remaining knights of the New Table, even the lower ranked ones."

"Don't tell me. They've all gone trick-or-treating in the land down under?"

"Yep. Take a look." Ashley handed the computer to Walter. "They're with knight number six in the second circle. At least forty of them."

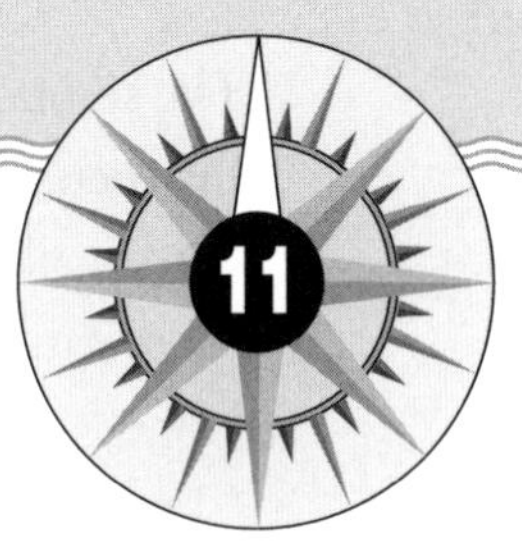

CHAPTER 11

The Passage Beetle

Billy and Bonnie walked across the meadow in the direction Joseph had vanished. It seemed that the trail sprouted more wildflowers than did the rest of the field. It looked as though a careless painter had shaken his brushes out as he walked the long green carpet, splashing the path with every colour of the rainbow.

When they passed over a rise in the field, the highway of flowers split into two colourful roads that slowly diverged across the plain. Billy stopped at the junction. "Now what do we do?"

Bonnie plucked a white flower and twirled it in her fingers. "Well, do you see any difference between the two paths?"

Billy studied the grass where the trail split. "There's a rock here. It looks almost like a road marker." He lifted the palm-sized stone. "It's flat on one side, and there's writing on it."

Bonnie leaned over Billy's arm. "What's it say?"

"It's faded, but I think I can make it out." He began to read out loud, hesitating at times as he changed the angle to cast light on the more illegible words.

The second circle's path of . . . blood
Instructs the . . . king his debt to pay,
For . . . all who seek a higher . . . call
Must patiently await their day.

"That sounds like Merlin's style!" Bonnie said.

"That's what I was thinking." Billy surveyed the two paths, his eyes picking through the splashes of colour. He pointed to the path on the right. "That one has red flowers, and the other one doesn't." He turned and looked at the path behind them. "See? Red flowers all the way to this point. Maybe that's what the 'path of blood' means."

Bonnie picked a red flower and held it next to her white one. "Makes sense to me."

Billy returned the stone to its place, and they marched down the path to the right, drawing in the faint scent of the tiny blossoms as their feet brushed the petals. Billy quoted the poem as they walked, making it sort of a marching chant. The bouncing rhythm helped him anchor the words in his brain. The sun warmed his skin, and the breeze blew constant refreshment, but the walk still seemed long and tedious, nothing but grass and flowers as far as he could see.

Billy plucked a yellow wildflower without breaking stride. "You know, I've been thinking about what Joseph said about perceptions, something about us seeing what we fear."

"Uh-huh. I remember." Bonnie touched her cheek, then quickly lowered her hand.

Billy halted and pulled her to a stop. "You don't have scales, Bonnie. Trust me. This creepy place is just playing tricks on you."

"But I can feel them, and the dragon saw them. I wonder why you don't."

"That's what I was thinking about. We have to be real careful and not always trust what we see or feel. We—"

"What's that up ahead?" Bonnie pointed toward the horizon.

Billy stepped in front of her. "Some kind of animal. A horse, maybe?"

"A horse would be great. I hope it's not just a perception."

As they continued on, the form became clear, a riderless horse ambling in their direction. When the horse drew near, it stopped, its gear clicking against a leather saddle.

"Seems friendly enough." Billy extended his hand slowly forward and stroked the horse's neck. "Maybe it's for us."

"Do you know how to ride?"

"Yeah. Dad used to own a horse, and I rode it once in a while." Billy put his foot in the left stirrup and vaulted into the saddle. He reached down to Bonnie. "Your choice. You can fly up here, or you can put your foot where I did, and I'll pull you up." With a heave, Billy helped her into place behind him, and she placed her hands lightly on his sides. He grabbed the reins and guided the horse down the path. "This should make our trip faster. Hold on. Let's see if he'll change gears."

Bonnie wrapped her arms around Billy's waist as he gave the horse a nudge with his heels. It broke into a steady trot, and the trail of flowers zipped by underneath. With the rhythmic beat of hooves drumming in his ears, Billy shouted, "Now this is the way to travel!"

Walter and Ashley tramped through the woods, Ashley with the computer near her lips. "Barlow, what do you see?"

"Young William has mounted a fine war stallion, and he is making haste down a trail of blood."

"How far have they gone?"

"Let's see. In your American measurements, I would say five miles or so."

"Five miles!" Walter repeated. "How are we going to catch up? We don't have a horse."

Ashley halted and squinted at the screen. "It looks like they're travelling in a wide circle. If we blaze a chord straight through the circle, maybe we can intercept them. The forty goons are probably near an entry portal setting up a trap, so if I calculate the speed and direction we need to intercept. . . ." She pushed her hand through her hair and shook her head. "I . . . I can't figure it out. These coordinates are relative, and there are too many variables. I can't compute our vector speed without—"

"Larry?" Walter offered.

Ashley nodded. "Yeah. Larry." She continued her march across the tangled undergrowth. "Karen, did you ever get that new mathematics engine loaded in Larry?"

"Yep. Trig functions last week, and advanced calculus theory two days ago. He's a geometric genius."

"Perfect." Ashley punched a series of keystrokes before speaking again. "Larry, I just entered Billy's approximate coordinates of origin and the central density point of the New Table knights. Take Billy's current coordinates and plot an arc to the location of the knights. Next, assuming Billy stays on his current pace, what direction and speed should we maintain to head him off at the knights' location?"

"Shaky assumptions, Ashley, but if you bear right nineteen point seven degrees and maintain your current speed, you should intercept him."

"How long will it take?"

"If you don't get tired and slow down, as humans often do, you'll intersect in twenty minutes and seven seconds."

Ashley angled to the right, keeping her exact pace while Walter followed in single file. "Okay, we're starting a right turn. Tell me when we're on target."

"Twelve degrees . . . eighteen . . . twenty!"

"So we're on target?"

"Just a hair back to the left."

Ashley cut back, stepping over a fallen log. "How's that?"

"Close enough for now."

"Okay, let me know if we have to speed up. Just correct me as we go along."

"Correcting you, Ashley, will be a pleasure."

Billy slowed the horse to a walk. A breeze had kicked up, blowing his hair back and cooling his face. The darkening horizon boiled in the distance. "Storm clouds?" he asked.

Bonnie's grip around his waist loosened. "Looks like it." She untied the sleeves of her sweatshirt and pulled it over her head. "It could get nasty real soon," she added.

Billy nodded toward a dense stand of tall trees to his left. "We could take to the woods. I don't want to get caught in the middle of a field in a thunderstorm."

"Being in the woods isn't much better, especially if we don't know what's in there. Besides, we'd have to get off the path."

Billy urged the horse closer to the trees and peered in through the gaps. A shadow dashed from one tree to another and hid behind the trunk. Its long, bony fingers wrapped around the smooth bark as its hate-filled eyes glared at them. Two other ghostly figures, dark, spindly men who seemed more skeleton than human, crept from behind a bush and slowly approached the edge of the woods. One of the men bared his angular teeth and howled like a lonely wolf.

Bonnie shuddered. "I hope those are more perceptions!"

"We're not sticking around to find out." Billy grabbed the reins. "Hang on tight!" He gave the horse a firm kick, and it bolted down the path, snorting like a wild bull in full charge. Bonnie's arms squeezed Billy's ribs, almost taking his breath away.

As the trail of red flowers zoomed by, the dark clouds rolled across the sky, covering the sun and stirring the breeze into humid swirls. Nickel-sized raindrops splashed on their faces, and peals of thunder rumbled all around.

"What's that up ahead?" Bonnie called out.

Billy pulled on the reins, and they slowed to a halt. "It looks like a bunch of riders. They're wearing black cloaks and hoods, like the guy who tried to kill me." Billy turned the stallion around, and another line of horses trooped across his path. "More riders!" Billy called. "We're surrounded!"

A muscular stallion in the middle of the pack took three steps forward. With a quick tug, the rider pulled off a hood, and long black tresses fell out from underneath, framing a delicate, feminine face. "Welcome to the second circle, young Arthur."

Bingo! You're right on the mark, Ashley. Billy and Bonnie are within a few feet of Apollo's location."

Ashley and Walter gazed at the computer together. "Yeah, I see that," Ashley said, putting her finger on a data reading, "but Apollo's not showing the frequencies we saw at the other portals. We have to find a way in, fast. Those New Table creeps are getting too close."

Walter held Apollo at his hip and kicked away the leaves near his feet. "Well, forty people have to leave some kind of trail. Let's just look around."

Ashley raised her finger. "Good point."

Walter and Ashley walked through the forest with their eyes focused on the ground. Walter circled a hefty oak and found a narrow strip of moist earth covered with shallow impressions. "Here!" he shouted. "Lots of footprints!" He and Ashley followed the trail, stopping at a point where the prints ended abruptly. He set Apollo on the ground. "Is this the spot?"

"Yep!" Ashley said, reading the computer screen. "The frequency we're looking for is maxed out."

Walter picked up Apollo and wiped the moisture off the base with the sleeve of his black cloak. "Can Larry give us another flash?"

"We'll need two flashes again." She turned and eyed their search path. "It looks like we walked about fifty feet from where we think Billy and Bonnie are. We'll have to get into their dimension, find them, and make another flash. What'll that take? Thirty seconds?"

"Sounds right. But we don't want to take forty bad guys with us."

"Another good point." Ashley spoke into the air. "Larry, can Apollo give us another pair of flashes, say, thirty seconds apart? Use the same frequencies, but give the second one about a third of the power. The portal door might be small, but we'll have to squeeze through it."

"Apollo needs time to recharge, and you have very little light there. It has enough juice for one flash. Given the current environment, it will take approximately two hours for it to be ready for two flashes."

"Two hours!" Walter moaned, pulling his hood from the cloak pocket. "That might be too long."

Ashley reached for the backpack and yanked out her hood. "Larry, will Apollo recharge in the other dimension?"

"If there is enough light, yes. The recharge time is dependent on available light energy, not on dimensional position, but I cannot estimate the necessary time in another dimension when Apollo is in this one."

"Barlow!" Ashley barked. "Is it dark or light where Billy is now?"

"There is some daylight, Miss. But storm clouds are brewing, and young William is in dire trouble. He is surrounded by horse-mounted knights clad in those dark cloaks."

"Horses?" Walter repeated. "Where did they get horses? I didn't see any hoofprints anywhere."

Ashley pulled her hood over her head and slipped off the backpack, letting it fall to the ground. "Larry, send us now. We'll let Apollo recharge there. Maybe we can help them while we wait."

"Ashley, I don't know if I can send the signal for the second flash across the portal, and I also don't know if I can detect when it is charged. I will program it, and you can press the manual switch when you think it's ready."

"But how will I know—"

"Just do it," Walter said, putting his hood on. "We're wasting time!"

Ashley and Walter stood hip to hip, and Ashley put her arm around Walter's shoulder. "Let's walk through this time, okay?"

Walter laughed. "Exactly what I was thinking, as usual."

"Okay, Larry," she said, closing her eyes. "Hit it!"

The lead rider dismounted and withdrew an ornate box from her saddle pack. Her companions pulled off their hoods, revealing young men with closely cropped hair and neatly trimmed beards. The host of male riders stayed put on their black stallions as the restless animals snorted and pawed the ground in a wide circle.

A peal of thunder rumbled across the sky. Black clouds churned overhead while drops of rain pelted Billy's hair and shoulders. He sniffed the air. The odour of sweating horses and ozone filled his nostrils; no hint of a scentser.

The lead knight walked toward Billy, presenting the box in her outstretched arms. "We have come so that we may put an end to this dangerous exercise, young Arthur." She set the box on the grass, opened it, and pulled out a gold crown trimmed with rubies and diamonds. She then dropped to one knee, extending the crown with both hands, her head bowed. "Our order recognizes you as the true Arthur, and we have the power to enthrone you in your rightful place." She lifted her head, raindrops streaming down her cheeks. "I am one of your New Table knights, and this garrison is your escort. With you and Excalibur leading the way, our full army will overwhelm any opponent." Bowing again, her voice trembled with passion. "We have long . . . awaited your coming, Your Majesty, and we hope . . . hope you will join our righteous crusade to free the captives in the seventh circle." She looked up once more, her lips quivering.

Bonnie grabbed a fistful of Billy's shirt and tightened her grip. Billy sat up straight and cleared his throat, attempting a deep, formal tone. "Speak plainly. What is in the seventh circle, and why should I join you? I'm already on a quest to rescue prisoners."

"To rescue prisoners, my lord?" A bright smile spread across the knight's face as she rose to her feet. "God be praised!" She spun in a slow circle and lifted her hands. "God be praised!"

The other knights shouted in unison, "God be praised!"

Another peal of thunder rolled across the plain.

As intermittent raindrops continued to splash all around, the knight stepped up and kissed Billy's hand. "Your Majesty, perhaps our journeys have intersected by divine providence, and you will use your mighty sword to break the chains of our comrades. They are the ones who will conquer your enemies and bring you to power."

Billy pulled his hand away. "No offence, but I think I'll stick to the original plan. Sir Patrick doesn't want us to join up with any New Table knights."

The woman stepped back, a wounded expression on her face. "I . . . I understand completely, my lord. You are wise to make decisions based on advice from those you trust." She bent down and placed the crown back in the box. A tear trickled down one cheek. "How long, my king, have you known Sir Patrick?"

Billy wiped the dripping rainwater from his eyes. "Professor Hamilton has known him for years, and he trusts him. That's good enough for me."

A weak smile crossed her face. "Professor Hamilton is indeed a trustworthy man, and you do well to honour him, but sometimes the most honest men can be fooled." Her face turned downward into a stern frown. "Your professor has trusted Patrick to watch over you in this realm while he journeys to London, but Patrick has already abandoned his post."

Billy doubled the horse's reins around his hands. "How do you know all that?"

She slid the box back into the saddlebag. "I will show you." Raising her hands high, she walked down the path in the direction Billy and Bonnie had been travelling. The line of horses parted, creating a gap about twenty feet wide. With a wave of her hand, the exposed canopy of sky and meadow blurred, creating what looked like a rectangular movie screen. The fuzzy picture sharpened, now showing a valley surrounded by mountains. The valley was rocky and dry with white bones littered across the floor. At the edge of the cliff overlooking the valley, a solitary man hid behind a crag in the mountainside. The view port seemed to zoom in on the man until his upper body filled the screen. Sweat poured down his face in narrow streams, and his hands shook as he gripped the edge of a boulder.

"It's Sir Patrick," Bonnie whispered.

"Yeah," Billy whispered back. "And he's all worked up about something."

"He is supposed to be watching you from his mansion," the knight went on, "but here he stands in the seventh circle, waiting for you to arrive. He heard about our entry into the circles, and now he wants to prevent you from rescuing our comrades." The screen went dark and then disappeared, allowing the grass and sky to return to normal.

The knight strode forward and extended her hand. "Come with me and take your rightful place on the throne of England. You pulled Excalibur from the stone, did you not? You have been called to rescue prisoners, have you not?" She took Billy's hand and kissed it again, her voice rising with enthusiasm. "Come with me, my lord! Let us break down the prison walls! Let us loose the chains of our powerful allies!" She bowed her head. "And I, myself, will stand at your side as your royal guardian when the crown of England is placed on your brow."

Bonnie let out a low laugh and whispered again. "Some royal guardian she'd make. That New Table knight in your bedroom tried to kill you."

"I heard that, Miss. Young Arthur's attacker was one of Devin's clan, traitors to our order. We could not control his lust for dragon blood, and he has met his fate, as has the young man who sought to harm the king." She paused and drew in a deep breath. "But you need not trust me. When we get to the seventh circle, you will meet someone I know you will trust."

Billy tried to speak, but his voice cracked. "Who . . . ahem . . . who is that?"

"Your father, the great dragon, Clefspeare, has entered the seventh circle, and he will vouch for us and give you instructions himself."

Billy put his hand on the long scar running across the edge of his scalp, the remains of a wound from his battle against Devin and Palin. It still sparked a twinge of pain, but it also carried a reminder of how his father, in dragon form, rescued him from the dark knights, risking his own life in the process. He nodded his head ever so slightly. *I trust my father now . . . I guess.* Bonnie's tense fingers clutched his shirt again. He reached back and gently grasped her wrist. *Bonnie's right. Even if I can trust my father, I definitely don't trust these riders.*

Billy straightened his back and gripped the reins with both hands. "You can keep your crown. That's not what I came for anyway. I'll just take my chances on my own."

The knight's smile vanished, her hair and cheeks dripping. "Far be it from me to force our king to take his throne." She guided her horse close to Billy and extended her open hand. "At least take this token. It is a symbol of our order that will grant you easy passage from one circle to the next as you accomplish your goals in each one. If anyone tries to interfere with your journey, this gift will be a dangerous weapon. I still have hope that you will fulfil your calling when you reach the seventh circle."

Billy reached for the token, a brooch with a golden insect on top, a shiny, winged beetle. He enclosed it with a loose fist. "I guess it's worth a try." As soon as the words came out, Bonnie's fist pulled on his shirt again, this time with more force.

"Very good," the knight continued. "Just stay on the path, and the passage beetle will transport you to the third circle in due time."

A bright flash enveloped the riders, and they dissolved into shards of light. The riderless horses shrivelled, their bodies shrinking toward the ground. Seconds later, they morphed into a circle of brown, scruffy rats scurrying in the grass. Billy's horse shrank too, and he and Bonnie slowly descended until their feet rested on the ground. Their horse, now a black rat, scrambled away between Billy's shoes and joined the others.

Walter jumped around in the grass like a tap dancer on a hot griddle. "Rats! I'm surrounded by rats! Where did the horses go?"

Ashley pulled off her hood. "There's Billy and Bonnie. C'mon!" She ran to their side. "Billy? Can you hear me? Bonnie?"

Walter tried to grab Billy's arm, but his hand passed through it again. "Nope. We're still just a couple of ghosts."

"Listen! I can hear them talking. Can you?"

Walter leaned over next to Billy's mouth. "Yeah. Barely. I think they're talking about something in Billy's hand."

"Shhh!" Ashley scolded. "Listen!"

"I don't think we should use it," Bonnie said. "We'd be asking for trouble."

"I guess you're right." Billy held out his palm. Fresh drops of rain pelted his skin and splashed on the beetle. "With this weather, it would be nice to get to the next circle the easy way, though."

Bonnie pushed wet strings of hair out of her face. "Maybe, but I don't trust that woman. I don't believe what she said about Patrick, and I sure don't want anything to do with that beetle thing."

"I know what you mean, but I didn't feel any danger from her."

"Maybe we shouldn't count on your danger sensor at all. It didn't work in the cave."

"That's true, but it sort of worked when I was near the dragon. I guess we shouldn't trust it while we're in the circles."

Bonnie rubbed her hands across her dampening sleeves. "Everything feels wrong here, like we're being watched. Let's just get rid of that bug and get going."

"Suits me." Billy threw the beetle on the ground.

Walter ran to where the scarab lay in the grass. He leaned over and tried to touch it, but it jumped into the air, beating its wings furiously. With a buzz-saw pitch, it darted back and forth like a crazed dragonfly, hovering for an instant and spitting blue sparks. With a final zip around Billy and Bonnie, it dug its razor teeth into Billy's neck and hung on like a tiny pit bull.

"Arrrgh!" Billy grabbed at his neck, yanked the bug off, and threw it to the ground. With a heavy stomp, he smashed it with his heel, and a splash of blue sparks rose around the edges of his shoe. He slapped his hand over the wound and dropped to his knees, his face locked in a painful grimace.

Bonnie squatted at his side and laid her hand on his back. "How bad is it?"

Billy removed his hand from the wound. A smear of blood painted his fingers. "You tell me. I can't see it."

Bonnie touched his neck. "There's only a little blood. It's just sort of oozing. But your neck's turning real red and swelling up fast."

Billy laid his palm on his forehead. "I don't feel so good."

"You're turning white as a ghost." Bonnie pushed on his chest. "Lie down! Now!"

"What? Why?"

She pushed harder, and Billy relented, laying his head back on the wet grass. She lifted his legs and supported them on hers. "Just stay calm and breathe easy."

"I . . . I think I'm going to faint."

Ashley pulled on Walter's shirt. "Anaphylaxis!"

"Anna who?"

Ashley paced back and forth waving her arms. "He's going into shock! We've got to get them out of here!"

Walter lifted Apollo. "Has Apollo had time to charge up?"

"We have to give it a try." Ashley pushed her hair back and pulled her hood over her head. "Billy may not last very long."

Walter drew his own hood from his cloak pocket. "But he can't walk. He won't be able to go through the portal."

"I think they're closer to the portal now, maybe right on it."

Walter shook his head. "No. I have the spot marked. They're still about ten feet away."

Ashley knelt at Bonnie's side. "Let's try what we did in the cave again. Maybe Bonnie will see the portal and drag Billy through."

"It'll be tight," Walter said, pulling his hood on. "We asked for a small window, remember?"

Ashley twisted her hood to align her eyes with its sockets. "We don't have any choice." She pulled open a latch on Apollo's base. "When you're set, push the button on the inside."

"Gotcha!" Walter hustled to the portal location, Apollo in hand. "Ready?"

"Let's do it!"

Instantly a blinding flash erupted from its centre and painted a new portal, smaller, about the size of a wall poster. Walter waved frantically at Ashley. "Let's go, girl!" Folding in their arms, they squeezed through one at a time. A few seconds later, the light dispersed into a million fleeing dots.

With torrents of rain pelting her head, Bonnie cried out. "God, help me! I think he's dying!" She bowed her head, shivering in the cold downpour.

A light flashed. Bonnie jerked her head up. Ahead on the path a shining rectangle hovered just above the flowers, casting a glow across their drenched petals.

Bonnie thrust her arms under Billy's shoulders, grunting, "C'mon. Let's get you out of here." Walking backwards, she dragged his body across the slick grass, flapping her wings to give more lift. She glanced behind her. She was almost there, but the window was shrinking.

She reached for Billy's scabbard and drew out Excalibur, igniting its sparkling glow with her touch. Tucking the hilt under her chin, she allowed the blade to rest across her shoulder, then regripped Billy's armpits. She slid him again, now only a foot from the flashing window. A buzz of electricity tingled on her scalp as she leaned back into the opening, the sword's blade leading the way. With a surge of strength, she lunged, but her hands slipped away, and she fell into the flashing window . . . without Billy.

Walter pulled off his hood and blinked away the black spots. Ashley knelt next to his feet and rubbed her eyes. The familiar woods surrounded him, oaks and beeches standing tall and the same gorse bush squatting at his side. He still clutched Apollo tightly in his grip.

Ashley yanked off her hood and jumped up, her head swivelling from side to side. "They didn't come! Billy needs medical help, fast!" Ashley snatched her computer and yelled. "Barlow! What do you see?"

"From what I could tell, an insane bug flew all around, a nasty little beast with blue spittle. William must have fallen to the ground. Miss Silver knelt at his side and looked very worried. Then, I saw a flash brighter than the sun, and all I have been able to see since the flash is a frightful storm boiling in a dark sky."

"You can't see Bonnie at all?"

"No, Miss. I have not seen her since the flash of light."

Ashley smacked her jaw and tilted her head upward. "Karen!" she yelled. "Are you there?"

A string of muffled words spilled through the computer speakers. A second later, Karen's voice became clear. "Sorry, I was eating a pickle sandwich. It's rilly dilly good."

"No time for comedy," Ashley barked. "Listen! Do you have an epinephrine kit handy?"

"Sure. I never leave home without it. But I guess since I'm home—"

"Get it, now!"

"Okay, okay. Don't be such a grouch." Karen's voice drifted away. "I have an EpiPen right over here in the . . ."

"Ashley, if I may interrupt."

Ashley let out a huff. "What is it, Larry?"

"Are you considering a cross-dimensional material collection?"

"Yeah. Do you have a better idea?"

"Not exactly. Your idea is valid. Apollo is able to receive a transmission, but its light creation engine is almost fully discharged. You can't go over there to administer the medication, not for at least three hours."

Ashley let out a groan. "He'll be dead by then!"

"Why don't you just send the kit?" Karen asked. "Bonnie knows how to use it. Remember? She watched you use one on me last month when I got stung in the garden."

Ashley snapped her fingers. "Right!"

Walter picked up Apollo and gazed into the inner glass enclosure. "Does Apollo have enough power to send it?"

"We only need a tiny portal." Ashley tilted her head up again. "Larry, how long before Apollo can open a small portal, say, six by two inches?"

"Approximately one minute."

"We were like ghosts in that dimension," Ashley said, "like the transfer wasn't complete. What will happen to the EpiPen?"

"When you and Walter transferred, my calculations relied on your estimates of the portal locations, and the results were off by the error in the estimation. If you are in the exact spot, I can be more precise."

"We have it pinpointed this time, but Billy wasn't right next to it. We'll have to hope Bonnie sees it somehow. Karen, put the EpiPen in Larry's transfer box."

"Already done!"

Walter set Apollo down next to the gorse bush. "The portal opened right here, but how can you send something to another dimension that we don't have with us?"

"Remember the button Karen sent when we were on the plane? Matter can be transformed into energy and energy into matter. Larry will analyse the hypodermic needle and its contents and send the atomic structure to Apollo. Apollo will grab available light energy and transform it into matter based on the atomic coding. Then we'll send the kit to the other dimension in a small portal."

"But the button didn't come across right. It just crumbled."

Sir Barlow's low baritone voice groaned from the computer. "The clouds in the scene are no longer moving! Could William have stopped breathing?"

"Larry!" Ashley shouted. "Give the adhesion factor a boost, and let's do it! Now!"

Apollo's platform light flashed on, and green sparkles danced inside the glass enclosure like iridescent pixies. The forest grew darker, as though a thick cloud had passed in front of the moon. The green sparkles swirled toward Apollo's base, like iron filaments flying toward a magnet, until a slender tube resembling a felt-tipped marking pen appeared.

Apollo's light flashed off. Ashley put her hand over the switch. "Let me do it on manual, Larry. Is it charged?"

"No."

"Give me a countdown!"

"Five seconds."

"Is the medicine thing solid?" Walter asked. "Will it crumble?"

"Three seconds."

"No time to test it. It's got to go!"

"One second. . . . Now!"

Ashley pressed the switch. A small flash erupted inside Apollo's glass case, and a portal window opened an inch from the EpiPen. Ashley tilted Apollo, and the pen rolled through the opening. It disappeared just before the tiny rectangle of light closed in a splash of sparks and a thin puff of smoke.

CHAPTER

AVALON

Bonnie fell through a shaft of light and landed on her back, her wings crumpling painfully under her. Still slipping on the wet ground, she grabbed Excalibur's hilt and scrambled to her feet. Except for the pouring rain, everything was different. The endless field had disappeared along with the trail of flowers. Now she stood amidst clumps of short, wiry grass next to a gloomy marsh. A motionless body lay just a few feet away, its feet extending into the dark water.

"Billy!" She rushed to his side and laid the sword on the ground. "You came through! But I know I dropped you!"

Billy gave no answer. His pale face didn't even twitch as rain streamed across his closed eyelids.

"Oh, no!" Bonnie laid her palm on Billy's cold cheek. She clutched a fistful of his shirt, her eyes darting around and her whole body shaking. "It can't be! It just can't be!" She lifted her head and wailed. "Nooooo!" With her fingers tightly intertwined, she cried out, "Help me! Oh, please help me!"

White sheets of rain snatched her voice and threw it against the ground. She pressed her ear against Billy's wet shirt and listened for signs of life. It was no use. Claps of thunder and beating rain flooded her senses, overwhelming any other sound.

She raised her head, lifting her eyes again toward the boiling black clouds. Water dripped from her soaked hair, joining with the merciless, needle-like raindrops to blind her tear-filled eyes. She yelled into the tempest with a breathless, pitiful wail, "God! . . . Please help me! . . . He's . . . he's dying, and I don't . . . I don't know what to do!"

A bright light flashed. She jerked her head around, wondering if another shining window had opened, but the desolate beach stretched out as far as she could see. She glanced at Billy's chest. Something new was there. It looked like a pen or a tube of lip balm, a familiar object but somehow out of place. She laid it in the palm of her hand and read the label out loud. "EpiPen?"

With a jolt of recognition, she gripped the pen in her fist, a fragile smile pushing through her trembling lips. She removed the cap and jabbed the needle into Billy's thigh, leaving it there a few seconds before pulling it out and massaging the entry point. With tears flowing to join the countless raindrops streaming down her cheeks, she breathed a silent prayer, joy and terror mixing in an emotional whirlpool. It was a miracle! A true miracle! It just had to work!

Walter kicked the gorse bush. "Not knowing what's going on is driving me crazy!"

Ashley glared at her computer. With one hand on her hip she shouted into it. "Barlow! What do you see now?"

"Ahem. The young lady lunged . . . toward William's chest, I think. Then she stared at something in her hand before lunging again, toward William's lower body, I believe, though I am not certain. The storm is still fierce, and I think she's crying, but she has a smile on her face."

"Any sign of change in Billy?"

"Aha!" Barlow cried. "The scene is moving! William must be breathing!"

Walter pumped his fist. "All right! You can't keep a good man down!"

"And now," Barlow continued, "Miss Silver is embracing William. I see his hands moving, and he seems to be rising."

Ashley smiled. The computer shook in her hand, her voice quaking to match her tremors. "That's . . . that's great, Barlow." She swallowed hard and whispered. "Keep us informed." She gazed at the ground for several seconds, a grim half-frown growing on her stiff lips.

Walter ripped a leaf from the bush, careful to avoid its thorns, and tossed it to the ground. Ashley's glistening eyes revealed hints of a deep mystery within, and he wished he could read her mind for a change. She was obviously determined to help Billy and Bonnie, but her options were running out as fast as Apollo was losing power. He held Apollo up and gazed into its glass enclosure. "It looks smoky in there, and the glass has some kind of sooty stuff on one side."

Ashley shook herself from her reverie and opened a door on the enclosure's side, letting out a stream of greenish-black smoke. "Larry, give me a status report on Apollo."

"I sent a status request, and Apollo responded rather tersely. To put it in blunt terms, Apollo's energy reserves are bankrupt. Even the ambient recharging unit is unable to function. You'll have to plug it into an AC source if you want to create another portal, if it's possible to do so at all."

Ashley caressed Apollo's cylindrical top as if it were a kitten's head. "Is Apollo too sick to read the light sources?"

"The data I'm receiving from Apollo at this moment are comparable to the readings I recorded earlier. Therefore, I assume Apollo is still able to accurately read input."

Ashley closed Apollo's door, then studied her tiny computer screen, her brow furrowing more deeply. "There's been a change. The signals are showing a large spatial displacement."

"You mean, they've moved?" Walter asked.

"Exactly. I don't think they're anywhere around here." She pressed a button on her computer. "Barlow! Another status report!"

"Yes, Miss. William is now standing at the edge of a lake or perhaps a marsh. I see an island, about a third of a mile from shore, but it is shrouded by mist. It seems that the storm has passed and left quite a fog behind."

"A big island?" Ashley asked. "Is there anything on it?"

"I cannot tell the size because of the mist. There is a building on top of a hill, perhaps a church or a monastery. I see a steeple at its apex."

"And the circles on the floor in your location? What do you see?"

"One moment."

Ashley tapped her foot on the forest floor. After several seconds, Barlow's voice came through the speakers again. "In the south-east circle, a light shines in the eyes of a dragon in a mirror, while another light pulses in the eyes of a man wielding an axe."

Ashley's lips almost disappeared into her tightening face. "An island with a church on a lake, Walter. What do you make of that?"

Walter closed one eye and scratched his head. "Well, supposedly this whole mess is about Arthur, so I do have a thought."

"Well, out with it. You think I'm a mind reader?"

"Don't get so bossy. I just thought you'd be way ahead of me, as usual."

Ashley's shoulders drooped. "Look, Walter, I'm sorry about getting on your nerves with the mind reading, and I know I've been barking a lot, but I'm wound up tighter than a drum. I can't help spitting out what I'm thinking sometimes."

"It's okay," Walter said, waving his hand. "Anyway, I was thinking the island sounds like something the professor mentioned. Do you know much about Avalon?"

"Just from storybooks. Any idea how we can find out for sure?"

"Let's ask Barlow. Maybe he knows something about it."

Ashley spoke slowly into the computer. "Barlow . . . do you know anything about . . . Avalon?"

"Oh, yes, Miss. I have seen the great tor from afar, from Camelot's zenith, but I never ventured any closer. Strange happenings. Witches haunt its regions."

"From what you remember, does the island you see in the window look anything like Avalon?"

"It's so foggy . . . it's hard to tell. But . . . it could be."

Ashley's mouth dropped slowly open, and the colour drained from her face. Walter prodded her elbow with his finger. "What's up? You look like a seasick ghost."

"I was just thinking about the King Arthur story." She grabbed Walter's cloak sleeve. "Don't you remember? Avalon is where Arthur went to die!"

Morgan folded her hands and rested her chin on her knuckles. "The scarab's bite was not meant for young Arthur's neck, Palin. Whoever interfered with our plans almost ruined everything, but they have also helped us by keeping the boy alive."

Palin stared at the brilliant oval shining over the abyss, his arms slack at his side and one hand clutching several pieces of paper. "How did the medicine appear? Did you do that?"

"I am powerful," she replied, shaking her head, "but not that powerful. If not for this coincidence, young Arthur would have died, and all would have been lost." She balled one hand into a fist and smacked her palm. "The plan was exquisite. A desperate boy brings a dying girl to Avalon and freely gives her into my healing hands, a host brought to my doorstep by special delivery. But now that the beetle missed its mark, we'll have to deal with the princess in another way."

The lady swung her long dark skirt and made waltzing steps toward the abyss. With a wave of her hand, the oval screen went blank. She turned her back to it, leaning against a boulder with her head down. "Our plans have been executed perfectly until this mishap." She looked up at Palin, her eyes flashing red. "The dragon girl's influence is too strong. Her spiritual eyes are older than the boy's, and he wisely follows her counsel. He is an exception to his gender's usual stubbornness."

"She's the one you want," Palin said, gripping the hilt of his sheathed sword. "Just give me the word, and I'll bring her to you."

Morgan banged her fist against the stone. "No!" She stood up straight and began pacing around the cave. "The girl will not be a fit vessel for me unless he delivers her body freely. Since her adoptive father gave her into the boy's care, he is now her surrogate protector. I am certain when he gives her to me, the transfer will be binding."

"To borrow a modern cliché," Palin said, "that will be like asking a mother bear for her cub."

Morgan halted, pressing her hands together as if praying. "Yes . . . yes, I know." She rubbed her palms against each other, and a cylinder of black clay appeared between them. Within seconds she moulded it into the shape of two humans conjoined at the hip. "Deception always dances on a fragile stage, Palin." She extended her hands, and the clay models hovered over her open palms. Although they stayed in place, the two figures seemed to be creeping along like a pair of dark shadows walking through a scary forest.

Morgan blew softly on the taller figure, and its edges slowly dripped like melting wax. "The boy's energy must be eroded before he enters the final circle." As the melting continued, the fusion point between the figures thinned to a sliver. "Each success will drain his resources, and he will be more willing to listen to other voices. If the girl helps him too much, he will not come to me in the weakened state I'm hoping for." The dark figures popped apart, and Morgan snatched them out of the air, gripping one in each hand. With a squeeze of her fingers, the taller one vanished in a puff of smoke. She caressed the smaller figure, lifting it close to her face and closing her eyes. As she breathed, the black clay evaporated, and its dark vapours rushed into her nostrils. Morgan's eyes glazed over as she let out a satisfied sigh.

Palin shuddered. He shifted his feet, barely able to keep his eyes on the morbid sight. "If your goal is to wear him down, then why were your knights offering him a crown and a quick exit?"

Morgan fluttered her lashes, and her eyes sharpened again. "They only appear to be helping him," she said, walking toward him. "Their gift offerings come from the tops of temple walls, and they open a gate of passage that is not the shepherd's."

Palin scowled. "You're just like Merlin. You spout your uppity poetry to make normal people look bad."

She grabbed his face, squeezing his cheeks together with an iron grip. "Oh, Palin, you are such a simpleton." She released him, patting one cheek like she would a baby's. "I speak and act in ways beyond your ability to perceive, and young Arthur has the same blindness. So I will simplify it for you. If Bannister had taken the easy path, he would not have been a worthy king, and he would likely have been unable to set the Watchers free. The rightful heir, the true son of Arthur, would never abandon his mission, so I expected him to turn down our offer. You see, I need him to suffer through the circles. His victories will come at great cost to his strength, but in those empty triumphs he will gain unwarranted confidence. That will be his undoing when the real trial begins."

She pointed at the papers in Palin's hand. "Did you examine them? Is it her handwriting?"

"Yes. They're the ones I took from her room back when I was alive."

She took the pages and strode toward the cave entrance. "Good. It's time for me to return to my island and separate the prince from his princess." She stopped, turned back toward Palin, and flashed a wicked smile. "I know you're dead, my dear, but you can still watch the screen for me, can't you?"

Palin glared at the ground. "I'll watch it."

"Good. If you see anyone you don't expect, you know what to do." She waved her arm toward the oval again, and an image of an island appeared. "I think I know who is interfering with my plans. Number three should have placed his scentsers in the fifth circle by now, so I will send him to collect the Stalworth girl. She will soon suffer Shiloh's fate."

Ashley held the cell phone to her ear, walking swiftly through the woods with Walter close behind. "C'mon, Professor, answer the phone! You were there just a little while ago!"

"This is Charles Hamilton. Evidently, I am either on another call or I have travelled out of range. I am confident, however, that I would like to receive your message. You see, I only give my number to people who are dear to me so—"

Ashley scolded the phone. "Prof, just get to the beep!"

"—in keeping with proper etiquette, please leave your name and number at the sound of the beep. There is no need to tell me the time of the call, because the messaging system provides me with that information."

Ashley rolled her eyes and whispered, "Patience . . . patience."

"Thank you for calling. . . . Beeeep!"

"Professor! It's Ashley. Listen. Walter and I need to get to Avalon. You said you were going there, but we don't know where it is, and we don't have a car." She bit her lip and glanced up at the full moon. "I guess that's it. You have my number. Give me a call ASAP. It's super urgent."

Walter caught up to Ashley's side. "Why don't you just ask Larry where Avalon is?"

Ashley slowed her gait. "It's a legend, not a hard fact. Would a computer have that kind of data?"

"Maybe Larry can do a search on the Arthurian legends and give us the closest possibility. Prof would have told us if he was going somewhere far."

"Good point." Ashley halted at the edge of the forest. "Larry, do a reference search and give me the best option for the location of Avalon."

"`Search completed.`"

"Great. What did you find?"

No answer.

"Larry?"

Karen's voice sounded from the speaker. "Uh-oh!"

Ashley crossed her arms. "Karen, I don't like the sound of that 'uh-oh'."

"Well . . . Larry's got a little problem. His response started scrolling on the screen, but his voice synthesizer blew out, which, if you ask me, isn't so bad. But then the screen froze. Think he's stuck in another code loop?"

Ashley grabbed a handful of her hair and pulled it back. "I doubt it. It's been weeks since the last one. Read me what the screen says and throw the diagnostic switch. I'll bet it's hardware."

"The stuff on the screen looks like a list of book titles," Karen replied, "but the last line says, 'Glastonbury Tor' ."

"Glastonbury?" Ashley repeated. "Isn't that where we are?"

Walter nodded. "Yeah. We're just a few miles outside of the main part of town."

Ashley aimed her penlight at her wet sneakers. "We can walk if we have to."

"How can you walk to an island?"

"We'll cross that bridge when we come to it." She punched a few keystrokes into her handheld computer.

Walter peered over her shoulder. "Whatcha doin'?"

"I'm checking an encyclopedia." She angled the computer screen toward Walter. "Here it is – the Glastonbury Tor."

"That hill with the tower?"

"Yeah," Ashley replied. "Kind of weird looking, but it's not an island."

"It wouldn't take much to make it an island," Walter said, putting his finger on the screen. "If this flat area flooded, that hill would stay dry."

Ashley nodded slowly. "Might be a possibility. Larry would be able to find the water levels back in the sixth century." She tilted her head upward. "Karen, any report on Larry?"

A muffled voice replied through the computer speaker, sounding far away. "I think you're right about the hardware. I smell a fried circuit."

Ashley raised the computer to her ear. "I can barely hear you. Where are you?"

"I crawled through Larry's access panel. I'm looking at the CPU array near the middle of Larry's innards."

"Watch out for the auxiliary power supply."

"I'm watching."

Ashley kicked through the damp grass. "What's your guess? Is he going to be up soon?"

"Can't tell yet. I'll let you know when I have a clue. At least the communicator's still working."

Ashley let her arm fall to her side. She flicked off her penlight and dropped it into her cloak pocket. "There should be enough light. I'll bet we can find that hill."

Walter squinted toward the dim horizon. "Is that it?"

Ashley followed his gaze and smiled. "Yep. Just like in the picture."

"Whew! It looks pretty far."

Ashley slipped her thumbs behind the straps and took off with a quick, marching stride. "Then let's start hoofing it, double time."

With Apollo in hand, Walter sprinted to catch up, then walked briskly at Ashley's side. "What'll we do when we get there?"

"We'll look for a portal. The grid on my computer may be able to locate Billy and Bonnie once we get close, but without Larry's help, and with Apollo on the fritz, we could be on a wild goose chase."

With the rain lessening to a light shower, Bonnie grasped her hair and wrung out the ends. "It's really a double mystery – you coming through the portal even though I dropped you, and the medicine showing up in the nick of time. I can't figure it out."

With a hard shake of his head, Billy slung a shower of droplets from his hair. "This place is so weird, I don't even want to guess."

Bonnie watched Billy squeeze water from the hem of his long-sleeved shirt. The moisture made the material cling to his arms and chest, defining his muscular frame. His months of training had chiselled an admirable physique. Bonnie quickly averted her gaze and folded her hands behind her back. "Can you walk?" she asked, glancing back through the corner of her eye.

Billy lifted his legs up and down, testing his weight on each one. "Yeah. I think so." He touched the wound on his neck with his fingertips. "That thing packed a wallop!"

Bonnie turned toward him again and ran her fingers across his cheek. "Your face is swollen. Did you know you were allergic to insect bites?"

"I never have been before, but I don't want any part of that bug again!"

Bonnie gazed across the mist-covered marsh. "I don't see a path anywhere, but Joseph said we wouldn't always be able to see one. Do you think we're supposed to go to that island?"

Billy pointed at a small, castle-like building on top of the island's hill. "I see a light in that second-storey window. Since we're supposed to follow the light, we might as well head for that one."

"Sounds good to me."

Billy scraped sand from the seat of his trousers and stepped toward the edge of the water. "I wonder if it's shallow enough to wade. We're already wet."

Bonnie stepped to the edge, letting the toes of her shoes dip into the marsh. "True, but the water's dark, and with all the vegetation, there's no way to tell what's lurking underneath." She expanded her wings and gave them a quick shake, throwing a shower of tiny droplets all around. "Why don't I just fly us there?"

Billy lowered his head. "No. . . . I don't think so."

"Why not?" she asked, waving a wing toward the island. "I've carried you before, and it's only a few hundred yards."

"Yeah, but I weigh more now, and with the sword on my back, it would be too clumsy."

Bonnie bit the edge of her tongue, trying to think of a way to soften her words. "Billy, that sounds like an excuse to me. What's really on your mind?"

Billy flashed an uneasy grin. "Am I that transparent?"

Bonnie cracked a smile and nodded.

"Well, it *would* be pretty dangerous to carry me, but . . ."

"But what?"

"Well, I know you came along to be my helper, but it doesn't feel right for you to be carrying me around. If anything, I should be carrying *you* around."

Bonnie crossed her arms over her chest. "Be careful what you wish for."

Billy clutched the wound on his neck and winced. His pupils expanded, and a light glaze coated his eyes. With his swollen cheeks turning crimson and his legs buckling, he seemed ready to topple over.

Bonnie clutched his biceps. "Are you okay?"

"Yeah, I'm fine." He widened his stance, and his eyes cleared up. "What were we talking about?"

"Me carrying you across the marsh."

"Oh, yeah. Well, I don't want you to get hurt. I really am a lot heavier now, especially since I'm all wet."

Bonnie pressed her fists on her hips and held back a grin. She decided not to touch Billy's "all wet" remark. "All right. I guess while you wade, I'll fly." She pointed toward the island. "I'll wait for you right there on the shore next to those two trees. Okay?"

Billy kicked at a clump of grass in the sand and nodded. "Okay. I didn't mean to make you mad or anything. I guess that bug zapped my brain." He lifted his head. "I'm sorry."

Bonnie smiled. "It's okay. I'll see you in a few minutes. If you run into trouble, just give me a yell." She launched into the air and zoomed low over the water. With the cloud cover keeping the marsh dim, and swathes of wiry grass coating the surface, there was no danger of seeing her reflection and violating the mirror warning. She watched for movement, ready to warn Billy if any strange creatures were hiding in the swamp. Raindrops pelted the inky stew, painting overlapping circles across the watery expanse. All else remained quiet.

Bonnie landed gently on a strip of soft grass that painted a skirt of green around the island. She found the trees she had pointed out to Billy and stood under one of the overarching boughs. The branches dangled a host of fist-sized apples just above her eye level, their red skin covered with streams of rain. She reached out and caressed one.

As soon as her fingers touched the peel, an image of the fruit tree in the first circle flashed into her mind. She jerked her hand away, remembering Joseph's warning that nothing would be fit to eat in the circles. So far, that was no problem. The meal Joseph provided had been plenty.

Bonnie shook her wings out again and gazed over the marsh. Billy's form laboured through the mixture of muddy water and weeds, his elbows raised high and his knees poking out of the water with each step. His slow progress told her that he was probably trudging through mud at the bottom.

Bonnie chewed on her bottom lip. *I wish he would've let me carry him.* The apple swung just above her head like a pendulum, and she bumped it with her fist to keep it going. *Is it pride? Or maybe it's a spirit of independence. Maybe he's just trying to learn how to get along on his own, without me to help him all the time.*

A coarse, squawking voice broke the silence. "He's a stubborn one, isn't he?"

Bonnie pivoted, searching the shore. The grass on the island beach stretched in both directions without a hint of movement. "Who said that?"

The voice croaked again. "I did. Look up."

Bonnie searched the branches of one of the apple trees. A large raven perched on the highest limb. Fluttering its wings, it hopped from branch to branch until it reached a thin offshoot just above the swinging apple. "I can see why you love him, Bonnie, but he has that stubborn male ego. If he doesn't learn to master it, he's going to get both of you in trouble."

Bonnie narrowed her eyes. "Who are you? How do you know my name?"

"I am the mistress of this island, and I am your friend."

"If you were a friend," Bonnie replied, clenching her fists, "you wouldn't be insulting Billy."

The bird cackled. "Oh, no! Not an insult . . . an observation. I am his friend, too. Should I not try to help a friend see his shortcomings? Should I not point out faults that may endanger his life?"

Bonnie pulled down on the branch and let go, flinging it, and the raven, straight up. "Then point out his faults to him. Telling me is just gossip."

The bird fluttered down to a lower branch, its eyes glowing a ghostly yellow-green. "So you say, my dear, but I beg to differ. It is not gossip if I'm trying to save his life."

A surge of heat rushed into Bonnie's cheeks. "Save his life? What do you mean?"

"His pride has endangered him, and it will be his death if he doesn't change." The raven flew down to the ground. It stretched out its wings, and its entire body elongated. Its feathers changed into a flowing gown, its head grew long, silky hair, and its face became thin and angular. Within seconds, a tall, slender woman dressed in black stood at Bonnie's side. She held out her hand. "Come with me," she said, her voice deep and silky. "When William nears the shore my guardian serpents will attack. I have a boat. If we hurry, we can reach him in time."

Bonnie unfurled her wings. "I'll fly to get him!"

The woman grabbed her wrist. "No! The serpents can stretch ten feet into the air. They'll grab you, too. I am their mistress. They will not attack my boat."

Bonnie jerked back but couldn't pull free from the powerful grip. "Let me go, or I'll scream!"

The lady snapped her fingers. A plume of bone-coloured vapour rose from her palm. With a wave of her hand, she fanned the cloud into Bonnie's face. "Be silent!" she growled. Her grip twisted, wrenching Bonnie's elbow. "You're coming with me!"

Bonnie's throat constricted. She couldn't scream. She could barely even breathe. Still caught in the woman's grip, Bonnie stumbled along at her side as they hurried down the shoreline. She tried desperately to wave at Billy, but would he understand her warning signal? And what did this evil raven have in store for her? Would Billy be her next victim?

Still marching briskly, Ashley turned up the speaker volume on her computer. "We're here, Sir Barlow. Did you say something?"

"William and the maiden have separated. She flew away, but I cannot tell where. William seems to be wading toward the island."

Walter wrinkled his nose. "Separated? That's got 'bad idea' written all over it."

"I'm with you, Walter." Ashley pressed a button on the computer. "Sir Barlow, I'm going to try to get a reading on their location again. Just pipe up whenever you see something new."

"Pipe up, Miss? I'm afraid I'm not familiar with that idiom."

"Your pipes are your vocal chords – your voice. Use it."

"Yes, yes, of course."

Ashley glared at the computer. "The signal's weak, but I think we're getting close." She held the device up against the horizon with the tor as a backdrop. The tower at the peak loomed in the darkness like a lonely sentry. A rising mist encircled the base of the tor, making the hill look like an island at sea. With the city lights casting an eerie glow across the fog, the tower resembled an abandoned lighthouse at the end of an elevated cape.

When Ashley's cell phone rang, she jumped. The computer slipped from her hand, and Walter lurched forward, snatching it just before it hit the ground.

Ashley smiled and grabbed the phone from her belt. "Nice catch, buddy!" She glanced at the number on the tiny glowing screen and pressed the phone against her ear. "Professor! We've been trying to call you."

The reply was scratchy, indecipherable. Ashley covered her other ear with her palm. "Say that again?"

"Cellular service . . . unreliable. . . . meet . . . tor."

Ashley squeezed her eyes shut and raised her voice. "You want to meet at the tor?"

"Yes . . . get . . . transportation."

Ashley's voice rasped as she shouted into the phone. "We're already on our way, not more than a mile or so from the base of the hill."

"Excellent. . . . with Apollo . . . Understand?"

Ashley wagged her head. "No, I don't understand. But we have Apollo. I think we can get to the top of the tor in about twenty minutes. We'll meet you there. Okay?"

A static buzz sounded from the earpiece.

"Professor?" Ashley shook the phone. "Professor?"

The connection fell silent.

Ashley snapped the phone shut and clipped it to her belt. "I don't know what's going on." She retrieved her computer from Walter. "My cell phone's showing that there should be a strong signal."

"Think it was another phoney call?"

Ashley shook her head. "I doubt it. They must know by now that we know about the phoney call, so it wouldn't make sense for them to try it again."

"True. But do they know that we know that they know that we know? Maybe they would try it again, because they know that we know it wouldn't make any sense."

"Stop it!" Ashley said, covering her forehead with her hand. "You're making me dizzy!"

Walter held out Apollo. "Wanna fire up our friend here and see what's cooking in the electromagnetic stew?"

"Yeah, but let's do it on the move." Ashley marched forward again and pressed two keys on her computer. "Okay, Walter. I'm ready. Wake up Apollo."

Walter pressed a button on Apollo's base and carried the unit like he would a handful of eggs. "Is it working?"

Ashley stopped and stared at her screen. "Amazing!"

Walter halted and cocked his head to get a look. "What? What's amazing?"

"The other portal areas were like pinholes that we had to punch our way through."

"Yeah. So?"

"If these readings are right, then this place is a hole the size of a meteor crater. It's like an interstate highway into Hades."

CHAPTER 13

Ascending the Tor

Billy pulled his foot from the sticky mud, making a loud, wet, vacuum sound in the ankle-deep water. The marsh should have been easy to wade, but the soft mud underneath swallowed his feet. Yes, it would have been easier to soar across the marsh in Bonnie's arms, but it wouldn't have been right. She was a great helper, and her advice never seemed to fail, but how could he use her as a crutch? This was his mission – his test. If she just carried him through the circles like he was her glass-eyed Teddy bear, he'd just be along for the ride. He had to do some of this himself!

Billy halted and took a deep breath. Light rain washed against his face as his shoes sank a few inches into the mud. He was about halfway across, and Bonnie stood under a tree on the other side. He pushed on into a deeper section, his gaze alternating between the water in front of him and Bonnie standing on the shore.

A woman dressed in black suddenly appeared next to the tree. She grabbed Bonnie by the wrist and ran along the island's shore until they disappeared around a bend that led into a cove. Billy pumped his arms and launched his body forward, pushing through the mud like a madman. Whoever that woman was, she looked like trouble!

As he struggled on, a wide ripple broke the water's surface near the shore. He planted his feet and slowed his breathing. Something was out there, and with his sense of danger still hibernating, he wasn't sure if he should plough forward or not.

Another ripple. Two more. Billy edged backwards, slowly pulling a foot up and placing it into the mud behind him. The water began to boil, curls of scaly flesh splashing to the surface and disappearing again underneath.

Snakes!

The boiling water moved toward him. Billy backed away another step, then two. A head popped up above the surface, its mouth open wide and lunging, dual fangs stretching out in attack. Billy yanked Excalibur out of its scabbard and swung the blade in one quick motion. He lopped the serpent's head from its body, sending its thick coils writhing in the marsh.

Another snake struck from the side. Billy dodged its fangs just in time. Two more attacked from the front. He swung his sword, neatly slicing one in half and hacking a deep gash in the other. The wounded serpent splashed in the shallows, its oozing purple blood mixing into the dark, soupy water.

Six ugly heads surfaced, protruding from the water like submarine periscopes. They approached from differing angles and skimmed along the water – fanged speedboats with glowing yellow eyes. Billy's heart thumped. Could he stop them all? He drew back his sword, but before he could strike, something jerked him out of the water, something with enormous strength. He landed with a thunk on a wooden surface, his legs flying upward and slinging muddy water in all directions.

Billy rolled to a sitting position. He was in a canoe! With Excalibur still in his grip, he braced his hand on the side and pulled himself upright on a bench. A slender woman sat on the other bench, her long black dress spattered with mud.

He wiped a smear of mud from his eyes. "Who are you? Where's Bonnie?"

The woman's voice crooned like a bedtime lullaby. "One question at a time, my friend. Which shall I answer first?"

Billy slid Excalibur back into his scabbard. "Where's Bonnie? Were you the one who took her away?"

She nodded, her eyes wide and sparkling. "Yes, young Arthur. I led Bonnie to a safe place on my island. She is quite well."

"Why do you call me Arthur?" Billy kept his eyes on her while taking off one of his shoes.

The woman waved her arm, and the canoe instantly moved toward shore, skimming slowly over the grass-covered water. "I am Morgan Le Faye, half-sister of King Arthur. I call you Arthur, because I sense the spirit of my brother in you, the same courage and combativeness that he displayed. You see, I carried the king to these shores many centuries ago in this very boat. But he has long since moved beyond my outer gates to his final resting place."

The boat ran aground on the grassy shore. Morgan stepped out so lightly it seemed that her bare feet didn't even press down the grass. She offered Billy her hand.

"I can make it." Billy lifted his leg over the boat's side and lumbered into ankle deep water before sloshing onto shore with his shoe in his hand.

Morgan let out a low laugh. "Must you always do things the hard way, Billy Bannister?"

Billy jerked his head up. "How do you know my name?"

Setting one finger on the bow, she drew the boat farther onto the shore. "Sir Patrick and I have discussed your coming. Although I disapproved, he delayed your mission for months. You see, I have waited many years for my land to be reborn, so I wanted to hasten your arrival and fulfil Merlin's prophecy."

After dumping a marble-sized mud ball from his shoe, Billy leaned over and slipped it back on. "What do you know about Merlin's prophecy?"

She spread out her arms, smiling like an excited schoolgirl. "Merlin and I walked these very shores together." Stepping over to an apple tree, she lifted a book-sized stone that leaned against a protruding root. "He carved his prophecy on this tablet when we last saw each other." She held the stone out for Billy to see as she recited the words out loud, her voice lilting in a melodious chant.

In circle three a raven lurks,
Deceiving all with words of scorn,
Yet two can find a hidden door
To take them to a land reborn.

She opened her eyes again, and her gaze riveted Billy in place. "I will show you the hidden door, and we will restore my land together."

"We?" Billy asked. "I think the two are supposed to be Bonnie and me. If we had stayed together, I'm sure we would have found the door."

Morgan laughed again. "Your interpretation is so short-sighted. Bonnie is a noble, valiant young lady, but she is not the subject of this prophecy." She put the stone back in place, then took Billy's hand. "You are to come with me back to your world to take your crown as the king of England and restore your authority over the lands that rightfully belong to the throne. But first we must rescue a group of warriors who will enforce your will on those who resist." She straightened Billy's shirt around his shoulders, and her hands lingered, touching his cheek with a tickling caress. "Your face appears to be swollen. Are you sick?"

Billy pressed his finger on his neck wound. "Some weird bug bit me. I guess I'm allergic to it."

She pulled his hand away and examined the bite, running a finger along the welt. "A passage beetle. Very dangerous."

"Yeah, I found that out."

"It is worse than you think. A passage beetle sprays an electromagnetic charge that allows its bearer to pass through the gates of each circle of this domain, but its bite creates unpredictable symptoms."

"Symptoms? Like what?"

She caressed his shoulder with her fingertips. "Are your muscles usually so well defined?"

Billy raised his arm and rubbed his triceps. "Well, I *have* been working out."

She twirled a lock of his hair at the back of his neck. "And your hair. Is it usually this long?"

Billy reached back and felt his hair. "That's weird. I just got it cut a couple of weeks ago."

Morgan's hand joined Billy's at the back of his head, and she caressed his fingers. "The bite has altered your metabolism. Destructive symptoms are possible – skin lesions, spontaneous bleeding . . . or worse."

Morgan's fingers felt like icicles. Billy bent down to tie his shoe, glad for an excuse to pull away from her touch. "You know so much about it," he said, looking up at her. "Is there a cure?"

"Yes, here on my island. You may have heard the legend about my healing powers. King Arthur was gravely wounded by his enemies at the Battle of Camlann, and I brought him here to nurse him back to health. After some weeks, he returned to Camelot, but forty months later, he came back to this island because of another mortal wound, and he lived here for many years. When he finally died, I became trapped, and now, since I can only serve the true king, only Arthur's heir can set me free." Morgan yanked Excalibur from Billy's scabbard, her eyes glowing with a fiery yellow hue. She held it vertically in front of her chest, letting the blade divide her feverish stare. "Take your throne, give me my freedom, and I will give you your cure."

Billy shot back up and grabbed Excalibur's hilt. For a brief second, Morgan resisted his pull, but she finally let go with a sigh. Billy glared at her, keeping a firm grip on the sword as he rested it on his shoulder. "I read that you just wanted to steal Excalibur from King Arthur."

"Steal?!" Morgan breathed a low, "tsk, tsk," shaking her head. "Oh, you are so ill informed. I am the Lady of the Lake, the one who gave Excalibur to Arthur in the first place. I am incapable of stealing. Part of my curse is that I am not able to keep anything that is not freely offered to me."

Billy loosened his grip on the hilt. "Look. Sir Patrick said I was supposed to find prisoners here and release them, not become a king in my own world. I'm here on a mission, not some quest to get a crown."

"Of course your mission is unselfish," Morgan said, placing her hand on his chest. "You have a noble heart."

Billy took a quick step back, and Morgan folded her hands at her waist, bowing her head. "I am under a curse only you can break, Billy Bannister." She looked up again, her eyes imploring. "Set me free, and I'll help you take the throne of England. Together we'll spread your goodness to all of humankind."

Billy's swollen cheeks grew warm. "Just . . . just take me to Bonnie. I want to talk to her."

Morgan bowed her head again. Her voice dropped off to a whisper. "Are you not able to make decisions without her counsel?"

"It's not that. Bonnie's my friend, and she's here to help me. I should be with her."

Morgan nodded, her hands still folded. "Very well. I will take you to her."

Bonnie sat on a low bench in a dank cell. Although the cube-shaped room was well lit by a lantern on the wall, she couldn't see much. There simply wasn't anything to see – only six-foot-high walls with a few corner cobwebs at the top to break the monotony of the damp, stone cage.

She felt like a fool for getting within arm's reach of that raven-witch. She had a feeling the dark-hearted woman was up to no good as soon as she started bad-mouthing Billy. Why didn't she just zoom away for help? She could have stayed away from the serpents. . . . If there really were any serpents. But, no; like a gullible little girl, she listened to a smooth-talking seductress and ended up locked in a dungeon.

And what would that witch do to Billy? When she bolted the door on the prison cell, her words were so creepy! *"Don't worry, dear. When young Arthur delivers you to me, then we'll become much better friends. We'll be so close, no one will be able to separate us."*

Bonnie let out a huff. *Friends with that ghoulish fiend? Forget it!*

But there seemed to be no way out. Bonnie had slammed her shoulder against the door at least five times, but it wouldn't budge. There was a grate in the ceiling for ventilation just inches above her head, but her fingertips could barely slide through the holes, and she had already given it a hefty shake. It was as solid as a rock.

Bonnie rubbed a sore spot on her forehead. The raven's goon, a burly, blonde bombshell of a woman, had really let her have it with the flat side of a sword. She was dressed like a knight, complete with chain mail and shield.

Bonnie put her chin in her palm. "Okay, Bonnie, time to think. You've already prayed a dozen times, so that's covered. But what am I forgetting? I'm supposed to be Billy's helper, so I shouldn't be in this predicament." She blew through her lips, making a low trumpeting sound. *This place is a house of cards compared to the candlestone. There's got to be a way to escape, but it sure isn't obvious.*

Bonnie poked her finger into the earthen floor and scratched away a thin layer of mud. The dirt underneath was dry and sandy except for one trail of moisture that disappeared into the layers of sediment. She dug a little deeper with the toe of her hiking boot. More moisture.

Hmmm. I wonder.

Switching from her toe to her heel, she kicked the dirt and gouged out a divot. She then tunnelled down several inches, following the moisture trail. Finally, she struck something solid, a metal grid.

Bingo! A drain!

Dropping to her knees, she excavated the damp soil with her hands, piling the mud up against the walls. As she scooped up another handful, her fingers brushed a smooth wood surface and a metallic lump.

Aha! A hinge. And where there's a hinge, there should be . . . Yes! A handle!

Bonnie grasped the handle and heaved open a trapdoor. The hatch stood on its hinges, partially shielding the lantern's light and casting a shadow across a hole about two-foot square. A miniature avalanche of surrounding dirt cascaded into deep blackness.

Bonnie knelt again and lowered her head near the opening, cupping her hands around her eyes to allow them to adjust to darkness below. *Nothing. Nothing at all.*

Muffled voices reverberated through the walls of the stone cage. Bonnie lifted her head. Footsteps clumped over cobbles, and the voices grew louder.

"You'd better not. Morgan won't like it," a woman's voice said. A jangle of keys clanked against iron.

"I'm just going to have a little fun with the girl," another woman said. "What Morgan doesn't know won't hurt her."

Fun? What could she possibly want with me? Does she consider it fun to beat me up?

Bonnie lowered her legs into the hole and braced herself on the sides. Folding her wings in tightly, she slid her body down, hanging on to the edges with her fingers.

She gasped. Cold darkness. A floorless chasm into nothingness . . . or worse.

The prison door creaked open. "What are you doing down there?!"

Bonnie closed her eyes and let go.

Walter pushed open a wooden gate. On the other side a long series of paved steps ascended a grassy hill in stages – about fifteen steps, then thirty feet of gently inclining concrete, then another dozen steps, and so on. A few sightseers ambled down the path toward them.

Walter rested Apollo on the top of the gate as he held it open for Ashley. "Looks like it's all uphill from here," he said.

Ashley marched right past him, hitching up her backpack and eyeing her computer. "We'd better get going."

After bending around the right side of the hill, the path curved back, and they laboured to climb the steepening grade. They clambered up several hundred feet, then stopped at a graffiti-laced wooden bench. Ashley sat on one end, and Walter plopped down on the other. As Walter caught his breath, he glanced over his shoulder to read the words etched in the weathered grain on the backrest, "No Religion – No Problems."

Walter set Apollo on the bench and rubbed a finger over the letters. "I wonder what they have against religion around here."

Ashley shrugged her shoulders. "Probably the same thing I did not too long ago." She spoke into the computer. "Barlow. We're near the top of the tor, and I need a status report. Can you hear me?"

Walter closed one eye. "You used to be against religion?"

"Shhh!"

A young couple walked by hand in hand, heading down the slope. When they passed out of earshot, Ashley brought the computer close to her face. No sound. She studied the flashing dots on the screen. "Very strange," she whispered.

Walter tried to get a peek. "What?"

She pointed toward the entry gate at the bottom of the hill, now shrouded in darkness. "Billy is right about there, where we came in, but Bonnie . . . ," she twisted her body and pointed behind her, toward the top of the hill, "is somewhere in that direction, maybe a hundred yards away."

"What's so strange? We knew they were separated."

Ashley rested her elbows on her thighs and cradled the computer with both hands. "Well, the vortex of light energy here may be messing up the data, but I don't think Bonnie's in Billy's circle at all. Her signal is way different now."

Walter peered at the upward sloping hill, barely able to see the outline of the tower at the tor's peak. He turned back and rubbed his hands across his upper arms. "This place creeps me out. Let's get to the top and find the professor."

"I know what you mean," Ashley said, throwing her hair back with a shake of her head. "You can almost feel the energy swirling around, like we're in the middle of a light-warping blender."

Walter grabbed Apollo and started up the slope with a bound. "Well, let's get this over with. I don't want to be part of an electromagnetic smoothie."

Morgan led Billy to a luxurious sitting room, complete with two plush sofas, a fireplace, and an oriental rug laid across a shiny marble floor. An afghan covered the back of one sofa, showing off an interwoven design – a red dragon breathing a plume of yellow fire. The other sofa sported a similar afghan with a white dragon spewing what looked like streams of ice.

A dog lay on the rug, its triangular ears perking as Billy walked in. Its coat shimmered, ribbons of orange, green, and purple rippling across its short hair as if a rainbow were petting it from head to tail.

Morgan twisted her head back and forth. "Bonnie's not here! Where could she have gone?"

Billy stepped toward a long hallway. "Could she have—"

"Elaine!" Morgan shouted. She pulled a braided cord that hung from the ceiling, and a loud bell gonged three times. "Come here at once!"

A lithe woman dressed in flowing silk ran into the sitting room, gliding gracefully on her bare feet. "Yes, Sister?"

"Where's Bonnie? I left her here just a few minutes ago!"

Elaine eyed Billy, then quickly looked back at Morgan. "She has chosen the wide path, Sister, just as you feared."

"The wide path?" Billy repeated.

Morgan glared at Billy. "I thought she was wiser than that."

"Wiser than what?" Billy asked, spreading out his arms. "What's the wide path?"

Morgan placed her hand on Billy's cheek, but he turned his head and stepped back. She balled her hands into fists and rested them on her hips. "I gave your princess the option of waiting for you or venturing out into a deeper circle. We call it the wide path, because so many have gone there before her. It seems that she has chosen to join them."

"I don't believe it. She would've waited for me."

Elaine gave Billy a half-curtsy and presented a folded piece of paper. "She left a note, Your Highness."

Billy snatched the note and flipped it open, reading silently. *"Billy, don't worry about me. I can't explain right now, but I have to go on. Trust me."* He refolded the note and repeated the closing phrase in his mind. *Trust me.*

His chin fell to his chest. "It's Bonnie's handwriting."

Morgan raised her hand again to caress Billy's cheek. This time he didn't step back. "Oh, Billy, I know you don't trust me yet, but you will learn. When the armies of the earth tremble at your feet, you will believe in me and my power."

Billy caressed the folded note with his thumb. "If you have so much power, why are you a prisoner here? Why do you need me?"

Morgan reached for Excalibur, but Billy twisted away. She turned her back to him, crossing her arms over her chest. "I brought the original Arthur here," she said, "and he went on to the eternal realm. I can only leave here permanently if I return to your world with the king." She spun around abruptly and extended her arm toward Excalibur. "Freely give me the sword, and I will prove to you my power. It was mine long before I bequeathed it to Arthur, before that thief, Devin, took it for himself, before it was restored into your rightful hands. Yet, in my hands, I can show you all its glory in unmasked brilliance. You have yet to see a fraction of its power."

Billy took one step back and planted his feet firmly. "No." He nodded toward the room's entry. "Just show me which way Bonnie went. I have to find her. If I decide you're really the prisoner Sir Patrick was talking about, I'll come back for you."

Morgan grasped Billy's upper arms, leaned forward, and kissed him tenderly on the cheek. "Very well, young Arthur. I will trust in my king's faithful word." She turned and gestured for him to follow. "I will show you the wide path." She stepped quickly down a corridor on the other side of the sitting room.

Billy hurried to catch up, and Elaine followed, staying a few steps behind. After making two left turns into adjacent halls and then a right that led down a long staircase, Morgan stopped next to a door at the bottom landing. The only light in the stairwell came from the door at the upper level. Billy halted halfway down the stairs. Elaine stood at the top and closed the door.

In the darkness, Billy heard Elaine's feet press the creaking stairs and then felt her soft breath as she drew close . . . too close. Morgan climbed back up, hemming Billy in. He drew in shallow, rapid breaths. He wanted to grab Excalibur and call upon its light, but Morgan's soothing voice washed over his senses.

"Young Arthur, do not fear us. We draw our bodies close to prepare you for the next circle. We will pray for your mission, and our prayers are best uttered in darkness."

Shivers erupted across Billy's skin. *Darkness? Why does a prayer need darkness?* As a gloomy heaviness filtered into his thoughts, his mind begged for light. Any light! He grabbed Excalibur and jerked it out. The sword's beam burst forth, filling the stairwell with brilliance. The laser ripped a hole in the centre of the lower door. A blast of air rushed up the staircase, pouring in from the gash.

Morgan and Elaine pressed against Billy's body. Loose, wrinkled skin covered their hideous faces, like skulls with leathery masks. Morgan's black lips drew close to his cheek.

Billy gasped and pushed Morgan out of his way. He threw open the door at the bottom of the stairs and dashed through, but his foot found no floor on the other side, and he fell headlong into an empty expanse.

Walter passed through a tall archway and stood at the centre of the tower's hollow base. "Well, we made it, but I guess the professor's gone AWOL."

Ashley kept her eyes on the handheld computer, her lips and cheeks taut. "It seems so."

Walter set Apollo on the ground. "You look like you swallowed a porcupine. What's the matter?"

Ashley held the screen where Walter could see it. "Billy's in a new circle, but it's still not the same one Bonnie's in. Their signals are way different."

"Explain something to me," Walter said, raising a finger toward the flashing dots. "If Billy's belt is the one spewing out a signal, then how can you keep track of Bonnie if they're separated?"

Ashley gave Walter a blank stare.

"Wow!" Walter exclaimed. "You're as stumped as a lumberjacked forest!"

Ashley pulled the computer back and turned away. "I guess you're proud of that, aren't you?"

Walter ran around to face her again. "Hey! Chill out! I'm on your side. Don't be so defensive."

Ashley pointed at herself. "*I'm* defensive? You're the one worried about me reading your mind all the time." She turned again, shaking her head. "If you were on my side, you'd cut the jokes and grow up."

Walter spread out his hands. "Grow up? Ashley, listen to yourself . . ." His voice trailed away. "Hmmm . . ."

"What?" Ashley said, tapping her foot. "Couldn't think of a joke?"

Walter grabbed his cloak and stripped it off. "No. I just thought of something." He tossed the cloak on the ground, closed his eyes, and took a deep breath. "I do feel different."

"Different? What are you talking about?"

"I think the cloaks are messing with our minds. Try taking yours off."

Ashley dropped the backpack and laid the computer on top. Walter helped her pull the cloak over her head, then rolled it up in a ball and held it against his chest. "Feel different?" he asked.

Ashley blinked her eyes and straightened her shirt. "Yeah . . . I think I do."

Walter stuffed the cloaks into the backpack. "Let's save them. They still might come in handy."

"I wonder why it affected me more than you."

"I don't know." Walter kept his eyes on the cloaks as he pushed them deep into the pack. "Every time you barked at me, I felt something, like I was supposed to bark right back, but I just ignored it."

After Walter helped her remount the backpack, Ashley took his hand. "Walter," she said, her voice pierced with remorse, "I'm sorry for being such an ill-tempered know-it-all."

Walter absorbed her heartfelt apology like soothing balm on a wound. "And I'm sorry for cracking too many jokes," he said softly.

Ashley drew him into an embrace and whispered, "Thank you for protecting me."

Walter held his hand above her back for a moment, then patted her gently. "Any time." After a few seconds, he pulled away. "Now we have to find Prof."

He retrieved Apollo and exited the tower through its tall archway, scanning the area as he walked across the tor's summit. The lights of Glastonbury cast a glow all around the eerie outcropping, illuminating a rising mist that dressed the hill in white raiment.

He walked to the tor's highest point and peered over the edge. Here, a second access trail descended a steeper slope than the one he and Ashley had climbed on the opposite side. The narrow path veered right, then plunged toward a faraway gate. Walter let out a quiet whistle as he surveyed the hill's expansive, tiered slopes. Flat strips of grass wrapped around the entire tor, creating wide terraces, like huge stair steps for a giant who might want to bound to the top. He tried to count the steps, but the mist veiled the lower levels. *Seven maybe?* he thought.

A beam of light flashed in a thicket at the base of the hill. Walter froze in place. Was it his imagination? No! There it was again! He kept his eyes on the spot and called out, "Ashley! I see a light!"

Ashley sprinted to his side. "Where?"

Walter pointed toward the dim outline of a group of trees. "It was right there, but I don't see it now."

"Let's check it out." Ashley stomped down the hill, choosing an especially steep part of the slope.

Walter hurried to follow, sliding at times to keep from pitching forward. He caught up with Ashley, then took the lead. "I think I still have it marked."

They tromped into the thicket, their feet crunching on a carpet of decaying debris. Walter kept his voice low. "With all the noise we're making, whoever was here probably knows he has company."

Ashley shone her penlight all around and whispered, "If we don't see the professor soon, we'll just have to shout for him." The thin beam darted from tree to tree. "What's this?" She steadied the light at a two-foot-high rock wedged into the ground at the base of an oak tree. The tree's low-hanging limbs seemed to stretch out and form a cradle.

"It's just a stone of some kind," Walter said.

Ashley bent down and placed her hand on the stone's smooth top. "No. It's carved, and it has writing on it." She shone the light on its flat face. "Born – 1948. Last seen at this tree on October 31, 1964." Ashley turned toward Walter. Even in the dimness he could see her alarm. "Walter! It's a tombstone!"

CHAPTER 14

The Forgotten City

Bonnie plummeted through cold darkness. She beat her wings, but they caught nothing, ripping through the vacuum in silence. With no air, she couldn't even catch her breath to gasp or scream. Her head pounded. Her skin seemed ready to explode.

Finally, she plunged into a blanket of air, and her lungs drank it in like a pair of thirsty sponges. Her wings pulled against the cool breezes and eased her body slowly downward, allowing her to survey her new surroundings from above.

The sun peeked over the horizon, casting narrow beams through pink and orange clouds. A city lay below – chimneys on low-rising roofs, empty horse carts parked at the sides of roads no wider than a dragon wing, and crates stacked in alleys between densely packed buildings. The chimneys gave no hint of smoke. No lights shone in the homes. No lamps lined the streets of cobblestone.

Bonnie scanned the city for signs of movement. Nothing. Not even hints of trash blowing down the street in the fresh, cool breeze. Each new part of this strange world proved colder than the previous one. Here, in the waking dawn, crisp, biting air chilled her bare hands, so she pulled them inside her warm, fleecy sleeves. Somehow her sweatshirt had dried during her descent.

She settled lower and performed an on-the-run landing in the middle of town. Letting out a long puff of white vapour, she stopped on the cobblestone road and scanned the area, her hands on her hips. The town looked like a cross between an Old West ghost town and a modern English village. Vacant businesses lined each side of the street, ranging from a dressmaker called, "We Are Not What We Seam" to a pub with a medieval-style bottle over the door that carried the words, "Good For What Ales You."

Bonnie whispered to herself, "No wonder it's a ghost town. These puns probably killed everyone." The wind whipped sand around her boots, loose doors creaked on rusty hinges, and dangling signs beat against warped roof lines. She half expected to see a tumbleweed roll by.

A shadow disappeared into an alley – quick, fleeting, like a startled animal, maybe a dog scampering away. Bonnie jerked her head toward the movement. Nothing else stirred. She hustled to a narrow walkway at the edge of the road, glancing up at the sign over the nearest door. "Sahara's Dry Goods." A dusty window revealed empty shelves lining the inner walls and broken crates littering the floor.

She prowled toward the side of the building, creeping nearer to the alley where she had seen the shadow. With her wings stretched out, ready to fly, she peered around the corner.

With the sun still low on the horizon, the sandwiched buildings kept the five-foot gap between them in dim shadows. About thirty yards back, the alley ended at a rough brick wall where stacks of crates reached a third of the way to the roof.

Bonnie bit her lip and took three cautious steps into the shadows. More boxes lined the side walls, ripped open and piled haphazardly, like a broken staircase leading to nowhere.

A stifled gasp squeaked from the wall to Bonnie's left. She crouched, her eyes searching for the source of the sound. She took a long, slow step and reached toward one of the empty crates. With a quick yank, she flung it to the side.

Bonnie slapped her hand against her chest. "A girl!"

Covering her face with a trembling arm, a young woman cowered in a corner created by the wall and a stack of crates. "Get . . . get away from me!"

Tears welled in Bonnie's eyes. The girl, about her own age, wore a tattered, frilly dress, her arm smudged with alley grime. Bonnie reached her hand out slowly, her voice pitching higher and quaking. "Don't . . . don't worry! I'm not going to hurt you."

The girl's frightened eyes peered out from underneath her arm. As she squished farther into the corner, her voice quavered like a shivering kitten. "You're a . . . a monster! Some . . . some kind of bat woman!"

Bonnie quickly folded in her wings, and her voice faltered again. "I'm not a . . . a bat woman. I'm a girl, just . . . just like you." Still in a crouch, Bonnie crept closer. "My wings are just extra. The rest of me is normal."

The girl squirmed back but couldn't slide any closer to the wall. "You're not normal! You have scales . . . like . . . like a lizard!"

Bonnie raised her hands to her cheeks and caressed the grooves in her leather-like skin. She closed her eyes and took a quick breath, opening them again to gaze at the girl. She was so pitiful. Her dress was no more than a rag, riddled with such gaping holes that she had to clutch the ratty fabric with her free hand to cover her exposed torso.

Bonnie tried to swallow a growing lump. “I . . . I don’t know how to explain the scales, but I’m really not a monster. I won’t hurt you.” She extended her hand again. “My name is Bonnie Silver. What’s yours?”

The girl’s lips trembled. “Sh . . . Shiloh.”

Bonnie leaned over slowly and slipped her hand into Shiloh’s. “Will you stand up and talk with me? Maybe we can help each other.”

Shiloh grasped Bonnie’s hand, and Bonnie hoisted her to her feet. Now that Shiloh was standing, the rising sun cast its morning glow on her face. Bonnie recoiled, letting Shiloh’s hand drop. “You look . . .” She swallowed hard. “You look just like me!”

Shiloh’s eyes narrowed under her wrinkling brow, and her voice sharpened, revealing a distinct British accent. “How can you say that? I don’t look anything like you.”

Bonnie gazed at Shiloh’s face – her blue eyes, her small nose, her blonde-streaked hair. She seemed to be a mirror – dirty and reversed – but still the reflection Bonnie recognized as her own. She raised her hand to touch Shiloh’s face, then pulled back and touched her own cheek. “I . . . I haven’t always looked like this. I don’t know what happened to me.”

Shiloh gave a thin smile. She tugged at the shoulder of her dress and clutched a hole closed in front, her face turning pink. “Then we’re in the same boat. I don’t know what happened to me, either.”

The cool morning wind gusted into the alley. Shiloh drew her arms in close to her body and shivered. The hem of her party dress dropped to just above her scuffed knees, revealing scratches on her left calf and blonde hair flourishing on both legs.

Bonnie glanced around. The alley was empty, and the entire street was still deserted. She pulled apart a pair of Velcro fasteners at the bottom of the back hem of her sweatshirt and began pulling it over her head. "Would you like something warm over your dress?"

Shiloh rubbed her bare arms, her gaze fastened on Bonnie. "I guess so."

Bonnie removed her inner shirt, then pulled her outer jersey back on. She handed Shiloh the white shirt and smiled. "Sorry it's not clean."

Shiloh popped her head through the neck hole and pushed her arms through the long sleeves, then hugged herself tightly. "It's nice and warm."

Bonnie straightened out her sweatshirt. "Good. And this will be plenty warm for me. I don't see how you could stand this cold the way you were dressed."

"It's cold, but at least my feet are warm." She raised one of her shoes on its toe, a dark blue sneaker with a "PF" logo on the side. "I'm glad I wore these instead of my patent leathers. They haven't worn out at all."

"So, what's this place all about?" Bonnie asked. "Do you live here alone?"

Shiloh rubbed her hands together and blew on her fingers. Her eyes seemed focused on the street behind Bonnie. "Alone? Sort of. This place is so weird, it's hard to explain."

"Try me." Bonnie made her wings shudder and pointed back at them with her thumb. "It's hard to get weirder than this."

"Yes, that is weird, all right," Shiloh said, nodding. "But you'll see what I mean when the people come."

Bonnie turned her head toward the deserted road. "People?"

Shiloh walked slowly out of the alley and looked both ways down the street, repeating her words in a stretched-out sing-song.

"You'll see." She followed the narrow sidewalk to the front of the dry goods store and sat on a two-person bench. Leaning against the backrest, she folded her slender arms over her new shirt's imprint, a sketch of a majestic lion with block letters underneath that spelled out, "He's not a tame lion."

Bonnie sat down next to her, tilting forward to make room for her wings. "How did you get here?"

Shiloh kept her eyes on her shoes and kicked at a pebble on the walk. "I was going to ask you that. I've never found a way out of this town. Every street hits a dead end."

"I flew here from . . . well, I guess you could say I came from another dimension. I was with a friend of mine, Billy Bannister, but we got separated, so he's probably looking for me now." She gripped her knee, massaging the soreness in an old injury. "I guess that sounds pretty crazy, huh?"

Shiloh picked at a splinter on the bench. "Not any crazier than what happened to me. I was kidnapped and locked in a little room, and I woke up in that alley three days later."

"Kidnapped?! Who kidnapped you?"

"You wouldn't recognize their names. It was a short guy with bad breath and a creepy lady with horrible taste in clothes, nothing but black."

Bonnie cocked her head to one side. "Black?"

"Black and slinky. She reminded me of Morticia from *The Addams Family*."

"*The Addams Family*?"

"Yes. On American television. I visited the States many times, and I enjoyed watching your programmes there."

"That show's been off the air for a long time." Bonnie narrowed her eyes at Shiloh. "How long have you been here?"

Shiloh put her finger on a series of gashes on the back of the bench. "I make a mark when the sunrise gets as far south as the old mill. I think that's when winter starts." She lifted her eyes toward the sun, which was now fully above the horizon. "It's heading that way, so I'm guessing it'll be winter again pretty soon."

Bonnie counted the marks, each group of five set off with a slash through it. "Thirty-nine?" She sat up straight and grabbed Shiloh's shoulder. "You've been here thirty-nine years?!"

Shiloh drew her head back and slid a few inches away. "Probably forty by now. I first noticed the sunrise point a couple of months after I got here, so I didn't start marking it until then."

"Forty years! Whoa! They need to bottle what you're using to stay so young!"

"Pretty strange, huh?" Shiloh placed a palm on each cheek. "I can see myself in the windows, and I still look fifteen."

"Fifteen?" Bonnie tapped her chest with her fingers. "I'll be fifteen in December."

"Really? What month is it now, about October?"

"Good guess. It was the thirty-first when I left England."

Shiloh bowed her head and laughed, but it seemed like a sad laugh. "Well, then . . . Happy birthday to me!"

"Today's your birthday?"

"Yes. If it's the same date in this world, I'm fifteen going on fifty-five."

"Wow!" Bonnie leaned back, her wings cushioning her body. "How do you survive? What do you eat?"

"I eat—" Shiloh sat up straight. "Look! Here comes someone."

A mustachioed man dressed in a black suit and bow tie ambled along the walkway, a cane hooked over his arm. A bowler hat covered his head, and brightly polished leather shoes adorned his feet. His lips seemed to be pursed for whistling, but no sound came out.

Shiloh jumped up from the bench and stood in the man's path, turning back toward Bonnie. "Watch this!" When he came within reach, Shiloh pulled on his sleeve. "Please listen to me, sir! I'm trapped here." The man kept walking, and Shiloh stayed at his side, still yanking on his suit coat. "Can you help me get home? Do you have any food?" The tugging seemed to have no effect on his clothes or his arm. He didn't notice at all.

Shiloh plopped down on the bench and spread her arms over the back. "I call that guy Bat, 'cause he reminds me of Bat Masterson." She winked at Bonnie. "That's another TV show. But it went off the air even before I left."

Bonnie nodded. "I've heard of him."

Shiloh leaned her head against the wall. "I give the people names and follow them around until they disappear." She shrugged her shoulders. "It gives me something to do to pass the time."

"Sort of like being invisible?"

"Yes." Shiloh closed her eyes. "I used to daydream about being invisible when I was little, you know, learn people's secrets, find out if they're talking about you." She sighed. "But it's not all it's cracked up to be."

"You asked him for food," Bonnie said. "Are you hungry?"

Shiloh patted her stomach. "I'm hungry most of the time. There's no real food here, but I do get one tiny meal a day."

"Just one meal? What's that?"

Shiloh glanced at the sun again. "It's almost time. C'mon, I'll show you." She jumped up from the bench and walked to the middle of the street. Bonnie followed, stepping quickly down the road, passing numerous boarded-up businesses, many with shattered glass in their windows and broken doors barely hanging on their hinges.

They arrived at the town's centre circle, in the middle of which stood a twenty-foot-tall statue of a man on a rearing horse. A dog dressed in a red sweater ran around the statue as though he were chasing pigeons. He seemed to bark, but all was quiet. A matronly lady sat on a bench reading a book, a white parasol over her head. She kept glancing at the dog. Her stern face and moving lips scolded him, though no words came out.

At the base of the statue, large, block letters on the foundation stone spelled out the name of the honoured man, "Captain Timothy Autarkeia." Just below the name, an eight-line poem was etched in cursive.

An urban prison lies in six
Where faithful soldiers e'er prevail,
And death will sprout in life anew
From seeds of light within the grail.

The faithful souls will learn the truth
That spoils of earth will never last.
Contentment holds eternal keys
To days of peace that never pass.

Bonnie read the verses twice, then tapped on Shiloh's arm. "Any idea what this poem means?"

"No," Shiloh replied. She flicked her head toward the statue. "Probably something to do with the soldier on the horse." She stepped up to a berm in front of the foundation stone and put her hand on an old-fashioned pitcher pump. "I found this little oasis the first afternoon I was here," she explained. "I use it for drinking water and washing up, but watch what happens." She pumped the handle three times, and a narrow stream trickled from the spout, spilling on a circular plot of grass underneath. Within seconds a thin green stalk erupted from the ground. Growing at a miraculous rate, it stretched up to knee height in less than a minute. The top of the stem sprouted a tulip-sized bulb with five dark green leaves wrapping the outside.

As soon as it stopped growing, Shiloh plucked it from the ground. She dug into the edge of one of the bulb's outer leaves, picking at it with her thumbnail until it peeled away. "The leaves are stubborn, but once I get the first one off the rest are easy." She stripped the last outer leaf and tossed all five into the wind. "Those are inedible," she explained. "When you're hungry, anything looks good, but the leaves are impossible to chew."

Now exposed, the inside of the bulb boasted a white, fibrous substance that looked like a cross between cotton and cauliflower.

"You eat that white stuff?" Bonnie asked.

"Uh-huh. I get one almost every day, but it usually grows only once a day no matter how many times I use the pump. Occasionally it works twice, but if it does, it always skips the next day." Shiloh pulled off a piece and popped it into her mouth, chewing and swallowing in rapid succession. "It's kind of soft, like overcooked beans."

"What does it taste like?"

"Sweet, like honey. Maybe a hint of ginger."

Bonnie watched a short, old man shuffling through the dust, waving a long stick at the pigeon-chasing dog. "Sounds delicious."

"Yeah. Not bad." Shiloh plucked off another marble-sized chunk. "You can have some if you want, but I don't think you'd like the after-effects."

The dog ran to the bench and sat next to his mistress, and they both disappeared, along with the old man. Bonnie turned back to Shiloh. "The after-effects? You mean like gas?"

"Worse. It always makes me sick. My stomach gets real bitter, and I get terrible cramps."

"That's awful!"

"Worse than awful, but I'd starve without it." She tossed the chunk into her mouth and spoke while chewing. "I skipped about two weeks and shrivelled into a scarecrow." She swallowed and picked at the bulb again. "It's all I have to eat, but it keeps me alive." She pushed another white lump into her mouth and chewed while watching a young couple passing by, staring at each other with loving eyes. The woman munched on a plume of pink cotton candy, and the man stuffed his mouth with a handful of popcorn from a red and white box. A kernel dropped to the ground and vanished.

Shiloh swallowed again and sighed. "I have all I really need." As she peeled off the last clump of food, a tiny luminescent bead remained in her palm, pale blue with purple sparkles within. "Oh, that's a pretty one!"

Bonnie leaned over to have a look. "It has a seed in the middle?"

Shiloh raised the bead, allowing the sun's light to shine through. It painted a bluish spot on the cobblestones. "I don't think it's a seed. I've tried planting and watering them, but nothing ever happens."

Bonnie gazed at the sapphire-like globule. "What do you do with them?"

"I save the prettiest ones." She gave the bead a gentle squeeze. "They're mushy enough to poke a hole through." She tugged a string that hung around her neck, then pulled it over her head and handed it to Bonnie. "I put some of them on a necklace."

Bonnie cradled the necklace in her palm. The multicoloured beads painted a kaleidoscope of blending hues on her skin.

Shiloh pushed a scarlet bead along the string with her finger. "Whenever I get a new colour, I put it on the necklace. Would you believe that after all these years, this is my first blue one?" She pulled a needle from her dress pocket. "I found needles in the seamstress shop down the street." She untied the knot and inserted the string through the eye of the needle. "I wish I could find some fabric. I'd patch my dress or make a new one." After poking a hole in the blue bead, she threaded the string through it. "There," she said, retying the string around her neck and letting the beads dangle over her shirt. "That makes forty different colours and shades."

Bonnie lifted the necklace. "I love the way the light makes them glitter. It's sort of like a rainbow, but with lots more colours."

Shiloh pushed the pump lever and let the stream pour over her cupped hands. She splashed her face and pulled up the hem of her shirt to dry her eyes. "Sleeping in that alley gets me dirty, but it keeps me out of the wind. And I can't sleep in any of the buildings. For some reason I have terrible nightmares unless I'm outside. It's worse than not sleeping at all."

Bonnie reached her sweatshirt sleeve up to Shiloh's face. "Here. Let me get a spot." She gently wiped Shiloh's cheek with the cuff. "Where did you come from? Your parents? Your hometown?"

Shiloh gave Bonnie a thankful nod. "Some of the details are fading away, but I do remember that I lived in Glastonbury, England. My father was a teacher, and Mum stayed at home. For all I know, they're both dead now."

As Shiloh talked, Bonnie couldn't help staring at her face. It was like watching a movie of herself, the way her eyes and lips angled with certain words. Shiloh's bright eyes and creamy, smooth skin made her face shine like an angel's. It was so strange. Somehow Bonnie had found her twin, a mirror image, a—

Bonnie's heart thumped. *A mirror!*

Shiloh lowered her brow. "What's wrong with you? Your jaw's hanging open."

Bonnie closed her mouth, pulling her bottom lip between her teeth. She snapped her wings out, stretching them to their full span. "I . . . I really can't explain. I just have to get out of here."

Shiloh dropped the empty stalk to the ground and clutched Bonnie's arms. Her voice pitched into a wail. "Don't leave without me!" Tears welled in her eyes. "I can't stand it anymore!" Suddenly, her eyes turned glassy, widening to panicked orbs. She clutched her stomach and dropped to her knees, gasping with deep, spastic grunts. "Ohhhh! . . . Augh!"

Bonnie knelt at her side and rubbed her back. "Cramps?"

Shiloh nodded, folding her arms tightly against her waist, breathing rapidly. "It . . . it only lasts . . . a few minutes."

Bonnie kept rubbing Shiloh's back, sighing to herself. "I can't understand why God would let you suffer like this." Several people walked past, none noticing the poor girl's misery. A lady in a tight dress sashayed within two feet of their crouched bodies but passed by without a glance. A stocky young man dashed across the street, starting and stopping a couple of times, as if he were dodging traffic. A short, elderly lady shuffled into a bookstore, vanishing just as she passed over the threshold.

Shiloh straightened and took in a deep breath. She stayed on her knees for a moment before lifting her hand. Bonnie stood and helped Shiloh to her feet. "You okay now?"

Shiloh kept her hand pressed against her stomach. "Just a twinge left. I'll be fine."

"Did you see that lady?" Bonnie asked. "She disappeared when she went in the bookstore."

Shiloh rubbed her hands across the shirt Bonnie had lent her, smoothing out the wrinkles. "I didn't see her, but they just go poof like that all the time, and it's usually at a doorway. But there's another door that's completely different. A lot of them end up going through that one."

"Where is it?"

Shiloh gestured with her head. "C'mon. I'll show you." She marched quickly down the road, finally slowing when she reached a teenaged boy carrying a bouquet of flowers in his arms. Shiloh followed him, keeping in step with the boy's careful gait. "I call him Frankie. He's one of my favourites 'cause he always seems so happy. He'll lead us to the main door."

"Don't you know where it is by now?"

Shiloh hooked her arm around Frankie's elbow, but he didn't seem to notice. "The main door is in a different building every day, so I never really know until they find it for me." Frankie took a sudden turn, pulling away from Shiloh's arm, and headed for the walkway. "Looks like he's going to the feed store," she said. "It hasn't been there in quite a while."

Frankie stepped up to a narrow building and paused, cradling the flowers in one arm while digging into his pocket for something. A sign dangled at the roofline, a single rope attached to a corner of a rectangular board that read, "From Bud to Cud Feed Store." Bonnie grimaced. "I wonder who came up with these horrible store names!"

"I know what you mean," Shiloh said, raising her eyebrows. "I'm not even going to tell you the name of the fertilizer store on the other side of town."

Frankie pulled a silver dollar from his pocket and gripped it in his fist, smiling. Light from inside the feed store's doorway spilled onto the grimy porch and out to the street, covering the young man's shoes. He tromped up three steps and marched across the threshold, his body passing through what appeared to be a barrier of liquid light. It seemed to envelop him, raising sparks that fell like fiery beads on the porch. They rolled around, fuming and spitting until they evaporated in puffs of vapour.

Shiloh turned to Bonnie, her eyebrows raised. "Groovy, huh?"

Bonnie lowered her chin and tried to swallow. "Yes. . . . Groovy."

Shiloh waved her hand and laughed. "Don't worry. Frankie's okay. He'll be back tomorrow."

Bonnie took a step closer to the door, eyeing the bright field of energy in the opening. "Have you ever tried to go through?"

Shiloh grabbed Bonnie's wrist and pulled her back. "I wouldn't try it if I were you."

Bonnie spun around. "Why not?"

"Watch." Shiloh ripped a stave from a rotting barrel that stood next to the door and gave it an underhand toss toward the opening. As soon as it reached the space, it sprang back like a shot from a rifle, leaving a trail of sparks behind it.

Bonnie ran to the street and retrieved the stave. One end emitted a plume of thick, curling smoke. "Wow! How did you know not to try it yourself?"

"Because I knew I wasn't like the ghosts." Shiloh took the stave and rapped it on the porch, detaching its smoky ashes. "So after I saw Frankie go through the main door, I tested it with a piece of wood just like this one. Then, about a month after I got here, a man showed up. He was a real weirdo, claiming to be the next King Arthur and that he was here to rescue me." She pointed at the door with the stave. "I showed it to the guy, thinking it might be a way out. Of course I warned him that it might carry a jolt, and I even showed him what it did to my stick, but he puffed up his chest and said, 'Stand back, fair maiden. If the ghosts can do it, I can do it.' " Shiloh rolled her eyes. "I was thinking, 'Fair maiden? What kind of crackpot is this?' But before I knew it, he was walking right into the doorway." Shiloh spread her arms and bulged her eyes. "His body stiffened, his hair stood on end, and he lit up like a throbbing X-ray screen. I could even see his bones! The door shot him like a daredevil out of a cannon, all the way to the street." She smacked her hands together. "He hit those stones and skidded thirty feet."

Bonnie held her breath, unable to speak.

"I ran over to check on him," Shiloh continued. She lowered her head for a moment, then looked up at Bonnie, new tears glinting in her eyes. "He was dead."

CHAPTER

NEW EDEN

Billy flailed in the darkness, hurtling through the void. He tumbled headlong, turning over and over, stretching out his arms. *Gotta . . . catch . . . something! Or . . . I'm history!*

Velvety fingers brushed by his hands, then his back and legs. He felt like he was rolling through soft bushes, being tickled by downy vegetation, yet he sensed no ground, nothing to support his weight. How could he fall and roll like this without getting hurt?

At last his momentum slowed, and he floated to the ground, his shoes gently pressing spongy earth. Feathery probes still prodded him, like sniffing hounds checking out a suspicious new arrival.

Unable to see in the dark, Billy swatted at the annoying tickle. As his hand flicked in front of his face, a dim stream of scarlet light passed by. His rubellite ring! It pulsed slowly, its light shifting between two slightly different shades of red, like a warning beacon atop a radio tower.

Billy grabbed one of the thin, fibrous probes and placed his ring finger next to it. The tickling feeler looked like a fern leaflet, but in the red light the colour skewed. The fern wiggled in his hand, feeling more like a squirming snake than a plant. He flung his fingers open, and the leaflet jerked away into the darkness.

An odd rumbling arose from the ground near his feet, gentle and rhythmic. He stooped and laid his palm on the grass. It felt like some kind of vibrating engine lay buried under the spongy earth, but it had a strange cadence, familiar, yet not like any motor he had ever heard.

He straightened again and rubbed his eyes. A faint glow slowly materialized in front of him, like the dawn of a new day. But the light didn't come from a brightening horizon; it seemed to materialize in the air itself, as though every particle emitted its own radiance.

Billy eased forward, allowing each step to press down carefully. A hose-like object jerked out of the way just before his foot squashed it. Was it a snake? Or maybe something worse?

He glared at the ground. Something down there was breathing . . . panting. His eyes adjusted, slowly recognizing the outline of . . . "A lion!" He leaped backwards, and his foot slipped into a hole. He yanked it up and squatted low. Did it see him? Would it pounce?

The cat lay curled up in a nest of leaflets just inches from where he had been standing. Its head perked up, and its narrow, feline eyes stared at Billy. Rising to all fours, it let out a wide, stretching yawn, baring its dagger-like teeth. With a flick of its tail it turned and followed a narrow path that led to the border of the garden. Billy laid his hand over his heart, trying to slow its rapid-fire drumming.

He reached back, searching for the hole. *Ah! Here it is.* As his eyes continued to adjust, he counted. Two, no, three holes! Three pits the size of manholes plunged downward with only a few feet of solid ground separating them. His fingers ventured a few inches into the middle one. A slight buzzing sensation crawled along his skin. *Could they be portals?*

He rose to his full height and stepped away from the pits. As the dawning glow spread, the scene sharpened. He stood in a field of lush ferns, each frond standing at least elbow high, some reaching above his head. They waved back and forth as if welcoming the new day. A fresh breeze blew over their feathery tops, creating a ripple of bowing heads. When the ripple reached the end of the field, the ferns waved again, as though they loved to celebrate every second of glorious light.

Enormous trees bursting with dark green leaves surrounded the circular field of swaying fronds, each tree nodding in the breeze as if agreeing with the morning adulation.

Stepping lightly along the path, Billy caressed the waving green stalks as he passed by. He could almost hear them purr as they arched their backs like satisfied kittens. When he reached the forest, he found a dome of earth next to a huge oak, a perfect place to rest. He sat and luxuriated in the bliss – perfect temperature, refreshing mists wafting through from unseen fountains, and pleasant aromas riding on gentle breezes.

For some reason his clothes had dried, even his shoes. Everything was comfortable, not an ache or pain, not even a hint of sweat on his skin. Could any place be more perfect than this? The forest stood in flawless beauty – without scar or knot on any trunk, without hint of mould on the myriad, multi-pointed leaves, and without sign of decay on the weed-free turf.

Although the air was saturated with pleasure, Billy felt a gnawing discomfort within. The simple delight of pure rest had pushed out nearly all distractions, but something was wrong. A single word kept prodding his conscience. *Bonnie?* He jumped to his feet and swivelled his head all around. *Bonnie! How could I forget? That witch must still have her!*

He gazed over the field of ferns and then into the forest. Although the tremendous tree canopy should have blocked normal sunlight, he still had no problem peering into the matrix of woods.

Nothing there.

He searched the ground for a clue, stepping to the edge of the ring of ferns. *Am I in another circle? Would this be number four?* He spotted something white where two paths crossed at the centre of the ring and dashed toward it. *Another stone!* Snatching it up, he drank in the words on its face, whispering each phrase.

New Eden lives in circle four,
Beginning new a world thereof,
But paradise is sealed for us
Who suffer now for those we love.

Billy carried the stone back to the edge, touching the fronds with the end of his finger as he passed by. *Eden? Like the Garden of Eden?*

A soft rustle sounded from the midst of the ferns. Billy spun toward it, trying to focus his eyes in the strange light. Someone was walking down the path – a female – petite, dainty, almost nymphean. Dressed in flowing silk she seemed to float through the garden, her bare feet brushing the ground like whispery kisses.

She smiled as she approached, radiant, chestnut hair draping her shoulders over her white gown. A leafy garland dotted with tiny white flowers crowned her head in a circlet. Without wrinkle, her skin told of less than twenty years of life. Without blemish, it told of spotless purity. As layers of thin silk flowed around her body, they accentuated her slender curves, giving hints through the translucent curtain that a girl had recently blossomed into a young woman.

Billy's heart thumped, and he swallowed hard. Was this a dream? He hid the stone behind his back, unsure if he should have left it where he found it.

When the girl drew near, she gave him a formal curtsy, then bowed her head. "Welcome, my king. I have been waiting for you."

Billy cleared his throat, trying to keep his voice from squeaking. "You've been waiting for me? Who are you?"

She lifted her head and gazed at him, her bright blue eyes sparkling. "I am Naamah, the maiden of this new world. Merlin told me you would come."

"Merlin told you?"

She rose to her feet. "Yes. You are the coming king, are you not?" Her eyes moved toward his arms. "I saw you pick up the stone you now hold. I assume you have read the prophecy."

Billy brought his hands forward and laid the stone gently on the ground. "I read it, but I'm not a king. . . . I mean . . . not really. I'm not a real king . . . not like a guy who sits on a throne or anything. I'm just Arthur's heir, and I'm here to rescue any prisoners I find."

"*Just* Arthur's heir?" Naamah let out a short, nervous laugh. "My lord, please do not blaspheme that fair name with such a word."

Billy shook his head. "I didn't mean it like that. I meant that I'm just a guy who's here to help. I don't want a throne."

Naamah's smile slowly dissolved, her eyes welling with tears as she turned her head away. "Then I must continue to wait for the true king. I trust in Merlin's prophecy. My king will come."

"Look . . . Naamah . . . I really am Arthur's heir." He pulled the sword from his back scabbard. "See? I have Excalibur. But I don't know anything about being your king."

She rushed forward and threw her arms around his torso. "Then you are the one I've waited for!" She tilted her head upward, gazing into his eyes. "And not just my king! You are my betrothed. We are to populate this new world and establish your good rule forever."

She laid her head against his chest. The warmth of her body radiated into Billy's, sending prickles of heat across his skin. He grasped her shoulder with his free hand and pushed her gently away. "Naamah," he said, his voice catching, "I . . . I don't think this is part of the plan."

She bent her knee in another brief curtsy. "Please, my lord, I beg your pardon. But Merlin has foreseen it. Do you not know the great prophecy of old?"

Billy slid Excalibur back into its scabbard. "I've heard a lot of prophecies from Merlin, but nothing about being your betrothed."

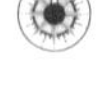

Naamah's brow furrowed. "How strange! Merlin said you would recognize his song."

"His song?"

"Yes. I'll sing it for you." She folded her hands across her chest and lowered her head, as if praying. Then, with a gentle smile, she began singing in a sweet, hypnotic voice.

The child of doubt will find his rest
And meet his virgin bride
To build a world of love so blest
Forever to abide.

For Arthur has a choice in hand,
To choose this lasting bliss
Or fly again to troubled lands
And toil through hell's abyss.

Billy shifted from one foot to the other. "I don't remember hearing that song."

Naamah lifted her gaze again and met Billy's. "You are the child of doubt, are you not?"

He nodded, barely able to blink. "Yeah. I've been told that before."

"Then release your doubts and believe. Why choose the toils of hell when you can live in bliss with me?" She spread out her arms, her eyes sparkling like dew-misted gems. "I am your virgin bride. Do I displease you?"

Billy gulped. "Uh . . . no. It's not that." Her smile penetrated his heart, joyful, yet sad at the same time. With her arms spread, her silky gown pressed closer to her body, outlining her lovely form.

Billy's heart raced wildly. Cool sweat slicked his forehead. He lowered his chin. "No. You don't displease me. I just—"

Naamah grabbed his hand. "Then come with me. I want to show you something."

Billy allowed her to lead him across the field of ferns and into the surrounding forest. What did she want to show him? Maybe it would be better if he didn't see anything more she had to offer, but he wanted to know what she had in mind. Maybe it was innocent. She seemed to ooze innocence, didn't she? He tried to push the battle out of his mind as they hurried past the nodding ferns.

Naamah stopped at a gap in the trees where two holes scarred the dark earth, each about ten feet across and five feet deep. She waved her arm over the expanse. Her smile and gleaming eyes sparkled in the forest's heavenly glow. "Here we are."

Billy set his hands on his hips. "What happened here? A couple of trees got uprooted?"

"Yes. The tree of life and the tree of the knowledge of good and evil once resided here. But this is *New* Eden, so we need only the tree of life. Our union will restore it to this place, and we will live in bliss forever." She pulled the garland from her hair and fashioned the strands into a figure eight. She looped one end around her wrists and extended the other loop to Billy, her face beaming. "Unite with me, my lord, under this eternal covenant, and we will build a new world together."

She stepped up so close, he could smell the sweet fragrance of her hair and sense the warmth of her body. Another aroma drifted past his nose. Something rich and earthy, like the sultry odour of clean sweat, permeated the air. She placed her palm against his chest and rested her head on his shoulder. As she sighed, her gentle breath penetrated his shirt and warmed his skin. "Will you stay with me?" she asked.

Billy's heart raced. A million needles pricked his skin. He swallowed a trickle of saliva through his parched throat. A bursting surge of heat erupted from within and roared through his body. It was too much . . . just too much. He bit his lip hard, and his mind cried out. *Help me!*

The words of Merlin's poem flowed through his thoughts. *But Paradise is sealed for us who suffer now for those we love.*

A hint of paradise lay on his chest, but she was not the one he loved. As far as he knew, she was merely a passion, not a promise. She was a flash of light, not an enduring flame. Her vows rested only on her ability to provide comfort and pleasure, and he could never pledge his heart to a girl who might be nothing more than a phantom.

Taking a deep breath, he grasped her shoulders and gently, but firmly, pushed her away. He reached back and drew out Excalibur, gripping it with both hands and raising it high. As his eyes absorbed its magnificent glow, soothing coolness penetrated his body like fresh rain on a sizzling sidewalk.

He slowly turned away. "I . . . I'm sorry, Naamah. I have to go." He took two steps toward the field of ferns and stopped. "I am prophesied to be the husband of someone else, and I have to find her."

"But if you leave me here without the tree of life, I'll die!"

Billy refused to look back. He could picture Naamah's beautiful, pleading face in his mind, and he knew it would melt his resolve. He began walking again, this time without hesitation, calling back, "Whoever put you in this garden is responsible for taking care of you. I have to move on."

Naamah's voice cried out in lament. "I'll be good to you. I promise." The sound of weeping followed, then sobs. She added, "Don't you like me?"

Billy paused again, but only for a second. Still clutching Excalibur, he marched down the path that crossed the field, his voice rising. "I guess I like you, Naamah, but I have to be true to someone I love. She's worth waiting for." He stopped in the middle of the field. The urge to turn around and see her face tortured his mind, but he knew looking back would be a mistake . . . his last mistake.

He swept aside a cluster of ferns and located the three pits. Full daylight revealed nothing inside. They seemed identical, completely black and apparently bottomless.

Naamah called out. "If you must leave me, choose the portal on the right. It will take you to your beloved. At least I can die knowing you found happiness."

Again, he refused to turn. He studied the pit on the right. Clean, sheer walls plunged into blackness. Rocks lined the middle hole's inner wall, but it was equally black. In the pit on the left, bugs and worms crawled along the walls, but a faint shimmer of light emanated from deep within.

He leaped into the hole on the left, but instead of plummeting, he drifted downward as though sinking into thick liquid. Particles of light erupted from underneath and formed a halo around his body, sending shivers from head to toe. As he sank farther, dazzling brilliance melted away the forest, the ferns, and the freshness of all that was New Eden. In a flash, Billy left it all behind.

A tombstone?" Walter said, crouching over the hewn rock. "What's a tombstone doing way out here in the trees?"

Ashley planted a knee next to a tree root. "Well, I guess it's really a memorial stone. It doesn't look like a body's buried here."

Walter read the inscription. "Shiloh Nathanson, beloved—" He looked up at Ashley. "The rest is worn away."

Ashley shone her penlight beam on the eroded word. "Looks like 'beloved daughter.' I can't read any more after that." She caressed the top of the stone. "Except down at the bottom it says, 'Last seen on October 31, 1964'. That's exactly forty years ago today. I guess a girl got lost, and her parents just marked the place where they last saw her." She flicked off her light and shook her head. "So sad!"

Ashley drew her computer up to her eyes. "And here's something else strange. It looks like Bonnie is now in this exact spot, or at least very close, not more than a few feet away."

Walter lifted the stone to test its weight, then settled it back in its bed of rotted leaves. "Creepy!"

A beam of light swallowed Ashley's feeble ray and washed over Walter's face, blinding him. He fell back on his hands, blinking.

"Walter!" The light jumped to Ashley's face. "Miss Stalworth!"

Walter jumped up. "Prof! We found you!

The professor jerked his flashlight back toward Walter. "Actually, I believe I found you."

Walter brushed a clump of leaves from his knee. "Well, we've been looking for you. Where's Mrs B?"

"I'm right here." Marilyn stepped to the professor's side.

Walter pulled Ashley to her feet. "So why did you decide to come here?"

"I was going to ask you the very same question," the professor replied, making a small circle on Walter's chest with his light. "I am here because I am aware of a certain local tradition surrounding this tor. This is the eve of Samhaim, and if not for the threatening weather, I would guess that many more pilgrims would be coming to the hill for a midnight visit. According to pagan tradition, the veil between the worlds of life and death is at its thinnest on this night. They believe contact with spirits of the dead is most accessible at this place."

"So it's Halloween night, and we're at Spook Central?" Walter asked.

"In a manner of speaking, yes."

Ashley rubbed her finger across her rubellite ring. "Do you believe in these . . . uh . . . pagan traditions?"

"Not as they do, Miss Stalworth. I am a Christian of the old school of faith, the faith of my fathers, which is based on revelation and reason. The religions of the earth, on the other hand, whether Celtic or otherwise, are based on experiences with the earth." He directed his light toward the tower on the hilltop. "I'm confident the locals have seen many strange events here in Glastonbury, but it is their interpretation of those events that actually begets their traditions." He pulled out his pocket watch and flashed the light on its face. "I, of course, have conflicting interpretations."

"Does Sir Patrick believe the traditions?" Ashley asked.

The professor snapped his watch closed. "Patrick has always been a mysterious fellow. He has great sympathy for the Druids in this town, though he steadfastly holds to the Christian faith. I believe he was likely once a Druid himself, so he sympathizes with the local legends concerning other worlds."

"But there is another world," Ashley protested. "We have empirical evidence."

"Indeed. Evidence abounds for such a place. The Bible speaks of Hades, but it is shrouded in mystery. What led me to the tor is the fact that Patrick believed at least one of the stories. You see, on Halloween night, a red dragon and a white dragon are supposed to fight in a chasm somewhere beneath the tor, symbolizing the climactic battle between good and evil. The tale, a fable at best, has a strong connection to the King Arthur legend, because the Holy Grail is said to be hidden in a spring near the dragons' battleground. When it was deposited there, the grail symbolically transformed the spring's waters into the blood of Christ, giving it restorative powers. I thought perhaps Patrick might have come here in search of a gateway into the battleground, believing Clefspeare would be used to fulfil the battle legend."

"Maybe. We know there are other ways to get in besides the window at his house." Ashley pulled her hood out of her pack. "Walter and I used the cloaks and made partial, dimensional crossings in a couple of other places." She hooked her finger through an eyehole and let the hood dangle. "We saw Billy and Bonnie there, but we couldn't communicate with them."

"Were they okay?" Marilyn asked.

"Well . . . they ran into some problems," Ashley replied, "but they made it through. Barlow's been watching them through the portal back at Patrick's house, so last we heard, they're still okay."

Ashley pushed the hood back into her pack. "I haven't tried to contact him for an update lately, because we've been busy looking for you two." She tapped the cell phone on her belt with her fingertip. "I tried to call, but it just buzzes now."

"Mine as well," the professor said. "It seems that communication devices are of no use."

Ashley waved her arm in an arc. "There's some kind of huge vortex of electromagnetic energy here, almost like a swirling tornado. We've seen the pattern on a smaller scale at the places where we entered the other world, so this is probably a bigger portal." She turned the computer toward the professor. "Have a look. Apollo mapped the energy magnitudes to my computer as we crossed over the tor."

The professor reached under his jacket for his glasses, fumbling with them as he slipped them over his eyes. "Am I reading it correctly? It looks like the highest readings are near the top of the hill."

Ashley pointed toward the apex of the tor. "That's what I thought – up near the top on the steeper side. It's not so turbulent down where we are right now. It's sort of like hiding in a ditch to stay out of a windstorm."

The professor pulled off his glasses and slowly folded them. "Then if I understand Patrick's stories correctly, there is probably an entry into the circles at the spot indicated on the graph." He returned his glasses to his inner pocket. "Can you pinpoint that, Miss Stalworth?"

"If we take Apollo up there and walk along the terraces, maybe."

"Then I shall go at once." The professor pulled his jacket zipper a few inches higher and extended his hand toward Apollo. "Walter, may I?" he asked, bowing his head. After grasping one of Apollo's dowels, the professor strode up the dark slope.

Marilyn opened her purse and fished through it. "Ashley, you mentioned contacting Sir Barlow. Is there any way to do that now?"

Ashley shook her hair back. "And check on Billy, right?"

Marilyn withdrew a pair of hair clips and fastened them into Ashley's unruly mop. "I'll fix your hair if you don't mind."

Ashley smiled and tilted her head back. "Sure, go ahead, if you don't mind me talking while you do it. I gotta see if I can get this data to Larry." She tapped her jaw. "Karen. You got your ears on?"

A voice came through the computer speaker, even more faint than before. "Well . . . sort of. I'm yelling at the microphone through the top panel on Larry's cooling duct."

"What're you doing up there? That's ten feet off the ground!"

"I'm soldering a connection on Larry's main I/O board. The lower access panel wouldn't budge so I had to climb into the upper hatch. I couldn't find the ladder, so I piled up your boxes of computer magazines on the ottoman and climbed up. When I finally jumped inside, my pile of stuff tipped over, so I'll have to figure out how to get down when I'm done."

"Be careful. Remember your leg."

"Ashley, I broke it almost a year ago. Give it a rest." The sound of banging metal clanked through the speaker. "And if this works, Larry will be as fit as a fiddle and back to his ornery self in a few minutes."

"Great work!" Ashley called.

Marilyn snapped a barrette closed. "That ought to do it."

Walter interlocked his fingers and cracked his knuckles. "Karen's really handy with the tools, isn't she?"

Ashley grinned. "She's talented all right, but don't go getting any ideas. She's too young."

Walter frowned. "Hey! I wasn't thinking—"

Ashley punched his arm. "It was a joke, Walter. I'm just trying to lighten up. Isn't that what you wanted?"

"Well, yeah. But—"

"Never mind. I'm calling Sir Barlow now." She lifted the computer close to her lips. "Sir Barlow, can you hear me?"

"Yes, Miss. I'm so glad you called. I heard you earlier, but I was a bit distracted. I was unable to answer."

"Distracted? What happened?"

"Three dastardly men in black garb accosted me. They insisted on speaking to you. Naturally, I refused to divulge your whereabouts, and they became a bit agitated . . . Well, more than a bit, I'm afraid. They drew swords and attacked. Fortunately, I was armed, not with my best sword, mind you, but a serviceable one. I dispatched two of the villains with ease, but the third was a stellar swordsman. He used a fake and advance I have never seen and tripped me with a sweep of his leg. With the point of his sword at my throat, he insisted that I, as he put it, spill my guts."

"That's terrible! What did you tell him?"

"Well, I wasn't quite sure what he meant, and I wanted to keep my guts intact, so I just stayed quiet. That's when your call came. He seemed pleased to hear your words."

"Uh-oh. Did I give away our position?"

"Yes, Miss. He laughed and said something about sparing such a great fighter, for which I was thankful, but he knew I would pursue him, so he slashed my lower leg before running from the room like a cowardly cur. While I was bandaging the wound with my sweater, I shouted into this computer, and I'm afraid I called it some unpleasant names in the process, but I couldn't get you to answer."

Ashley's eyes darted back and forth. "It's okay, Barlow. At least we know he's coming. Is the injury very bad?"

"It is merely a flesh wound, Miss. I am able to walk, but chasing the scoundrel was out of the question. I wish he had taken his trash with him. Now I have to dispose of these two hooded hacks."

"Have you been able to watch the screen?" Ashley asked.

"It was difficult to watch while engaging in mortal combat, but I did see William speaking to a young lady, a splendidly beautiful lass, if you will forgive me for saying so."

"Go on."

"She seemed to be making romantic advances, but I can't be sure. She drew close to the camera, so my view was dark much of the time. After the intruder left, I was able to continue my surveillance."

"And . . ."

"Allow me to check again." Ashley, Walter, and Marilyn waited through several seconds of crackling static, each one fidgeting in the cold darkness. Finally, Barlow's voice erupted from the speaker again. "William is now standing next to a chasm filled with fire."

CHAPTER

Something Wicked

Billy rubbed his eyes. The forest and ferns had vanished. Naamah was gone. The brink of a deep chasm lay a few feet away, and a river of flaming lava crept slowly by at the bottom. A field of barren rock spread out behind him, a stark contrast to New Eden's glory. Now, instead of hidden fountains spraying refreshing mists, lava pots spewed orange glops of superheated ash. Slithering snakes replaced purring predators, and the only green he could see was the skin of a hissing lizard perched on a rock, proudly extending his purple dewlap. Rather than the intoxicating aroma of Naamah's silky hair, the air smelled of ozone and coated Billy's lips with a bitter film.

On the other side of the chasm, a lush forest lined the rim, looking almost like a postcard photo from New Eden. Was he now in another part of circle number four, or had he moved to number five? Could this chasm be the gap between the two circles?

A girl dressed in white strolled out of the forest and stood at the opposite edge of the gulf, her head turned downward. She gazed into the gorge, slowly rocking back and forth until she let her body tip forward and fall.

Billy shouted, "Noooo!"

The white form shrank as it tumbled downward, head over heels in a haphazard cartwheel. In a silent splash, she disappeared in the river of fire.

Billy yanked the front of his shirt up to his mouth, biting his thumb through the material. Was it Naamah? Why did she do it? Was she despondent over his rejection of her? Had she given up hope of ever finding her beloved?

Billy leaned over the edge, gazing into the fire, searching the clumps of ash for signs of body parts in the glowing gorge. Suddenly, a huge shape burst from the river, a giant red bat zooming up parallel to the sheer rock face. Billy lunged backwards just before it could ram his chest. He spun a one-eighty arc, whipped out Excalibur, and held it in ready position, scanning the crystal blue skies for the winged rat.

He spotted it high in the air to his left, darting around like an angry hornet. The bat suddenly plummeted, its scarlet wings beating furiously and its razor teeth snapping. It swiped by Billy's neck just as he hacked with his sword. He sliced across its claw-barbed wing, shearing off the outer third. The claw tumbled to the ground and writhed on the hot stone like a decapitated snake. The bat careened, flying in an awkward circle before it crashed and rolled between two bubbling lava pools.

Billy dashed to the creature and raised his sword, ready to hew it to pieces, but it didn't move. The wings shrank, morphing into human arms, one with a missing hand. The red, leathery skin faded to white and transformed into a silky dress. The hideous face softened to the creamy complexion of young, unspoiled beauty – Naamah's face, sad and still.

Billy dropped to his knees, gasping. He laid Excalibur across her torso and grabbed her wounded arm. Blood poured to the ground, but there were no rhythmic spurts of red that would indicate a beating heart. As he caressed Naamah's cold skin, he noticed something strange, a bluish mark on her arm. He snatched Excalibur and held it close to the mangled limb, waving it over her skin from her shattered wrist to her bruised elbow. The mark shone like a beacon. *A letter M!*

Billy shot to his feet and backed away. With trembling hands he slid Excalibur into its scabbard. A New Table knight? If they could take the form of a beautiful girl or a raging bat, how could he ever hope to tell who they were?

He kicked a pebble and watched it bounce across the barren rock. So what should he do now? With New Table knights popping up everywhere, he felt like the rules had changed in the middle of the game. It was like playing basketball, and the other team suddenly added five extra guys . . . and they were all ten feet tall!

He was alone in a vast expanse of desert. A young woman's body lay crumpled in bloody carnage, the sleeve of her white gown soaking up the red pool under her arm. Billy gritted his teeth. He had to forget about Naamah. He had to find Bonnie. But where was she in this layered maze? Maybe back at number three, but how could he get there?

He scanned the bare, stony ground. *I've gotta find this circle's rock and read the next poem. Maybe it'll help me figure out what to do.* Except for the pebble he had just kicked, this barren place didn't even have any loose rocks.

Billy snapped his fingers. He sprinted to the last place he had seen the little stone bouncing across the hardened lava field and found it lying at the base of a three-foot-high spatter cone.

Droplets of molten rock splashed all around, like a Fourth of July sparkler's fiery shower. To avoid the splattering lava, he kicked the pebble away from the cone, but he wasn't quick enough. Several drops rained down on his trouser cuff but just rolled off without even scorching it.

The marble-sized white pebble came to rest next to a sheer mountain face. Billy snatched it up and held it close to his eyes. Words wrapped around its smooth surface in a spiral. He turned it as he read the tiny words out loud.

A shore afar is circle five;
A captive waits in chains of greed.
Each bite conceals the toxic lust
And veils the demon's bread and mead.

Billy dropped the pebble into his pocket. *A shore afar? Okay, that makes sense. I'm at the edge of a gulf, so that's a shore. But it doesn't tell me what to do next. There's no captive here.*

He kicked the side of the mountain, sending a shower of grit onto his feet. He shook the sand from his shoes, too much, really, for the feeble tap he'd given the sheer wall. He scratched the back of his head. There had to be more to this mountain than met the eye.

Placing his hand on the face of the massive rock, he pushed his fingers into the loose sand. His index finger sank in more than an inch. *Bingo!*

Using both hands, he scraped away the sandy mask. Soon, he detected a pattern, block letters standing more than a foot tall. He cleared away more dirt in the lower rows, then planted his feet in the excavated letters to reach the upper rows. Finally, he could read the entire message.

Not all applaud the king's brave quest
To rescue men from savage chains,
Yet still he foils the raven's plot
With tables turned from food to flames.

When weapons fail and faith survives,
In sacrifice the king expires,
But rising from his river grave,
His flame revives to kindle fire.

Billy set his hands on his hips. *Well that certainly makes it all clear.* He kicked the mountain again. *As clear as mud!*

Bonnie covered her mouth with her hand, then spread her fingers to speak. "He was dead? What did you do, drag him away and bury him?"

Shiloh drew a line in the dust with the barrel stave. "No. His body was gone the next day. But I'm sure he was dead. He wasn't breathing, and he laid there like a log for hours."

"Any idea what happened to him?"

"Nope. Not a clue for almost forty years." Shiloh tossed the cooled stave into the barrel. "Anyway, that's why I never tried the main door. It's deadly." She stooped less than a foot from the entry, staring into the electromagnetic field. "But sometimes I wondered if I should try it anyway. Could dying be worse than living here?" She tilted her head up toward Bonnie. "You can't imagine how lonely it's been. The sun rises, and I crawl out of my nest of crates. I try to talk to Bat, but he never answers." She rose again and half-sat on the barrel, gripping the rim with her hands. "Sometimes I hold out a handful of beads for Frankie and ask him to play a game of marbles with me, but he never stops.

He never even answers. He just plucks out his silver dollar and carries his flowers away like I'm not even there, and I draw a circle in the dirt and play marbles by myself." Her voice faltered, lowering to a sad whimper. "But . . . after a few years . . . I couldn't come up with any new games. No matter what I played, I always won . . . and lost."

Shiloh stood and sniffed in a deep breath. "Then I go to the statue and pump the water to wash my face and arms and eat the plant. After my cramps, I wander around until the sun sets and the air turns cold. I make my nest again and curl up in the alley until I fall asleep."

She bowed her head, and a tear dripped to the porch. She hugged herself with both arms, and her voice quaked. "But . . . but I have all I really need."

Bonnie placed a gentle hand on Shiloh's back and glanced around the feed store's porch. "If only I could find a board, something flat and solid." She reached up and grabbed the hanging sign, lifting her full weight and dangling with it. The frayed support rope snapped, and with a quick flap of her wings, she landed softly with the sign in hand. "I have an idea." She propped the sign on end. "Have you ever tried to block the light in the doorway?"

Shiloh wiped the tears from her cheeks. "Sure. You saw what it did to the stave. It kicks like a mule."

"Does it make a gap in the energy field?"

"Uh-huh. But since the field always yanks anything out of my hand, the gap only lasts a second. I never could see anything on the other side." She rubbed the heel of her hand with her fingers. "The jolt hurts so much, it gets pretty discouraging. I just quit trying."

Bonnie patted the top edge of the sign with her hand. "How about if I push this in while you try to look through the gap? I'm willing to take a jolt."

Shiloh shook her head. "Not like this one. The shock will make your split ends have split ends."

Bonnie curled her fingers into a ball. "I've been crushed inside the fist of an electric monster. I doubt anything could be worse than that."

"An electric monster?"

Bonnie laid the sign on its longer edge. "I'll explain later. I'm going to slide this through, so you'll have to get on your knees to look. If it's as bad as you say, we may have only a second or two before this thing gets kicked out of my hands."

"Well . . . if you're sure." Shiloh dropped to her knees, bending over until her nose nearly touched the dusty wooden planks. "I'm ready. Don't let it smack me on the head!"

Bonnie pushed the sign up to the edge of the doorway. "I'll brace the side with my foot so it doesn't kick back. Be ready to duck, just in case."

"Okay."

Bonnie gripped the sign with both hands. With a quick thrust, she slid the sign forward, blocking the bottom third of the doorway's light field. Immediately, a tremendous rush of energy surged through her body. She gritted her teeth and held on, but the sign kicked up and banged against her head. She fell backwards and landed on the porch with a loud grunt.

Shiloh rushed to her side. "Are you okay?"

Bonnie propped herself on one elbow and rubbed her forehead. "I think so." She brought her fingers down to check for blood. "That's the second time I've been smacked there today." She sat up, rubbing her head again. "Did you see anything?"

Shiloh's face had turned pale, and she nodded slowly, her eyes glazed. "I saw my tree."

"Your tree?"

She nodded again. "It's an oak tree I used to climb at home near a big hill. It looks a little different now, but I'd never forget my tree. It's where we were having my birthday party when 'Morticia' and her gang kidnapped me."

Bonnie grabbed Shiloh's hand. "So this *is* the way home for you!"

A man reading a newspaper passed by and disappeared through the door. Shiloh pulled her hand away from Bonnie's. "A lot of good it does me. I can't get there from here."

"What if I—" Bonnie clutched her chest.

"What's wrong?"

"My heart. It's beating funny." She gasped, taking in short, quick breaths.

"Must've been that jolt. I told you it was a brute."

Bonnie took a deeper breath. "Whew! It's better now." She braced herself with her hands and stood up, holding her palm on her head again. "I'm dizzy, too. I felt like I was back in that monster's fist." She picked up the sign and propped it on its short end. "As I was about to say, what if I hold the board up there vertically? That'll open it enough for you to jump through."

"Maybe. But it'll put you closer to the field. It might knock you clear across the street!"

Bonnie tapped her shoe on the porch floor. "You've been here forty years. Don't you want to go home?"

"Part of me does. I miss my mum and dad, but what if they're dead? What if everyone I know is dead? And will I still be fifteen if I go home? Or will I be over fifty?" She turned and faced the street as two policemen passed by, swinging batons on thin ropes. "Part of me just wants to stay here. You may not believe it, but I've actually gotten used to it."

Bonnie put a hand on her hip. "You're right. I don't believe it. I saw you crying."

Shiloh spun back, her face glowing red. "Living in the other world was no picnic, either!" She let out a long breath and laid her hand on the edge of the sign. "Look, my father was always hiding, always running from something. We moved all over England, and I hated it. One day, I heard him and Mum talking, and I figured out they were running away to protect me." She sniffed, and a tear emerged as her voice cracked. "I prayed and prayed that God would just take me someplace no one would ever find me, that He would somehow show me how to stop whoever was chasing us." She wiped away the tear and sniffed again, letting out an uneasy laugh. "I guess I got my wish, didn't I?"

"But why was someone chasing you?"

Shiloh looked out at the street again. "Well . . . I'm different."

"Different? How?"

Shiloh propped her elbow on the sign and shook her head. "You wouldn't understand."

"Me? Not understand 'different'?" Bonnie laughed. "Listen, sister. I've been hiding dragon wings in a backpack for years. I know about 'different' ."

Shiloh lowered her head. "And I guess kids laugh at the scales on your face, right? That must be awful."

Bonnie's heart fluttered, and a tingling sensation ran up her spine. "Yeah. . . . The scales."

The two policemen passed by again followed by a man carrying a bucket. The trailing man looked at Bonnie and quickly turned his face away.

Bonnie's mouth dropped open.

Shiloh squinted. "What's wrong?"

Bonnie gave a slight nod with her head and whispered. "Did you see that guy with the bucket?"

Shiloh lowered her voice. "What about him?"

"Have you ever seen him before?"

"Yeah, but only recently. Why?"

Bonnie wrapped her fingers around Shiloh's wrist. "I could have sworn he looked at me. I mean, he looked right at me, but only for a second."

Shiloh's eyes shifted toward the street, but she didn't turn her head. She stretched out her words, her lips barely moving. "Okay. . . . That's different."

"So what do we do?"

"I have an idea."

"What?"

Shiloh cupped her hands around her mouth and shouted. "Hey, you! What's the matter? Never seen a girl with dragon wings before?"

The man jerked his head around, alarm flashing across his face. He dropped the bucket and dashed away, turning onto a side street and out of sight.

Bonnie jumped down the steps, and with a mighty flap, she leaped into the air. Within seconds, she was soaring over the buildings and descending toward the narrow street where the man had disappeared. Dozens of phantom people lined the sidewalk in front of a theatre, apparently waiting for the show to begin. Strangely enough, there were no young children. Every man and woman seemed to be at least eighteen years old, maybe older.

Bonnie pulled up and made another circle, then dove to the street and landed with a trot. The man who had been spying on her was likely posing as one of the moviegoers, but how could she tell which one? She had only caught a glimpse of him. He was wearing black, but so was just about everyone in line.

She hurried to the box office window and stomped on the toes of the first man in line. No reaction. Watching the eyes of the thirty or so people behind him, she methodically tromped on the foot of each male. After eight hefty stomps, a man near the back stepped out and drew a sword. "Back off, Dragon Girl! Just let me go on my way, and I won't hurt you."

"Not before I get some answers!" Bonnie crossed her arms over her chest. "Who are you?"

The man snorted. "Oh, you're a brave one . . . for a girl, that is."

In a flurry of feet and wings, Bonnie lunged into the air, then cut a tight circle back toward the man. She swooped behind him, snatched his collar, and lifted him high above the road. "Talk fast," she yelled, "before my grip gets too weak. I'm just a girl, you know."

The man tried to swing his sword behind him, but to no avail. "Go ahead, Demon Witch!" he shouted. "Drop me! See if I care!"

She glided down and dropped him from about eight feet above the road. He hit the ground feet first and tumbled over, dropping his sword and planting his face in the cobblestones.

Bonnie landed and grabbed his weapon. She leaped on his back and pressed the sword's tip into his scalp. "Are you ready to talk now? I'm pretty good with a sword . . . for a girl."

The man raised his hands. "Okay, okay! I get the point! Don't rub it in."

"I'm going to let you go, but don't try anything." Bonnie released him and flew several feet away. She then rammed the blade into a crease between two stones. "You're a slayer, aren't you?"

He brushed off his clothes. "Your brilliance is exceeded only by your arrogance." He lifted his head and grimaced. "Or your ugliness."

Bonnie plucked the sword from the street. "Have you ever heard the word 'impertinence'?"

"Many times, from my master . . . and my mistress."

She gripped the hilt tightly. "You're Palin, aren't you? You look a lot like a picture a friend of mine drew."

Palin reached into his pocket and pulled out a handkerchief. "So you recognize me, do you? They say that dead men tell no tales, but it seems there are no secrets in Hades."

"Hades?" Bonnie tilted her head. "What are you talking about?"

Palin wiped a smudge from his chin. "I see that you're ignorant as well as arrogant. Didn't your brilliant professor tell you that the circles are the seven levels of Hades?"

"He mentioned something about the afterlife, but he never finished."

Palin rolled his eyes. "Oh . . . I see. He never finished. How convenient."

Bonnie balled her hand into a fist. "If you're so smart, what are you doing here?"

"I'm supposed to be here. I'm dead. And I was assigned to keep an eye on a prisoner."

Bonnie rested the sword on the cobblestones. "Shiloh? Why?"

"The invisible spirits that roam these streets at night take notice of sleeping little girls." He folded his handkerchief and stuffed it into his pocket. "My mistress takes very good care of Shiloh."

"Yeah, right. One tiny meal a day that makes her cramp up. I'd hate to see what bad care looks like."

"If you're referring to that silly little plant," Palin spat on the ground, "I was told that Merlin conjured it up the day Shiloh arrived." A column of black smoke erupted around his feet. "My mistress offered her a royal banquet, but she refused it." The smoke rose above his head, enveloping his body. "It looks like my mistress has come to take me away, but I'm sure I'll be back for my guard duty tonight. Cheerio!" The black cloud suddenly dispersed, and Palin was gone.

Bonnie flapped her wings slowly, lifting her feet off the ground. Still carrying the sword, she propelled herself high into the air. *As long as I'm airborne, I'll take a quick look around. It was pretty dark when I got here. Maybe there's a way out I couldn't see before.*

She rocketed higher, surveying the land from horizon to horizon. The ground curved sharply, bending until it met a transparent barrier on all sides, as though the whole world was a ball that had been jammed into a glass cylinder. Higher up, the sky seemed to narrow to a tube, but as she flew to investigate, she met thinner air, making it hard to breathe. She beat her wings rapidly and stared at the mirror-like dome surrounding her. The reflection of her upright figure grabbed her gaze. Bonnie's image was strong and shapely, yet the horrible scales on her face seemed to glow, pulsing in time with her throbbing heart.

Bonnie gasped, but the thin air starved her lungs. She collapsed her wings and dropped, spreading her arms out in free fall. She closed her eyes to chase her reflection from her mind. It was hideous! But she had to shoo it away. It wasn't real. It was just a perception. It was . . .

A tear squeezed past her eyelid and trickled down her cheek. She sniffed and wiped it away.

Extending her wings again, Bonnie slowed her descent. As she settled on the cobblestones, she pulled to a stop at the statue in the town square. The shadow of her wing covered the poem on the base except for the final two lines. "Contentment holds eternal keys to days of peace that never pass."

With the sword in hand, Bonnie ran toward the feed store, where Shiloh stood at the top of the porch steps. Suddenly breathless, Bonnie halted a dozen yards short. Her knees buckled. She dropped to her seat and clutched her chest.

Shiloh ran out to the street. "Bonnie! What's wrong?"

Bonnie took several short breaths before trying to speak. "I think it's . . . it's my heart again. Flying must have . . . taken a lot out of me."

Shiloh pushed her shoulder under Bonnie's arm. "Come on. Let's get you out of the wind."

Bonnie leaned on Shiloh as she hobbled back to the porch. Once there, they both sat cross-legged near the portal. "Let's just rest," Shiloh said. "I think you probably scared that creep half to death. He won't be back for a while."

Bonnie smiled and folded in her wings. "I guess looking like a dragon is good for something."

"Well, I think it's cool. Watching you fly like that was a gas." Shiloh lowered her head and drew a circle on the dusty porch floor with her finger. "I suppose I spilled the beans about my family. Do you want to hear the whole story?"

Bonnie drew her knees up and grasped them with both arms. "Sure. I love a good story, and it'll give me time to recover."

Shiloh scooted close to Bonnie. "I love stories, too, but since there's no one to tell me any, I just make them up and tell my own. I've gotten pretty good at storytelling, if I do say so myself."

Bonnie lifted her eyebrows. "Really. You're a good storyteller?"

"Yes. What's wrong with that?"

"Nothing. It just seems like we have so much in common."

Shiloh's smile trembled. "If you say so." She fingered the hem on her borrowed T-shirt and draped it over her bare legs. "Anyway, some of the story isn't mine. My dad told me the first part, because it happened way before I was born."

Bonnie pulled her knees closer to her chest and rested her chin on top. "Okay. Let's hear it."

CHAPTER 17

SHILOH'S STORY

Shiloh wrapped her arms around her knees and rocked back and forth, her eyes rolling upward. "It all started about fifteen hundred years ago . . .

Merlin pulled an oar silently through the murky water, sitting low in the dugout canoe. He whispered, "Valcor, if we want to save the king, surprise is our only hope. We must keep our heads and our voices down."

The crisp air carried the sound of crickets across the water along with the melody of tree leaves rustling in the gentle wind. Merlin gazed at the sky, picking out the stars and drawing the constellation lines. "King Arthur's chariot," he whispered. "He guides us to the southern shore."

At the rear of the boat Valcor patted the ornate hilt of a splendid sword. "We have Excalibur, but I think I would prefer a chariot right now." He dipped his oar into the moat and pushed against the shallow bottom. "Are we nearing the serpents?"

"Yes," Merlin said, drawing in his oar. "I hope our momentum will carry us past their nests. Keep your arms well inside, and I will sing."

Valcor raised the sword. "Shall I summon your audience? I prefer raising a battle hymn for slashing their throats to crooning a lullaby that keeps them tucked in their beds."

Merlin chuckled. "You have no idea what we're up against, my friend. And you're not yet familiar with how to use Excalibur's power." The old man rolled up the wet sleeves of his scarlet robe and gripped the edge of the canoe. Beginning with a low hum, he closed his eyes and sang a haunting melody.

Thou servants of the blackest soul,
Asleep in Av'lon's shallow bowl,
Wake not as skies above thee break
With ripples sounding in our wake.

While sleep enfolds you in your lair,
We pass you by without a care.
So in your dreams protect her doors,
While safely we approach her shores.

The canoe drifted slowly across the grass-coated water, both men staring hard at the black surface.

Valcor whispered, "I thought you were going to say, 'While praying for your lasting snores.' "

"Shhh!" Merlin scolded.

A tiny splash broke the silence. Merlin spun toward the sound. Valcor raised his sword. The moon reflected on the dark water, tiny waves rippling the white disk.

"A frog," Valcor whispered.

Merlin nodded, sweat streaming down his cheeks.

The boat slowed to a stop. "Not quite enough," Merlin whispered. "Two more strokes, and we will pass their nests." With a surgeon's care, he slid his paddle into the marsh and pulled against the water. The boat started forward and coasted across the grassy surface. Merlin pulled again, but when he lifted the oar, a scaly tentacle looped around the wood and jerked it into the water. A fanged, gaping mouth shot above the surface and flew toward Merlin.

With a lightning-fast swing of the sword, Valcor severed the snake's thick neck, and its head landed in Merlin's lap.

Merlin lunged for Valcor's oar. "Keep swinging!" He drove the oar into the water and heaved against the muddy bottom.

A second scaly creature wriggled its body over the canoe, then coiled around the entire vessel. As it constricted, the floor of the boat cracked, sending a thin spray of water into the air. Valcor swung the sword down hard, slicing cleanly through the snake's midsection. Purple blood mixed into the spray, coating Valcor's shirt.

The bisected creature slid away, separating the front and back of the boat. Merlin balanced on one half and Valcor on the other as the bobbing wreck began to sink. "Run for it!" Merlin shouted, leaping toward shore.

Valcor bounded over the snake's body and splashed into the moat. More snakes surged across the surface. Sloshing through hip-deep water, Valcor swung Excalibur. Another head lopped off. And another. He spun around and sliced a snake's throat, making its head flop backwards.

Valcor waded forward until he reached the shallows, then dashed to shore, mud, blood, and water dripping from his clothes.

Merlin sat on the grassy beach with his head bowed over his crossed legs, still clutching an oar. Valcor dropped down next to him, breathing heavily. "So much . . . for our . . . surprise visit."

Merlin gasped for breath. "If Morgan . . . is not alerted to our presence by now . . . she is a heavy sleeper indeed."

"Maybe you should sing your magic song to her," Valcor said, wiping Excalibur's blade on his sleeve. "It worked so well on the snakes."

Merlin let out a quiet, "Harumph," then rapped Valcor on the leg with his oar. "The song is not magic. The melody and rhythm lull the beasts of the earth to sleep. But since this is not an earthly place, I was not sure how effective it would be." He rose to his feet. "Come. Morgan's sister, Elaine, often haunts these shores at night. We would be safer with the snakes than in her clutches."

Valcor stood and sheathed his blade. "I will not feel safe until I leave this place. I know what you promised, but no one has ever returned from the underworld."

Merlin's pupils grew, shining like obsidian. "All who enter willingly may leave without cost. Those who come against their will, however, can never depart unless an innocent one perishes in their place."

"And the king? Will he be able to leave?"

"Yes. He came willingly to be healed, though he is now under Morgan's spell." Merlin pulled on Valcor's arm. "Let us waste no more time."

The two men stole through the mist, passing under the branches of several apple trees before ascending a steep hill, leaning forward as they dug their feet into the grassy slope. After crossing several terraces, they approached a dark building at the apex. They skulked past twin turrets to a rear entrance of the church-like structure. The short steeple in the centre of the roof cast a long shadow over the moss-speckled black door. A thick vine grew along the door's side, seemingly embedded in the wall and leading up past a window on its meandering climb to the roof.

Merlin reached into his robe's deep pocket and drew out a small flask. Putting one hand on the vine, he handed the flask to Valcor and whispered, "On my signal, pour this into the crack under the door. When you hear the dog slurping it up, return my signal and ascend the vine. By the time you reach the window, I should have it open."

Valcor nodded and took the flask. Kneeling at the door, he watched Merlin climb the thick vine, hand over hand, his sandals pushing against stony outcrops in the wall. The old man reached the window and swung his body into its recessed opening. When he had settled into a comfortable position, he waved his arm.

Valcor pulled a stopper from the flask and poured a thick liquid under the door. A foul odour, a cross between stale urine and rotting flesh, assaulted him. Pinching his nose, he scooted back and listened. Within seconds a snuffling sound penetrated the wood, then a long, multicoloured tongue thrust itself under the door, slurping every drop of liquid.

Valcor jumped to his feet, waved at Merlin, then clambered up the vine. He stretched his leg and planted his foot in the window's ledge. Taking Merlin's hand, he swung gracefully into the recess. He grabbed one of the window's iron bars for balance, and the whole network of rods pulled loose from the frame.

Merlin tightened his grip on Valcor's hand until he steadied himself. "I applied a corroding agent to the metal," Merlin whispered. He pushed a stopper into a vial and slipped it into his pocket. "Carry the bars into the room and set them down quietly. The dog will sleep, but a sudden noise may arouse him."

Valcor stepped through the window and winked. "I hope your sleeping spell works better than your song."

"It is not a spell," Merlin countered, copying Valcor's movements. "It is simple chemistry – a herb concentrate and a strong opiate mixed into pork drippings. I know you lack trust in my skills, but I am neither witch nor wizard."

The two men dropped silently to the floor. Merlin opened his palm. In its centre, a fluorescent stone emitted a bluish-green glow, giving just enough light to guide them to a bed on the far side of the room.

An uncovered man lay on the bed, girded only in a loincloth. Beads of sweat on his face and chest reflected the eerie light, covering his skin with an illusory green pox. His torso rose and fell in an easy rhythm.

Merlin stooped at the side of the bed and pulled Valcor down beside him. He lowered his voice to a faint whisper. "We are not too late. You will carry the king to the shore, and I will borrow Morgan's skiff and meet you there. Perhaps the serpents will allow her boat to cross the swamp."

"The king looks well," Valcor whispered back. "Why not awaken him and let him walk? It would be much safer."

"He is not well, and he will not awaken easily. Her food is poison to the living, and she must have somehow tricked him into eating it. Every bite makes him more and more a part of this dark realm. It will take him many days to recover."

A light flashed, and the severed head of a huge snake rolled up to the bed. Merlin and Valcor jumped to their feet, Valcor with Excalibur drawn.

A torch-bearing woman stormed into the room, her voice booming. "How dare you violate my private residence!"

Merlin squared his shoulders. "When you hold the king hostage, Morgan, you have no rights!"

Valcor charged, his sword ready to swing. Merlin reached out. "Valcor, no!" But it was too late. Morgan waved a dark-sleeved arm, and Valcor flew backwards as though punched in the face by a gargantuan ogre. He slid on the floor, coming to rest at Merlin's feet.

Morgan thrust her torch into a stone vase and spread out her arms, her face twisting with rage. "Give me one good reason why I should not slay you where you stand."

Merlin held up his hand. "Wait!" He glanced at the king, still sleeping on the bed, then at Valcor, struggling to get up. Merlin placed his hand on Valcor's head. "Allow my squire to take the king back to Camelot without hindrance, and I will make sure that Sir Devin acquires Excalibur."

Morgan's sneer melted into a smile. With waltzing steps, she glided toward Merlin. "You would give me Excalibur?"

Merlin shook his head. "You know you can receive nothing unless it is given to you by its rightful protector. Arthur would never give you the sword, so Devin will have to use it in your stead. But since he is your obedient doormat, that arrangement should be quite useful to you."

A new flame burned in Morgan's eyes. "I am unable to take what I wish only because of the curse your God put on me!"

"I do not control my God," Merlin shot back. "He controls me." He helped Valcor to his feet. "Nevertheless, I am able to tell you how to restore your spirit to the world of the living. Will that information ease the pain of not holding the great sword in your own grip?"

Morgan intertwined her fingers at her waist and glided toward King Arthur's bed. "Why would you risk giving me such information?"

Merlin picked up Excalibur and ran his thumb along the edge of its shining blade. "Ours has been a strange friendship, Morgan. Through the years we could have killed each other countless times." He pushed the sword into Valcor's scabbard. "Yet we have always shown mercy." He lowered his head. "I have long hoped that you would be redeemed, but in your current condition, it can never be so."

A wry smile crossed Morgan's face. "So you want to offer me a second chance? A new body and a new life?"

Merlin nodded toward Arthur. "To save the king . . . and to save you."

Morgan strode to Merlin's side and stretched her long fingers across his chest. "Your wish is granted. Tell me more."

Weeks later, two quiet forms, one male and one female, huddled around a flickering candle. A tent draped across three short poles broke the chill wind. They rubbed their fingers in the candle's fragile warmth, and as each exhaled, the flame trembled. As they sat cross-legged on a threadbare grey blanket, tension creased each worried brow. They glanced from time to time at the tent's entrance flap and then at each other as snaps of twigs and owl hoots penetrated the silence.

With his hands clenched over his mouth, the man took in a deep breath and whispered between his thumbs. "If he is not here soon, Irene, we have to assume the worst. Valcor is no match for Devin."

Irene placed a gentle hand on his forearm. "He is no match in battle, Jared, but my brother is wiser by far. Do not give up hope. I would not have arranged this meeting had I thought this a fool's errand."

Jared raised his head. "Did you hear that? A nightingale?"

Irene shushed Jared and whispered, "It is the signal." She pursed her lips and blew a warbling bird whistle.

Within seconds, the tent flap flew open, and a man bustled in, water dripping from his wet sleeves.

Irene grasped the man's arm. "Valcor! Are you hurt?"

He shook his head, stooping under the low ceiling, panting. "Devin . . . Devin tracked me to the river's edge, so I swam . . . swam upstream a thousand cubits." He took a deep breath and continued. "I ran the rest of the way. It will be some time before the dogs pick up the trail again."

"Still, we must hurry." Valcor pulled a scroll from his vest and sat beside Jared. "I found the letter." He rolled it out on the blanket. "And I managed to keep it above water."

Irene glanced upward and clasped her hands together. "Thank the Maker!"

Valcor wrapped his arms around himself and shivered. "Yes. It is a miracle that I escaped. I guess my bribe wasn't quite big enough, and the guard tipped Devin off." He rolled up his wet sleeves and ran his fingers across the parchment, smoothing out the wrinkles. "But this information is worth all the trouble."

Jared eyed the letter. "It is lengthy. Please give us a summary."

Valcor gazed at his friend, a former dragon, and his only sister, who was once Hartanna, the next queen of the dragons. He held the letter close to the dancing flame. "It is clear that Devin is now more dangerous than ever."

"But he failed," Irene said. "Arthur and Merlin squashed the rebellion."

"Devin didn't fail completely. He took Excalibur, and now Merlin has vanished. Who can predict how powerful Devin and Morgan will become?"

Irene straightened her back and placed her hands on her knees. "But will he give the sword to her? Devin is evil, but he is not stupid. Once she possesses the sword, she will have no more use for him."

Valcor slid the candle closer to the letter and shook his head. "When Merlin and I journeyed to Avalon to rescue the king, I learned that Morgan cannot keep Excalibur, or anything else, unless its protector freely hands it over to her." He pressed his finger on the page. "This letter explains what I believe is an even greater danger. You see, in order to secure the king's freedom,

Merlin promised to tell Morgan how to restore her wandering spirit to a body, but he refused to give her the information until His Majesty and I arrived safely in Camelot. The promise, it seems, has been fulfilled in this letter, which I recently learned was in Devin's possession."

Irene shifted to Valcor's side and draped her shawl across his shoulders. She eyed the letter's exquisite penmanship. "Why would Merlin make such a promise to a witch?"

Valcor took her hand. "I asked Merlin that very question. He said the plan is of divine origin and extends well beyond his vision, but we should not worry; God knows what He is doing. In any case, it seems that Morgan is not a witch, at least not the common variety we have seen. She was the wife of a Watcher."

"A Watcher!" Jared repeated. "I thought they were all banished to the abyss!"

"They were, but Morgan's husband taught her the Watchers' crafts, the evil arts of the fallen angels. She did not know that practising these arts would cause her to lose her humanity. She actually took on the nature of the Watchers. She has no hope of redemption without becoming human again and giving herself in obedience to the Christ. She craves a new body. But obedience to the Christ?" Valcor let out a low snort.

A peal of thunder rolled across the sky. Valcor's gaze flashed toward the tent entrance as he rolled up the scroll and thrust it back into his vest. "There is much to explain, and time is short." He held his hand over his vest pocket. "It seems that Merlin told Morgan she needed a *hostiam viventem*, a living sacrifice, in order to become human again. That sacrifice has to be a legal, female relative of the king – a wife, a daughter, or perhaps even a niece. Well, Morgan had her evil eye on Guinevere, but not even demonic arts could persuade Arthur to give up his wife. So, it seems that she changed her plan, hoping Devin could take the throne."

"But how would that further her cause?" Jared asked. "Devin has no wife and no female relatives that I know of."

"Who would have him?" Irene sliced her hand across her throat. "I would kill myself before I let that piece of filth touch me!"

Valcor smirked. "Even dead, you might still be a target. Merlin said that a deceased woman could be a hostiam if she sacrificed herself for the cause of love, assuming, of course, that the body has not been dead long. But Devin would have no need to hunt for corpses. If he had succeeded in usurping the throne, he would have had his choice of women. Morgan would have entered his wife and become queen, and Devin would gain enough power to rule the world. I believe Devin would have put up with a witch of a wife for a prize like that."

A distant howl drifted into the tent. Valcor pushed the entrance flap to the side and leaned out, then ducked his head back in. "So Devin and Morgan have an understanding. She provides him with power, with influence in high places, and he, in turn, uses that power to become king, gets married, then provides Morgan with a body to live in."

Irene raised a finger to her chest. "But if any legal female relative would serve as host, then I really would be a candidate, would I not, since I am an adopted daughter?"

Valcor nodded. "You would be, yes."

"Then why does Devin seek to kill me?"

"Because," Valcor replied, stroking his chin, "he has identified you as a former dragon. He hasn't yet made the connection that you are also in the royal line. So you have peril either way. If you are a dragon, Devin wants you dead. If you are an heir, Morgan wants you alive, yet in such a way that you would be better off dead. I believe, however, that Devin's bloodlust will override his desire to search for Morgan's hostiam, so he will likely try to kill you until the day he dies."

"If he ever dies," Irene added.

Jared's bushy eyebrows lifted. "If? Why do you say if?"

"Haven't you noticed his new youthfulness?" Irene asked. She brushed her finger across her calf. "He shows no sign of the leg wound I gave him when I fought with him as a dragon. If Morgan's evil handiwork has made him like the Watchers, then who knows how long he might live?"

Valcor firmed his chin. "Then I was right. We should all go into hiding. Although your friendship is dear to me, we must separate. The farther apart we live and the less we communicate with each other, the more difficult it will be for Devin and Morgan to find us all."

He began to rise, but Irene pulled on his sleeve. "Wait. I have something for you." She opened her palm. Two spherical red stones rolled to the edge of her hand, looking like a pair of polished cranberries at the peak of harvest. She plucked them from her palm, handing one to each of the men. "You know what the rubellite means to the dragon race. I ask you to keep it. Always remember what we once were. If you ever procreate, pass it along to your progeny at the appropriate time." She gazed up at them, her blue eyes sparkling. "As these gems reflect the vitality of your mortal essence, may you always reflect the nobility of our race through your courage, your integrity, and your sacrifice."

Valcor stood and bowed, tears streaming down his cheeks. He rolled a tear onto his finger and held it out for Jared and Irene to see. "How rare were the tears of a dragon. We once lived in Paradise, and because of the corruption of an angel disguised as a dragon, all the world was cast into darkness. Now, as humans, we shed many tears – for what was lost, for what might have been, and for the end of friendships. Goodbye, my true friends." He bowed again and hurried from the tent.

"We had better go as well," Jared said, holding the tent flap open for Irene.

She raised a finger. "We must wait for his signal that all is clear."

They waited, listening so intently they could hear a faint sizzle from the candlewick. Another howl pierced the night. Jared wet his fingers and snuffed the flame. "That's a good enough signal for me." He and Irene shuffled from the tent and folded it up.

After inhaling deeply, Jared tucked the bundle under his arm. "It's a new world, Hartanna, if I may call you that one last time. We will now be alone and friendless, perhaps for many years. This knowledge of Morgan's intent to capture a hostiam is vital in helping us understand our enemies, but it also casts a heavy burden on our shoulders." He took Irene's hand. Her eyes glittered in the moon-washed night. "If Valcor speaks the truth," he said, "you are in the greatest danger. You must go into hiding as far away as possible, and it would be best if I never learn where you are."

Irene intertwined her fingers in his. "Valcor speaks the truth. Of that we can always be sure."

Jared kissed her hand. "May the Maker grant you safe passage." He bowed and marched quickly to the north. Irene closed her eyes briefly, then hurried away toward the south.

Valcor, hiding behind a tree, watched them depart, listening to the mournful howls of the approaching dogs. He jogged a hundred paces or so toward the sound, rubbed his hands on the grass, then dashed away to the west.

Fifteen hundred years passed. In the town of Glastonbury, England, a man and his wife celebrated their daughter's fifteenth birthday in the shade of a lush oak tree. A magnificent, grassy hill towered over them as they spread out a chequered blanket in a copse that grew near the base of the steep slope. The mother set a double fudge, two-layer cake in the centre of the blanket, and the three sat in a circle as she lit the candles, cupping her hand around the match to keep the cool breeze from snuffing out her efforts.

As soon as the last candle came to life, the parents sang a hurried version of "Happy Birthday to You." The girl then leaned forward and blew the candles out. Her father clapped his hands. "All fifteen in one blow!"

The girl pushed back her blonde-streaked hair and smiled. "I think the wind helped me."

"And now for your gift!" He pulled a small, velvet-covered box from his jacket pocket, and, carefully lifting the hinged lid, he presented it to her.

As she drew out a delicate gold chain, a wide smile spread across her face. An octagonal bronze pendant dangled at the bottom of the chain with a bean-sized white stone glimmering at its centre.

Her mother ran a finger along the chain's links. "Do you like it?" she asked.

The girl leaned over and kissed both her parents on the cheek. "I love it! Thank you!" She settled back and examined the gem in the pendant's centre. "What is this? A pearl?"

Her father helped her fasten the chain around her neck. "It's a rubellite, the rarest kind. It was once red, and it suddenly turned white before you were born. It's a family heirloom my sister gave me a long time ago."

The girl rubbed her thumb across the smooth stone. "You mean Irene? From your stories about the dragons?"

"Yes. It represents our life essence. Irene—"

A man burst into the copse. "Here they are!" He drew a sword from a scabbard and ran toward the birthday gathering.

The father leaped to his feet and stood in front of his wife and daughter, spreading his arms as a shield. The intruder halted and pricked the father's throat with the point of the sword. The mother jumped up, but her husband lifted his hand, signalling for her to stay away. He angled his head back. "Palin!" He swallowed hard, feeling the sting of the blade. "What is the meaning of this?"

A female voice answered. "You know the meaning, Valcor."

Palin stepped aside, lowering the sword. A slender, dark-haired woman appeared from behind a tree. Her ghostly form seemed to float, though her legs moved in a normal cadence.

Valcor smirked and nodded. "Morgan. How typical of you to pollute the pristine like a walking weed."

A scowl flashed across Morgan's face, but she recovered quickly, her dark red lips stretching out over her teeth. "Poetic, as always, my old friend, but your insults are misplaced. I have a wonderful birthday gift for Shiloh, and I would like for her to come with me to receive it."

Shiloh stood behind her father and wrapped her arms around his waist. He grasped her hands in front, intertwining his fingers with hers. "When pigs fly, Witch!"

Morgan's smile melted into a thin horizontal line. "I thought you would come up with a more original quip, Valcor, but your denial was expected."

Valcor nodded toward Palin. "Where is your other pet gorilla? Has Devin finally given up hunting for your hostiam?"

Morgan reached for Palin's blade and pricked her finger on its tip. "Devin is not known for handling these matters delicately. You would fight. He would kill you. All would be lost." She held out her hand, palm down, allowing a drop of blood to fall to the leaf-strewn grass. A wiggling brown sliver crawled out of the ground, like an earthworm squeezing up from a narrow hole. As it emerged, it lengthened to the size of a man's foot, then doubled, constantly growing in girth, and its end morphed into the head of a snake as it continued to stretch.

Morgan grasped the snake's midsection and wrapped its body around her shoulders and torso, carrying its neck in her hand as the hissing head bared its fangs at Valcor. "So when we finally tracked you down," she continued, "I sent Devin to make sure the place I prepared is ready for your daughter's arrival." She stepped toward Valcor, and the snake lunged. Its fangs latched onto Shiloh's forearm.

She screamed, shaking her arm until the snake finally released her and dropped to the ground. Valcor stomped on its head with the heel of his boot, pounding it flat. Shiloh's mother pulled her daughter away and hustled to the nearby oak tree.

Morgan shook her head in mock lament. "What a shame! Now I'll have to take Shiloh with me." She picked up the dead snake by the tail. "You see, I have the only cure for the serpent's venom."

As Valcor's wife tried to tend to their daughter's wound, he spun toward Morgan, his red face taut. "What good is she to you?" he shouted, spitting his words. "She can't be your hostiam without my approval!"

"Don't worry. I will keep her safe in the sixth circle until you change your mind. I'll let you decide which is better for her. Will you allow me to take her body and send her soul to God, or will you condemn her to live an eternity of tortured loneliness? For now, though, you have to answer a more urgent question. Will you allow the serpent's venom to rot her flesh over the next three days until she suffers an excruciatingly painful death?"

Valcor shot her a threatening glare. "For healing only. Not as your hostiam." He ran to the tree and scooped Shiloh into his arms, whispering as he carried her back to Morgan. "Will you trust me, dearest angel?"

Amid streaming tears, she nodded. "Yes, Daddy."

He gazed into her eyes, his own tears falling to her dress. "Will you remember what I've taught you? Never lose faith, no matter how long it takes. Above all, never eat Morgan's food. God will provide for all your needs."

She shook her head, breaking into a sob. "I won't forget, Daddy! I'll never forget!"

CHAPTER 18

ESCAPE

Shiloh released her knees and extended her arm, displaying two tiny snakebite scars near the crook of her elbow. "So Palin carried me up the hill and threw me down near the top. My parents followed, and when Palin dropped me, Mum ran up and tried to help me. Then Morgan shoved Mum with her foot, and she fell, but I couldn't see what happened to her. Morgan clamped her arms around me, and everything went black, like I fainted or something. When I woke up, I was locked in a cramped bedroom for three days, and this weird doctor kept showing up to make me drink some awful tea. I knew I couldn't eat what she gave me, but I figured that drinking was okay. Then, one morning, I woke up in my alley."

Bonnie held out her own arm and caressed her scars, needle marks from the dozens of times her father had drawn blood. "You and I really do have a lot in common." She took Shiloh's hand. "Irene is . . . was my mother. We're cousins."

Shiloh's mouth dropped slowly open. "Cousins?"

Bonnie smiled, nodding her head excitedly. "We're both dragons. Isn't that awesome?"

Shiloh released Bonnie's hand and folded hers together. "I . . . I guess it's awesome that we're cousins, but I'm not a dragon."

"But if Valcor's your father, then you must have dragon blood."

Shiloh shook her head. "He told me he found a way to become fully human before I was born, so I'm fully human, too."

Bonnie lifted her hand and caressed her scaly cheek. "Wow!" She quickly dropped it, folding her hands and matching Shiloh's pose. "So you still don't know what happened to your mum and dad?"

"No," Shiloh replied, her head drooping. "I can't even remember what my mother looked like. But even after all these years, I still see my daddy's face in my dreams, the same way it looked when he put me in Morgan's arms, tortured, like he was about to crumble into pieces. And I still wake up in the middle of the night, hearing him call in that same voice, 'Never lose faith, no matter how long it takes.' "

"That's what's kept you going, I'll bet."

Shiloh pulled up a thin chain around her neck and held the pendant in her palm. "That and my father's gift. As long as I wear it, I'll never forget his love for me." The pendant's rubellite centre pulsed between red and white, painting her fingers in alternating hues. "It just started flashing like this last night. I was hoping it was a good sign, and now that you're here, I'm sure of it."

Bonnie spread out the fingers of her own right hand. The stone in her ring strobed, too, but at a slightly faster rate than Shiloh's. "It's almost like a heartbeat, isn't it?" She placed her left hand on her chest and compared the rhythmic pulses. "But it's not the same pace as my heart." She folded her fingers into a fist and covered it with her other hand. "Strange. It's never done this before."

"Mine was solid white for years, so maybe the pulsing's got something to do with you coming here."

Bonnie nodded slowly. "Maybe." She smiled and extended a hand to Shiloh. "Ready to try to get back home?"

Shiloh grinned. "Ready!"

Pulling on each other's hands, they stood up together. Bonnie picked up the sign, propped it up lengthwise, and slid it close to the door. "Now, when I slide it in, if everything looks clear, jump through the hole."

Shiloh crouched next to the opening. She licked her lips and swallowed. "Okay . . . I think I can do that."

Bonnie took a deep breath. "Ready?"

Shiloh held up her hand. "Wait! How are you going to get home?"

"Don't worry about me. I told you we came to rescue prisoners, and that's what I intend to do. Even if Billy doesn't find me, I'm sure I'll get home somehow."

A tear slipped down Shiloh's cheek. She rose to her feet again and untied her bead necklace. "Okay," she said, fastening the string around Bonnie's neck. "We'd better do it before I change my mind."

Bonnie gripped the sign with both hands and shoved. The edge penetrated the doorway. Sparks shot out, enveloping Bonnie with a surging electric buzz. "All clear?" she grunted.

Shiloh peered into the gap. "I see the tree!"

The sign ripped out of Bonnie's hands and flew toward Shiloh. Shiloh ducked just in time as the board spun like a rectangular frisbee out into the street.

Shiloh lowered her head to the porch floor and pounded the boards with her fist. "No! I'll never get out of here! Never!"

Bonnie firmed her chin and spread her wings. She leaned into the doorway and thrust her right wing into the energy field. Waves of shock tore across her skin, boring into her flesh like a thousand power drills. She erupted in a guttural scream. "Go! Goooo noooowwww!"

Shiloh stood and leaped into the gap in one motion. Her body slipped through a thin, jelly-like membrane and disappeared from sight. A new jolt of electricity slammed into Bonnie like a runaway truck, shooting through her heart and tossing her body into the air. She tumbled across the dirty road like an old rag doll – arms, legs, and wings flopping haphazardly through the dust.

When she came to a stop, everything seemed dark – the cobblestones, the buildings, the sky – but she could see a solitary man slowly approaching.

Her heart thumped wildly in her chest, but she couldn't move anything. Her whole body tingled. Her head swam in the swirling mix of darkness and sparks of colourful light. She could barely breathe, gasping for a mere puff of fresh air. She heaved her chest, whispering a desperate prayer. "Jesus, help me!"

The words of the poem at the base of the statue drifted across her ears like a song, "Contentment holds eternal keys to days of peace that never pass."

"Contentment," Bonnie whispered. The whole world exploded in light – a single brilliant flash – and then blackness.

The professor jogged back to the stand of trees with Apollo in hand. "Did you get enough data?"

Ashley studied her computer. "Plenty of data, maybe too much for this computer. If Larry were up and running, he could map this in a heartbeat."

Walter, the professor, and Marilyn huddled around Ashley and watched the screen draw lines on a graph, slowly illuminating one pixel at a time. Ashley groaned. "This will take forever!"

A static-filled voice sputtered through the computer's speaker. "Your graph is complete. I'm sending the image to your screen."

"Larry!"

"In the flesh. . . . Or rather, in the silicon."

"Karen!" Ashley shouted. "Good job!"

Karen's voice sounded through the speakers, loud and lively. "Thanks. It wasn't the I/O board after all. I found a trail of little black pellets at the bottom of Larry's casing and followed it to a nest of mice next to the secondary exhaust fan. I guess all the trash they gathered gummed up the outflow. Larry just overheated and tripped a breaker on the Omega panel."

"Great detective work!" Ashley held the computer out for everyone to see. "Here's the image!" A graph flashed on the screen showing a series of lines growing closer and closer together as they reached a solid point.

The professor placed his finger at the focus of the tightening circles. "Can you find this point on the tor?"

"Larry," Ashley called, "can you guide us to the maximum vortex point?"

"With pleasure."

The foursome ascended the steeper side of the tor, correcting their course a few times based on Larry's directions. As they neared the top of the hill, they slowed their pace.

"Okay, Ashley. You are standing at the max point."

Ashley braced one foot on the steep slope and the other on a terrace. "Good. Can you tell if Apollo is able to do a flash?"

"Apollo is . . ." Larry paused.

"What?" Ashley said, shaking the computer. "Apollo is what?"

`"Ashley, my programming instructs me to report an anomaly."`

"An anomaly? What is it? No! I mean . . . go on."

`"Apollo is currently reading an electromagnetic field disruption at the focal point. I suggest you step back."`

Ashley wedged Apollo's base into the ground, then backed away, pushing the other three with her. She pulled the computer close to her ear. "Keep me up to date, Larry."

"To quote *Star Wars,* Ashley, 'There is a great disturbance in the force.' And it's growing to an unstable level. I predict a significant cross-dimensional rift."

A flash of light exploded in a hail of sparks. A brilliant white rectangle appeared, floating a few inches above Apollo, too bright to see through. Seconds later, a body dove out of the light. It struck the ground head first and tumbled down the tor, twisting to the side and rolling to the edge of the trees.

Walter dashed down the hill. The new arrival, a young female, sat up, holding her hand against her forehead. Walter skidded to a stop and extended his hand. "Are you okay?"

The girl accepted his hand and pulled herself up, her eyes focused on a nasty elbow abrasion. "Yes. I'm fine." Her voice was low and very British. She lifted her head, and her eyes met Walter's. "Who are you?"

Walter grabbed her shoulders. "Bonnie?" The professor, Ashley, and Marilyn caught up and surrounded the girl.

She pulled away from Walter's grasp. "I'm not Bonnie!" Placing her palm on her head again, she moaned. "Ohhh! What a trip!"

Ashley peered into the girl's eyes as the moon illuminated her dirty face. "Bonnie, don't you recognize us?"

The professor shone his light on the girl's forehead, then her clothes. "Miss Silver, your dress is not the one you wore when you left, but I recognize the Narnia shirt I gave you for Christmas. I believe you are suffering a bout of amnesia. That was quite a spill you took."

She smiled and turned her back to the professor. "I'm not Bonnie. Look. No wings." She took a deep breath and spread her arms out, slowly turning. She let out a long squeal, ending with, "I'm home! I'm finally home!"

"Home?" Walter repeated. "Where have you been?"

The professor turned off his light. "I believe, Mr Foley, that her accent indicates a local origin. She must have been one of the prisoners of the circles."

The girl extended her hand toward the professor. "Shiloh Nathanson. Pleased to meet you."

The professor shook her hand. "Charles Hamilton, at your service."

"Wait a minute," Walter said, pointing at Shiloh. "If you know about Bonnie's wings, then you must know Bonnie."

"You bet I do! She's the one who got me here! There's this strange doorway, and she opened a hole in some kind of electric fence so I could jump through."

"So where is she now?" Marilyn asked.

Shiloh flicked her thumb toward her entry point upslope. "Still in there. But she said not to worry; some guy named Billy would find her and get her out."

Walter smacked his fist into his hand. "Then they're still separated!"

Shiloh nodded. "I'm afraid so."

The professor gazed into Shiloh's eyes. "Miss Nathanson, where is your home?"

"Here in Glastonbury . . . well, on the outskirts of town, really."

"Perhaps we can take you there. I'm certain your parents are beyond merely worried about you."

"That's for sure . . . If they're still alive."

The professor leaned over, lowering his voice. "I am puzzled about your striking resemblance to Bonnie Silver. Who *are* your parents?"

"Robert and Sarah Nathanson, but I'm sure they've changed names again by now. That was forty years ago, and they were always on the run."

Walter's foot slipped, but he quickly righted himself. "Forty years! But you're my age!"

Shiloh shook her head and laughed. "Not exactly. I guess I'm fifty-five now. I left on my fifteenth birthday."

The professor pinched his chin. "I know of a Nathanson in Glastonbury, but he is childless. Perhaps he is your father's relative. If your parents are no longer here, I can take you to him."

"Ashley, I must report another anomaly."

Ashley lifted the computer. "Let's hear it, Larry."

"Apollo is reporting a fully-charged flash engine."

Ashley swung her head and looked up toward the portal. The door of light had vanished, and the moon shone on the hillside . . . the empty hillside. "Apollo's gone!"

"Impossible, Ashley. Invisible to you, maybe, but not gone. Its signal is somewhat warped. I conclude that it has moved through the portal."

"That big flash must have recharged it!" Walter exclaimed, leaning over the computer. "Can you program it? Can Bonnie use Apollo to get home?"

"Yes, I have made the proper adjustments. My communications with the unit are now completely in sync. The subject, however, will have to see the rift in the dimensional barrier and know how to use it."

Ashley fingered the clips in her hair. "A hole in an electric fence? So that's why she didn't need a cloak." She tilted her head upward. "Karen. You listening?"

"Are you kidding? This is better than *Star Trek* reruns!"

"Listen! Fire up the word processor. You're going to send a note to Bonnie, special delivery!" Ashley jerked the computer up to her mouth. "Barlow! What's up with Billy?"

"It's hard to tell, Miss. I think his shirt has overlapped his belt and has obscured most of the view. I can tell that he's moving, but I see only rocks on the ground."

"Check the circles. Which drawing is he in?"

"One moment."

Shiloh stared at the handheld computer. "This Barlow guy can tell where Billy is?"

"Yes," Ashley explained. "There's a drawing of circles on a floor, and two lights show up in the circles, one for Billy, and one for Bonnie. Bonnie was in what we're calling the sixth circle. I suppose that's where you were, too. Anyway, whenever they go somewhere else—"

Barlow's voice interrupted. "He is in the south-west circle. The eyes of the child in the picture are glowing. But there is no longer a light in the western circle."

Ashley bit her lip. "Bonnie's not in number six anymore?"

Shiloh pushed her head between Ashley's face and the computer. "Are you sure, Mr Barlow? I just saw her there two minutes ago."

Ashley leaned away from Shiloh and pulled the computer closer. "Check all the circles, Barlow. She has to be there somewhere."

"Very well, Miss."

Shiloh folded her hands behind her back. "I've got . . ." – she swallowed, and her voice rose to a trembling pitch – "a sick feeling in my stomach."

"Yeah," Ashley agreed. "Big-time."

Barlow's voice rattled through the speaker. "Miss Stalworth!"

"I'm here! What is it?"

"The circle at the north end! The child in the king's lap! Its eyes are glowing!"

"Okay, Barlow. Don't get so excited. At least we found her."

The professor gripped Ashley's shoulder. "Miss Stalworth. The child in the northern drawing is in the lap of the Lord. That circle is a vision of heaven."

Ashley's face turned ghostly white. "Heaven?"

Billy turned away from the edge of the chasm and gazed out over the endless expanse, a field of black, rippled lava rock, dappled with rolling mounds of cooled flows. A few active, bubbling craters dotted the black plain, like pots of soup waiting for the chef to return.

His stomach growled. The thought of soup exposed a gnawing void in his belly. He sniffed the air. Was he really smelling food? Beef stew? He sniffed again. Garlic? A loud gurgle sounded. He pressed his hand against his stomach. *Quiet! Now's not the time.* Still, he couldn't ignore the pain. Acid churned in his oesophagus – sizzling, burning. How long had it been since he'd eaten?

He shook his head to throw out thoughts of food, but he couldn't chase away the smell. It was real. It had to come from somewhere, but he couldn't see a single building – only wasteland and a burning chasm that seemed to travel for miles, biting a deep trench into the never-ending flat terrain. With its sheer walls and superheated floor, nothing could be hiding there.

In the opposite direction, a range of mountains loomed miles away, one of the peaks boasting a wide, volcanic cone. Billy sniffed the air again. Could there possibly be homes near the source of all this lava? That wouldn't make sense. But even if there were, could the aroma travel that far? Maybe the portal to the sixth circle was nestled in a pass between the mountains or even beyond the range. Bonnie wasn't here, so why stick around at a dead end?

He took a last look at Naamah's crumpled body. No time to bury her. It would probably take hours to reach the volcano, so he wanted to get started right away. Who could tell how long he had before darkness fell? Although the day was clear and bright, he couldn't find the sun. He let out a sigh and set off into the basaltic wasteland.

After a dozen or so paces, he spotted a flash of light from the corner of his eye. He whirled around and snatched out Excalibur. A solitary man sat at a picnic table poised at the edge of the chasm. Tall and slender, he leaned over with his elbows propped on each side of a plate, greedily gnawing on a leg of fried chicken. A black cloth covered the table, with steaming dishes spread from one side to the other – an oval serving dish piled with slices of turkey, grilled chicken legs, and sirloin steaks; thick pepperoni pizza on a stoneware disk; roasted ears of corn stacked in a pyramid; a mountain of mashed potatoes in a wide vat; an oversized gravy boat and ladle; and thick beef stew in a monstrous casserole dish.

Billy licked his parched lips. *That's where the smell came from! Why couldn't I see it before?* He stepped slowly toward the table. The man looked up, and without taking his mouth away from the chicken leg, he motioned for Billy to sit next to him.

Billy swallowed an eruption of burning liquid. "Uh, no thanks."

The man dropped the stripped bone on his plate and wiped his mouth with his sleeve. "Come on! I won't bite!" He grabbed a slice of pizza, and a string of melted cheese stretched over his hand. He stuffed half of it between his chomping teeth and shook his head, talking with his mouth full. "This is the best food you can find anywhere in this God-forsaken land. Of that, you can be sure."

Billy took a step closer but stayed out of reach. "Who are you? Why are you here?"

"I am Francis Peabody, but you can call me PJ."

"PJ? That doesn't fit Francis Peabody. Wouldn't it be FP?"

PJ shoved the crust into his mouth and grabbed another slice. "It's a childhood name that stuck, so to speak. I was called PBJ by my parents and six brothers because of my love for peanut butter and jelly sandwiches. Over time it shortened to PJ."

"Okay. I'll buy that." Billy extended his hand. "My name's Billy Bannister."

PJ kept both hands on the pizza and nodded. "Pleased to meet you BB."

Billy withdrew his hand and shifted his weight from foot to foot. "So, what are you doing here?"

PJ licked a string of cheese from his chin. "I'm a traveller, much like yourself. I entered the circles about forty years ago in search of a lost girl."

"A lost girl? Who?"

"A young lady, really – Shiloh Nathanson. I found her soon after I entered, but I had a bit of a mishap. My mind is fuzzy on the details, but when I tried to lead her home, I hit a wall of electricity and blacked out. After that, all I could remember was being carried by strong arms. I finally woke up in this place."

Billy pressed his hand against his gurgling stomach. "I don't get it. Why didn't I see you when I got here?"

PJ tipped up a bottle of dark liquid and downed several gulps. He belched loudly and wiped his mouth with the edge of the tablecloth. "It's the way of this world. Passing through dimensions doesn't always happen cleanly. I travelled through six circles, and going from one to the other was never the same."

"So you're stuck in this one now?"

PJ took another bite of pizza, his voice muffling as he chewed. "Seems that way, but I'm not complaining." He gestured toward the food with a wide sweep of his arm. "There's always plenty to eat."

"But what else do you do? Don't you get lonely?"

"Not really. I pretty much just eat most of the time. I'd watch the sunrise and sunset, but there's no sun to watch."

"Yeah. I noticed that." Billy sat at the opposite side of the table. "Are you always hungry?"

PJ belched again. "Not really, but I never get full or fat. The food's so good, why stop? It just keeps reappearing, and I'd swear it gets tastier every day." He slid the pizza toward Billy. "C'mon. Join in."

The smell of tomatoes and cheese surged into Billy's nose, setting off a five-alarm belly fire. The foodless hole in his stomach burned, begging for just a taste of the dripping mozzarella. He slid the plate away. "No. . . . No, I can't."

"Oh. Gas, huh?" PJ grabbed a bowl and scooped a ladle full of beef stew from the pot. "Here," he said, pouring it into the bowl with a slow swirl, "this'll settle your stomach." He stretched out his lanky body and placed the bowl right under Billy's nose, dropping a spoon into the stew.

The steamy vapours washed over Billy. Oh, the aroma! A breath from heaven! He tipped up the end of the spoon, revealing chunks of beef and potatoes swimming in luscious broth. Saliva squirted so hard, his glands ached. Pain gripped his stomach, demanding that he fill his fiery chasm and give it something to gnaw on instead of his own flesh.

Billy pushed the bowl away and tried to stand up, but the pain doubled him over.

PJ rushed to his side and gripped his arm. "Come, boy. You need nourishment. And this food is to die for."

Billy groaned, shoving his fists into his belly. "That's what I'm afraid of. I was told that no food here is fit to eat." He pulled free from PJ's hold and wiped a stream of sweat from his brow. Feeling his ring slide across his skin, he dropped his hand down and checked the rubellite. It no longer pulsed as it had before.

"Not fit to eat?" PJ nodded with his eyes half closed. "I'll bet Joseph told you that."

The pain eased a bit, allowing Billy to straighten his body. "You've met Joseph?"

"Indeed! He gave me a fine meal in the second circle and warned me not to eat again. But am I supposed to wait forty years to eat? I think not."

Billy eyed his ring again, rubbing the gem with his thumb. "How long did you wait?"

PJ shrugged. "Oh, a day or two."

Billy narrowed his eyes. "A day or two? That's not so long when you know the food's not fit to eat."

"Oh, so now you're the expert on what's fit to eat? Who do you think you are, Julia Child?"

Billy slid his foot across the lava flow. "Uh, no. I don't even know who that is. It's just that Joseph said—"

"Joseph said!" PJ interrupted in a mocking tone. He set his hands on his hips. "But did Joseph ever tell you why it was unfit?"

"No. I didn't ask—"

"Well!" PJ extended his hand. "See there? There *is* no reason. Unfit, indeed! Bunch of nonsense." He beat his chest with his fists. "As you can see, I am alive and well."

"Yeah, but what's the good of that? You're stuck here like a cat in a cage. Don't you want to try to leave?"

"Not really. You see, I was once like you – anxious, ambitious, adventurous. Oh! That's alliterative. Very good!" PJ swivelled his head from side to side. "Now, where was I? Oh, yes. I am embracing my fate, BB, which is really not a bad one, you see." His eyes brightened. "Oh! That rhymes. Excellent!"

Billy ground his molars together. Talking to this guy was a waste of time. He wasn't a prisoner who needed rescue; he was a candidate for a padded cell. Could the food have addled his brain? "But why would you want to live here?" he asked. "It's just a world of endless lava fields and no one to talk to."

"Not so." PJ pushed his hands into his armpits and flapped his elbows. "A bird comes by every day, a raven, in fact, and I talk to it."

"You talk to a bird!? Isn't that a little bit crazy?"

PJ shrugged. "Not if the bird speaks first. It would be rude not to answer."

"What do you talk about?"

"Why, food, of course! The raven asks me what I wish to eat, and I tell it. When it leaves, the food appears."

Billy nodded slowly. "I see. . . . A raven." He gazed out over the chasm, lowering his voice to a whisper. "Yet still he foils the raven's plot . . .Tables turned. . . . Hmmm." With his stomach pain easing further, he took a deep breath, trying to figure out this odd man in this equally odd world. It didn't make sense. Food, no matter how good, shouldn't be enough to make him want to stay. Life here had to be more boring than watching mannequins play chess.

He kicked at a black ripple on the stony ground. Turning back, he edged close to the bench and pinched the corner of the tablecloth.

PJ's brow furrowed, and his square chin grew tight. Billy knew he had to make this quick. Leaning over, he grabbed the edge of the table and lifted, pushing it, food and all, into the chasm. After watching it bang against the wall and splash into the lava, he turned back, brushing his hands against each other.

PJ's face blazed scarlet. He lunged toward Billy and pinned his arms to his sides. "Idiot! That food was mine!" PJ lifted Billy off his feet and walked him toward the chasm's edge. "Now you'll pay, you fool!"

Billy tried to spew fire in PJ's face, but no flames came out. He strained his arms against the pressure and grabbed two fistfuls of PJ's shirt, hoping the crazed glutton wouldn't throw him in if he hung on.

With Billy clamped to him, PJ threw his own body into the gorge. They plummeted, PJ releasing Billy as they tumbled through the scalding air. Billy let out a blood-curdling shout, tensing every muscle as he plunged toward the river of lava.

Rolling his body into a ball, Billy tucked his face between his arms. He hit the river bottom-first and splashed into the thick, red lava, throwing his head back and opening his eyes. PJ, his face frozen in terror, splashed right next to him, and his body burst into flames on impact.

Billy felt nothing – neither the sizzling torment he expected, nor the viscous, molten rock that surrounded his body. He floated near the edge of the river, and the lava next to his body began changing colour, from red to purple to black. The thick liquid hardened into crusty soot, giving him a solid foundation underneath. He stood up, and his feet sank into gritty, black dust until he was knee deep in volcanic ash. He waded to the edge of the river and shook the powder from his shoes. Drawing in a deep breath, he suddenly felt strong, invigorated, almost wild with energy. His insides boiled, and with a giant heave, he spewed an enormous stream of fire from his mouth, blasting it out in one long breath.

When the fire ceased, he crossed his arms and grasped his biceps, flexing them to test his bursting strength. He felt ready to conquer the world.

Tightening his muscles, he drew out Excalibur, his fingers strangling the hilt. The laser beam shot out brighter than ever before. The beam curved back toward him and twisted around his body like a spider spinning a net around its prey. The web of light grew into a radiant cocoon, and the flaming river seemed to melt away.

He felt like he was floating in nothingness – brilliant white nothingness. Except for a gentle breeze wafting across his face, he sensed no movement. His vision slowly cleared, the white light dissolving into grey, then sharpening into fuzzy objects – a cobblestone street, dilapidated buildings, and a muscular man dressed in black standing in the distance.

Billy rubbed his eyes, then shook his head. *Okay, what now? I hope it's not another crazy glutton.*

He marched forward, the scene taking shape with each step. The man in black straddled a curled-up body, his feet set as though he had conquered a foe.

Billy quickened his pace, trying to focus on the body. It looked strange, like it had . . . *It does! It has wings!*

Billy regripped Excalibur's hilt and ran, screaming, "Bonnie!" But just before he came within striking distance, the man drew his own sword and shouted, "Halt, foul dragon!"

The force of the voice rattled Billy's brain. He screeched to a stop, his legs suddenly feeling like two Slinky springs. His arms drooped, but he managed to hang on to Excalibur. He recognized that voice, the voice that haunted and hunted him through months of sweat-filled nightmares. His eyes cleared. Glaring back at him was the evil face of Palin!

I'm ready," Karen said. "What do you want me to type?"

"Let's see . . ." Ashley latched onto a handful of hair at the back of her head and spoke slowly. "Bonnie, this device is called Apollo. Hold it in the spot you found it. When you're ready to leave the circles, slide the metal flap on the base, and press the button. A shining door should appear, and you should be able to walk through the interdimensional passageway. That's all for now." She released her hair and raised a finger. "Wait! Add this. . . . Too much information can make your brain choke."

"Hold it. How do you spell 'interdimensional'? It's not in my spell checker."

Ashley spelled it out in rapid-fire fashion: "I-N-T-E-R-D-I-M-E-N-S-I-O-N-A-L."

"Got it! I'll put it in the transfer box."

The professor grasped Ashley's arm. "We should also send the song to Miss Silver."

"The song?"

"Yes, the one I believe Merlin implanted in my mind. Perhaps she'll be able to give it to William."

Ashley handed the computer to the professor. "Okay, sing it to Larry; he'll transcribe it and attach it to Karen's document, then he'll print it all out."

The professor raised the handheld computer to his lips, like a stage singer with a microphone. He cleared his throat and closed his eyes, his throat beginning to waver as he crooned.

A dragon chained in darkest pits
Will not behold pure freedom's light,
For dragons claim a lofty perch,
Yet cannot reach the highest height.

For even now in pits of gloom
The dragon's pride will never bow,
Until redemption's sword sets free
The dragon's heart to kneel and vow.

He cleared his throat again and handed the computer to Ashley.

Ashley swung it up to her ear. "Larry, did you get it?"

"Yes. Bravo! If I had legs I would give him a standing ovation."

"Cut the comedy and print it out with Karen's note. She'll zap it over to Bonnie."

`"Will do. One fantastic, far-fetched fax coming up!"`

Marilyn whispered into Ashley's ear. "Can we get an update on Billy?"

Ashley lifted the computer again. "Barlow, do you have any Billy news for us?"

All five gathered around, waiting for Barlow's reply.

"Yes. It's good news and bad news, Miss. It seems that somehow young William survived a fall into a river of fire, but now he is standing in front of a stocky swordsman, who holds himself and his sword in excellent form. But even worse is what I see on the ground – a body . . . with wings."

"Bonnie?" Walter asked.

"I cannot say for sure," Barlow replied, "but I know of no other human with dragon wings such as these, and the swordsman is standing over her as though she is his vanquished foe."

"He must be that guy we saw!" Shiloh shouted. "He was carrying a bucket, and Bonnie scared him away."

"Is Billy moving toward him?" Marilyn asked.

"Not yet. He seems to be standing still."

Walter pressed closer. "Does the swordsman look like anyone you've seen before, Barlow?"

"Now that you mention it, he does. Devin had a squire, an expert warrior who remained in his lowly position in spite of his talents, but I have forgotten his name."

Walter clenched his fist. "I'll bet it's Palin!"

"Yes, yes. It *is* Palin. I'm sure of it."

"I think Billy can take him," Walter said, tightening his jaw. "He's worked out so hard, I can't imagine anyone beating him."

The professor shook his head. "But he's never faced the likes of Palin in his training."

"Well . . . no. But I'm still betting on Billy. I just wish I could help him."

Barlow's voice returned through the computer speaker. "I fought him myself, Walter, in the king's annual tournament. Even in my prime, he bested me in under a minute."

Billy straightened his failing legs and shouted, "Get away from Bonnie!"

Palin laughed. "Bannister, you are the comic, aren't you? You killed me, and now you expect me to just give this witch's body over to you."

Billy's heart skipped a beat. "Her body?"

"Oh, yes. She's quite dead. But she's freshly dead, so my mistress will still be able to use her."

Billy raised his fist to eye level. His rubellite stared back at him without a hint of a pulse, cold and lifeless. His legs shook again. Tears welled in his eyes. Was Bonnie really dead? He clenched his fist so tight, his nails dug into his hand. Palin couldn't be trusted. He had to be lying. Billy tightened his grip on Excalibur's hilt. "This is your last chance, Palin. Stand aside or else."

Palin snorted. "Or else what? You'll kill me? You've already done that." He scowled, and his voice spat out like a hissing snake. "Why don't you try a blast of your fiery breath? That worked before when my back was turned, you half-breed coward!"

Billy felt the fire boiling in his belly, but he knew Palin was baiting him. For some reason, he wanted the fire. Would it energize him? Billy drew back his sword, but no beam came out. It didn't matter. He could beat this scoundrel without the light. His leg muscles strengthened, and his arms rippled with power. "Your back's not turned now. Defend yourself!"

Palin stepped in front of Bonnie's body and raised his sword. "You have no chance, pye-dog. You're just a kid who believed an elaborate lie. Patrick's been playing you like a violin. He wants you to set his minions free so he can take over the world. My mistress has been trying to stop him, and if you let me deliver Bonnie's body to her, she will foil his plans."

Billy shouted, angry sparks flying from his mouth. "You're a liar!" He gritted his teeth and charged forward, swinging Excalibur with all his might. Palin met the blow, parrying with a powerful swing of his own. The blades flashed as they slammed together and locked in a stalemate, each warrior leaning in and grunting. The dark knight suddenly lowered his blade and ducked down, sending Billy rushing forward. He swiped at Billy's legs, but Billy leaped over the deadly blade just in time. He slid on his heels and turned to face Palin again. Billy swung immediately, but Palin lifted his sword, knocking Excalibur upward just before it could slice his throat.

Striking empty air, Billy's arms followed through, exposing his undefended right side. Palin thrust his blade toward Billy's ribs. Billy collapsed his legs, bending his body backwards as the knight's sword tip passed right over his eyes. He pulled his own sword back and sliced Palin's wrist, but no blood came out, only a trickle of black slime.

Palin toppled over, and Billy rolled away to avoid his falling body. He jumped to his feet and leaped toward Palin, who had fallen flat on his face. He planted a foot on the knight's back, digging in with the heel of his boot. "Drop the sword!" he commanded.

Palin's hand opened, and his sword fell to the street. "Go ahead and run me through, you coward. Stabbing in the back is what you do best."

Billy pushed all his weight on Palin's back and kicked the sword with his other foot. "You're already dead." He stepped away from Palin, avoiding his opponent's hands, and picked up the vanquished sword. "Stay put if you know what's good for you."

Billy hurried toward Bonnie, keeping a wary eye on Palin as he laid both swords on the street. He dropped to his knees and turned her body on its side, his fingers pressing her wrist.

No pulse!

He leaned over and laid his ear against her lips.

No breathing!

Billy's heart raced. He coughed fiery spittle, choking on scalding liquid. He laid his cheek on her chest, his skin burning as his face tightened into a twisted mask. He gasped, crying through spasms of roaring pain. "She's . . . she's dead! Oh! . . . Oh, dear God! . . . Dear God, don't let her be dead!"

Palin lifted his head and yelled, "I told you she was dead, Dragon Boy."

Billy picked up a stone and flung it at Palin. "Shut up! Just shut up!"

The stone glanced off Palin's leg. The dark knight rose to his knees, laughing scornfully.

Billy snatched up Excalibur and jumped to his feet. A new stream of sparks flared from his mouth as he roared, "I oughta cut your head off right here and now!"

"I didn't kill your girlfriend, you fool! She killed herself."

Billy screamed. "You're a liar!" A stream of fire spewed out, barely missing Palin's head.

The knight stood and dusted off his clothes. "Call me whatever you want, but I saw her do it."

Billy held Excalibur back with both arms, ready to strike. "Talk fast. In ten seconds, your head will be looking up at your body."

"Keep yapping, mongrel. Your mouth is bigger than your brain. You can slice me to pieces, and Bonnie will still be dead." He pressed his thumb against his chest. "I know how to give her new life."

Billy's muscles wilted, but he forced himself to hold Excalibur up. "Why should I believe a single word you say?"

"Because we both want the same thing. We both want to revive Bonnie."

Billy slowly lowered Excalibur and let its tip rest on the ground. He kept his voice firm. "What's in it for you?"

Palin took a step closer. "I'll have new life in the world of the living."

Billy edged back. "How?"

Palin crossed his arms over his chest. "It would be impossible to explain. If you want her to live, you'll just have to believe me. I know you don't want me back in your world, but at least Bonnie will be alive again."

Billy twisted the sword, drilling the tip into the dust. "I'm still listening. What needs to be done?"

Palin pointed toward an abandoned feed store. "Take her body through that door over there. It will lead you to the seventh circle. But make sure you put Excalibur into the doorway first, or the passage will do to you what it did to Bonnie."

"Are you planning to go with me?"

Palin extended an open palm. "Not unless we both hold Excalibur while we pass through."

Billy thrust Excalibur into his back scabbard. "I'd rather chew glass."

"Then you'll have to go alone." Palin began walking in the opposite direction of the feed store. "When you get to the seventh circle," he called, "you'll meet someone who will tell you what to do."

"How will I know him?" Billy yelled.

Palin turned, a crooked smile bending his lips. "Oh, you'll know him, all right. He's your father."

CHAPTER 19

BREATHLESS

Hot tears flowed down Billy's cheeks as he knelt at Bonnie's side. He snatched Palin's sword from the ground and heaved it toward the feed store. It clanked against the wall and bounced back to the street. He slid his arms under Bonnie's legs and back and cradled her body. With a low grunt, he lifted her and lumbered to the doorway. Out of the corner of his eye, he kept watch over Palin as he marched toward the opposite side of town.

Billy stopped a few feet in front of the door. A curtain of agitated light crossed its opening, and a strange object sat on the floor between his shoes and the threshold. The object's wooden frame reminded him of an old-fashioned hourglass, except the inner enclosure was a tall rectangle rather than curved glass with a pinched middle.

He laid Bonnie down and grabbed the frame, gazing into the glass as he straightened his body. *What's this? A piece of paper?* He found a hinged door on the glass, flipped it open, and pulled out the four-inch-square scrap. Through his tears he read out loud,

"Bonnie, this device is called Apollo. Hold it in the spot you found it. When you're ready to leave the circles, slide the metal flap on the base, and press the button. A door should appear, and you should be able to walk through the interdimensional passageway. That's all for now. Too much information can make your brain choke."

Billy recognized the author immediately. "Ashley!"

The rest of the note was printed in a smaller font. Billy pulled it closer to read.

A dragon chained in darkest pits
Will not behold pure freedom's light,
For dragons claim a lofty perch,
Yet cannot reach the highest height.

For even now in pits of gloom
The dragon's pride will never bow,
Until redemption's sword sets free
The dragon's heart to kneel and vow.

He folded the note and shoved it into his hip pocket. *Too many poems!*

Billy tipped Apollo at an angle. *Ah! Here's the flap.* He opened the door and put a quivering finger over the button. With his heart racing, he swallowed away a new lump. *But if I go back now, everything's lost. There'll be no hope for Bonnie. I have to get to the seventh circle. But what if Palin's lying? Could things get any worse?*

Miss!" Barlow called through the speakers, "the battle is over, and William is now approaching Bonnie."

Walter, the professor, and Marilyn huddled around the handheld computer. "Is she all right?" Ashley asked. "Can you tell?"

Barlow's voice lowered to a barely audible whisper. "No . . . No, Miss. She is not all right. I . . . I am quite certain that she is dead."

Ashley's voice squeaked. "How can you be so sure?"

"Miss, . . . I have seen many dead bodies, and . . ." A long sigh sounded through the speaker. "The young lass is no longer among the living."

A surge of heat shot into Walter's face. "And Billy didn't whack Palin's head off?!"

"No, Walter," Barlow replied. "I saw Palin walking away a free man."

Walter balled up his fists and kicked the turf. "I don't believe it!" he shouted. "Billy wouldn't let Palin go free if he killed Bonnie! He would have chopped the little rat to bits!" He punched the air. "There's just no way it's true!"

Marilyn put her arm around Walter, barely able to speak. "But . . . but Barlow saw her body, and . . . and you heard what he said. Nobody knows what's really going on in there. We have to trust Billy."

Walter jerked his cloak and hood out of Ashley's backpack. "If Bonnie's really dead, Billy can't possibly be thinking straight." He raised the hood in his shaking fist. "Send me in there. I'll find out what's going on."

"How?" Ashley asked, wiping her tears, her voice still pitched high. "Apollo's in the circles."

"Circles, smircles. Where there's a Larry, there's a way!"

Ashley bit her thumb, then raised her eyebrows. "I guess it can't hurt to ask." She tilted her head upward. "Larry, based on the last readings of the electromagnetic flux here, what would it take to open a portal? Can you make Apollo do it from the other side?"

"Affirmative. Apollo is fully charged and functional, and since I know the precise positioning of the portal and Apollo, the transfer should be perfect this time. But my programming instructs me to inform you of a risk tolerance limit. If I open a portal now, Apollo will have to recharge again, rendering it inoperative for a time."

"How long?"

"That depends on the power of the flash. If Walter intends to pass through, I suggest a flash that would delay the next one by an hour."

"An hour?! But Billy might need it before an hour. What kind of flash would delay the next one by say . . . fifteen minutes?"

"A very small one. It would create a short-lived rift in the dimensional barrier. He might be able to squeeze through it, but the danger level is high."

"How high is 'high'?"

"Impossible to calculate. I have no units of measure with which to communicate a level of danger. My analysis merely suggests the crossing of a risk tolerance boundary."

Walter pulled the cloak on and slid his head into the hood. "Get me in there. Billy's my best friend, and he needs me. Don't try to talk me out of it."

"Why?" Marilyn asked. "Billy seems safe right now, and you can't help Bonnie."

Walter spread out his hands. "I can't explain it. Something's wrong, and I have to go in."

Professor Hamilton peered through the holes in Walter's hood and gazed into his eyes. "I understand completely, Walter. I support your passion, but the prophetic poem doesn't allow for William to have any more helpers."

Walter closed his eyes to hide his tears, but pain erupted in his voice. "His helper can't help him anymore!" He grabbed the professor's shoulders, his tears now breaking through. "What if she really *is* dead, Prof? I . . . I have to . . . to take her place!" Walter wrapped his arms around his teacher.

The professor pulled Walter close and patted his shoulder, holding one hand on the back of his head. He sniffed, and his hands trembled. "You're right, Walter. The events have seemed a fantasy of sorts, but if Bonnie has really died, it's . . . it's a terrible tragedy."

Walter pulled away. "Then I have to go *now*." He lined up the hood's eyeholes. "Tell Larry to fire up that puppy." He ascended the slope to the place where Apollo had disappeared.

Ashley's smile quivered. "Larry. Give us . . ." She swallowed and took in a deep breath. "Give us the small flash on my command!"

"Ready and waiting for your word."

"Ready, Walter?"

Walter flashed an "OK" sign with his fingers.

A hand slapped over Ashley's mouth. She let out a muffled shriek. A tall, hooded man in a black cloak held her from behind, one arm around her waist and the other angling her head back. His deep, malice-filled voice shouted, "So you're the one who's been interfering!"

The professor lunged, but the intruder pulled away. "Back off, old man, or I'll snap her neck like a toothpick."

Walter dropped to a crouch and began skulking toward Ashley, hoping his own black cloak would keep him hidden. He followed the flat terrace, staying as low as possible.

"Just stay quiet," the man growled, "and no one else gets hurt." He began walking slowly toward the portal area, half-dragging Ashley with him.

Walter made a bending course around the man and sneaked up from behind. He could tell that Shiloh had seen his manoeuvres. She hopped into the man's path, walking backwards, apparently trying to keep him distracted.

"Where are you taking her?" Shiloh demanded.

The man kept walking. "To a pleasant little village. Peaceful and quiet."

"I think I know the place," Shiloh continued. "Why don't you take me instead?

"Shut up, wench!" When he arrived at the portal, he released Ashley's mouth and yanked back a fistful of her hair. "I heard you yapping to that machine. Give the order! Open the portal!"

Walter saw Ashley's eyes shift his way as he crawled up to the intruder's side. He nodded and flashed another "OK" sign at her.

Ashley's voice rattled, shaking almost beyond recognition. "La . . . Larry. Gi . . . give Apollo the . . . the signal."

"Ashley, my AI programming suggests that you are suddenly distressed. I am switching to high security mode."

"Karen!" Ashley screamed. "Switch Larry to manual! Now!"

"Sure thing, Boss."

Holding his breath, Walter rose slowly behind Ashley's captor.

"Whew!" Karen said. "Got it just in time. He's now on vocal override."

Walter lifted his hand toward the man's head. His timing had to be perfect.

Ashley's throat squeezed almost completely shut. "Larry," she choked out, "Flash . . . Apollo."

A splash of brilliance sprinkled across the grass, drawing a rectangle from just above the ground up to Ashley's waist. The man unzipped his cloak in front and began to wrap it around her body as he edged toward the portal.

Walter snatched off the man's hood and shoved him backwards toward the glowing rectangle. He wrenched Ashley away as the man toppled to the grass, his head striking the electromagnetic barrier. The intruder writhed on the ground, shrieking.

Walter pulled Ashley close and shut his eyes as a series of pops and sizzles overwhelmed the man's dwindling screams.

The professor shouted, "Go Walter! Before the portal closes!"

Walter opened his eyes. The professor and Marilyn were dragging the intruder's body away by the ankles, and the portal window had shrunk to half its original size. Walter squeezed Ashley's hand and dropped down to all fours. As he crawled ahead, Ashley called out, her tears streaming, "You can tell me any jokes you want, Walter." She began sobbing. "Any time you want."

Walter gave her one last "OK" signal before covering his hands with his sleeves. He then lowered his head, and scurried through the portal in a splash of sparks.

Billy straightened his body, straddling Apollo on the feed store porch. Bonnie lay curled in a foetal position at his feet, one wing wedged under her side. The electrified door sizzled nearby, drawing chaotic ripples of light across Bonnie's sweatshirt.

Billy lifted Excalibur and tried to summon the beam. It hadn't worked against Palin, so who could tell if it would work now? But he had to know. Without the sword, Apollo was his only option.

After a brief electrical spurt, Excalibur burst with light, its laser shooting up and burning a hole through the porch ceiling. After a sigh of relief, he stooped, trying to figure out how to carry Bonnie without zapping her.

Apollo suddenly flashed at Billy's feet, blinding his eyes. He dove over Bonnie's body, keeping the sword's light safely away. The scene around him shattered into shards of light, as if someone had broken a huge glass window with the old town's image painted on the surface. The pieces crumbled, dropping out of sight, leaving behind a new scene, steep mountainsides that plunged into a narrow valley.

Billy lifted himself from Bonnie's body and looked all around. *What happened? I didn't push Apollo's button!* He knelt on a gigantic flat rock at the low point of a mountain pass.

White vapour clung to the mountainsides, like thin clouds struggling to scale the rocky crags. A rock-filled gully led into the heart of the pass where two mountains formed a *V*, leaving barely enough room for a man to walk, much less a man who had to carry a dead girl.

A cool breeze dried Billy's cheeks. His chest heaved, cutting off his breath, leaving him only rhythmic spasms. The urge to just sit and cry was overwhelming, but he had to go on. Bonnie's only hope lay in a liar's dubious promise, but as fragile as it was, even a skeleton of hope was better than none at all.

He looked all around the flat rock for Apollo. The strange device had sparked new hope. It proved that Ashley was somehow tracking their progress. She had sent them a message from their own world, a ticket to a high-tech, interdimensional bus ride home, but now their link was broken. Apollo was gone.

Billy clenched his teeth. This was too much to take! Nobody said his mission would be impossible! Nobody said Bonnie would die!

He pushed his hand through his unnaturally long hair, now drenched with sweat. He placed his palms on his cheeks. Still warm and puffy. He reached across his chest and grabbed his rock hard biceps. Hauntingly strange!

He gasped for breath. With his chest heaving like a wild animal's, he didn't even feel like the same person anymore; he felt like his whole body had morphed into a hideous creature.

So where should he go? Was this the seventh circle?

A light glimmered through the narrow opening in the mountains and disappeared, like the sun striking the mirror of a speeding car. He scooped Bonnie up again and headed for the gap, trying to follow the light, glad at least that his abnormal strength was good for something. As he entered the mountain pass, the two slopes seemed like a pair of hands poised to slap together at any second and smash him like a pesky housefly.

Pebbles and grit tumbled down as he navigated the narrow path. He had to walk at an angle to keep Bonnie's head from striking the side. Sure, she was dead, but he couldn't bear to let a hair of her head scrape against the rocks.

After several minutes the path opened into a wide ledge that overlooked a deep canyon. The ledge wrapped around the mountain to his left, looking like a protruding bottom lip from a gigantic rocky face. With careful steps, he followed the lip, keeping his eyes wary for the glimmer. Something had to cause it, and maybe it, too, had gone this way. There really wasn't any other way to go.

He rounded a curve, and a bridge came into view, an arching span of stone with waist-high parapets on either side, each wall notched with a series of square cogs that resembled a row of rocky molars. The bridge crossed the canyon, ending at another ledge protruding from the mouth of a massive cleft in the opposite mountainside.

He gazed down at the valley to the left of the bridge. Morning sunshine cast bright rays across the bridge and down into the depths, illuminating a dry gully filled with strangely shaped skeletons. With some of the skeletons partially intact, he recognized their form – long necks, spiny ridges riding on thick backbones, and remnants of leg bones, narrow skulls, rib cages, and wing structures. *Dragons!*

To the right of the bridge, an enormous red stone lay impacted between the two mountains. It looked like a river dam, perhaps drying out the valley many years ago, but now it seemed that the river no longer flowed at all. Huge white letters covered the face of the boulder, rows of etched poetry. He read the words silently.

The final circle numbers seven,
And beasts await your sword's command.
The greatest danger tests your faith,
And wisdom's touch will make you stand.

The bridge of faith still lies in wait,
The narrow path of answered prayer.
Restore the fountain from the stone,
Regenerating souls laid bare.

Billy pulled Bonnie's head close and rubbed his cheek against her hair. "I wish you could see all this," he said out loud.

A man in a black cloak appeared from behind a solitary boulder just inside the yawning mouth of the cleft on the other side. He waved his arms frantically. "Billy! Come over here!"

Billy hoisted Bonnie's body a bit higher and squinted across the valley. "Sir Patrick?"

"Yes, yes!" Patrick stepped up to the edge of the bridge. "I heard what happened to Bonnie. Bring her to me. There is still hope for her."

Billy put a foot on the bridge and tested his weight on it.

"It's sturdy!" Patrick shouted. "I would come and help you, but it's a one-way bridge." He spread his fingers on an invisible wall and leaned against it. "You can come to me, but I can't come to you."

Just as Billy stepped forward, a huge shadow enveloped the entire span. An enormous dragon swooped down and landed gracefully on the bridge, straddling the left parapet. His reddish brown scales reflected the sun's glory, and his long neck curled over, placing his head in front of Billy. His red eyes flashed, and his wings beat the air like two whipping sails. "Billy! Stop! You must not cross this bridge!"

Billy gulped. "Da . . . Dad?"

Walter yanked off his hood and rubbed his eyes. The blinding light slowly faded away to reveal a row of deserted buildings lining a cobblestone street. He stuffed his hood into his pocket and swung his head around, quickly taking in his surroundings. Apollo sat at his feet, and a sword lay near the front wall of the nearest building. He snatched up both of them. A solitary man about a hundred yards away marched toward a horse stable. Billy didn't seem to be anywhere around, so Walter tiptoed after the man, staying in the shadows of the buildings.

The man disappeared through the stable's open double doors. Walter ran up to the outer wall and inched close enough to the door to peer inside. As his eyes adjusted to the gloom, he could see the man standing next to an eerie light that illuminated his sinister face.

Palin!

Walter sneaked into the stable, quiet as a stalking cat. He crept as close to the dark knight as he thought safe, and crouched, barely breathing.

Palin squatted in front of a short barrel. A glowing statuette stood on top, a feminine figure, about a foot tall, with a long, flowing dress. Its arms were spread out as if making supplication, and its head was angled upward. Walter swallowed a gasp. The statuette moved! Its arms waved in jerky motions like a movie projection with missing frames, and its lips seemed to be forming words.

Walter crawled closer and pressed his ear between two crates. The statuette's voice poured out a mixture of sweetness and poison. "I keep you here, my dear Palin, for my good pleasure. I know letting young Arthur win your little swordplay wounded your pride, but I care nothing about that. The fact that he thinks he defeated you fulfils my purpose, and you will have another chance to take your revenge. Very soon he will deliver the virgin bride to me, and I will have my hostiam. After that, you can slice him to pieces for all I care."

"What if he doesn't deliver her? What will you do?"

"He will deliver her. How can he not trust his own father?"

"But did you foresee Patrick's interference?"

"I expected Merlin's fools to meddle somehow, but it will not matter. You see, every test in the circles actually works in my favour. If Bannister fails, Merlin's plans to revive his precious menagerie in the seventh circle will also fail. If the young king succeeds, he will be bursting with pride, making him perfectly ripe for harvesting the girl from his arms. You will see."

"And when do I get to skewer the mongrel pup?"

"Patience! I want our victory to be as sweet as possible. When I take over the girl's body, I will pronounce the boy's death sentence myself. Won't it be a delight for Billy Bannister to hear the command for his death from the lips of Bonnie Silver, his prophetic bride?"

Palin leaned his head back and laughed. "Oh, yes! Perfect! I can see his face now! And he will die believing he was forsaken by the one he held most dear!" He laughed again, almost cackling with pleasure. "Morgan, your plan makes me feel positively alive again!"

Walter strangled the sword's hilt. With his jaw locked tight, he was ready to leap out and hack that hyena's head off with a single swipe. But he had to wait. He had to find a way to warn Billy, and attacking Palin now would ruin everything.

The statuette continued. "Come, then. We will plunge together into the seventh circle and prepare to receive our army. The Watchers will rule the earth again!"

Palin straightened his body and closed his eyes. Walter retrieved his hood and pulled it over his head, grabbing up Apollo and the sword as he rose to his feet. A stream of light poured out of the statuette and shot around the room dozens of times, creating a blinding vortex of radiant energy, like a tornado of lightning.

Hot fingers grabbed Walter's frame, knifing through him like electric sabres. He cried out as the flashing cyclone lifted him into its swirl and flushed him through the floor. Hurtling feet first, he zoomed down a rollercoaster of light, rushing wind trying to snatch away his hood as he bit the material to keep it in place.

After a few seconds, the rocketing plummet slowed, and the swirl of light placed Walter on solid ground as gently as an old farmer would set down a newborn chick. Being numbed from the electric jolt, he couldn't feel Apollo and the sword still clenched in his fingers. He set them down and jerked the hood off. With long strokes, he tried to rub feeling back into his hands and arms while he scanned the area.

He spotted Palin, walking away on a ledge, treading lightly over a carpet of pebbles. A steep mountain rose to his left, a deep canyon plunged to his right, and rocky terrain lay all around. Seconds later, the dark knight disappeared into a yawning archway in the mountainside. In the opposite direction, far in the distance, a bridge crossed the canyon. Walter bit his lip. *No time to check that out. I gotta follow Palin!*

He grabbed Apollo and the sword and headed for the archway. The ledge was level enough, but a layer of talus littered the path. His shoes crunched down on the sand and pebbles, forcing him to tiptoe to mute the noise.

When he reached the mouth of the cave, he flattened himself against the side, creeping in inch by inch. His eyes adjusted slowly. Two forms took shape. One was obviously Palin. The other was more slender, a bit taller, and seemed to be wearing a dress. Both had their backs to the cave entrance.

Walter leaned forward and narrowed his eyes. *The statuette!* But now she was normal size, and the only light surrounding her came from the rising sun's beams that splashed on the cave's vestibule. *Hmmm. He called her Morgan back at the stable. I've heard that name somewhere before.*

Morgan and Palin leaned over, peering into a wide hole, and smatterings of their conversation trickled into Walter's ears. He sneaked as close as he dared and listened. Morgan's voice echoed off the rock walls. "Don't be ashamed, Palin. Viewing Tartarus for the first time would make any man tremble, and I understand your frailties. It is difficult for you to gaze upon utter hopelessness."

"Yet they have endured it for thousands of years!" Palin exclaimed. "Your husband must be amazing."

"Now you understand why I have gone through so much to get him out. It has taken all these years for my plans to come together, but it will be worth it."

"What if the mongrel won't come?" Palin asked. "Do you have a plan B?"

"I do. But don't worry. He will come. He will trust his father, and Clefspeare will deliver his son and Bonnie directly to me. Then, when Billy gives the girl up, I will be able to possess her." Morgan swung away from the hole, her silky dress spinning with her, and took several steps toward Walter's hiding place. Walter pressed his body against the wall and held his breath. She set her hands on her hips, her eyes fixed on Palin. "It's time you had a dragon history lesson. You and Devin battled them all your lives, but did he ever tell you why he lusted for their blood?"

"Is that a trick question?" Palin rolled his fingers into a fist. "Because they're evil."

Morgan turned and glided back to the edge of the hole. "Oh, yes. They were evil, at least by your definition of the word. Back when you first strapped on your sword, most dragons did the deeds of their spiritual father, the one to whom I bow the knee." She spread out her arms. A shaft of light rose from the floor, creating a flat, oval disk that hovered over the opening like a vertical flying saucer. She curled her finger, gesturing for Palin to join her. "I have a story to tell you. It's time you learned the mysteries behind my power."

The disk flared with a burst of light and slowly transformed into a moving image, a winged humanoid creature with flashing blue eyes and a dazzling white robe walking among an adoring crowd of humans. Its shining head towered at least two feet above its worshipers.

Walter rubbed both eyes with his fists. *Is that an angel?*

Morgan stood beside the display, like a teacher ready to give a lecture. "Long before your day," she began, "when the Watchers came to earth and united with us, we had to purge the skies of dragons in order to rule the world, for they were the only race with the power to destroy the Watchers."

The oval screen switched to three dragons flying over a canyon. A river of flame shot from their mouths and nostrils and slammed against the angel. The angel absorbed the fire and tripled in size, finally exploding into thousands of sparks of light.

"The ensuing battle was cataclysmic," Morgan continued, "igniting the great deluge that flooded the earth." The screen filled with images of floodwaters ravaging homes and dragging people, along with the shining angels, into raging rivers. Morgan's voice rose to match the terror of her story. "The rush of water swept the Watchers into the abyss, into the depths of Tartarus, where they have been imprisoned ever since, but Noah rescued two juvenile dragons in his ark, allowing them to multiply once again."

The screen went blank. Morgan took a deep breath and placed a hand over her heart. "In the meantime, we, the wives of the Watchers, sank in the floodwaters and perished. Yet, because we had become united with the Watchers, a few of us survived as wandering wraiths, immortal, but with no hope of life beyond our cursed existence."

Morgan gazed into the dim cave, a bare glow from the entrance illuminating her gaunt face. Walter held his breath again and squashed his body against the wall harder than ever. Now was no time to get caught in the clutches of the black queen of Spooksville.

Morgan placed a tender hand on Palin's head. "As you know, the other wives bore offspring to the Watchers, a race of supermen sometimes called the Nephilim. They also died in the tempest, but the flood could not destroy their spirits. They lived on and inhabited the new brood of dragons, conquering their minds and controlling their actions."

"And that's what made dragons evil," Palin added.

"If you mean that they began to serve my master, yes, most turned to our side. But a few were protected from the Nephilim, and they remained our enemies." She rubbed Palin's hair like she might a child's and laughed. "What's so comical is that you hunted dragons with Devin, thinking all dragons were evil, while Devin had a different agenda. You see, I prophesied that when the last dragon was eliminated, Devin would become like one of the Nephilim and help me rule the world. As he learned our ancient crafts, he became more and more like us, able to wield power and influence among the feeble-minded. And being infused with the power of dragon blood, he lived an unnaturally long life. Devin has survived the passing of his body, and like one of the fallen spirits, he awaited a new body."

Morgan chucked Palin's chin. "But what you didn't realize, was that when I sent you and Devin out to kill dragons, I really wanted you to kill the so-called good dragons. If you eliminated some of my pets along with them, it would be worth the effort.

I knew that only the good dragons could prevent the Watchers from ruling the world once I set them free, so I chalked up my losses to what you might call a 'queen's gambit'."

Palin gripped the hilt of his sword and tightened his fingers around it. "So you just used me like a pawn for over a thousand years?"

Morgan pressed her palms on his temples and kissed him tenderly on the forehead. "Exactly, my dear Palin, but you received your reward. I showed you how to live through it all. Even now, because you also took dragon blood for so long, you have become a wraith like me, and you're safe from the judgment seat . . . at least for now. When my plans succeed, you will be restored to the earth to serve me once again."

Palin loosened his grip on his sword. "And if you fail?"

Morgan drew back. A frown deepened her sunken cheeks, and she punctuated each word with venom. "I . . . will . . . not . . . fail!"

"But your plans count on Clefspeare betraying his own son. How can you be sure he'll do it?"

Morgan spread her hands horizontally, palms up, and interlocked her "pinkie" fingers. A puff of black smoke arose from her skin and formed into the shape of a dragon. A pair of wings flapped slowly on the back of the six-inch effigy as it hovered over her hands. "Like all dragons, Clefspeare trusts in the old ways – in nature, in earthly forces that came into being by the Maker's hand. He trusts in fire and scales, in claws and teeth. What he doesn't realize is that the ways of the earth are my ways, so his scales cannot protect him here." She clapped her hands together. The dragon crumbled into a shower of fine dust, and her evil grin returned, pushing dimples into her ashen face. "You will see. Clefspeare will unsheathe my greatest weapon and administer young Arthur's final test."

CHAPTER

Blasting Through

Ashley used one finger to tap the keys on her computer. "Okay, Apollo's moving, so we can assume Walter picked it up. That's cool, because it means we can follow his progress." She cocked her head to one side. "What was that? . . . A scream?"

The professor took three quick steps up the tor's slope. "I heard a scream, but there is no one around, not even any sightseers."

"That's odd." Ashley leaned closer to the computer. "For some reason, all the signals are getting clearer. I wonder if—" A sudden gust of wind blew Ashley's hair over her face. It continued in bursts, beating on her like a helicopter's downdraft.

Shiloh hunkered behind Ashley. "Don't worry," Ashley said. "It's okay. It's our friend Hartanna."

The great she-dragon landed softly on the tor's slope, her claws digging into the turf. She growled softly. "Clefspeare is near. I can feel it. I tracked the sensation to this haunted hill."

"Did anyone see you?" the professor asked.

"Unfortunately, yes. At least five people were ascending the tor from the other side. They screamed and ran away, but a boy had a camera. I fear he may have taken a picture of me." She stretched her long neck toward the professor. "I assume you are here for the same reason I am. Do you know where Clefspeare is?"

The professor shook his head. "No. Our search has also led us to the tor, as you assumed. It's a long story, but there is a portal to another dimension here, and we believe Clefspeare may be within it. Billy and Bonnie are also there . . . at least Bonnie *was* there."

"*Was* there?" Hartanna repeated.

The professor grasped his jacket lapels, then parted his lips as if to reply, but nothing came out. He pulled his handkerchief from his pocket and wiped his eyes.

Hartanna's growl deepened. "What happened to Bonnie?"

Marilyn placed a hand on Hartanna's flank, her own voice shaking. "We're not sure how." She gulped and took a deep breath. "But . . . she . . . passed away."

Hartanna whispered, "What?" Her eyes flamed red, and she shouted, "She died?!" She lifted her head high and let out a thunderous roar. Deep sobs wrenched her head up and down, and her entire body heaved. Marilyn laid her cheek on Hartanna's side and stretched her arms over her scales, moving with the dragon's rhythmic mourning.

While Hartanna wept, Shiloh pulled on Ashley's sleeve from behind, whispering into her ear. "Why is the dragon so upset about Bonnie?"

Ashley wiped a tear from each eye with the back of her hand. "Hartanna is her mother," she said softly.

"Her . . . her mother?" Shiloh sniffed, and her face contorted.

Ashley put an arm around her shoulder, but when Hartanna's groans clutched her heart, she stepped in front of Shiloh. "Better not let the dragon see you, at least not yet. Wait till we get a chance to tell her your story." She glanced back at Shiloh. "Any idea why you look so much like Bonnie?"

"That's the part I don't get. She says we're cousins, and you think I look like her, but the person I saw was covered with scales."

Ashley tilted her head. "Scales?"

"Yeah. Do you think she changed when she got into the other world?"

"Maybe. . . . I guess. Barlow didn't mention that, though." Ashley straightened her body, trying to make herself a screen for Shiloh. "Just keep your head down. Right now we have to deal with a huge, grieving dragon."

Sir Patrick's voice shrieked from the other side of the bridge. "Billy! Yes, this dragon is your father, but you have to trust me! You must cross the bridge to save yourself and Bonnie! It's the only way!"

Clefspeare spun his head and blew a stream of fire at Patrick. "Silence!"

Patrick covered his face with his cloaked sleeves. The flames splashed on his torso, making the mesh lining glow orange.

Clefspeare stretched his neck, bringing his head within a dozen feet of Billy. He spoke in a low growl. "Patrick's way is narrow of mind and focus. He doesn't understand the ancient ways of the earth." The wide dragon eyes seemed to soften, and the growl smoothed into a gentle whisper. "If you want to save Bonnie's life, give her to me. I will take her to someone who can revive her. But we must hurry. Since Bonnie has been dead for so long, time is of the essence."

Billy took a step forward but hesitated. "Where are you going to take her?"

Clefspeare opened his massive claws. “To the mistress of Excalibur, the lady who first gave the sword to Arthur. She understands the healing power of light energy.”

“Billy!” Patrick yelled. “Don’t listen to him. That woman is your enemy. I don’t know what her plans are, but they can’t be good.”

Clefspeare blew another stream of fire at Patrick, this time straight at his face. Patrick ducked below the flames, covering his head with his arms.

“Be gone, you pretender!” the dragon roared. “I’ve had enough of your meddling! Billy doesn’t need to hear you disparaging the lady. He needs to get Bonnie to her, and time is running out.”

Patrick bolted upright again. “Then he should ask you why you oppose his crossing the bridge. What harm could it do?”

The dragon swung his head back toward Billy. “It could do great harm. This bridge is the border between mortality and immortality. If you cross it, Bonnie’s fate is sealed. It will not be possible to revive her.”

“He lies, Billy! The bridge is the only way. Didn’t you see Merlin’s poem? Doesn’t it say, ‘The bridge of faith still lies in wait, the narrow path of answered prayer?’ You have followed Merlin’s path this far. Don’t turn aside now!”

Clefspeare spat out a baseball-sized sphere of flame, propelling it like a meteor toward Patrick. It grazed his cloak’s sleeve, lighting up the metallic lining around his elbow. The dragon growled. “Look who speaks, a man dressed in the robes of the unrighteous, a New Table knight asking you to obey a false prophet.” The dragon lowered his rumbling voice. “I, too, followed Merlin’s prophecies, far longer than you have. But they failed at every turn.” He extended his neck over the parapet. “Look into the valley and see the results. Merlin’s miracles didn’t save these dragons. They would have been better off keeping their claws and scales and fighting the slayers. Becoming human made them easy prey, and now they are dry bones in this valley of death."

Clefspeare lifted his head high, raising his voice as though he wanted Patrick to hear. "I am told that you have seen the letter branded in the skin of every New Table knight. Did anyone tell you what it means?"

"You mean the *M*?" Billy replied. "No. No one told me what it stands for."

"It stands for Merlin. He fooled me for years, but I discovered that he has been directing the New Table knights all along. How else could they have infiltrated this place so easily? Merlin set a trap to destroy the line of dragons, and his minions have killed Bonnie. Now we must get her to someone who can truly help, a faithful ally of the dragon race."

"No, Billy!" Patrick yelled. "The *M* stands for Morgan, Merlin's eternal enemy. Merlin is good and noble. You and Professor Hamilton know this to be true. Don't let this dragon's cheap trick fool you! The only way to rescue the prisoners in the valley is by crossing the bridge. Search your heart. Let your faith guide you."

Billy clenched his fists. "I'm trying to have faith!" he shouted. "But faith in what? How do I know who's telling the truth?"

The dragon stepped between Billy and Patrick. "Exactly! Faith in what, indeed! Your faith should be in your strength. Morgan allowed me to watch your accomplishments. In circle after circle you faced a different kind of evil. You overcame temptations so horrible any other human would have given in." Clefspeare puffed out his chest. "Yes, I saw you outwit the devil and plunge your sword into his heart. I saw you reject a crown of glory on that trail of blood. And would any other young man have turned down Naamah's advances? Yet, you, my son, remained a solid rock. And when I saw you overcome your rage and defeat

Palin face to face, I was so proud! You could have made a pincushion out of him, but you granted him mercy."

Clefspeare let out a guttural howl, seeming to laugh with joy. "Billy, you *are* the new King Arthur! Reach out now for his sceptre. The world is yours! You have come through victorious, and the winner takes it all!"

His whole body shaking, Billy dropped to one knee and placed Bonnie gently on the ground, careful to avoid damaging her wings. He raised his hand high. "Just let me think a minute." He bit his lip hard. Scenes from the seven circles flooded his mind – spearing the heart of the dragon and watching its blood drip to the ground like black tar, spurning the tearful entreaties of the raven-haired crown-bearer as she begged on bended knee, tearing his fragile heart away from the lovely temptress in New Eden's seductive web, and conquering the scornful warrior, the mocking phantom that haunted his dreams night after night.

He crossed his arms and squeezed his hardened biceps. He really was strong. He really had won all those battles. Could Clefspeare be right? Could Merlin have fooled everyone? Should he give Bonnie over on the chance that the dragon was telling the truth?

Bonnie's head lolled to one side, exposing her ear and a deathly pallid cheek. He leaned close and whispered, sobs breaking through. "I . . . I don't know what to do. . . . I guess you've got good connections where you are now, so . . . so if you can hear me . . . I could sure use some help. I'm . . . I'm not very good at this. I need a sign or something." A tear dripped from Billy's eye to Bonnie's cheek. He brushed it away with a lingering thumb. "You are my virgin bride . . . my immortal beloved." He wiped his nose with his sleeve and sniffed hard. "Somehow . . . some way . . . we'll be together again."

He straightened his body, ignoring the tears rolling down his cheeks. He tried to steel himself as he stood and faced Clefspeare again, but his arms and legs quivered. "Okay. What do you want me to do?"

The dragon opened his claws again. "Allow me to take Bonnie to Morgan."

Patrick screamed. "No, Billy!" He grabbed the edge of a boulder, his voice faltering. "You . . . must . . . not!"

Clefspeare extended one of his claws toward Bonnie. "It's the only way to save her." He flipped his tail toward the other side of the bridge. "Ask Patrick yourself. Does he know how to bring her back to life?"

Billy waited for Patrick to answer, but the grey-haired gentleman just leaned heavily on the boulder, his face ashen.

"You see!" Clefspeare roared. "His silence speaks volumes! I'm telling you to trust in what you have seen, your victories here in the circles, the tests you have passed to prove yourself king. I'm telling you how to save Bonnie's life. Patrick asks you to sacrifice an innocent lamb, to throw away a precious life just to fulfil an empty promise scrawled on an ancient stone."

Patrick struggled to the edge of the bridge, looking weak and frail. "Billy, you do indeed have great power and talents, but have faith in the One who gave them to you. Merlin wouldn't lie, nor would Professor Hamilton. The bridge is the only way."

The dragon launched another ball of fire, missing Patrick by inches. "Back off, pretender, or I will make you a human torch!"

Patrick tore off his black cloak and stood up straight. "Fire away, Clefspeare. I'm willing to sacrifice myself to make sure Billy sees the light of truth."

Billy kicked a pebble at his feet. "You two could argue till Doomsday, and I still wouldn't know who's telling the truth. I have a feeling both of you are hiding something. Maybe you're both lying."

Clefspeare unfurled his wings and roared. "I am your father. When have I ever lied to you?"

Billy stepped back. A surge of heat rushed into his face, and stinging drops of sweat trickled into his eyes. His voice pitched higher. "When have you lied to me?" He bent down and picked up Bonnie again, letting her head droop against his shoulder. His passion erupted in a mournful lament. "My whole life was a lie, and you're the reason! You should have told me what you were a long time ago!" His tears dripped on Bonnie's sweatshirt, but he didn't care. He lowered his voice. "I thought I had forgiven you, but I guess I haven't."

Billy stepped up to the bridge and began crossing the span. Clefspeare blew a lightning stream of fire over his head. "No, Billy! Bonnie's life is at stake!"

The heat of the flames radiated over Billy's face. He halted, anger erupting in his voice. "You said to trust in myself. Are you going to stop me and prove yourself a liar?"

With a flap of his wings, Clefspeare leaped to the side and perched on the parapet like an enormous vulture, his long neck stretching over the span. "If you want Bonnie to die," he waved his head toward Patrick, "then proceed."

Billy walked slowly forward, glancing up at the dragon's noble head and fiery eyes. The sun's rays washed over his reddish scales, making them glisten like sequins. Shadows fell across Billy's path, outlines of the notches on the parapet. At the crest of the bridge, the sunlit areas of the walkway formed a cross.

Billy stopped at the centre of the bridge and dropped to his knees. He set Bonnie's body on the stone surface directly on top of the cross and looked up to the sky. "My decision is to let God take care of her. If He's going to restore her life, I'm sure He can do it from here." He cradled Bonnie's head for a moment, then set it down. "I know *I* can't do it."

Billy stroked her hair, his hand lingering on a purple bruise on her forehead. He looked up at the dragon, then at Patrick. Both seemed perplexed.

The dragon let out a long, "Hmmmmm." He lowered his head and looked Billy in the eye. "So are you giving up all rights to her?"

"I guess so. I'm not—"

"That's all I wanted to hear." Clefspeare unfurled his wings, then leaped from the parapet and snatched Bonnie up with one motion, wrapping his talons around her body and vaulting into the air.

The wind from his wings knocked Billy backwards. He grabbed a notch on the parapet as the dragon soared over the valley, making a beeline toward a mountain at the far end of the pass.

"Billy!" Patrick yelled, his arms waving. "I can't cross the bridge. You have to follow him!"

Billy spread out his hands. "What did I do wrong?!"

"Nothing! You acted in faith, and God will honour that. Now go!"

Billy sprang back down the arch and dashed across the ledge, his eyes pinned on the flying dragon in the distance. Would he be able to keep up? Would the path lead to a dead end? Billy pumped his arms and sprinted as fast as he could. Path or no path, he would find a way.

Ashley stood in front of Shiloh, reaching back to hold the girl's hand. Hartanna had settled down, and Marilyn and the professor knelt near her head, whispering to her.

Ashley spoke to Shiloh in a hushed tone. "Sounds like they're explaining how we know Bonnie's dead, that her light stopped glowing in the sixth circle, and how Barlow was watching through Billy's belt."

"Watching through his belt? Maybe you could explain it to me, too."

"Well, when Billy went in—"

Barlow's voice crackled through the computer speaker, weak and faltering. "Miss Stalworth, I . . . I hesitate to convey the terror I've seen."

Ashley jerked the computer up to her mouth. "Go ahead, Barlow. It can't be worse than Bonnie dying."

Barlow's voice strengthened. "A dragon has snatched Bonnie's body from William and has flown away with her. William is chasing the beast even as we speak!"

"All right," Ashley said, grimacing. "So it *is* worse."

Shiloh whispered, "Is there any way I can go in there again?"

Ashley leaned back, angling her head. "Why would you want to do that?"

"I know why Morgan wants Bonnie's body, and I think I know how to stop her."

"Can't Walter do it? Maybe I can get a message to him."

"No!" A hint of impatience spiked Shiloh's voice. "We're not completely sure Bonnie's dead. There might still be a chance to save her, and I'm the only one who can do it."

"Okay, okay! But I don't know for sure which circle Apollo's in. You might not go back in the right place, and you'd be alone."

"Ashley, you have programmed me to interrupt when my AI engine calculates a need to give you information."

Ashley spoke into the air. "Go ahead, Larry."

"Apollo's signal has changed dramatically, so it has likely moved into the deepest region of that domain. It is safe, therefore, to assume that Walter has carried it into the seventh circle."

"There!" Shiloh said, nodding at Ashley. "If you can get me through to Apollo, I won't be alone."

"That might be a big 'if,' but I have another idea." Ashley punched several keys on her computer. "Larry, can you still flash Apollo?"

"Yes, but Apollo is no longer close to the existing portal. If we could simultaneously create a flash on your side, the two flashes could produce a cross-dimensional corridor straight to Walter's location. But you should hurry. Apollo has been moving, so I cannot tell you how long it will stay where it is."

Ashley eyed Hartanna, who was now rising to her full height and stretching out her wings. "I think I might be able to get a flash on this side," Ashley said, "but it'll be tricky. Can you send the numbers for the light spectrum I'll need to produce?"

"Coming right up."

The chart on Ashley's computer screen filled with coloured bars. She read the numbers under each one. "Wow! This may be doable." She shrugged the backpack straps off her shoulders and let the pack slide down. "I was thinking of using biofeedback to get a certain fire-breather to create the spectrum. I'll need another chart with the desired amplitudes at the top for each frequency. Are you with me, Larry?"

"Understood, Ashley. We're on the same page, so to speak. I can monitor Hartanna's fire penetration from Apollo's position and send you back the corrected data, but can she hold a stream of fire long enough to adjust the frequency of the light she produces?"

Ashley drew her cloak and hood from the pack. "I think I can provide just the motivation she needs." She smiled. "Never doubt a mother's love."

"Understood again. This should be fun . . . in a calculated sort of way, of course."

Ashley whispered to Shiloh. "Okay, I have a plan." She spread out the bottom opening of the cloak. "You'll have to wear this."

Shiloh raised her arms and allowed Ashley to drape the cloak over her head. "No zipper on this one?" Shiloh asked.

"You mean like the one on the guy who grabbed me?" Ashley pulled the hem down to Shiloh's ankles. "That must have been a newer model." She straightened the material with a brush of her fingers. "Okay," Ashley continued, handing her the hood. "Put this on when you're ready to go and cover your hands with your sleeves. Got it?"

"I think so." Shiloh pinched the corner of Ashley's backpack. "Can I borrow this?"

"Sure." Ashley helped Shiloh put on the pack. "I think I see what you have in mind."

"Yep," Shiloh said, hoisting the pack in place. "I'm going to be dragon bait."

Walter waited several minutes after Morgan and Palin left before allowing himself to breathe normally. He set Apollo down near the wall of the cave and tiptoed to the edge of the hole in the floor, keeping a firm grip on the hilt of Palin's sword. As he approached, the room grew darker, as though light itself was being sucked into the abyss.

With his feet firmly planted, Walter leaned over the edge and peered down. A strange mixture of light and darkness swirled like a black-and-white striped whirlpool deep into the recesses of a narrow funnel. The walls of the abyss sparkled, as though embedded with crystals, and the vortex of light revealed a higher density of crystals the deeper it went. Each crystalline facet seemed to draw in the light, slurping its energy and darkening the tornadic stream as it passed by.

Walter lay on the floor and scooted his torso forward until half his body extended over the edge of the pit. He pressed his finger on the closest crystal. *I'll bet I know what this is. It could really come in handy.*

Tired moans drifted up from far below, barely audible, and a foul stench filtered into his nose. He lowered the sword inside and dug out the gem with the point, grabbing the golf ball-sized stone with his free hand when it popped loose.

He scrambled back to his feet and dropped the gem into his pocket, then leaned over and whispered into the hole. "Anyone down there?"

A rumbling moan erupted from the depths of the pit. Walter jerked back, stumbled for a second, but caught himself and froze in place near the abyss, his heart pounding wildly.

The light stream slowed, finally pausing and collecting on top of the abyss like a bubbling fountain. It formed itself into an upright oval, shining like a mirror in a sunlit field, though foggy and indistinct. Walter lifted his hand to shield his eyes. The oval dimmed slightly and sharpened into a bright, elliptical ring.

The moaning clarified into words, each syllable vibrating the ring with pulses of light. "Who calls upon Samyaza? I do not recognize your voice."

Walter tiptoed backwards, one careful step at a time, keeping his eye on the oval and feeling the space behind him with his hands. There was no way he was going to answer this thing.

The oval vibrated again, the voice louder and angry. "There is an intruder in our midst! Let us send a call to Morgan!"

Walter backed up to the wall and flattened himself in a slight crevice. He gasped, shallow breaths pumping his chest in and out. He gripped protrusions in the stone wall and searched the floor for Apollo. His trembling fingers finally touched its familiar outer frame.

Just before he could snatch it up, a flapping sound reverberated through the cave. Walter plastered himself against the wall again. A dragon flew into the opening, a limp body dangling from its talons. The bright oval illuminated the dragon's face. The beast's red eyes flashed, and its long tongue darted like a striking snake.

Walter grabbed his knees to keep them from knocking together. The dragon looked just like . . . *Clefspeare?*

The dragon stumbled, spilling its load and falling to one side. It struggled back to its feet, seeming fatigued and disoriented. The body rolled into the light, a winged girl, as still as death.

Walter's belly churned. Could that be Bonnie? He was about to jump from his hiding place to help, but the oval shook, its radiance streaming in all directions. "Ah! It is not an intruder. I hear the sound of a dragon. Do you have the girl?"

Clefspeare gasped. "Yes. I will go now and alert Morgan."

"Excellent! Is the boy following?"

"Yes. I must go before I collapse."

"Indeed. And hurry. Morgan must arrive before the boy does."

"If he comes too quickly, I will delay him." The dragon retreated, crawling to the entrance like a wounded dog. When it reached daylight, it spread its wings and flew away.

Walter ran quietly to Bonnie's prostrate body and knelt at her side. He turned her head and placed his palm on her smooth, pale face. *Cold. Too cold.*

He turned her over, and pressed his ear against her chest. *Come on! Give me something!* He lifted his head, breathless, his brain screaming in terror. *No! It can't be!* He released her shoulder, and her face turned back toward the floor.

Walter lurched to his feet and backed away, his mouth agape, his legs shaking. He dashed to the wall, smacking it with his hand.

He then dropped to a crouch, biting his fist as his tears flowed. It couldn't end this way! It just couldn't!

A distinct shuffle, like a foot slipping on gravel, disrupted Walter's anguish. He jerked his head up. A new shadow veiled the cave entrance.

Ashley pointed at a boulder nestled in the tor's slope. "Hide there for a minute. I'll be right back." She quick-stepped to Hartanna and held the computer out for her to see. "Hartanna, I talked to Sir Barlow, and I'd like him to repeat what he told me."

Hartanna's ears twitched, but her voice was barely more than a whisper. "Is it about Bonnie?"

"Yes." Ashley firmed her chin and spoke into the computer. "Barlow, tell me again what you saw in the sixth circle. Who was standing over Bonnie with a sword?"

"It was Palin, Devin's squire."

The dragon's eyes burned red. "Palin?"

"But you can't be one hundred per cent sure Bonnie was dead, right?"

"Miss, I beg your pardon, but as I said before, I've seen many dead—"

Ashley shouted into the microphone. "One hundred per cent, Barlow! Are you one hundred per cent sure?"

"Well . . . no. But the lights in the circle—"

Ashley injected more passion into her voice. "And did Palin take her body?"

"No. William defeated Palin and carried her away, but the lights—"

"Yes, the lights," Ashley repeated, her agitation growing. "I know all about the lights. Didn't you tell me one of them turned on in another circle?"

"Yes, it did, but—"

"And it wasn't Billy's light, was it?"

"No, Miss, it was in—"

"Thank you, Barlow." Ashley turned down the volume on her speakers. "Hartanna, I love Bonnie like a sister. As long as there's one molecule of a chance she's alive, we have to try to rescue her. Are you with me?"

"With you?!" The dragon gave her wings a mighty flap, sending a blast of air into Ashley's face. "Show me what to do!"

Ashley swiped a vagrant strand of hair out of her eyes, then reached up and pulled on Hartanna's wing. "Come this way." She led the dragon to the portal location. "Look right here." She drew a rectangle in the air with her finger. "I need you to blast fire at this target, and you'll need to keep up a stream long enough to open a portal to the other world." She held up the computer. "While you're blowing, watch the three bars on this graph. They'll adjust according to the kind of light spectrum you're creating. All you have to do is alter the flame to make all three reach the top of the chart. Think you can do that?"

Hartanna arched her tawny brow. "If it is possible, I will do it."

"Now," Ashley continued, "I want you to be ready for a shock. I'm going to show you a girl who looks just like Bonnie. She was a prisoner in the other world and saw Bonnie there. She wants to go back and try to find her. If you two can go into the circles together, you can provide the firepower she may need. So you have to bust that portal wide open to get yourself through it." Ashley waved toward the boulder. "Come on out, Shiloh."

Shiloh emerged and stepped timidly forward.

Hartanna reared up, her eyes growing to the size of baseballs. She slowly extended her neck, drawing her head close to Shiloh. She sniffed three times, then pulled back. "She has a familiar scent, but I cannot place it. Nevertheless, I will accompany her."

"Okay," Ashley said. "That was easy enough." She lifted the computer shoulder high. "Now I'll hold the graph where you can see it while you get the flames going."

Hartanna took in a deep breath and blew out a concentrated stream of yellow fire, as thin as a laser. The stream drilled into the slope of the hill, igniting the grass.

"Okay, Hartanna. You're doing great on the white light, but we need a lot more ultraviolet. Alter the flame, and let's see what happens."

The stream slowly transformed to a reddish torrent, thickening into a lava-like river. The flames crawled along the grass, spreading out across the hill in a smoky circle.

"Great! Keep tweaking it. You're getting closer."

From red to purplish scarlet, the stream blossomed into a massive wave of shimmering fire. Hartanna's face darkened. Her eyes bulged as she watched the tiny computer screen. After a few more seconds, the light seemed to spread out in mid-air as though it had hit a bank of fog.

"The portal's coming into view!" Ashley shouted. She released the computer with one hand and tapped her jaw. "Larry, flash Apollo now! I want the biggest blast you can give me!"

`"Coming right up!"`

The stream of fire splashed against a barrier, as though an invisible wall had formed. The flames splattered around a tall, pulsating rectangle of brilliant white light.

`"Apollo has flashed. The door is open on the other side, and Apollo is reading your light stream more clearly. You're almost there."`

Ashley pumped her fist and yelled. "Break through it, Hartanna! Break through it now!"

Hartanna heaved an enormous burst of flame. A purple ball of fire smashed against the portal, sending sparks of light shooting in all directions like a thousand flaming meteors. The professor, Marilyn, and Shiloh dropped to the ground as slivers of streaking light zipped over their bodies. Ashley crouched while trying to hold the computer in place. Hartanna collapsed, her head striking the slope with a thud.

A jagged rectangle hung in the air like a window to a world of light, pulsating, throbbing with energy.

Ashley sprinted to the front of the portal and lifted a clenched fist. "We did it! It's open!"

"The corridor is complete, Ashley. We now have a connective tunnel to the other world. But you must hurry. It is already deteriorating."

Ashley waved her arm frantically toward the opening. "Shiloh! Hartanna! Go!"

Shiloh jumped up and ran to the portal, pausing there for Hartanna to join her, but the great dragon didn't budge.

Ashley leaped to her feet and rushed to Hartanna's side. The dragon's body heaved, breathing chaotically, her eyes flashing yellow. Ashley spun toward Shiloh. "I think she's out cold, or maybe in shock!"

The professor shone his flashlight into Hartanna's eyes. "See how her eyes absorb the light? She must have spent all her energy. I think it will take more than my flashlight to revive her."

"Ashley, the corridor's safety is quickly becoming compromised."

Shiloh pulled on the straps of her backpack, her face solemn. She firmed her chin, her lips quivering. "If you find my parents, please tell them that I love them." Without another word, she threw on her hood, jumped into the portal, and dashed out of sight. Seconds later, the window of light began shrinking, dimming to a ghostly aura, then finally disappearing in a tiny flash.

CHAPTER

The Hostiam

Walter, still in a crouch, kept his head as low as possible. A shadow – tall, slender, and feminine – strode into the cave with long sweeps of her arms and legs. Walter clenched his fist. *Morgan's back. Now how am I going to get out of here with Bonnie's body?*

Morgan halted at Bonnie's feet. A wicked smile spread across her lips, then a laugh broke through, low at first, but it grew to a loud cackle and carried across the cave. The shining oval vibrated, creating a reply. "Morgan, hearing you laugh is the most delicious sound that has come to my ears in centuries."

"Yes, my love. My hostiam has arrived, and the time of possession is upon us."

"Let us not delay another second. The pain of this prison never ceases."

Morgan lifted her arms, straightening her body into a vertical column. As her eyes turned glassy, she uttered a string of unintelligible sounds and vaporized into a stream of black smoke. It tightened into a thin line and zoomed toward Bonnie's body. Splitting into two streams, it poured into her nostrils. Her head jerked around, and her chest heaved into spasms. Pushing on the floor with her hands, she sat up. Her eyes snapped open, wide and flaming. A smile slowly crept across her face. She stood, her head turning from one side to the other as she strutted toward the abyss.

Walter's heart thumped in his chest, and nausea torqued his belly. Was that witch now inside Bonnie?! But something was different. Bonnie's skin had suddenly changed. It was rough and scaly now, more like a lizard's than a human's.

Bonnie's wings stretched out and flailed wildly. Morgan crowed in Bonnie's voice. "I've done it! I'm alive again!" She patted her body with both hands. "Solid and shapely. Just what a woman needs."

Walter squeezed his sword so tightly, he could feel his pulse tap dancing on the hilt. Should he jump out and challenge this . . . this creature? Yes, it sounded like Bonnie, but whatever it was, it wasn't Bonnie anymore. Somehow this was really Morgan in a scaly Bonnie suit.

A new shadow appeared at the entrance, and a bright light pierced the darkness. Morgan whispered something at the abyss, and the aura vanished.

Billy ran in, holding Excalibur in both hands. As soon as he saw the winged form standing in the shadows, he slowed to a stop and let Excalibur droop at his side. Its light faded completely away, casting the cave in darkness except for a hint of sunlight peering in from the entrance. Billy squinted. "Bonnie? Is that you?"

Morgan rushed forward and threw her arms around his waist. She laid her head on his chest. "Yes! Oh, yes, Billy. Your father told me what you did. You made the right decision. You saved my life!"

She pulled back and took him by the hand. "Now let's destroy this place. It will never be a prison again." She led him to the edge of the abyss. "Strike this pit with Excalibur, and everyone will be set free."

Billy suddenly crumpled to his knees, dropping Excalibur as he grabbed his midsection. "Ohhhh! I feel sick."

She grabbed his elbow and pulled. "You're sick because the pit is filled with candlestones. Only Excalibur can destroy them. Hurry!"

A bright light erupted at Walter's side. He fell back, rapping his head against the wall. Reaching out through the blinding rays, he latched on to one of Apollo's outer dowels. It blazed like a supernova, casting beams of light throughout the cave, illuminating both Billy and Morgan.

Billy pulled away from her grasp. "Bonnie. Your skin! What's happening to you?" He clutched his belly more tightly and groaned.

Morgan reached up and caressed her cheek. "What?!" She yelled at the abyss. "Samyaza! Give me a mirror! Now!" The aura reappeared, and she gazed into its reflective surface. She pressed her hands on her temples and screamed. "I'm hideous!"

A girl's voice shouted at Walter's side. "You got that right!"

Morgan spun around. Her scaly jaw dropped open.

The girl pulled the hem of her shirt down low, hitched up a backpack, and marched forward. Halting about ten feet from the pit, the girl hooked her thumbs under the backpack straps. "Hey, Morgan! Where did you dig up that dragon's body? You must have been desperate to find a winged girl if you took that ugly carcass instead of me."

Morgan's face tightened into a scowl. "Who gave you power to perform such magic, Demon Witch?"

The girl ran toward the cave entrance. Morgan lunged after her. Billy extended his leg, tripping Morgan just before her fingers could grasp the girl's hair. He scrambled for Excalibur, shouting, "Run Bonnie! I'll take care of this . . . this thing!"

Rising to his knees, Billy pushed Morgan's head against the floor and raised Excalibur high, reviving its glow.

Walter dashed out of hiding, screaming at the top of his lungs, "Billy! No! Don't stab her!"

Billy squinted as he slowly lowered his sword. "Walter?"

Black smoke poured out beneath Billy's hand. It rose in a column and solidified into Morgan's body. She pushed Billy over with her foot. "Fool!" She ran toward the cave entrance. "I'll take care of you later!"

Walter threw his arm around Billy and hoisted him up. "C'mon buddy. Let's get you away from this pit. The one with wings is Bonnie's real body. Don't ask me to explain it." Before they could take two steps toward the archway, Morgan's laugh echoed against the walls. Walter helped Billy sit down, then raised Palin's sword and planted himself in front of his friend and Bonnie's body.

Morgan re-entered the cave, leading the girl with the backpack, a fistful of hair in her grip. "Your father is so helpful, Billy. Look at the present he found for me!" She threw the girl down to the floor and instantly transformed to black smoke again. The smoke enveloped the girl's head, but this time, it didn't penetrate. The girl sprang back to her feet, and the smoke resolidified.

Morgan slapped the girl across the face, leaving a red imprint on her cheek. "You deceived me!" the sorceress screamed. "You are not my hostiam!"

Walter jumped up and tackled Morgan, pinning her to the floor. Billy, still clutching his stomach, stumbled toward Morgan, raising Excalibur. A laser beam burst from the sword's tip. "Stand back, Walter, I'll turn her into a million dots of light."

Walter threw himself to the side. Just as Billy swung the beam, she vaporized again, her stream of smoke flowing toward Bonnie's body.

Billy screamed. "No! You can't have her!"

Morgan materialized at Bonnie's side. She scooped the limp body into her arms and walked to the edge of the abyss. "I'll give you one chance to change your mind, young Arthur. Either give her to me, or she's lost forever. No one has ever escaped from the depths of Tartarus."

Billy's face turned lava red. His body wilted. The candlestones had sapped all his strength.

Walter grabbed his arm. "No, Billy! Don't give Bonnie's body to her. She's dead. What good would it do if she could breathe and walk again? It would be Morgan, not Bonnie."

Billy panted. "But . . . but Patrick said there might be a chance to revive her."

"You'll never revive her if Morgan's inside her body."

The girl threw off her backpack and cloak and stepped between Billy and Morgan. "You can take me as your hostiam. I give you my permission."

"Take you?" Morgan sneered. "You're not in the royal line."

"Have you forgotten Shiloh Nathanson, daughter of Valcor, brother of Irene, adopted daughter of Arthur?" She lifted the hem of her T-shirt, revealing a frilly dress. "Does this old party dress look familiar? Or do you just toss your victims into prison and forget about them?"

Morgan took a step back from the pit. "Shiloh? But you're not of age, and no guardian is present. You can't give your own permission."

"I'm fifty-five years old. That's plenty old enough to consent." She walked to the edge of the abyss and stood toe-to-toe with Morgan, looking up at her with steely eyes. "Now are you going to take me or not?"

A new, wicked smile spread across Morgan's face. She vaporized, dropping Bonnie to the ground. Shiloh closed her eyes, and the black smoke blasted into her nostrils. Her chest heaved, and her arms flailed wildly. After a few seconds, she stood still. Her eyes glowed red – evil and filled with hate. She turned toward Billy and Walter and spread out her arms. "Now young Arthur, you will do what I say or your friend Walter will—"

Shiloh's eyes suddenly flashed back to normal. Her face twisted with terror. She pushed her hand down her shirt and pulled out a pendant on a chain. A gem in the centre pulsed red and white. She gripped the pendant in her fist, her arm trembling like an earthquake. She spun back around, pulling her hair and stamping her feet. With a sudden lunge, she jumped into the abyss.

Walter rushed to the edge of the pit, just catching a glimpse of Shiloh's body as it plunged into the darkness. He turned toward the cave entrance and fell to his knees. Billy sat on the floor, his hands covering his face.

Walter thrust his arms under Bonnie's body and hoisted her up. Her skin had returned to normal, but it was still deathly pale. He stumbled toward the exit arch, blinking back his tears. He stopped and nudged Billy with his knee. "C'mon. Let's . . ." He swallowed away a lump. "Let's get out of here."

Billy pushed himself up and wobbled on his weakened legs. He slid Excalibur into its scabbard and grasped Walter's shoulder to keep from falling. They exited the cave side by side and stopped on the ledge that skirted the mountain. Billy slid his back against the face of the cliff and dropped heavily to his seat.

Walter laid Bonnie down and headed back inside. "I have to get Apollo."

With Apollo still emanating a faint glow, he found it easily, snatched it and Palin's sword, and dashed back through the cave. When he returned, Billy was standing near the rim of the ledge, his eyes fixed on something in the sky.

Walter set Apollo and the sword down while trying to follow Billy's line of sight. "Got your radar locked on something?"

"It's my father. I see him patrolling out there, but I think he's coming this way." Billy bent toward Bonnie. "There's definitely something wrong with him, and I don't think we should stick around to figure it out." He rose to his feet and pointed toward a distant part of the valley. "Dad was guarding a bridge over there, and he didn't want me to cross it with Bonnie. But now I know I have to." He slid his arm under Bonnie's knees. "We'd better get in the cave until he goes away."

Walter pulled Billy's arm back. "No way! The candlestones will sap you dry."

"But we can't leave Bonnie . . . I mean . . ." Billy searched his mind for the other girl's name. ". . . Shiloh trapped in that pit."

"Well, yeah, but how're you going to get her out?"

"Morgan wanted me to strike the pit with Excalibur to destroy it. She said something about setting everyone free."

"Bad idea," Walter said, shaking his head vigorously. "One of the things in that pit talked to me, and he sounded like the president of 'Demons Are Us' ."

"You want Shiloh to stay in there with him? It'll be pure torture, especially if Morgan's still inside her. I can't leave her like that."

"Good point." Walter cocked his head upward. "But we'd better decide soon. Your father's almost here."

Billy stood, leaving Bonnie on the ground. "Watch her. I'm going back in the cave. With the candlestones in there, he's not likely to follow me." He drew out Excalibur and rested the blade on his shoulder. "Tell him Morgan's got a different hostiam and I'm in there getting ready to bust open the pit. That ought to keep him in a good mood. Just remember not to call him Mr Bannister. He's Clefspeare now."

Walter closed one eye. "You want me to face a ticked-off, fire-breathing dragon alone and convince him that I just happened to be strolling through the pits of Hades?" A grin broke out on his face. "I love this plan!"

A few seconds after Billy disappeared into the cave, Clefspeare landed on the ledge with a flap of his huge wings. After he settled himself, he growled. "Why are you here with Bonnie's body?"

Walter tried to act confident, but he felt like he was going to heave his guts. He clenched one fist behind his back and shoved his other hand into his pocket. He slowly withdrew the candlestone he had chipped from the wall of the abyss, allowing his fingers to spread out just enough to expose the dragon to the gem. "I'm so glad you asked that. You see, Billy and I were just talking about why we're here. Billy said, 'Hey, Walter, nice day for a stroll through the underworld, don't you think?' And I said—"

"Cut the nonsense!" the dragon roared. It suddenly paused, seeming confused, but its eyes burned like erupting volcanoes. "Or I will . . . I will use you as a torch!"

Walter opened his fingers just a hair further. "Be cool, Mr Dragon. Morgan's got herself a different hostiam now." He pointed back to the cave with his thumb. "And Billy's in there getting ready to blow that candlestone pit. Everything's under control."

The dragon blinked, and his head wobbled. "You know about . . . about the hostiam? What's your part in this?"

"C'mon, Clefspeare. I know you. Don't you remember me?"

The dragon stretched his neck downward and gazed into Walter's eyes. "You look . . . familiar."

Walter scratched his nose, then looked away with a shrug of his shoulders. "Well, I guess Morgan hasn't kept you informed."

"Impossible! Morgan tells me everything!"

Walter rolled his eyes. "If you say so." He flicked his thumb toward the cave again. "Then go on in and see for yourself if you want." He opened his fingers as widely as he dared. "I'll wait."

The dragon unfurled his wings. "There is no need. I will go back to the bridge and wait for her instructions." Clefspeare lifted off the ground, faltering at first and losing altitude over the valley, but he quickly recovered and shot into the sky.

Walter collapsed to his seat at the cave entrance and wiped his brow. *Whew!* He tried to peer into the arched entryway, but it was too dark inside. He cracked his knuckles and bit his bottom lip. *C'mon Billy. You got one more minute before I come in after you.*

Billy hurried toward the edge of the abyss, guided by Excalibur's radiance. Shafts of light from the cave entrance collapsed into slithering, glowing snakes and swept by his feet as they swirled into the pit. It felt like his own energy was being slurped along with them, cramping his stomach and legs. As he slowed down and inched closer to the edge, he let out a low groan. *I have to do it! I have to!*

The sweeping light gathered at the surface, and the oval-shaped aura appeared, floating above the surface of the pit. The image congealed into a familiar face, sharpening until he recognized it easily. His father's face. His father's human face.

Billy gulped. "Dad?"

The aura vibrated like a gently plucked harp string. "Yes, son. I felt your presence earlier, so I figured out how to make an image appear on the surface after watching Samyaza do it. I'm really still at the bottom of this pit. The Watchers have huddled in a corner, but I'm not sure how long they will allow me to speak to you."

"Then who is the dragon outside the cave?"

"Our old enemy, Devin, has taken over my dragon body. Once they brought me into the seventh circle, I had no power to stop him."

"Are . . ." The pain ripped through Billy's chest. He gasped for breath and grabbed a fistful of his shirt. "Are you trapped in there with Samyaza and the Watchers?"

"Yes, but since I have no body, they are not able to touch me. I have only spiritual perception, so all I can do is manipulate the light."

"Is Shiloh in there with you?"

"Yes. She is a delightful girl; a bit sore from her spill into the pit, but not badly hurt. Since she has a body, I have to protect her from the Watchers."

Billy's lungs ached, ready to collapse. He took three steps back, enabling him to breathe again, but he had to cough out every word. "Why . . . can't you . . . just leave?"

"I can't escape because the entire pit is lined with candlestones, and I exist only as a spirit. My energy gets pulled into the abyss by the gems, sort of like gravity on a physical body. It's all I can do to keep from being drawn into the gems themselves. Shiloh can't escape, because the pit is simply too deep, and its walls are sheer."

"But is . . . is Morgan still inside her?"

"No. Light and darkness can have no fellowship, and the light in Shiloh was too powerful. Morgan had to leave her body. Apparently the two fought for control while they were up there, and Shiloh jumped in to take Morgan with her. Unfortunately for us, but fortunately for you, Morgan is trapped in the abyss with us. Even she is unable to climb through the energy fields that seal this chasm."

Billy raised his sword, using both weakened arms to hoist it. "Well . . . I'm going to . . . get you . . . out of there . . . with Excalibur."

The aura flashed. “No, Billy! Don’t! You’ll release the Watchers. That’s what Morgan has been wanting all along.”

Billy let the sword’s tip fall to the ground. “The Watchers?”

“Fallen angels, far more powerful than you can imagine. They will make earth into a living hell, and you, Billy, as the new Arthur, would be their first victim. They’ve corrupted the world once before, and God brought the great flood as a result. Who knows what would happen if the Watchers took control again?”

Billy took two more steps back. “But how . . . how else will you get out?”

The aura turned pale blue, and ripples spread out from the centre like splash rings in a pool of water. “We are content to stay here. To sacrifice ourselves for the benefit of the entire world is a small price to pay. Although Shiloh has nothing, no food or water, she keeps saying, ‘I have all I really need.’ She is willing to suffer and die. Her love is amazing!”

With pain roaring through his heaving chest, Billy cried out, “Dad! I have to get you out! I have to!” He sniffed and wiped his sleeve across his nose. “It’s . . . it’s just not the same without you! I tried to pretend you were dead, but . . . but Mum never smiles anymore. She needs you . . . and I . . .” He drooped his head, and his voice died away in a pitiful lament. “I need my dad.”

Billy wrung Excalibur’s hilt like an old mop. He inched backwards, his legs stiff and cramping. “I’ll be back. . . . I’ll . . . I’ll find a rope or something, and . . . and I’ll come down there and get both of you out . . . somehow.”

A red hue splashed across the aura. “The candlestones would kill you! You’d never make it halfway down.”

Billy neared the cave’s entrance, still backing away. “Then Shiloh can climb out on the rope.”

"If Shiloh tried to climb, the candlestones would prevent me from following. I wouldn't be able to protect her from the Watchers."

With renewed strength, Billy raised his sword again. "Then I'll be the one to do the sacrificing. Let the Watchers do what they will to me. I'll be ready." Excalibur's beam shot out through the tip. He charged toward the abyss and swung the beam down into its depths, illuminating the entire cavern. The embedded candlestones in the walls of the pit filled with flaming light and exploded like over-juiced lightbulbs, popping and sparking in a fireworks grand finale. With the candlestones getting zapped, Billy felt sudden relief. The constant draining of energy vanished.

The abyss began filling with liquid light. It looked like a lava tube with boiling energy rising toward the top. As the bubbling light drew closer, something dark moved at the surface, something with arms and legs flailing about. Billy dropped to his chest and stretched his arm into the pit, wriggling forward until his entire upper body was suspended over the precipice. "Shiloh! Grab my hand!" Shiloh flapped her arms, but she couldn't seem to turn the way she wanted. The cauldron of light was more like mist than water, thin and vaporous. She looked like a Golden Retriever paddling in the fog.

Other forms seemed to congeal in the glowing soup, rising up and snapping at Shiloh like attacking sharks. Were they the Watchers? Billy stretched out, reaching so far his joints felt like they were ripping apart. It wasn't enough. Her desperately floundering hands grasped empty air.

Billy's body slipped an inch, then another. He dug the toes of his boots against the cave floor, but it didn't help. He heard his belt buckle scraping the stone as his hand dropped lower and lower. Shiloh's writhing fingers drew within a hair's breadth of his own. If he grabbed her now, would she just pull him in? Would the Watchers get both of them?

Dirt fell across the back of Billy's head. Something clamped down on his legs. A familiar voice shouted out. "Grab her Billy, and let's blow this place!"

"Walter!" Billy grunted. "Great timing!" He slid farther down and latched onto Shiloh's wrist. "Got her!"

Billy's body heaved backwards. He kept a vice-grip on Shiloh's wrist as her fingernails dug into the heel of his hand. As soon as Billy rose to his knees, Walter grabbed Shiloh's other arm, and the two hoisted her to solid ground.

Billy brushed a clump of dirt from Shiloh's hair as she knelt in front of him. "Are you okay?"

She nodded, grimy tears flowing down her cheeks. "I'm all right."

Billy picked up Excalibur and thrust it into his back scabbard while glancing at the rising light in the pit. "I don't think I want to be around when that stuff hits the surface."

"Yeah," Walter replied. "Pardon the language, but I think all hell is about to break loose." He spread his feet apart. "Do you feel something?"

Shiloh slapped her palms on the rocky floor. "Yeah, the ground's shaking."

"This volcano's gonna erupt with spooks!" Walter shouted, grabbing Shiloh's arm. "Let's get out of here!"

The trio bolted out of the cave. Billy scooped up Bonnie's body and lumbered along the ledge in the direction of the bridge. Her limbs had stiffened. Even her back wasn't as flexible as before. She was long dead. Who could hope for a miracle now? And what would become of his father? Would he just disperse in the light? Would he disintegrate and scatter into the great beyond?

Billy tried to shut the possibilities out of his mind as he laboured up an incline, forcing his legs to push him into a quick march as the bridge came into sight. He kept his eyes fixed on it. The dragon was perched on the side at the apex of the arch, but Patrick was nowhere to be seen.

Walter draped an arm around Shiloh, who had lost one of her shoes. As the slope steepened, he half-carried her to offset her unbalanced strides. When they reached the bridge, he helped her sit with her back to the mountainside, and he plopped down next to her, setting Apollo between them.

Billy laid Bonnie in front of Shiloh and Walter and stood in front of them. The dragon unfurled his wings and hopped halfway down the bridge, balancing on the parapet. "Why have you come back, Son?"

Billy drew out Excalibur and squared his shoulders. "Cut the 'son' stuff, you mongrel lizard!"

The dragon drew its head back. "Billy! What are you talking about? I'm your father."

"I know who you are, Devin. You're Morgan's little lapdog." Excalibur's beam flashed from its point, and Billy flexed his biceps. "You've called me a mongrel a hundred times for being the son of a dragon, but now you're a dragon yourself! Looks like you'd do anything to please your mistress, you disgusting cur!"

The dragon roared and blew a river of fire at Billy. Excalibur's beam slapped against the flames, and the fire wrapped around it like a snake winding around a pole. The beam absorbed the dragon's breath in a sizzling bath of rising smoke.

Suddenly, the ground began to shake. Rocks tumbled down the mountain, raining dirt pellets on their heads. Walter jumped up and pointed at the cave entrance. "The pit just blew its top!"

A rush of light burst from the cave entrance, gushing out like a horizontal geyser. At least eight ghostly shapes, multi-winged humanoids, separated from the flow. With glowing eyes and a silvery aura, they stretched their double-sized bodies, flexing chiselled arms and legs and expanding their massive chests with the air of newfound freedom. Their wings unfurled, and they flew toward the bridge, a shrieking raven leading the way.

Billy held up Excalibur and waved it in front of him, hoping to fry at least a couple of the gargantuan ghosts before they descended on them like a pack of wolves. The brilliant beam spread out into a wall of light, creating a shimmering dome over himself as well as Walter, Shiloh, and Bonnie. The raven pulled back, flapping its black wings madly, but the humanoid creatures slammed against the barrier, bending it like rubber and rebounding in all directions.

Excalibur's beam diminished, but the umbrella of light hovered a few feet over their heads. The creatures flew all around the edges, screaming and biting at the shield. Their wild eyes glowed red. Pointed fangs overlapped their lips, top and bottom.

The raven fluttered to a landing on the mountain ledge, transforming into Morgan as soon as her feet touched down. The dragon joined her, standing just behind with its head perched above her shoulder. She crossed her arms over her chest. "Very clever, young Arthur. Who told you a photo-umbrella would stall the Watchers?"

Billy knew he hadn't done it on purpose, but he wasn't going to let Morgan in on the secret. "Let's just say I've got a few tricks up my sleeve no one knows about yet."

Morgan pressed her finger against the shield. A splash of sparks showered back over her hand. "You'd better have a few more tricks than this little bubble of yours. You're stuck in the bowels of the underworld with a dead princess and two useless friends, and the only mortals ever to escape this land are not here to guide the way." She dipped into a mock curtsy. "In the meantime, Your Majesty, I'm going to take my friends to the upper world. We have a few surprises in store for the folks back home."

Walter jumped to the edge of the shield. "Go ahead, you Goth-babe wannabe! We'll see you up there and kick you and your uglies back to Hades faster than your breath will curdle milk!"

Morgan raised her head and scowled, but a crooked grin washed away her frown. "Oh, Walter, you're such a brave little man. Just because I like you so much, I'm going to show you and your friends mercy. You won't have to suffer here after all." She turned to the dragon. "Devin, your fire should be able to penetrate the shield. Kill them all. We'll wait for you at the portal."

The dragon grumbled. "But Excalibur—"

"Don't fret over his toy light sabre!" she yelled. "Just grab the living girl! Love is his weakness. Threaten her, and he will do whatever you ask." She signalled with her arm. "Amazarak, lead the way to Avalon." She then lifted her head to the sky, her eyelids fluttering. "Samyaza, my love, I think it's time you carried me to our threshold."

The largest of the silver-haired creatures flew down and lifted her into his arms. "With pleasure, my wicked pet."

A man leaped down from an upper ledge and landed feet first next to the dragon, bending his knees to absorb the impact.

Walter nudged Billy's elbow. "It's Palin! What's he up to?"

Swinging a sword, Palin lunged at Morgan. Samyaza pulled her away from Palin's attack and flew away with her in his arms. The other Watchers followed, zooming through the sky until they disappeared over a mountain.

Palin waved his sword and shouted at the dragon. "Morgan has played us for fools, Sir Devin! Let us follow them to the third circle and stop this madness before it's too late!" He dropped to one knee and bowed his head. "Forgive my boldness, my liege. I will do whatever you wish."

The dragon raised a claw and laid it on Palin's shoulder. "Whatever I wish, my old friend?"

"Yes, my liege, as always."

The dragon drew his head back and took in a deep breath. "Then die!" He blew fire into Palin's chest, igniting his clothes. Billy lit up Excalibur and charged through the shield. He swung the beam across the flames and slammed the stream of fire into the ground. Billy pivoted, ready to slash Devin, but the dragon leaped into the air and flew down into the valley. Seconds later, he was gone.

Billy threw down his sword and dove toward Palin. Wincing as the blaze leaped toward his face, he slapped Palin's chest with his hands. Walter dashed through the dissolving shield, stripped off his cloak, and smothered the fire with it. The flames quickly died away.

Billy leaned over Palin's charred face. "What can I do?"

Palin sputtered his words through half-melted lips. "It seems . . . we've done this before . . . Dragon Boy."

Billy pushed Palin's hair out of his eyes. "Yeah, and I'm sorry. I was a coward."

Palin shook his head. "Not . . . a coward. I . . . deserved it." He coughed. A stream of blood oozed from the corner of his mouth. "I was wrong about you . . . Billy. You're not just like me. You're . . . you're a better man than I."

Billy slid his hands under Palin's body. "Maybe if I get you across the bridge—"

Palin grabbed Billy's wrist. "No! Don't!" He slowly relaxed his grip, and his voice became steady and low. "It's too late for me. I'm already dead, remember? I had my chance to cross the bridge long ago. I—" His body arched upward, and he exhaled slowly, releasing Billy's arm. As his body settled down, his extremities began to crumble, first his fingers, then his hands and legs, dissolving into ashes.

Billy and Walter rose to their feet. A fresh breeze cut across the top layer of Palin's ashes and carried them down into the valley, biting away at the pile until it disappeared.

Walter patted Billy on the back. "C'mon." He snatched up his cloak and pushed his arms through the sleeves. "We still have to get Bonnie across the bridge."

CHAPTER 22

The Holy Grail

Marilyn rubbed Hartanna's neck with long strokes. "Your scales are still cold."

Hartanna exhaled, and a few tiny embers shot from her nostrils. "I never had a chance to build a regeneracy dome after the long trip over the ocean. I was exhausted when I arrived, and breaking through the portal sapped my reserves."

The professor descended the slope from an upper terrace. "We have to get you out of here. A crowd is gathering near the entrance, and, believe me, you have not seen a true media feeding frenzy until you've seen a British one. I expect lights and cameras all over this place before we know it."

Hartanna pushed up on her forelegs. "I don't think I can fly, but I might be able to crawl to the trees in a few minutes."

Ashley sat down on the grass and checked the time on her computer. "Let's see. Shiloh's been gone half an hour now. I'll check with Barlow again." She pressed a button and spoke into the microphone. "Hey, Barlow. Anything new, or is it still too dark to see?"

"They are in the light now, Miss, but I feel that I am still in the dark. What I have seen is so amazing, I cannot describe it."

Ashley propped her forearms on her knees. "Well, give it your best shot."

"I saw a floating head made of pure light, but I did not recognize the face. I saw hideous creatures bouncing off a shield of light. I saw a dragon burn Palin to a crisp, and his ashes blew away in the wind."

Ashley pressed her lips together. "Did you see Shiloh and Walter?"

"Yes, I caught glimpses of both of them. They seem well."

"That's a relief! How about Bonnie?"

"William carries her body from time to time. She still appears dead to me. And, before you ask, I checked the lights. They are still glowing in the drawings in the seventh and eighth circles."

Ashley pushed against the ground with her palm. "I understand. I'll ask the professor—"

A voice shouted from the top of the tor. "There it is!"

Ashley spun her head. Someone turned a powerful beam of light down the slope and waved it over Hartanna. "Keep the light right there! We've got it!"

With a heavy grunt, Hartanna leaped into the air. Her wings flailing wildly, she rose over the tor, bounding off the top of the tower as she leapfrogged the peak. The professor and Marilyn sprinted in pursuit, following just behind the low-flying dragon as they followed the path toward the entrance.

"Quick!" the voice yelled. "It's getting away. Roll the camera!"

A young man jogged down the slope, a TV camera hoisted on his shoulder. The man with the light followed, keeping it trained on the escaping dragon. The professor halted, stepping in front of the pursuing cameraman and raising his hand. "Stop this nonsense! Don't you know what night this is?"

"That's no Halloween costume, old man. Get out of my way!" The cameraman pushed the professor roughly to the side, knocking him to the floor, but the professor managed to stick his leg out. The cameraman tripped and tumbled down the slope head over heels, and his camera followed behind, rocking to a stop at one of the terraces.

The professor hustled down the slope and grabbed the camera, but when he looked up at the sky, he let the camera drop to the grass. A helicopter buzzed overhead with a high-powered spotlight aimed at Hartanna. The dragon landed and bustled into a cluster of trees while Marilyn followed. The professor hurried back to the portal area and found Ashley. "There's no use trying to hide her now."

Ashley nodded toward another helicopter far in the distance. "Yep. Let's hope they don't have live feeds to the networks."

A voice buzzed from the computer, but the chopper's engine drowned it out. Ashley raised it to her ear. "Karen, did you say something?"

"Yeah. I'm watching you guys on TV right now. Except for a Scooby Doo marathon on the Cartoon Network, you're on every channel."

Ashley kicked at the grass. "Oh, great! The dragon's out of the bag!"

The professor's mouth dropped open, and he took a wobbling step backwards. "In the name of all that is holy!"

Ashley pivoted on her heel. The portal had reappeared, bursting with streams of light flying in all directions. An enormous, glowing creature had stepped out with muscular legs as thick as an elephant's. His body, a human form at least nine feet tall, solidified, shaking off the glow as he stomped along one of the tor's terraces. His angular jaw opened, and he let out a warrior's cry that shook the earth as several other creatures, just as massive, poured through the shimmering rectangle and lined up in a row.

"Ashley," Karen's voice shouted. "What are those things?"

Ashley's jaw froze. She could only stare in stunned silence.

"They are the Watchers," the professor whispered, "ancient demons more powerful than any other evil creature."

A dragon flew through the portal, his wings beating the air. With a quick snuff, he shot a stream of fire at the helicopter, sending it hurtling to the ground in flames. He then took a place at the end of the line of creatures.

Finally, a slender woman dressed in black emerged from the portal followed by a smaller woman and a vicious looking, striped dog. She walked in front of the line with long, confident strides.

"All hail Morgan!" they cried.

Morgan stopped at the centre of the line and raised her arms. "We're free at last!"

"Free at last!" they echoed.

She balled her hands into fists. "Now Elaine and I will help you regain the world! Samyaza will be revered once again, and all who oppose him will die."

"What's happening?" Karen called. "There's no picture. Everything went dark."

Ashley squatted low and tried to swallow. She could barely spit out her words. "I think it's . . . it's the end of the world." She pulled the computer closer and whispered. "I love you, Karen. Say goodbye to Beck and Stacey and Pebbles for me."

"Goodbye? But—"

Ashley turned off the computer and whispered. "Sorry, Karen. Can't risk any noise right now."

Morgan stalked back and forth along the terrace. "As you know, our only real enemy is the dragon race, and the only two dragons remaining are Hartanna and this one whom Devin now occupies. When we find Hartanna, she will be easy prey, because she will trust the dragon she believes is Clefspeare. Devin will destroy her. Then, after we find a more suitable vessel for Devin to inhabit, he will destroy the dragon body he now occupies."

The creatures shouted their approval in a cacophonous wail, sounding like a choir of howling dogs and bleating sheep.

The professor crouched at Ashley's side and put his arm on her shoulders. "Can you speak to Larry?" he asked.

"Probably. But what can he do?"

"I suggest the biggest flash Apollo can possibly produce. Perhaps we can bring Billy and the others back here, or perhaps we can send these monsters back to hell where they belong."

Ashley tapped her jaw. "I'm on it, Professor."

Billy bent over slowly, picked up Excalibur, and slid the blade back into its sheath. He trudged back to Bonnie and lifted her into his arms.

Carrying Apollo again, Walter helped Shiloh to her feet, and the two of them joined Billy at the edge of the bridge. "Well," Billy said, "I guess I'll just try to cross and see what happens."

Walter slapped him on the back. "I'm right behind you, buddy. You can count on that."

When Billy reached the apex of the arch, he saw an old man on the other side, his arms held out in a cradle, much like Billy's.

"Joseph?" Billy asked.

The old man, now dressed in a long robe, nodded. "Yes. Come now. Give the precious lamb to me. I will take her to the Holy Grail."

Billy descended the arch, quickening his pace. Walter and Shiloh trailed him by a couple of steps. Billy reached the opposite ledge and laid Bonnie in Joseph's arms. "Be real careful with her, okay?"

"She is a precious treasure, I know, but don't let your heart be troubled. I have carried a lamb even more precious than she."

Joseph turned toward a huge boulder behind him. "Come out Patrick. I know you are weary, but I will need help with my burden. I am not as young as I used to be."

Patrick emerged from behind the mammoth rock. When he caught sight of the three young people on the ledge, he fell to his knees. His lips quivered, and he held his hand to his chest. "Sh . . . Shiloh?"

Shiloh lifted her head. Three deep lines dug into her brow as she leaned forward. "Daddy?"

Patrick's face lit up. He jumped up and spread out his arms. "Shiloh!"

Shiloh leaped into his embrace. "Daddy! It's you! It's really you!"

He spun her around, laughing and crying, kissing her cheek over and over again. "Shiloh! My dear Shiloh!" He wrapped her up in his arms. "My daughter is alive from the dead! Praise the King of Heaven! My daughter is alive!"

After a final spin, Patrick turned to the others, his face bursting with joy. "She's alive! Can you believe it? My daughter's a—" He suddenly dropped his chin, and he turned slowly toward the dead body in Joseph's arms.

Shiloh pressed her cheek against Patrick's. "She gave her life for me, Daddy. Bonnie died to set me free."

Patrick let Shiloh slide down to the ground. He strode forward and pushed his arms under Bonnie, joining hands with Joseph and making a two-man cradle. As they began descending a path that led into the valley, Joseph looked back at Billy. "Follow us into the grail, and bring Apollo . . . and your faith."

Billy took Apollo from Walter and trailed the two men as they wound their way into the valley, following a narrow, switchback path. The valley was littered with bones, dusty, crumbling bones, many still pieced together in the shapes of dragons. When Joseph and Patrick finally arrived at the bottom, they laid Bonnie's body down in the midst of the densest collection of whitewashed dragon remains. Billy tramped through the dust and set Apollo next to an arching set of blanched ribs.

Joseph shook Patrick's hand. "Go and be with your daughter." Patrick bowed and hurried away.

Joseph spread out his arms and turned his head from side to side. "Young man, can these bones live?"

"What?" Billy squinted at the unearthly scene, a strange old wanderer standing in the midst of a valley of dry bones. "Why are you asking me? I thought you'd tell me what this is all about."

Joseph folded his hands at his waist. "Do you not remember what your professor sang to you after your adventure with the candlestone?"

"Well, I remember his singing, but I don't remember the song."

Joseph bowed his head. "Then listen to the words again."

A voice rose from the valley floor, the professor's gentle tenor somehow pouring forth from the bones as if they themselves were singing.

A valley deep, a valley long
Lay angels dry and dead;
Now who can wake their cold, stone hearts
Their bones on table spread?

Like wine that flows in skins made new
The spirit pours out fresh;
Can hymns of love bring forth the dead
And give them hearts of flesh?

O will you learn from words of faith
That sing in psalms from heaven
To valley floors where terrors lurk
In circles numbering seven?

The beautiful song left Billy breathless. He placed his palm on his chest as if to keep his heart from leaping out.

"And you have seen Merlin's verse, have you not?" Joseph continued, his head still bowed. "Speak it to me."

Billy pivoted and gazed under the bridge at the red boulder on the other side. Although it was a few hundred feet away, its huge letters were easy to read. With trembling lips he spoke the prophecy.

The final circle numbers seven,
And beasts await your sword's command.
The greatest danger tests your faith,
And wisdom's touch will make you stand.

The bridge of faith still lies in wait,
The narrow path of answered prayer.
Restore the fountain from the stone,
Regenerating souls laid bare.

Joseph lifted his head. "I ask you again, can these bones live?"

Billy firmed his chin and nodded. "Yes, they can live." He then squinted at Joseph. "But how?"

"Turn now," Joseph said, "and approach the prophetic stone. Then raise your sword and strike it."

Billy pivoted and urged his tired legs into a lumbering jog. As he approached, the red stone seemed to grow, towering over him like a scarlet skyscraper. He slid Excalibur from its scabbard and lifted it in the air with both hands. The white letters suddenly blazed with fire, flames dancing in the deep etchings. Billy hesitated and glanced back at Joseph.

"Strike the rock!" Joseph yelled. "Strike it with all your heart!"

Taking in a deep breath, Billy pulled back his arms and lunged toward the heart of the stone. With a mighty swing, the blade cracked against the face, slicing a gash from the top of his stroke to the bottom.

Red liquid gushed out, spilling over Billy and knocking him down. Torrents of crimson carried him along the valley floor, sweeping him toward Joseph. As the rushing tide slowed, the old man waded over and helped him to his feet. Billy held tight to Excalibur, and the blade dripped red, as though freshly drawn from a kill.

The flood abated to a shallow stream that covered the valley floor, flowing gently around Bonnie's body and the dragon bones. Joseph held Apollo in one hand and gripped Billy's wrist with the other. "Now lift up your sword and paint the skies with the visions of the night, the dreams that have prophesied all that you are about to see."

Billy aimed Excalibur toward the sky. The beam exploded from the blade and seemed to rip into the hazy blue backdrop, scarring the heavens. Billy's recurring dream flooded back into his mind – the muddy water, the bone-filled cemetery, the electric fence.

Billy guided Excalibur, drawing line after line in the sky until he had emblazoned a shimmering fence on his sparkling canvas that hovered hundreds of feet above the entire valley.

Excalibur's beam died away, but the fence remained. A rift in the sky near one edge created a gate that swung open, leaving a gap in the fence. From the centre of the gap, another beam of light shot out and drilled into the valley floor, spreading out until it covered the riverbed like a silver carpet.

The beam expanded into a huge dome of swirling luminescence, like an inverted funnel of pure light. From all around the cone, tiny rays shot out toward Bonnie's body, striking something sparkling on her chest. The rays bounced back in dozens of colours, filling the dome with a kaleidoscope of reds, yellows, and blues.

Shiloh leaped to the edge of the cliff, shouting excitedly at Billy. "It's my necklace! That's what's making all the colours!"

Tears rolled down Billy's cheeks. He tried to call back, but he could only whisper. "It's a regeneracy dome. The light's creating a regeneracy dome." He sighed, then laughed, more tears slipping down his cheeks.

The colourful streams multiplied and wrapped around the skeletons. Moisture oozed from the bones, and their ashen shade turned gleaming white – fresh, clean, and new. Jumping off the ground, the bones seemed to dance, rattling against each other and piecing together, joint to joint. Soon, a menagerie of skeletal dragons stood motionless on the valley floor, like statues in a science museum.

In a flurry of bubbles and ripples, the red liquid from the riverbed began crawling up the beasts' leg bones, coating them in scarlet as it ascended and tying the skeletons together with ligaments, tendons, and muscles. The reddish coat thickened into leathery skin and scales, turning beige as it dried and hardened.

The process stopped abruptly. The red river dried up, and the regeneracy dome shrank, enveloping only Bonnie's motionless body in the midst of its swirling colours.

Billy lowered Excalibur and glanced at his rubellite ring. The colour was static. No pulsing. He scanned the valley again. Now, instead of a bunch of bones, the riverbed was full of lifeless bodies – fully formed, but still lifeless.

Joseph scooped up a handful of dust and scattered it into the breeze. "Speak to the prophetic rock, son of man. Say, 'Come from the four winds, O breath, and breathe upon these slain, that they may live.' "

Billy slid Excalibur back into its scabbard and turned toward the boulder, now alabaster white instead of red. He took a deep breath and repeated Joseph's words, his voice shaking like an earthquake. "Co . . . come from the four . . . four winds, O breath, and . . . and breathe upon these slain, that they may live."

A song rose from the valley floor. This time, instead of the professor's solo, a choir of angelic voices sang an ecstatic chorus.

> Whither shall I go from thy spirit? Or whither shall I flee from thy presence?
> If I ascend up into heaven, thou art there: If I make my bed in hell, behold, thou art there.
> If I take the wings of the morning, and dwell in the uttermost parts of the sea;
> Even there shall thy hand lead me, and thy right hand shall hold me.

Billy gave a short laugh, mixing it with a stifled sob. "It's . . . it's Bonnie's song. They're singing Bonnie's song."

Long tails began swishing. Wings stretched out like taut parachutes. Great mouths opened in yawns and roars, fire spitting out in weak streams. Eight dragons lifted and dropped their legs as they lumbered around on the dusty valley floor.

Billy clenched his fist and shifted his gaze from his rubellite to Bonnie's motionless body. The song continued, bursting out in rapturous crescendo.

> If I say, Surely the darkness shall cover me; even the night shall be light about me.
> Yea, the darkness hideth not from thee; but the night shineth as the day:

The rubellite's red eye never blinked. All the bones were gone, and eight dragons stood here and there, still stretching and testing their newly restored bodies, but Bonnie lay deathly still in her dome, hundreds of sparkling hues bouncing off her body.

Joseph laid a strong hand on Billy's shoulder. "I don't know why she was excluded from the regeneration, Son. My understanding was that the plan called for her to be revived with the rest of them."

Billy shivered, nausea boiling in his stomach. He could barely speak. "Did . . . did I mess up something?"

"Mess up?" Joseph tilted his head. "Perhaps you could use that idiom. I would say you just didn't recognize the light at the bridge, so God gave you another one to follow. It proved to be a longer path, one that I am not familiar with, so I have no idea how it will end."

"Isn't there anything I can do to make it right?"

"I know of nothing," Joseph replied, handing Apollo to him. "Do you have an idea?"

Billy took Apollo and hugged it with both arms. "Well . . . I read a prophecy about a dragon chained in darkest pits. Maybe it means I should go back to the pit and try to find my dad. But I don't know how that will help Bonnie."

"You crossed the bridge," Joseph said. "You cannot return to the other side, not without a new portal."

Billy jerked his head up. "What's that noise?" A buzzing racket seemed to rise from the direction of the valley's boulder dam. He rotated on his heels. A mass of fluttering wings swarmed at the base of the white stone.

Joseph shouted over the din. "Passage beetles!"

Billy pulled out Excalibur and waved it back and forth, creating the dome of light. "Will they attack?"

"So far, it seems not, but if they do, not even the dragons are safe. Their bite can pierce armour . . . and your photo-umbrella. Neither blade nor beam will hinder such an army."

Billy allowed the beam to diminish and sheathed Excalibur. "Is the bite fatal?"

"Not to souls already dead. All victims pass to a deeper circle where they face greater torment, but a bite to a living human is likely to be a fatal wound."

Billy rubbed the welt on his neck. "Would someone who's already been bitten be immune?"

"I cannot say. I don't know if it's ever hap—"

The buzz suddenly grew louder. "They're coming this way!" Billy shouted.

Joseph clutched Billy's shirt collar. "You must mount a dragon and fly! I will send the other dragons to collect your friends and follow."

Billy jerked away. "I can't. There's something I have to do." He marched toward the bridge, Apollo dangling from his hand. The fluttering beetles charged toward him in a thin stream and encircled him, like vibrating yarn spinning around a spool. In seconds they knitted a shroud of tiny armoured bodies, wrapping his legs and torso. As they crawled on his skin he waved his arms at Joseph. "Get everyone out! Now!"

A sharp sting on his hand jolted his brain. Another shot across his neck. More bites dug into his arms, sending a tidal wave of ripping agony along his spine. Through the mass of buzzing antennae and wings, he could still see Bonnie's body lying in the dome . . . motionless. He blew two beetles from his lips with a fiery spurt. "Goodbye, Bonnie. I'll see you again . . . someday."

The entire scene began to dissolve before his eyes – Joseph, Bonnie, the dragons, the valley – all melting to the ground. The sky swirled like a black tornado, and the ground collapsed beneath his feet. He plummeted down a slippery tube at breathtaking speed.

The beetles peeled off his body, stripping upwards like flakes of dead skin. His shirt flopped up into his face, and his sleeves tried to ride up his arms. Seconds later he slowed to a stop, landing gently on his feet. He straightened his shirt and patted his hands on his chest. The beetles were gone, but his skin felt like fire.

The ground radiated intense heat, rising into his face like steam in a sauna, and his toes chafed in his shoes. Lifting his feet one at a time, he tested the ground. Although it gave a little bit, it seemed solid enough. He looked up. High in the dark sky a tiny circle of brightness peered down. He set Apollo near his shoes and drew out Excalibur, creating an ambient glow that illuminated his immediate surroundings in the oven-like chamber.

A stony ceiling capped the room just out of arm's reach. Directly over Billy's head, a six-foot-wide tunnel with sheer, vertical walls exited the chamber. Far above, a ray of light shone down like a distant full moon, the same circle of brightness he had noticed before.

Billy moved Excalibur toward his feet. "Auggh!" He jerked his knees up and down, dancing in place. The floor was crawling with worms, long, orange and black striped worms slithering in a knotted mass, thousands, maybe millions. His feet squashed a dozen or more, sending streams of worm juice spraying all around. A ripple of fire passed across the surface, igniting the injured worms, but they kept right on squirming, apparently unable to die.

Billy settled his feet in the writhing quagmire, his skin tingling as hot worms oozed between his socks and trouser cuffs. He summoned Excalibur's beam and stirred it into the wormy soup, but it had no effect. The blade's glow was enough, however, to illuminate the chamber. A column of fire shot up, spewing a geyser of flame that splattered the arching roof with a sparkling coat of orange luminescence.

Far away to his left, two walls came together to form a dark corner. Lifting his feet high, he strode to the nearer wall, squishing more worms and dodging another fountain of fire. He ran his hand along the wall's surface and poked his finger into one of its many deep divots. Did candlestones once occupy these little holes?

As he approached the corner, he found a sneaker with a PF logo on the side. Worms slithered across the outer lining and crawled through the eyelets, chewing on the frayed laces and canvas. A sparkle of light caught his eye. He stooped, finding a spot on the floor clear of worms. A glow pulsed on the clean stone tile, strobing between two distinct shades of crimson. He picked up a chain next to the glow, lifting a gold ornament with a pulsing red light in the centre. *Shiloh's pendant!*

Walter gulped, backing away from the edge of the cliff. "Billy disappeared!"

Shiloh grabbed his elbow. "I think those bugs ate him!"

"They couldn't have! They disappeared, too!"

"Walter!" Joseph shouted from the valley. "Come down here!"

Walter leaped toward the cliff and zipped along the path, Palin's sword in hand, skipping most of the hairpin turns and sliding down the slope. He sprinted up to Joseph's side, breathless. "What happened? . . . Is Billy okay?"

Joseph laid his hands over Bonnie's regeneracy dome as if warming his fingers. "I do not know. This development was not in Merlin's plan. Only the Almighty can guide Young Arthur now."

Walter gazed inside the kaleidoscopic aura. "But what about Bonnie? Wasn't bringing her back to life part of the plan?"

One of the dragons stretched out its neck, hovering its head over Bonnie. Joseph reached over and stroked its tawny scales. "It was part of the plan," he replied, "but events arose that I did not expect. I honestly don't know what will happen next. But for now, you must do your part."

Walter pointed at himself. "My part in the plan? I'm just here to help Billy and Bonnie!"

Joseph knelt and scooped up a stray passage beetle, gripping it by the outer shell to avoid its blue spittle. "That is the way of prophecy," he said, rising again. "Purposes are always fulfilled, though individual participation and outcomes vary."

The dragon draped the end of its tail over Walter's shoulder. Walter eased his hand over it, pressing his fingers in between the spikes. "Okay," he said slowly. "Confusing, but okay." He gazed at Joseph's dark eyes. "What do I do?"

"First, help me with Bonnie. Dead or not, her body doesn't belong in the circles. We must get everyone back to the world of the living as soon as possible."

"Suits me," Walter said, hoisting the sword over his shoulder. "Show me the door, and we're outta here."

Joseph lifted his eyes toward the sky. "The gate is up there."

Walter squinted at the shining fence Billy had drawn with Excalibur. "I love a challenge!" He thrust the sword between his belt and waistband. "Well, we have a bunch of winged dragons here. What are we waiting for? Let's launch them!"

Joseph patted the dragon on the flank. "This is Thigocia. She is a war dragon and a healer. If anyone can still help Bonnie, she can, and she is delighted to have a chance to go to war against the Watchers." He stood on tiptoes to speak into the dragon's ear. "Round up your troops. You must collect Bonnie and the living humans and fly through the gate." He cupped his hands around his mouth and called up to the ledge. "Patrick! Shiloh! Come down here!"

Thigocia lowered her head, making a stairway with her spiny neck. "Young man, climb on my back and hang on tight. I am accustomed to carrying a warrior, but I assume that you are not experienced yet."

"Nah. I'm a rookie, but I'm ready to ride." Walter climbed up the scales and grabbed hold of a spine near the dragon's neck. "My name's Walter. I guess you don't have any—"

"Reins to hang on to?" Thigocia finished. "No. I need no guidance. I will lead the way, and I will appoint two others to carry your friends."

Walter half closed one eye. "Did you just read my mind?"

"I do not read minds. I make calculated assumptions."

Walter pushed his seat up higher on Thigocia's back. "That sounds way too familiar."

Patrick and Shiloh ran onto the valley floor hand in hand. Joseph directed each of them to a dragon, helping them climb aboard.

Thigocia unfurled her wings, stretching them out into a mammoth pair of leather-like sails. "We must keep Bonnie's regeneracy dome intact." She flicked out her long, forked tongue and banged her tail on the ground. "Ladies! Form the hammock pyramid! Firedda! Yellinia! We three will take the lower position."

"The hammock pyramid?" Walter repeated.

Thigocia turned her body, pointing her tail toward the regeneracy dome. "Yes. It is the way we transported a wounded dragon through the air in order to prevent further injury."

The dragons carrying Patrick and Shiloh stationed themselves on each side of the dome, completing the triangle with Thigocia. Three other dragons took to the air and flew in a tight circle right over the triangle, beating their wings furiously.

"That's it!" Thigocia shouted over the flapping racket. "Now alternate your downbeats, and we'll be off."

A strong updraft nearly pulled Walter off Thigocia's back. With dust flying everywhere, he clutched her spine with both hands, squinting through the debris. Bonnie and the entire sparkling dome lifted slowly off the ground.

The three lower dragons stretched out their wings, allowing the updraft to fill their sails and slowly draw them into its flow. With gentle strokes, like oars through water, their wings lifted them higher and higher. The final two dragons flew below the pyramid, acting as a safety net, and the team of eight dragons angled toward the shining fence in the sky.

Walter glanced back at Joseph and freed his hand to wave. "What's going to happen to you?" he yelled.

Joseph waved back and shouted. "When all has been fulfilled, I will be taken home to the eighth circle." His voice began fading away. "Farewell! Godspeed to all of you!"

Walter refastened his hand on Thigocia, his black cloak flapping around his arms. Would the others need cloaks to pass through the portal, or was this one safer than the others? Should he put on his hood?

He gritted his teeth. *I'll just trust Joseph. He would have told us if we needed protection.*

The dragons, flying in a swirling, triple-stack formation, plunged through the shining gateway. Walter held his breath as they passed through a flashing, viscous membrane, popping out on the other side into a gloomy, night-time sky.

Ashley whispered into the air. "Okay, Larry. I know it might take a while, but when Apollo's charged to the calculated point, hit it!"

`"Flash sequence countdown has commenced."`

Ashley grabbed the professor's arm. "It'll take at least a few minutes. We'd better find those Watchers and see what happens."

They scurried up the hill and gazed around the summit. Even in the darkness, the shining creatures were easy to see as they made their way down the slope toward the entrance to the tor. Ashley and the professor trailed them, bending low to stay out of sight.

A new crowd had gathered at the gate, and many were streaming up the path. Morgan, Elaine, the dog, and the Watchers marched into the throng. The Watchers waved their massive arms, as if expecting the adulation of the crowds. Lightning flashed at their feet as they stomped along the path, and black clouds rushed over the tor, boiling up into a colossal thunderhead, blocking out the moon.

The dragon trailed behind, flapping his wings to steady his descent on the slope. "Hartanna is near," it roared. "I can feel it."

At the sound of the dragon's voice, the mob scattered, dozens of people retreating to the entry gate.

"Then hunt her down and kill her!" Morgan shouted. She grabbed Samyaza's hand. "Let us not risk facing Hartanna's flames. Take to the skies, and I will guide us to our new base of operations."

Samyaza swept Morgan into his arms and launched into the air. Another Watcher cradled Elaine, then scooped up the prism dog as the mass of shining beings streamed into the turbulent clouds.

The professor pulled Ashley's wrist. "I know it could be suicide, but we must do all we can to prevent Hartanna's murder. I don't know if the dragon will harm Marilyn, but we can't risk it." Ashley gritted her teeth and nodded, but a loud buzzing sound made her turn. "Professor! The portal!"

The professor ran down the slope, waving back at her. "You see to that, Miss Stalworth. I must help Marilyn and Hartanna . . . or die trying."

Ashley dashed over the hill, retracing her steps back to the portal terrace. The door to the other world burst open in a dazzling explosion of light, washing the entire side of the hill in a pulsating sapphire glow and bathing Ashley's face in an icy wind. Six dragons popped out of the blazing rectangle, three over three, followed immediately by two more that zoomed upward and circled overhead. Of the first six, the three lower dragons settled to the ground, a colourful dome of light floating in their midst. A male rider clambered down the lead dragon's back, a sword in his hand. The others found level spots on the terrace to land.

Ashley sprinted toward him, her arms spread out. "Walter! You made it!"

Walter received Ashley's embrace, smiling broadly when she kissed his forehead. She pressed a clump of grime on his cheek and smeared it down to his chin. "You're a mess!"

"Yeah, I had to do some dirty work, but I—"

"Wait!" Ashley interrupted. "Hartanna needs your help. She and Billy's mum went over the top of the hill and down the path. There's another dragon over there trying to kill her!"

Walter gave her a tired salute. "I'm on my way. Tell the dragons where I'm going. I'll probably need their help." Lifting his sword, he hustled to the crest of the tor and disappeared over the top.

Ashley ran toward the shimmering dome. Patrick and Shiloh climbed off their mounts and joined her. "What's this?" Ashley asked, drawing closer and peering inside. She threw her hands over her mouth. "Oh, no!" She grabbed Shiloh's arm. "Is she . . . ?" She swallowed down a painful lump. "Is she dead?"

"I'm afraid so," Patrick said. "The regeneracy dome doesn't seem to be working."

"Can't we do something?" Ashley asked. "Can't we—"

A loud ruckus ripped away Ashley's words. The lead dragon shouted commands as the others lined up on the terrace, flapping their wings to get in place. "That's right. Attack positions. We will fly as one in battle formation. I sense the Watchers nearby. We cannot allow them to escape!"

Ashley forced herself to shout. "The Watchers just left." She pointed up the slope. "They went over the tor, then flew away! But can't you stay and help—"

"That is all the information I need, young lady. I assume the dead girl is your friend, so I apologize for having to rush away. Her chances are so slim, it would not be wise for me to spend the time to attempt a healing." Thigocia beat her wings, sending fresh breezes across Ashley's body, rippling her clothes. The great dragon lifted into the sky, and one by one the other dragons followed, their commander leading the way into the clouds.

Ashley covered her mouth again. *That dragon said . . .* She gasped. *Can it really be true?*

CHAPTER 23

FOLLOWING THE LIGHT

Billy draped the chain around his neck, tucked it under his shirt, then trudged slowly back to the centre of the room where he had left Apollo. He pulled the folded sheet from his pocket and read the poem again.

> A dragon chained in darkest pits
> Will not behold pure freedom's light,
> For dragons claim a lofty perch,
> Yet cannot reach the highest height.
>
> For even now in pits of gloom
> The dragon's pride will never bow,
> Until redemption's sword sets free
> The dragon's heart to kneel and vow.

Billy crumpled up the paper and flung it on the mass of undulating worms. "Why couldn't you bow?" His voice echoed against the scarred walls. "You bow . . . you bow . . ."

Billy thrust the sword back into its scabbard. Darkness enfolded the room. He spread out his arms. "But where are you now?" The echoes continued. "Where are you now? . . . where are you now?"

A faint glow appeared in Apollo's enclosure, sending a ray of light across the wadded paper as it rose and fell on the wiggling carpet. Two worms had latched onto it and were slowly gnawing away the edge. Billy nudged the paper with his toe, then snatched it up again. With tears welling, he refolded it neatly before sliding it into his back pocket.

A deep, mocking voice reverberated in the room. "Where are you now? Where are you now?"

Billy jerked Excalibur out and used its ambient glow to search the room. "Who said that?"

"Who said that?" the voice mocked again. A dark shadow grew out of the floor, rising toward the ceiling and solidifying into the shape of a dragon. "I'll tell you where he is, Billy Bannister!"

Billy summoned Excalibur's beam and slashed it across the shadow. The laser wrapped around the dragon, illuminating his reddish scales, but the light sputtered and dissolved. Excalibur dimmed, glowing no more than a child's nightlight.

The dragon laughed. "Your understanding of that sword is not deep enough to defeat me." Its tail snapped forward and cracked like a whip. "Behold! The tree that killed your Genesis father and you along with him!"

The chamber shook, rattling Billy's joints. He fell to his behind, clutching Excalibur like a lifeline as hundreds of worms slithered over his legs. The worms suddenly transformed into moist dirt and a hole began opening at his feet, filling rapidly with water. He pushed against the mud, trying to slide away, but another hole ripped open behind him. He scrambled up and stood between the two growing holes, then slowly backed away to safer ground.

The water in the first hole bubbled to the surface and streamed across Billy's shoes. The other hole gushed like a geyser, sending a misty spray across his face. A dark green stalk sprouted between the holes, growing into a tree in a matter of seconds. Two red, oblong apples popped up at the end of a branch and dangled within reach.

The dragon's tail snaked around Billy's wrist. It dragged him to the tree and pulled his hand toward the fruit, making him drop his sword. "Through seven circles," the dragon growled, "I have drawn you toward the desire of your flesh. Why have you resisted? You are but a worm who longs to feast on Adam's apple."

Billy yanked his hand away. "You're the worm, you lying snake!"

"Oh, you're the clever one," the dragon snapped, "but you won't be feeling so witty after a few days alone in this chamber." Excalibur, now lying in the mud, suddenly blinked off completely, turning everything black. A stream of fire shot from the dragon toward the tree, covering one of the apples with flame. When the fire abated, the fruit glowed cherry red. "Darkness will seep into your soul, and despair will conquer your spirit. But my tree will always be here to keep you company. As soon as you take the fruit, I will set you free and reunite you with your father."

The dragon backed into one of the pools and began to sink into the water, its scales reflecting the crimson glow of the dangling apple. As the dragon's head approached the bubbling surface, it snaked out its skinny, orange tongue. "I leave this reminder of one of your dead girlfriend's favourite quotes." It flashed a long row of razor teeth. "Call to me, and I will answer you." Just before its mouth touched the water, it added, "My name . . . is Lucifer." It disappeared in an eruption of steaming bubbles.

Billy stood motionless, staring into the dim chamber. The glowing apple cast an eerie halo, bathing everything in a bloody mask. Excalibur lay cold and dark, and Apollo sat upside down next to the blade without a hint of life. He retrieved his sword, turned Apollo upright, and stalked toward the tree, pulling Excalibur back with both hands.

"Die, you foul weed!" He swung at the trunk, but the blade clanked on the petrified bark and bounced back, rattling his bones. The apple shook, sending circular waves of energy across the crimson light field.

His head still vibrating, Billy sat down at the edge of one of the streams and let the cold water run through his shoes, soothing his scorched feet. As he rested, the red glow washed over his body, pricking the skin through his wet clothes like a gorse bush brushing his arms and back with its nettles.

He slid farther from the tree and turned his eyes away from the fruit. The stinging eased up a bit, but the darkness seemed to envelop him in a dirty red blanket, making it difficult to breathe. The stuffy air filled with putrid odours, a mixture of every foul scent he had experienced in the circles. He knew the painful sensations were part of the dragon's attack, but with Excalibur powerless in his grip, he had no defence. He was alone.

Billy buried his face in his hands, shutting out the relentless red glow. "I'm not alone," he whispered. "I'm never alone."

The dragon's echoing voice replied. "Call to me, and I will answer you."

Billy shook his head violently. "No! I'll never call to you!"

"Just take the fruit, and your suffering will end."

Billy stamped his foot in the water. "No! Get away from me!"

The voice deepened, and his words echoed through the chamber. "Your father abandoned you and is gone forever . . . forever . . . forever. You long for help, but Bonnie is dead . . . dead . . . dead. Walter is trapped in my realm and will die there . . . die there . . . die there. And even if the professor searches to the ends of the earth, he will never find you . . . find you . . . find you. All is lost . . . lost . . . lost. There is nothing left to do but despair . . . despair . . . despair."

Billy closed his eyes and slapped his hands over his ears. "Get away from me! Just . . . go . . . away!" After several seconds of total silence, he opened his eyes and slowly uncovered his ears. The odours vanished. The glow from the apple dimmed, then blinked off, leaving the chamber in complete darkness. Only the gentle splashing of water gave any hint that there was more than pure nothingness all around.

He mopped his damp forehead with his even wetter sleeve, then tried to look at his hand. Nothing. Total blackness. Even his wiggling fingers were invisible. He bit his lower lip and grabbed a handful of dirt. No light at all! It wasn't supposed to be this way! Where was the guiding light the professor promised would always be there? And Joseph mentioned something about not recognizing the light. What could he have meant? Billy drooped his head between his knees. It was all so confusing! The mission wasn't supposed to be *this* hard!

The sound of bubbling water washed through his brain. The splashes formed words in his mind, giving speech to his thoughts. The professor seemed to whisper in trickling prose. "God always provides a guiding light, William. No matter how dark it seems or how terrible the situation, you can always count on finding a glimmer, a spark of light in the deepest blackness that will tell you which way to go. . . . Don't give in to darkness, for the dawn will eventually break."

Billy stared into the void. Where was the light? There was no glimmer, not even a . . . A glint of red penetrated the darkness. *What was that?* He swung his head back and forth. A faint reddish glow raced across the lower half of his field of vision, then vanished, only to reappear an instant later. He dropped his chin to his chest, trying to track the fleeting beam. Again it flashed. *Aha!*

Grabbing the chain around his neck, he drew out Shiloh's pendant. The gem at the centre still pulsed between two shades of red, illuminating his hand and his dark rubellite ring. He curled his fingers over the edge of the pendant and stared at it. *Okay. I found a light. Now what?*

His gaze drifted from the pendant to his ring. Barely visible in the pendant's strobing aura, his reflection stared back at him from his rubellite. In the darkness his image seemed more like a phantom than a photo, a floating misrepresentation of his features. It looked more like . . . *Dad?*

He rose to his knees, his back straight. He closed his hand into a fist and tightly shut his eyes. "Dad," he said out loud, "how am I ever going to get over you if you keep haunting me like this?" He reopened his eyes. "You've been around, but . . . but you turned into a dragon. You're not really my dad anymore." Tears rolled down his cheeks. His voice grew, pitching higher. "If you want to leave me, just go away! You're tearing Mum and me apart!" He sniffed and clutched the pendant against his chest. "But if you want to come back and . . . and be my dad again, I'll . . ." He gasped, "I'll search . . . I'll search for you from one end of the earth to the other!" He raised his clenched fist. "Nothing will stop me from finding you!"

He dropped the pendant under his shirt, picked up the sword, and gripped it tightly, but the blade remained dark. The lack of light opened an old wound in his mind. The day he pulled Excalibur from the stone back in West Virginia, the sword stayed cold and lifeless in his hands. It seemed like years passed before he finally learned the secret of its power. He had been lying half-unconscious on a cold laboratory floor in the midst of a collapsing mountain when the professor asked him, "What now is your weapon?" And on that fateful night he had replied, "Truth is my sword." At that very instant Excalibur's laser had burst forth, enabling him to defeat the slayer.

Truth. The word triggered the memory of his dilemma at the bridge and of Patrick stripping off his black cloak. "Fire away, Clefspeare," Patrick had said. "I'm willing to sacrifice myself to make sure Billy sees the light of truth." The man was ready to lay down his life for someone he barely knew. The expression of pure love on his face was a beacon.

Billy nodded. The guiding light was at the bridge after all.

He ran his finger along the edge of Excalibur's darkened blade. "Sacrifice," he whispered. "Isn't that what love is really all about?" The blade sliced through his skin. "Ouch!" He felt a trickle of blood oozing down his finger. He let it flow, feeling it drip onto his palm. Wasn't this the very symbol of sacrifice? Wasn't this the element that extended the life of Devin and Palin, of Ashley's grandfather, and of dragons themselves? Did the spilling of blood mean something more than he could ever understand?

Billy squeezed his finger, drawing more blood. He stared at his wound, trying to see through the darkness. A faint glow, almost undetectable, traced a line down his hand. What could be the source? Was his blood actually emitting light? He gasped. *Photoreceptors! They carry light!*

Carefully, reverently, he smeared blood on the face of the blade. The faint glow spread across the metal, filling the etched design until it blushed with radiance. Two dragons were locked in combat, one blazing red, the other shimmering white. Light streamed from the white dragon's mouth, pouring over the entire blade until Excalibur burst with brilliance.

Billy's eyes drank in the glorious splendour of the flaming sword. He flexed his muscles, gripping the sword's hilt with all his strength. The power was back!

The dragon, liar though he was, had said, "Your understanding of that sword is not deep enough to defeat me." But now Billy knew. Excalibur's blade was forged long ago in the fires of love and sharpened daily by the blood of sacrifice. He had understood so little of that truth, but now he would never forget. He brought the blade close to his face and let it rest on his forehead. It was time to go to war!

With light now flooding the chamber, he bounded through the stream, screaming a battle cry. He attacked the tree, slicing through the thick trunk with a single blow. The branches erupted with fire, and the apples exploded, sending black muck splattering all around. Billy raised his arm to block the slime as he slowly retreated. The tree toppled, striking the ground with an earth-shaking thud.

The jolt sent Billy stumbling backwards, tipping Apollo on its side. Its inner cavity suddenly flashed, then exploded in a blaze. The felled tree disappeared in a dazzling splash of sparks, leaving no trace of trunk, roots, or branches. The stone in Billy's belt, the camera to the real world, shattered and flaked to the ground. Excalibur's laser blasted upward, ripping an enormous hole in the ceiling. An avalanche of dirt rained down. Billy hustled to the middle of the chamber and covered his head with his arms, laughing and crying at the same time.

Walter stormed down the other side of the hill, holding his sword out to the side. He followed the narrow, paved path until it turned sharply to the left at a natural ledge. Two men and a lady pointed toward a field near the base of the tor and shouted almost in unison, "The dragons are down there!"

Walter wiped his brow and gazed down the slope. The path curved back from the left and bordered a field to its right. "I see them!" The moon had reappeared, and in its glow, the two dragons seemed to shimmer, each one crouched as if ready to strike. Two human forms stood between the combatants, but shadows veiled their faces.

Walter charged ahead, taking a shortcut straight down the steep hill to join the path again. As he sprinted into the field, Hartanna roared, "Clefspeare, if you kill me, no man or beast will protect you from the Maker's wrath."

The professor stepped up boldly, as if trying to protect Hartanna, but his uplifted arms looked feeble in the shadow of the enormous dragon. Mrs Bannister stood behind him, her hands on his back. The professor's voice boomed. "Have you gone mad, Clefspeare? What demon has possessed you?"

Walter jumped in front of the professor, brandishing his sword in both hands. "The demon is Devin, Prof. He's inside Clefspeare's body."

Devin reached out and snatched up Mrs Bannister in one of his scaly claws, squeezing his talons around her waist. She screamed, pushing against his grip with both hands.

"Hartanna, fighting you here would take too long. Come with me as a prisoner of honour or she dies!"

Walter pulled back his sword. "We don't make deals with demons!" He jumped up and hacked at the dragon's forearm, penetrating the flesh between two scales. Mrs Bannister flew out of Devin's grip and tumbled to the ground in a heap. The professor rushed to her side, pulled her to her feet, and led her behind Hartanna's body.

Dark blood streamed from Devin's forearm. The dragon roared, whipped his tail around, and looped it around Walter's body. With a snap, he flung Walter into the air, then followed with a blast of fire. Hartanna caught Walter with her wing, shielding him just before the flames could slam into his body.

As soon as Hartanna set Walter down, he pushed the wing aside. Devin took a heavy step toward them. Walter raised his sword and waved at the she-dragon. "Get Prof and Mrs B out of here! I'm going to end this now!"

Hartanna scooped up the adults with her claws and tried to fly, but she could only skitter along the ground. When Devin gave chase, Walter sprinted around the dragon's flank and sliced off the back quarter of his tail. Devin screamed and shot up into the air. He soared higher than the treetops, then plummeted straight toward Walter, his rear claws bared.

Walter flattened to his stomach and rolled clear. Devin slammed to the ground, cracking the surface. The earth crumbled beneath Devin's body, and he slid into the widening chasm. A laser beam shot upward through the hole, narrowly missing the dragon, then streaked along the ground in a hundred directions like branches of lightning.

Walter pushed up on all fours and scrambled away from the brink. The chasm ripped open even wider, swallowing more dirt and catching Walter's kicking feet. He sprawled forward, frantically scratching the ground for something to grab. Anything!

He snagged a root and hung on, his body sinking below ground level as the gulf widened. He tried to call for help, but dirt spilled into his mouth. As he spat it out, a loud splash sounded behind him. *Oh, great! Water! Drowning is next!*

Digging into the chasm wall with his feet, he pulled on the root hand over hand, but he was still a good five feet from the top. His body hung over a pit, and all he had was a stringy root keeping him from a precarious plunge.

A sturdier tree root dangled just inches over his head. If he could only let go long enough to grab it, he would be home free. His root began tearing away from the wall, inching him lower. He slowly released it with one hand. *Okay! Here goes!*

Ashley knelt at Bonnie's side and wept. The regeneracy dome shrank, barely enveloping Bonnie's curled-up form. The inner sparkles slowed, falling to the ground in tired sizzles as the dome finally collapsed and vanished.

Ashley scooted forward on her knees and laid a hand on Bonnie's ashen cheek. It was cold and slick, more like glazed pottery than skin. She slid her hand under Bonnie's back and pulled her into an embrace, laying Bonnie's head against her shoulder. She cried bitterly into the mass of tangled, blonde-streaked hair. "Bonnie . . . I . . . I love you so much! . . . If I could take your place . . . I would." She lifted her head. "God . . . if you're listening . . . give me a sign. Show me if there's anything I can do."

Larry's voice crackled through the handheld computer lying on the ground. "`Apollo's flash completed.`"

Patrick and Shiloh stood at Ashley's side, arm in arm. "We should not linger here," Patrick said. "With the Watchers prowling—"

The ground suddenly quaked, sending violent shivers through their feet. A flash brightened the sky. Streaks of light zipped across the ground, one stripping the grass along the terrace and sending a path of sparks flying straight up. The bolt shot into Bonnie, enveloping her and Ashley in a vibrant halo. The aura buzzed. Ashley shook violently, Bonnie still in her arms.

Ashley's teeth ground together. Spots danced in her vision, and her world faded to black. A thousand images flashed before her eyes – her childhood bedroom, her father and mother, a fire, a hospital, her grandfather, kids at school cruelly laughing at her – all spinning on a high-speed merry-go-round.

She felt a cool touch on her cheek. "Ashley?" a gentle voice said.

Ashley forced her eyes open. Three smiling faces stared down at her. Patrick, Shiloh, and . . . "Bonnie?" She pushed herself up to her seat. "Bonnie! You're alive!"

Bonnie grinned and offered Ashley a hand up. Letting out a loud squeal, Ashley leaped to her feet, then wrapped her arms around Bonnie's neck and rocked from side to side. "I can't believe you're alive again! We thought we'd lost you!"

Bonnie pushed Ashley back gently. "Where are Billy and Walter?"

"Billy's still in the circles, but I'll tell you what I know about that later." Ashley pointed up the slope. "Right now Walter needs our help over that hill. A dragon's after your mum."

"A dragon!" Bonnie stretched out her wings. "The one from the circles?"

"It came out of the circles, but I don't know who it is." Ashley reached down and rubbed her tingling thighs. "Can you fly?"

Bonnie balled up her fists. "I'll soon find out! I have a bone to pick with that dragon."

Dirt poured on Billy's head, spilling into the stream at his feet, and light poured in from above. A huge splash in the hole in front of him sent water washing over his face. He stumbled backwards and fell into the hole behind him, now a pool of frigid water. He thrust his feet downward into the biting cold and found the bottom. Standing on tiptoes, he propped up his body and kept his head and torso above the surface. He raised Excalibur, and its light flashed back to life. He summoned the beam once again and aimed it skyward.

The sword's light radiated across his wrists. For some reason his skin had turned milky white. A pasty film coated his arms and shirt, making him look like a glowing ghost. With a mental command, he doused Excalibur. If the dragon was still around, he didn't want to be a neon bullseye in its fire-breathing cross hairs.

Billy looked up at a new gaping hole in the ceiling a dozen feet or so above his head. It was way out of reach, but he could see the sky – the big dipper, the glow of the moon, and . . . a jet? No, two jets. And a transport helicopter. Was he back on earth? Could Apollo's flash have sent him away from the circles and the dragon?

Finding an upward slope, he sloshed ahead, but his shoes slid on the white residue, making the going slow. Finally, after plodding into ankle-deep water, he summoned Excalibur's beam once again and guided it around the room, now a gaping crater.

Pools bubbled up in both holes, and he stood in one of the outflow streams. Chalky residue coated the rocky bed, making it look like someone had spilled a hundred gallons of milk into the water. The other spring bed, however, wore a coat of reddish-brown, like the skin of a freshly rusted nail.

Bubbles in the red spring floated to the surface and multiplied, like a volcano about to erupt. A curtain of vapour shrouded the pool, growing into a billowing cloud. Slowly, the head of a dragon emerged, the fire from his breath boiling the water and sending blasts of steam into the air.

A river of flame burst from the pool and hurtled toward Billy. He jumped out of the way of the inferno and swung Excalibur's beam across the dragon's neck. The beam wrapped around its head, buzzing like an army of chainsaws. The shaft of light separated into a million sparks and adhered to the dragon's scales, but the sparks quickly fizzled out, leaving the crater bathed in the light of the moon and the dragon unharmed.

His scales even redder than before, the dragon lunged out of the spring. In the white light from above, Billy studied the glowing monster. Something was different. The shape of its head was wrong, not the same as it had been when it presented the fruit tree and then submerged in the pool. Was this even the same dragon? Or was this . . . Devin?

The dragon blasted another jet of fire. With a hyper-fast sweep, Billy parried, catching the jet with the sword's beam and quenching it in the white spring's water. A plume of steam rose, filling the chamber with fog.

The dragon roared, his six-inch teeth bared and his forked tongue lashing out. "You can't keep blocking my flames forever! Give up and be my hostage, or die!"

Devin's voice!

Billy held Excalibur in front of his face with both hands. "No way! I don't know how we got here, but I'm not about to give up! I can create a barrier with Excalibur for as long as I want." He gestured upward with his head. "Besides, I think the British government has sent a welcoming party for you."

Devin glared at Billy. "Trust me, the military won't be on your side. They'll investigate everything. You'll be a caged white rat in a top secret laboratory with tubes sticking out of your body from your head to your belly." He paused, his body dripping red, as though thin blood streamed from every scale.

Walter's voice popped in from above. "Billy! You made it back! You okay?"

Billy jerked his head upward. "Walter!" He turned his gaze back toward Devin. "I'm fine. I just have to dispatch this stinking lizard. What's up with you?"

Walter propped his hands on his knees and leaned over the twenty-foot-wide opening. "There's about a hundred soldiers lining up, armed way past their teeth, but I don't think they know where you are yet. All the dragons flew—" Walter grimaced and pounded the dirt with his fist.

"Ahhh!" Devin said, letting out a sinister laugh. "So you revived the other dragons, and now they've flown the coop!" He thrust his tongue out at Billy again. "Looks like you're alone in this fight."

Walter threw a rock at Devin, hitting him square on the snout. "Alone? What are you talking about, you ugly hunk of snakeskin? I'm here, remember?"

Devin blew a jet of fire, but Walter jumped to the side. "Missed me, you overgrown tin can! Why don't you come out here instead of crawling in the dirt like a slimy little worm?"

The dragon roared. "I'm not a fool to be baited, you idiot! I know you want me up there where the soldiers can see me."

Walter stuck out his tongue. "You couldn't hit a knight with your breath if he kissed you on the mouth!" He hopped up and down and waved his arms. "C'mon give it another shot!" He put his thumbs in his ears and wiggled his fingers.

"Oh, trying to use me to signal the military, are you? I know I'm trapped in this hideous body, but I'm not as stupid as Clefspeare. Forget it, boy. Billy's alone, a captured fool, just like his father."

Billy growled under his breath, but he kept his anger in check. What good would it do to attack now? Something was keeping Devin safe from the beam. Was it the red coating? Some kind of residue that repelled the translumination?

A new splash erupted from one of the pools. Walter stepped out of the white spring and stood at Billy's side, drenched and looking like a wet, glazed doughnut stick. He shook his head like a dog after its bath, sending white droplets in all directions. "Don't ever try to abseil into a pit with a root."

Billy lifted Excalibur and set his feet. "I'll make a note of it."

Walter glared at the dragon. "Billy's never alone as long as I'm around." He dug into his pocket and held up a closed fist. "You think you're so smart, can you guess what's in my hand?"

Devin's good claw reached toward Walter, but Billy grabbed his friend and stepped back to avoid the lunging dragon. Devin tumbled into the white spring face first and thrashed around until he was able to right himself. As Devin's head rose above the surface, Billy waved Excalibur, creating an umbrella shield.

Devin stalked slowly toward Billy and Walter. The two boys inched backwards, both keeping their eyes pinned on the milky white dragon. Walter held his fist higher and whispered, "Let's drop that curtain, and send this snake to the moon."

Billy stilled his sword, and the shield collapsed into a single beam. Devin reared back to heave another blast of fire, but before he could let out a spark, Billy slashed his body with Excalibur's beam. This time, the laser ate through Devin's hide, disintegrating him into a spinning stream of dazzling light. Walter opened his hand, and the stream rushed toward it and plunged into the candlestone that lay in his palm.

When the light vanished, all was silent except for the gentle slap of running water. Walter tossed the gem into the air, caught it in his hand, and wrapped his fingers tightly around it. He gave Billy an impish smile. "Know of any pawn shops in Glastonbury? I'm willing to let this go cheap."

Billy tucked Excalibur in its sheath and splashed Walter with a swift kick. "I oughta sell you at a pawn shop!" He then hooked his arm around Walter's neck and pulled him close. "But you're worth a whole lot more than the couple of farthings anyone's likely to pay for you."

A female voice drifted into the pit. "Well that looks cozy!"

Billy pulled away from Walter and looked up. That voice! Could it be? He could barely whisper. "Bonnie?"

Walter waved. "Hey, girl! You finally decided to wake up?" He kicked up a splash of water and grinned. "About time, you lazy thing!"

Billy felt tears in his eyes, but he didn't bother to wipe them away. His voice shook. "Don't . . . ahem . . . don't listen to him,

Bonnie! We both know better!" He spread out his arms. "You know what? I think I need to get a ride from a certain, awesome girl I know. It's your turn to carry me for a while."

Bonnie's face beamed. She fluttered down into the cavern, settling into the ankle-deep water streaming from the pool. Billy stared at her, his arms slack and aching. Bonnie folded her hands at her waist and lowered her head, whispering, "I learned something really important today."

"What's that?" Billy whispered back.

She lifted her gaze, and her eyes sparkled as she stepped closer. "You remember how we were supposed to follow the light?"

"Sure. I remember."

"Well, I saw the Light." She sighed and hugged him. "And now I know. I have all I really need."

Bonnie's love wrapped around him like a purring tiger, driving out the chills and warming his soul. Her heart pounded against his chest, the most beautiful rhythm ever drummed. She released Billy and turned to Walter, embracing him briefly before pulling away and glancing around the dark pit. "Where's Devin?"

"I'd show you," Walter said, holding up a fist, "but you'd probably get sick."

Billy shook his drenched arms. "Explain it later. We have to get out of here. The soldiers are bound to find us soon."

Bonnie rubbed Billy's cheek with her finger. "Ewww! What's this stuff?"

"Just think of it as icing on the cake," Walter replied, holding his arms out. "And it's time for you to deliver a pair of fruitcakes to the top floor."

CHAPTER 24

A Final Song

Billy sat cross-legged facing a crackling campfire, resting his weary bones under a clear, starry sky. The silhouette of West Virginia's rural skyline under the waning moon set his mind at ease. Most of the pain was gone – his bruises were shrinking, his self-induced cut had closed, and even his passage beetle bites had healed. Since his hair had quit growing so fast and his cheeks were no longer swollen, his body had probably purged the beetle venom.

He sniffed the smoke-tinged air, detecting the faint hint of a skunk's musky scent. For some reason, even that was pleasant, the aroma of the real world, far removed from the counterfeit odours of scentsers and the smell of scorched worms in the depths of Sheol.

Yet, not all was right in this world. The emotional wounds seemed to bleed without remedy. Without any idea of what happened to his dad, the emptiness and mystery were almost unbearable, like plunging through a dark void in a nightmare that never ends.

His friends sat in a circle beside him, chatting and laughing together as they roasted hot dogs and marshmallows, each voice massaging his heartache like loving fingers. He gazed at Walter to his left, then his mother, Ashley, Karen, and finally Bonnie on his right, her wings wrapped around her body. She looked exhausted. After Patrick sneaked her out of England on a private jet, she had flown to Castlewood on her own. Billy had hated to let her make that trip. If only he could have gone with her somehow.

Walter poked a stick at the fire. Bundled in his heavy jacket against the cool mountain breezes, his skin glowed with sweat as the fire threw an extra blanket of heat across the group. The flames shrank to a few crackling tongues, and puffs of white mixed in with the campers' sighing breaths. Their enthusiastic conversation seemed to evaporate with the dying fire.

Billy held a forked branch, stained at the end with grey and black ashes. His bold voice broke the silence. "I'll just go ahead and say what everyone's thinking. We're stuck out here in the mountains, at least until Sir Patrick, the professor, and the dragons come up with a plan to stop the Watchers." He tossed the branch into the fire. "I hope Shiloh's holding up okay. Those reporters will be demanding DNA tests or something before they'll believe she's Bonnie. Prof said he wants Shiloh to throw them off the trail, but they smell blood, and they're not about to give up easily."

Karen pressed a gooey marshmallow and a chocolate wafer between two graham crackers to make a s'more, then used her tongue to catch the delightful mixture oozing through the gap. She shifted her body higher on a rolled-up sleeping bag, licking her lips. "So, Ash, where are the dragons now?"

In the flickering light, Ashley's face looked tired, her reddened cheeks punctuating her half-hearted smile. She slowly turned a skewered marshmallow over the nearest embers. "Last I heard," she said softly, "they were resting in Iceland and hope to be here sometime in the next few days. With the military searching for them, they have to be super careful."

Bonnie picked up her last bite of hot dog. "Any sign of the Watchers?"

Ashley pulled the toasted marshmallow from her skewer. "I haven't had time to search news reports for signs of what they might be up to." She squeezed the white goo between two crackers and handed it to Bonnie. "It didn't take long for the media to find you at my house. They swooped in like a flock of vultures."

Billy kicked a stray ember back into the fire. "Yeah, thanks to Adam Lark ratting on her. Now we might have to stay out of sight for weeks!"

Peering out from under the bill of his Baltimore Orioles baseball cap, Walter swallowed his third s'more, then licked his lips. "It's not so bad. We have food, lots of sleeping bags and blankets, and a great chef." He nudged Billy's mother with his elbow. "Right Mrs B?"

Mrs Bannister squeezed her own s'more and grimaced at the dripping mess. "I wouldn't call hot dogs and s'mores the work of a great chef, Walter."

"Remember the beans," Walter added. "I loved the beans."

Billy pulled Walter's cap farther down over his eyes. "As long as you don't make me remember them all night. Don't forget. I'm sleeping next to you."

Walter straightened his cap and began digging in his pocket. "Oh, yeah? Well, I have a secret weapon for a middle of the night attack."

Billy's mum squawked at Walter. "You didn't bring the candlestone, did you?"

"Nah, Mrs B." Walter held up a small, foil-wrapped cylinder. "They're just gas tablets. My dad's got the candlestone back in his office safe. We figured we couldn't destroy it. Devin's still got the only body Mr B can get into."

"But how are we going to squeeze Devin out and leave the dragon intact?" Billy asked. "Even Ashley's restoration machine couldn't separate a spirit from its body."

Ashley bent forward and stoked the fire with a stick, sending up a plume of sparks. "Give me time. I'll figure out something."

Karen elbowed Ashley. "What's up, Sis? You've been sulking all evening."

Ashley sat back and dug her hands into her pockets. "Not really sulking. I've just been thinking." She paused, and her voice pitched up half an octave. "One of those dragons is my mother."

Karen hooked her arm around Ashley's elbow and leaned against her shoulder.

Bonnie swung her head toward the woods behind her. "Did you hear something?"

Billy whispered, "Don't worry. I don't sense danger, but I do think someone's walking this way."

A tall, slender form in a black trench coat stepped into the circular glow of firelight, followed by a shorter companion dressed in jeans and a lavender hooded jacket.

"Professor!" everyone said at once.

"And Shiloh," Bonnie added with a smile.

Shiloh hustled over and sat by her new-found twin. Bonnie unfurled a wing, wrapped it around Shiloh, and handed her the box of grahams.

Billy's mother patted a blanket on the ground next to her and raised a coffee thermos. "Any news, Professor?"

The professor slipped into the space between Mrs Bannister and Ashley and waved his hand at the thermos. He picked up a stick and poked the fire absent-mindedly. "A great deal of news, both good and bad." He raised the stick in the air. A tiny flame crawled along its end and dwindled into a red ember. "Shiloh and I had to escape from your home. The reporters were simply wearing her out with questions, and the television networks are constantly playing the tape from the tor. They seem to get their jollies from freezing on a close-up of Bonnie and her dragon wings in all their glory."

Shiloh pulled Bonnie's wing over her lap. "The professor found the cave Billy's father used in the Otter Creek Wilderness, so your mother and the dragons will have a place to hide when they get here." Shiloh slid out two cracker squares. "Or should I call your mum Aunt Hartanna?"

Bonnie handed Shiloh a skewer and a marshmallow. "I guess you can, but it's kind of confusing. Your father was named Valcor as a dragon, and he was Hartanna's brother back then. That much I have straight. But if he was a dragon, why didn't he ever change back like all the others? Does it mean they're not related now?"

Shiloh threw her hood back. "I don't know. He said he doesn't have dragon blood anymore and that it was real complicated. He didn't have a chance to explain."

Billy's mother pulled the edge of her blanket over the professor's lap. "So the media vultures are still circling our house. What's the good news?"

"Oh. That *was* the good news, that I was able to get Shiloh away from them."

"Ouch!" Walter said, ready to pop another cracker into his mouth. "What's the bad news?"

The professor wrapped his fingers around his calf. "Sir Barlow's leg wound was more severe than he indicated. Infection has set in, and he will require surgery to repair the damage. Even as we speak, he is being flown to Johns Hopkins Hospital in Baltimore at Sir Patrick's expense."

“Why Hopkins?” Bonnie asked.

“A surgeon there is a member of our circle of knights, so he is aware of our circumstances. Hopkins is also close enough to easily fulfil Patrick’s request that an anthrozil donate blood for the procedure. He believes your photoreceptors will aid his healing.” The professor glanced at Billy, Bonnie, and Ashley in turn. “Are there any A positive anthrozils here?”

Ashley raised her hand. “O positive. But it’ll work in a pinch.”

“Me, too,” Billy added, extending his arm. “Just lead me to the needle. I can spare a gallon or two.”

Bonnie pushed Billy’s arm down, grinning. “Me first! My blood is grade A-plus.”

The professor clasped his hands together. “Excellent! I’ll take Bonnie there myself later tonight. When we return in the morning, perhaps we’ll know more about Morgan’s plans. She has been plotting for hundreds of years, fuelled by hate and revenge, so I doubt that she’ll wait long to act. Patrick has heard rumours of a covert operation in both England and the States, but it would do no good to speculate about the unknown. ”

Billy threw another stick into the fire. “Has Patrick learned anything about my dad?”

The professor shook his head. “I’m afraid not, William. His first priority was to get the children in his care to safety. I’m sure he’ll begin the search as soon as he can.”

Billy propped his chin on his palm. “Dad must still be trapped down in that place. It’s hopeless.”

Shiloh unfastened the top button on her jacket. “My father says there’s plenty of hope left.” She pulled her necklace from under her jacket and dangled the pendant. “Thank you for finding this for me. Bonnie’s mother gave this rubellite to my father hundreds of years ago, so it’s a family heirloom.” She grasped it by its edges and held it up for the others to see. “Look. It pulses two different shades of red.”

Billy stared at it. "Yeah. I noticed that when I found it."

"It used to be white," Shiloh went on. "Daddy says it might mean that your father's still alive. The pulsing could represent his life force. We just have to find him." She pulled the necklace over her head and extended it to Billy.

Billy let the pendant dangle against his palm. He rubbed his finger across the shining gem. "You're giving it to me?"

"A rubellite is a symbol for a dragon, and I'm not a dragon. It's better if you keep it. I'm sure my father won't mind. Maybe it'll help you find your father. Barlow's knights are coming back to the States tomorrow to help you."

Billy draped the chain over his head and tucked the pendant under his shirt. "So . . . where do we start? Here? Back in Glastonbury?"

Shiloh cast her gaze on the ground. "I don't know. I don't think my father knows, either."

"Well, if my opinion matters," the professor said, "I think William's father is no longer in the circles. All indications are that the portals to that realm have disappeared. The window screen went blank, and even the electromagnetic vortex at the tor has vanished. The other world is no longer accessible, and I refuse to believe that he would be trapped there forever."

Shiloh snuggled inside Bonnie's wing, and the circle of eight fell silent.

Billy grabbed another stick and whacked it against the ground. "So we failed! Morgan got what she wanted. The Watchers are free, and she's huddled up with them somewhere planning Armageddon."

"No, William!" The professor strode to Billy's side, and after Walter scooted over to make a space for him, the professor sat elbow to elbow with Billy, a new burst of firelight flickering in his eyes. "You and Bonnie did not fail. Your mission was to rescue prisoners, no more, no less, and you succeeded magnificently against the most extraordinary odds." He spread his arm toward Shiloh. "A poor girl has been set free after forty years of miserable bondage. The dragons are alive, fulfilling Merlin's great prophecy that they would someday live again. Also, Morgan failed to obtain the hostiam she desperately needs to live in this world. She will likely suffer soon enough, since the world she normally inhabits seems to have lost its doors. And to top it off, you are now the head of the Circle of Knights. The spirit of Arthur has returned at our time of greatest need. Patrick will soon preside over a formal coronation and hand you the Great Key."

"The Great Key?" Billy asked. "What's that?"

"Patrick said that he stored it in the safest place possible along with his most valuable treasure, so I have never seen it. But I have heard that you will use it when you lead your army in the war."

"The war? How can I possibly lead an army in a war?"

The professor enfolded Billy's gloved hands in his. "You have fulfilled your role to this point, but an even greater battle looms. For now, we take much needed rest in the peace of this wilderness, away from the fevered distractions of media madness. When the time comes, however, you will need to go to battle as the warrior you have proven yourself to be. If you lack faith that God has brought all of these miraculous events to pass, you will surely fail when the greatest test arises."

Billy stared at the four interlocked gloves, then shifted his gaze up to the professor's steely eyes – old, sagacious eyes that had seen hundreds of trials and countless miracles. He felt a spiritual connection with this wonderful gentleman, as though his teacher's tested faith flowed from eye to eye and hand to hand.

Billy closed his eyes and nodded. "I guess you're right . . . as usual." The circle fell silent again. Another new flame erupted in the campfire, crackling the fuel and playing harmony for a chorus of crickets chirping in the woods.

The professor slapped his knees. "I think it's time for a rousing song. We need something to cheer us up."

Billy shook his head. "I don't really feel like singing, Prof."

The professor stood up and straightened his coat collar. "Not you, William," he said, his eyes half closed. "I will sing."

Walter snorted. "Not another one of those weird, prophetic songs no one can understand, I hope."

"Why, yes, Walter," the professor replied, clutching his lapels. "It *is* one of those weird, prophetic songs. This one came to me in a dream, and I think I shall not forget it as long as I live."

"A dream?" Billy almost laughed in spite of himself. "Were there any penguins in it?"

"As a matter of fact, there was a penguin, a friendly chap who gave me an umbrella. I was appreciative, because I was walking through a dreadful storm at the time. He told me to sing, and sing well, or he would take the umbrella back."

Billy knew the story was supposed to be funny, but he could only nod. He had a strange feeling this song was going to shake him to the core.

The professor stood, warming his hands over the fire. "It has no title, as far as I know, but it conforms to Merlin's distinctive pattern. Here goes." He lifted his gaze toward the star-filled sky.

When dragons flew in days of old
With flashing scales and flame,
They soared in scarlet droves of fear
With hearts no man could tame.

The Watchers sang a siren's chant,
Seducing tickled ears,
Ensnaring girls with heads laid bare
And dragons far and near.

While most fell prey to Satan's song,
A few held fast their birth
And worshipped God's created realm,
Religion of the earth.

Content to suffer wrapped in chains,
A dragon leaves the skies.
Content to bleed for souls unknown,
A dragon bows and dies.

But can such faith repel the wrath
When evil is reborn?
Can sacrifice alone endure
When scaly hearts are torn?

A warrior comes with sword and shield,
With truth and faith in hand,
Exposing lies and cutting through
The darkness in the land.

Has eye not seen, has ear not heard,
The love that sets men free?
From scales to flesh he softens hearts;
From red to white he bleeds.

And when the warrior rests his blade,
With virgin bride he kneels.
The dragons fade from scales to dust
And bless the golden seal.

The professor straightened his trench coat and sat down. "I think that should be a welcome song, William. I find the words quite optimistic."

"Yeah," Walter agreed. "It's almost like a promise. Except for that bleeding part, it sounded pretty good."

Bonnie hooked her arm in Billy's and pulled him close. "It *is* a promise, Billy, and we'll figure it all out together."

Billy gazed into Bonnie's eyes. They glistened like the stars in the sky. Her love and sincerity poured forth like a refreshing fountain. He smiled and cocked his head toward the professor. "Hey Prof. What happened next in the dream?"

The professor sat back down. "Strangely enough, before I could finish, the penguin yanked the umbrella from my hand, smacked me on the head with it, and walked away."

Walter laughed out loud. "I guess the penguin doesn't understand your *Prof*-etic songs either."

A shower of marshmallows and loud "Boos!" rained on Walter's head. "Okay, okay!" he said, catching one of the marshmallows. "I know when I'm not appreciated." He popped the marshmallow into his mouth, then stuffed his hands into his pockets. His face suddenly brightened. "Oh, yeah." He lifted a short red cylinder. "Prof, I found this wax thing in the pocket of the black cloak. Any idea what it is?"

"Walter!" the professor shouted. "That's a scentser! Its effects are unpredictable!"

"Well, I'll just get rid of it, then." Walter flung it into the fire.

The professor lifted his hands. "Don't panic! It could just be a sleep inducer. At this point, it might be more beneficial than harmful."

Bonnie sniffed the air and started giggling.

Billy detected the odour of popcorn, smooth and buttery. He smiled at Bonnie. "What's so funny?"

Bonnie burst out laughing, and Shiloh joined her. Both giggled like schoolgirls at a slumber party.

Soon, everyone around the fire was snickering, chuckling, or bending over with loud belly laughs. "This is perfect!" Walter said, standing up, barely managing to stifle his own laughs. "Now, there was this fish who loved to play golf. One day, he flopped up onto the seventh green . . ."

Appendix
The Poems and Prophecies of Circles of Seven

Merlin's Song

With sword and stone, the holy knight,
Darkness as his bane,
Will gather warriors in the light
Cast in heaven's flame.

He comes to save a remnant band,
Searching with his maid,
But in a sea of sadness finds
His warriors lying splayed.

A valley deep, a valley long
Lay angels dry and dead;
Now who can wake their cold,
stone hearts
Their bones on table spread?

Like wine that flows in skins made new
The spirit pours out fresh;
Can hymns of love bring forth the dead
And give them hearts of flesh?

O will you learn from words of faith
That sing in psalms from heaven
To valley floors where terrors lurk
In circles numbering seven?

Merlin's Lullaby

Thou servants of the blackest soul,
Asleep in Av'lon's shallow bowl,
Wake not as skies above thee break
With ripples sounding in our wake.

While sleep enfolds you in your lair,
We pass you by without a care.
So in your dreams protect her doors,
While safely we approach her shores.

The Compass Room Poem

Young Arthur holds the window's key
To ancient realms that bear his quest.
The circles know where lie the beasts
Who crave the light, who crave their breath.

The prison world awaits a king
To rescue souls who have no hope,
Yet evil spirits also wait
To ride the sword's redeeming stroke.

The beasts conceal the ancient truths
That dwell behind divided tongues,
But dragons' hearts reveal their flame
From shining light and psalms well sung.

In circle one there lies a belt,
The camera's eye to watch your tale,
A tale as old as man's first tears
When Adam donned the devil's veil.

The stone recalls the tale of threats
That lie in circles deeper still.
In letters giving aid and hope
They guide the souls with steadfast will.

You cannot bear this test alone
For faith is edified in pairs,
And bearing witness two agree
Survival rests on faithful prayers.

Beware of mirrors found within
To quell your rival's fiery darts,
For mirrors sketch our shallow shells;
They cannot fathom human hearts.

Yet mirrors can reflect the truth
And overcome the darkest night;
The perfect law resides in those
Who live by faith and not by sight.

When thinning shadows fade to black
Polaris greets the standing bear,
Then raise the sword to pierce the veil
And strike the pose of saints in prayer.

The Poems of the Circles

The second circle's path of blood
Instructs the king his debt to pay,
For all who seek a higher call
Must patiently await their day.

In circle three a raven lurks,
Deceiving all with words of scorn,
Yet two can find a hidden door
To take them to a land reborn.

New Eden lives in circle four,
Beginning new a world thereof,
But paradise is sealed for us
Who suffer now for those we love.

A shore afar is circle five;
A captive waits in chains of greed.
Each bite conceals the toxic lust
And veils the demon's bread and mead.

Not all applaud the king's brave quest
To rescue men from savage chains,
Yet still he foils the raven's plot
With tables turned from food to flames.

When weapons fail and faith survives,
In sacrifice the king expires,
But rising from his river grave,
His flame revives to kindle fire.

An urban prison lies in six
Where faithful soldiers e'er prevail,
And death will sprout in life anew
From seeds of light within the grail.

The faithful souls will learn the truth
That spoils of earth will never last.
Contentment holds eternal keys
To days of peace that never pass.

The final circle numbers seven,
And beasts await your sword's command.
The greatest danger tests your faith,
And wisdom's touch will make you stand.

The bridge of faith still lies in wait,
The narrow path of answered prayer.
Restore the fountain from the stone,
Regenerating souls laid bare.

A dragon chained in darkest pits
Will not behold pure freedom's light,
For dragons claim a lofty perch,
Yet cannot reach the highest height.

For even now in pits of gloom
The dragon's pride will never bow,
Until redemption's sword sets free
The dragon's heart to kneel and vow.

Merlin's Promise

When dragons flew in days of old
With flashing scales and flame,
They soared in scarlet droves of fear
With hearts no man could tame.

The Watchers sang a siren's chant,
Seducing tickled ears,
Ensnaring girls with heads laid bare
And dragons far and near.

While most fell prey to Satan's song,
A few held fast their birth
And worshipped God's created realm,
Religion of the earth.

Content to suffer wrapped in chains,
A dragon leaves the skies.
Content to bleed for souls unknown,
A dragon bows and dies.

But can such faith repel the wrath
When evil is reborn?
Can sacrifice alone endure
When scaly hearts are torn?

A warrior comes with sword and shield,
With truth and faith in hand,
Exposing lies and cutting through
The darkness in the land.

Has eye not seen, has ear not heard,
The love that sets men free?
From scales to flesh he softens hearts;
From red to white he bleeds.

And when the warrior rests his blade,
With virgin bride he kneels.
The dragons fade from scales to dust
And bless the golden seal.

Excerpt from volume four

This excerpt taken from *Tears of a Dragon*

Published in the UK by Candle Books,
(a publishing imprint of Lion Hudson plc)
Wilkinson House, Jordan Hill Road,
Oxford OX2 8DR

Published in the USA by AMG Publishers
6815 Shallowford Rd.
Chattanooga, Tennessee 37421

This is a pre-publication excerpt.

Scheduled release date: October 2009
ISBN: 978–1–85985–794–6

Merlin's Promise

When dragons flew in days of old
With flashing scales and flame,
They soared in scarlet droves of fear
With hearts no man could tame.

The Watchers sang a siren's chant,
Seducing tickled ears,
Ensnaring girls with heads laid bare
And dragons far and near.

While most fell prey to Satan's song,
A few held fast their birth
And worshipped God's created realm,
Religion of the earth.

Content to suffer wrapped in chains,
A dragon leaves the skies.
Content to bleed for souls unknown,
A dragon bows and dies.

But can such faith repel the wrath
When evil is reborn?
Can sacrifice alone endure
When scaly hearts are torn?

A warrior comes with sword and shield,
With truth and faith in hand,
Exposing lies and cutting through
The darkness in the land.

(Continued)

Has eye not seen, has ear not heard,
The love that sets men free?
From scales to flesh he softens hearts;
From red to white he bleeds.

And when the warrior rests his blade,
With virgin bride he kneels.
The dragons fade from scales to dust
And bless the golden seal.

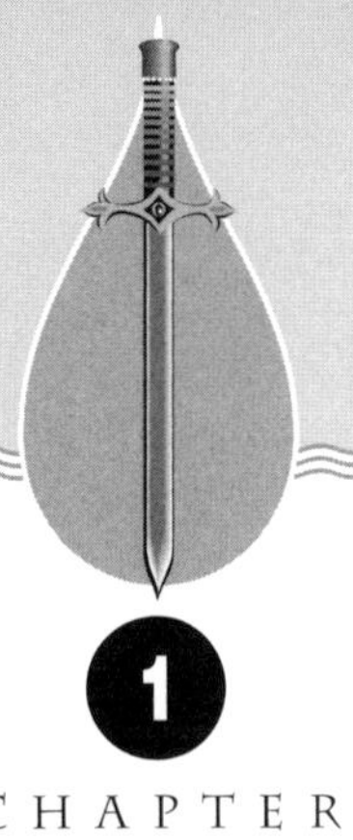

1

CHAPTER

Fama Regis

Bonnie leaned against the bedrail and clutched Sir Barlow's burly hand. "I'm glad you're feeling better."

Barlow smiled, lifting his moustache. His dark eyes sparkled. "Yes, Miss. Thanks to an infusion of your blood, I am as fit as a fiddle." The knight's brow furrowed under thick strands of unkempt hair. "That is the correct idiom, isn't it?"

Bonnie tightened her grip on Barlow's hand and laughed. "That's the perfect idiom for a true gentleman!"

Barlow's smile broadened, revealing a chipped front tooth among a half-dozen yellowed incisors.

A new voice filled the room, strong and cheerful. "Indeed it is the correct idiom. A fine violin well played is fit for heaven itself."

Bonnie spun toward the sound. Professor Hamilton, her teacher and friend, ambled into the hospital room, unbuttoning his black trench coat. She glanced at a clock on the wall. "Did you run into trouble somewhere?"

"Only minor annoyances." The professor clipped a cell phone to his belt and leaned a wet umbrella against the wall. "I'm afraid the foul weather has caused the entire populace to forget customary manners. There seems to be a general uneasiness, an underlying anxiety weighing down every man, woman, and child." He pulled a wrapped sandwich from his coat pocket and handed it to Bonnie. "The restaurant queue seemed interminable, and several pushy fellows insisted on . . . ahem . . . butting into the line." The professor nodded at Barlow. "I could have used the services of a battle-trained warrior." He withdrew another sandwich from his opposite pocket. "This is for you, but Dr. Kaplan said you must maintain the hospital diet until tonight, so I'll save it. Was your noontime meal sufficient?"

Barlow mumbled something unintelligible under his breath, then added in a louder voice, "A ghost couldn't survive eating the paltry servings here."

Bonnie put her sandwich in the side pocket of her backpack. "I'll go outside to eat this later. No use torturing our good knight." She hitched up her pack to make her hidden dragon wings more comfortable. "Did Sir Patrick have any news?"

"Quite a bit." The professor ran his hand through his unruly white hair. "It seems that the Great Key, as he calls it, is now in William's possession. Apparently Shiloh gave it to him last night at the campfire."

Bonnie caressed a colourful string of beads around her neck. "The pendant with the rubellite? How is that a key?"

"Patrick says he will tell us more when he comes." The professor squinted at the intravenous tube stretching from a dangling plastic bag to Barlow's arm, then pulled a pair of spectacles from his shirt pocket. "He did tell me that Merlin called it the Great Key in a prophecy, indicating that it would be crucial should the Watchers ever emerge from their prison." He slipped the glasses on and read the label on the IV bag. "Patrick confirmed our thoughts, that we should locate the king's chronicles. The book will help us unlock the mystery of the key." He lowered his head and sighed.

Bonnie tried to make eye contact with the professor. "Is something wrong with Sir Barlow's IV?"

The professor's gentle smile quivered. "No, no. That's not it at all." He slid his hands into his pockets. "It just reminded me of days long past when I spent many hours coaxing instruments like these to work just a little bit better." Drooping his head, he pushed an electrical cord under the bed with his foot. "Those were times of shadows, the darkest days of my life."

Bonnie took a step closer. "Do you mind telling me what happened?"

"Oh, no. Not at all." The professor pulled a wallet from his back pocket and fished out a locket-sized photo from inside. He bent over and showed it to her.

Bonnie studied the photo, a black-and-white picture of a man in a tuxedo and a woman in a wedding gown. She felt the joy of the smiling faces and the oneness of the clasped hands. "She's beautiful, Professor. You look very happy."

"Yes, we both were." He returned the photo to his wallet and straightened. "It has been more than twenty years since she passed away."

"I knew she died, but I didn't know when." She took the professor's hand in hers, trying again to catch his faraway gaze. "It must have been very sad for you."

The professor finally looked down at her and smiled, but it was a sad smile. "Indeed. She was the light of my life. We were as close as two people can be, one mind, one spirit. Our daughter, Elizabeth, was about to be married, and the evening before the wedding, we attended the rehearsal dinner, a beautiful affair at a posh restaurant—white tablecloths, crystal, silver, fine china—all the trimmings of an elegant feast. Later that night, my wife became deathly ill—food poisoning of some sort—and she had to go to the hospital. She insisted that the wedding go on as planned, and since one of my students, Carl Foley, whom you know, of course, as Walter's father, volunteered to stay with her, we decided to set up a live video feed to the room so she could attend the ceremony from her hospital bed."

"Then she got to see the wedding?"

"Yes, but by the time I returned to her side, she had worsened. The doctors had no explanation, but it was as if she were drifting away; her mind was leaving her body. She would cry out, 'Help me! I'm falling!' though she lay securely in bed. As you can imagine, I was beside myself, but God did not answer my prayers according to my desires." He straightened the intravenous tube, his bottom lip quivering as his voice began to crack. "She . . ." He swallowed and wiped a tear. "She passed away that very night."

Bonnie slid her hand around his elbow and leaned her head against his arm. "I'm so sorry, Professor."

He leaned over and kissed Bonnie gently on the top of her head. "As were many others, little angel. It was such a lovely funeral with hundreds of gracious mourners. And so many people brought flowers! We both loved our flower garden, so I made sure I flooded the funeral home with her favourite, the carnation, and I added Easter lilies, of course, but the guests brought dozens and dozens of bouquets and laid them against the casket. And, strangely enough, people also brought dresses and skirts my wife had made for their daughters." He laughed under his breath, his eyes glistening. "She couldn't bear to make trousers for them. She believed young ladies should look like young ladies. In any case, the visitors expressed their thankfulness for my wife's skill and generosity in sharing her love with so many friends and neighbours. It was as if the story of Dorcas in the book of Acts were being replayed at the funeral." A new tear made its way down the sage's wrinkled cheek, and his voice pitched up ever so slightly. "But there was no apostle Peter to come and awaken my precious one from sleep." The professor raised his hand and bit his knuckle, closing his eyes as his body heaved with stifled sobs.

Bonnie wrapped her arms around his waist and held him close. She glanced at Sir Barlow. Tears streamed down the knight's face, too.

After a long pause, the professor spoke again, his voice now much stronger. "So I will have to go to her when I finish my course here on earth, and I look forward to that day with great anticipation."

Bonnie gave him a strong hug. "I know you miss her, but I hope your course isn't finished for a long time." She pulled away, looking up at the professor with the brightest smile she could muster. "So she was a seamstress? What a wonderful gift!"

"Yes. What she could do with a needle and thread!" He sighed again, his lips tightening. "But that is in the past, and there are new dark days to deal with, I'm afraid." He strolled to the window, sliding his hands into his pockets again as he gazed at the wet landscape through the foggy glass. Raindrops pelted the windowpane, sounding like a hundred soft fingers tapping for permission to enter. "I am concerned for Patrick. He seems weak . . . exhausted." He withdrew one hand and sketched a square on the condensation. "He is many centuries old, even older than I knew. And now, being fully human, he will certainly die. I fear his days are coming to a close."

He wiped away the condensation with his sleeve. "And Patrick informed me that this is no ordinary weather event. These monsoon conditions are spreading over the entire North

American continent, and a similar phenomenon is beginning in Europe. While I was walking in the downpour, it seemed that each drop emitted a popping noise as it struck the sidewalk, much like the sputter of a droplet on a hot fryer, yet so faint that I doubt I would have noticed if I had not leaned over to pluck a quarter from the walk. With thousands of droplets popping, it reminded me of Rice Krispies in a bowl of milk."

"Do you think that's what's making people so irritable and jumpy?" Bonnie asked.

"Very possibly. If this is demonic work, stirring fear in the hearts of people would certainly fit their modus operandi, but there may be more substance to this rain than simple fear mongering."

Barlow sat up in bed and threw off his sheets. "There is no time to lose." He stripped the tape that held his IV tube in place. "Those scoundrels from the abyss are a step ahead of us. We must summon my knights to battle!"

Bonnie wrapped her fingers around Barlow's wrist. "Wait! The nurse will do that."

The professor jumped to the bedside and grasped Barlow's shoulder. "Patience, my good fellow. Dr. Kaplan has already ordered your discharge. We will get you out of here as soon as possible."

Barlow laid his hand over Bonnie's, an apologetic look on his face. "I'm sorry for my outburst, Miss, but I'm anxious to lead my men into battle against the demons."

Bonnie gently fastened the tape back on Barlow's arm. "It won't be long now. If we can get you out of here soon enough, we can all go and get Sir Patrick and your knights at the airport."

"That reminds me," the professor said. "We couldn't possibly carry everyone in my car, so I called Marilyn this morning and asked her to fly here and ferry some of us back to West Virginia."

Bonnie straightened the IV tube and draped it around the bed. "Did you ask Billy to search for King Arthur's book?"

The professor patted her on the shoulder. "Yes. He said he would search for it right away."

"Right away? In this downpour?"

"Yes. With the Watchers on the move, we must act quickly. If they are able to manipulate the weather, the magnitude of the disasters they can wreak is incalculable." He ran his finger along the IV tube and sighed, his eyes wet with new tears. "Are you ready to face more danger, Miss Silver?"

Warmth surged through Bonnie's body, as if an oven-heated blanket wrapped around her and chased away the autumn chill. She gazed at her teacher. If only there were some way she could give him a glimpse of all the wonder she had seen in heaven after dying in the sixth circle. What earthly words could possibly express the joy of perfect bliss? "Professor, I have been in the arms of my Lord in heaven, and I saw a reflection of my face in his laughing eyes." She felt her own tears welling up as she folded her hands at her waist. "I've never been more ready in all my life."

Billy tiptoed across the rocky cave floor, guiding Excalibur with both hands. The sword's energy pierced the darkness and spread out into a glowing sphere, surrounding him in a wash of alabaster light. As he glided under the bright shroud, the cave's shifting air penetrated his skin like the grip of a life-devouring phantom.

The professor's call had already delivered a numbing bite to his senses. "Locate *Fama Regis*," he had said. "And guard the pendant well. The fate of the entire world could hang in the balance."

Billy shivered hard. His journey to the dragon's den had begun under gloomy skies that quickly deteriorated into a torrential downpour. Now, in the cave's cool draft, his wet clothes sapped his body heat. He freed one hand and blew a stream of superheated breath on his fingers, making them toasty warm in seconds.

As he advanced deeper into the expansive cavity, a hint of danger pricked his mind, prompting him to creep more slowly, one gentle step after another. A trickle of water echoed nearby. That was new. Clefspeare's cave had always been perfectly dry before. But now a steady plink, plink, plink troubled the silence, slowly escalating in frequency. The sound racked his nerves. He couldn't see any water yet, but those drips had to collect somewhere, and that meant trouble. If a growing pool reached the ancient book . . .

He stopped and sniffed the damp air. After his experiences with scentsers in the circles of seven, he vowed never to let one of those mind-altering odours sneak up on him again. This was no time to get waylaid by sleepiness or anger, or even worse, fits of laughter. The needle on his danger meter pushed toward the yellow-alert zone, but he had no way to tell who, or what, might be lurking in the shadows. It was time for silence.

He dimmed the sword's glow and crept forward again, mentally shushing the crunching pebbles under his hiking boots. At the back of the cave, the walls came together in a crease. A collection of marble-sized stones lay in a pile where the corner met the floor. Billy crouched, picked up one of the stones, and brought it close to the sword. Its polished facets shimmered red, sending streaks of crimson across his fingers. A laser-like beam shot toward an octagonal pendant dangling from a chain around his neck. The gem in the pendant's centre seemed to answer the stone's red aura, pulsing vibrantly with its own shade of crimson like the heart of a ready warrior.

"Yo! Billy!"

Billy dropped the gem and jumped to his feet. He extended Excalibur and brightened its glow. "Walter? Is that you?"

"Who else?" Walter stepped into the sword's corona. "Thanks for the light. It would've been hard to find you without that overgrown mosquito zapper." He extended a dripping umbrella. "It's pouring out there. I thought you might want this." He pulled down the hood of his olive drab rain slicker. "Something wrong?"

Billy tucked the pendant under his shirt and took the umbrella. "My danger alarm's working overtime, so you kind of spooked me. But it couldn't be you setting it off; you're not dangerous."

"Who says so?" Walter unbuttoned the front of his raincoat. "I'll bet Devin thinks I'm dangerous by now, sitting in that candlestone with nothing to do but twiddle his claws."

Billy poked his friend's lean belly with the umbrella and grinned. "You're only dangerous at the buffet line." He propped the sword against his shoulder and tilted his head upward. "I hear water dripping, and it's getting louder."

"No wonder. It's raining so hard out there I had to ask directions from a fish." Walter glanced all around the dim chamber. "The cave probably has a leak somewhere."

"Yeah, could be." Billy tapped the floor with the umbrella, shaking out a spray of droplets. "I thought you were staying with the womenfolk. That's more important than keeping me dry."

"Your mum decided there was enough room for everyone to head for Baltimore." Walter began counting on his fingers. "Prof will drive back with Barlow, Fiske, Standish, and Woodrow, and your mum will fly back with Bonnie, Ashley, Karen, Shiloh, Patrick, Newman, and Edmund." He shrugged his shoulders.

"Sounded like a boring trip, and besides, Karen stays glued to me like old chewing gum, so I decided to hike up here where the action is."

"It's dull as dirt here," Billy said. "I was hoping the dragons would fly in. That'll stir things up."

"Yeah. Ashley said they could get here today if they hurried. I told her we'd go dragon riding as soon as they finish off the Watchers, but who knows how long that'll take." Walter bent down and kicked some loose gravel. "Any luck finding the book?"

Billy pushed the top of the pile of stones with the umbrella tip. "Not yet. I thought Dad would've hidden it in his cave, but all I've found is this pile of gems."

"Gems? Cool!" Walter held up a black square of leather. "If you cash those in, I guess you won't be needing this."

"My wallet?" Billy took it and stuffed it in his back pocket.

"Yeah. Your mum put some money in there in case you needed it." Walter shoved the pile of gems with his shoe, then knelt and leaned close. "Well, Sherlock, I guess you didn't look right under your nose."

Billy lowered the sword, lighting up the stones. An old leather binding protruded from the toppled pile. "I didn't have a chance," he said, dropping the umbrella and grabbing the book. "You sneaked up on me before I could." He blew a coat of sand from the cover.

Walter stood again and craned his neck to read the raised script. "What does *Fama Regis* mean?"

"The acts of the king, or something like that. It was written by Arthur's scribe." Billy opened the heavy cover. "Believe it or not, the scribe was Palin for a while." He flipped through several pages of thick parchment. "And he drew some awesome pictures. Take a look." He gave the book to Walter and held Excalibur close. In a drawing, a knight draped in chain mail raised his sword and shield against a lunging dragon. The dragon blasted the shield with a tsunami of flames, its wings fully extended in battle. A young lady dressed in silky white stood close by, her delicate hands covering her ivory cheeks.

Billy tapped on the parchment. "Let's get this to camp. Maybe when Prof gets back we'll find some clues and—" He spun around, pointing Excalibur toward the cave entrance.

Walter slapped the book closed and whispered. "What's up? Danger getting close?"

"Big time." He lit up Excalibur like a blazing torch and nodded toward the entrance. "Come on. I'm tired of waiting for danger to sneak up on me. Let's give our visitor a greeting he'll never forget."

Billy charged ahead, Excalibur's beacon leading the way. As they neared the entrance, muted daylight mixed into the darkness, brightening with every step. Billy halted at the archway and glanced all around, sniffing, listening. Walter skidded to a stop at his side. A curtain of rainwater cascaded from the top of the entry arch, pelting the ground and streaming down the slope, away from the cave. Billy whispered, "You smell something?"

Walter wrinkled his nose. "Yeah. Smells like a wet dog."

A twangy voice rose in the distance. "Now, Hambone, ain't nuthin' to be skeered of in that cave. Do you want to get colder 'n a nekkid rat in Alaska?" A skinny, long-legged man pushed through a thicket, a shotgun poised on his shoulder and an old hound trailing behind on a leash.

Billy laughed. "It's just Arlo Hatfield!"

Walter tucked *Fama Regis* under his coat and fastened the buttons. "Cool! I've been wanting to meet him."

"Danger's still close," Billy whispered, "but I don't want to explain Excalibur to Arlo." He thrust the sword into his back scabbard and waved at the old hillbilly. "Pssst! Arlo! Get in here, quick!"

Arlo tightened his grip on his gun for a second, but when his gaze found its way to the cave entrance, he relaxed. He spat out a stream of tobacco juice and stepped up his pace. "C'mon, Hambone. Looks like we'll have comp'ny."

The blue tick hound hesitated, prompting Arlo to pull him along. "What's wrong with you today? Ain't you got a lick o' sense? You remember Billy, donchoo? The boy what lost his pa?"

Arlo jerked Hambone's leash, nearly dragging him forward. He gawked at Billy, water streaming from the bill of his baseball cap. "Whatchoo doin' here?"

Billy gestured for Arlo to come inside. He stooped and petted

Hambone, still whispering. "I was looking for something that belonged to my . . . uh . . . my pa." As he stroked the dog's ears, his pendant fell outside his shirt again and dangled on its chain. "Why are you here?"

"Hambone and me were out huntin' squirrels near the crick when the rain commenced to gettin' mighty fierce. I remembered the cave up here, so we came lookin' fer it. But Hambone's actin' awful queer, like he's skeered of somethin'."

Billy stood again. "Maybe the weather has him spooked. I haven't seen it rain like this in . . . in a coon's age."

Arlo scratched his head through his cap. "Could be. But I don't rightly know how long a coon lives." He reached out and slipped his fingers behind Billy's pendant. "Now here's a purty thang. It's flashin' like a radio tower light. Where'd you git it?"

Billy's danger sensation suddenly jumped to red alert, a thousand needles pricking his skin. The pendant's glow washed over the hillbilly's face like a pulsing laser. His wrinkled skin seemed to melt, rivulets of flesh pouring down like bloody sweat until a new face appeared, a shining, ghostly visage with cruel red eyes.

Billy jumped back and yanked out Excalibur. Walter leaped at Arlo and twisted the shotgun from his grip, giving the hillbilly a hefty shove as it pulled away. Arlo stumbled back into the downpour, leaving Hambone in the cave. As water splashed on his head, the hillbilly's face reappeared as if painted on his skin by the windswept rain.

Excalibur's beam shot out from the tip and waved over Arlo's head. "I don't know who or what you are," Billy shouted, "but if you take one step, I'll zap you to kingdom come."

A glowing foot stepped forward, leaving Arlo's foot behind. Then, an entire body emerged from the hillbilly, a nine-foot-tall goliath of a man dressed in brilliant silver mail. Arlo's body collapsed behind him, motionless.

"Go ahead and strike!" the man shouted. "I've already been to kingdom come."

Billy tightened his grip and whispered to Walter, "I hate it when someone dares me to strike. It usually means it won't work."

Walter broke open the shotgun barrel and peered inside. "No shells." He tossed the gun on the ground. "You got any fire-breathing ammo?"

"Yep. It's been brewing in my belly for a while."

"Then let's fry this pig and start makin' bacon."

Billy dimmed his sword and launched a torrent of fire at the creature, splattering his shining body with biting orange flames. The man swelled in size, growing to at least twelve feet tall. Plumes of steam shot into the air as sheets of rain cooled the inferno.

Walter grabbed Hambone's leash and backed away. "So much for that idea."

"No! Wait!" Billy pointed with Excalibur. "Something's up!"

The humanoid creature stumbled on shaky legs, smoke rising from his scorched torso. He dropped to his knees and spread his arms wide. He shouted, "Be closed!"

A rolling wave of darkness flew from the creature's hands. It splashed against the cave entrance and spread out, laying a sooty coat over the archway.

Billy lit up Excalibur again and swiped the beam against the black curtain. It tore across the expanse, and sparks of light ate away the darkness like buzzing termites.

"He doesn't like the fire!" Walter shouted. "Hit him again!"

Billy launched another fiery salvo, but it bounced off the entrance and shot just past his head toward the inner recesses of the cave. Hambone whined a mournful lament.

Walter hovered his hand over the archway. "A force field?" He kicked at the base of the field, sending out a splash of sparks. "Owww!" he yelled, jumping on one foot. "These things are such a pain!"

The shining creature stood and laughed. "That should keep you in there long enough."

"Long enough for what?" Billy yelled.

"You'll soon find out." An evil smile grew on his face. He opened his enormous palm to the sky, allowing the rain to pool and drip over the sides. "These waters are courtesy of my lord, the prince of the power of the air. He sends his greetings, young king, and hopes you will enjoy a refreshing swim."

Walter slung a baseball-sized rock at the force field, but it ricocheted harmlessly back. "You're a big talker for someone who's scared of a couple of kids and a hound dog!"

A pair of wings sprouted from the back of the creature. "We are wise enough to know our weaknesses. Why battle against your strengths?" He laughed and launched into the air, disappearing from sight.

"Coward!" Walter shouted. "Come back and fight like a . . ." His voice trailed off to a whisper. "Like a man . . . I guess."

Billy gazed at the hillbilly's body on the ground outside. Rain poured over the still form without mercy. "I sure hope Arlo's okay." He touched the field with Excalibur's tip. The contact point sizzled and threw the blade back. "The blade won't pierce it." He summoned the beam and let it slowly approach the field. As soon as it brushed the surface, the beam angled away as if bouncing off a mirror. He doused the light. "It must not be like the portals in the circles. The beam doesn't faze it either."

"It's not soundproof," Walter noted. "We heard that ghost creature, and I still hear the storm."

Billy turned slowly toward the back of the cave. "I hear something else."

"The dripping sound again?"

"More like gushing now."

Hambone let out a howl. A stream of shallow water had pooled all around, lapping against the dog's paws. It flowed to the cave entrance and stopped at the force field, unable to drain through the exit.

"We'd better think fast!" Walter shouted. "Can that beam of yours go through rocks?"

"It only transluminates organic stuff!" Billy lit up Excalibur again. "But it's worth a try."

The beam drilled into the ceiling as if trying to bore a hole through the solid stone above their heads. Steam poured from the contact point, masking his efforts.

Walter grimaced as sparkling light rained on his head. "Is it working?"

Billy moved the beam, dimming it slightly. The steam dispersed, revealing solid rock, clean and shiny, as if polished by a buffing brush. "No. Not even a dent."

"And the floor's hard as concrete, so we can't dig under the field." Walter marched in place, sloshing in the calf-deep water. "I'm running out of ideas. You got any?"

Billy grabbed Hambone's leash from Walter, yelling to compete with the sound of rushing water. "Just keep *Fama Regis* dry." He waded toward the back of the cave. "Hambone and I will try to find the source. Maybe we can block it up somehow. See if you can find a big, loose rock."

"I'm right behind you." Walter dragged his feet through the knee-deep water. "Maybe I can kick up a rock while I'm walking."

Lifting his legs high, Billy trudged into the darkness, lighting his way with Excalibur. When he reached the rear wall, cold mist sprayed his face. Water rose past his thighs, and Hambone paddled frantically to keep his head above the surface.

Walter shouted over the din. "Sounds like it's coming from the ceiling." He lifted a rock the size of two fists. "This is the best I could do."

Billy raised his sword, guiding the glow upward. Torrents of water gushed from a back corner and plunged into the flood. "I can't hold the sword and try to plug it at the same time."

Walter handed *Fama Regis* to Billy. "Don't worry. I can handle it." He clambered up the wall, clutching stony projections with his free hand. As he pushed the rock into the gaping hole, the fountain split into dozens of fingers and splashed across his face. The stream slowed for a second, then spat out the rock like a shot from a rifle. "There's no way!" he shouted. "It's too fast!"

Walter jumped, splashing down into waist-deep water. He took *Fama Regis* back and held it high. "I say we try the entrance again!"

"Yeah. We're not doing any good back here." Billy scooped up Hambone under one arm. "C'mon, boy. You're getting tired."

They forged ahead into the more illuminated part of the cave, reaching the archway once again. Billy lifted Hambone over a wall protrusion and set him down on a ledge just above the flood. The water now crested at the bottom of the pendant as it dangled over Billy's chest. "I'm going to try Excalibur," he yelled, "and a blast of fire at the same time."

Walter balled one hand into a fist. "Give it all you've got!" He rested the book on top of his head. "Even a little hole might keep the water from rising."

Billy charged up the sword's energy, making it so bright he couldn't keep his eyes on the blade. He slashed the beam against the entry and launched a ferocious salvo of fire. The flames bombarded the field, spreading out over the entry space, making ripples of orange along the plane. The laser beam bounced off the field again and struck the water, lighting up the surface with dancing sparks of white.

"Turn it off!" Walter yelled. "The water's like electrified ice!"

Billy shut down the sword and stopped the flames. The force field shimmered like a disturbed pool, then turned crystal clear again. With water rising to his armpits, he resheathed Excalibur and lifted his elbows over the dying sparks. "Got any new ideas?"

"Just one." Walter placed the book on Billy's head, and Billy instinctively grabbed it. Walter stepped toward the force field, took a deep breath, and leaped into it. A tremendous explosion of sparks sent him flying back through the water, like a torpedo shooting through the depths. When he stopped, he lay floating on the surface, face down and motionless.

Billy lunged for him and screamed. "Walter!"